The Deluge Scrolls

By

Benn K. Leavenworth

PublishAmerica
Baltimore

© 2007 by Benn K. Leavenworth.
All rights reserved. No part of this book may be reproduced, stored in a retrieval system or transmitted in any form or by any means without the prior written permission of the publishers, except by a reviewer who may quote brief passages in a review to be printed in a newspaper, magazine or journal.

First printing

All characters in this book are fictitious, and any resemblance to real persons, living or dead, is coincidental.

ISBN: 1-4241-5747-1
PUBLISHED BY PUBLISHAMERICA, LLLP
www.publishamerica.com
Baltimore

Printed in the United States of America

*To Tom, Jim, Jan, and Doug for their help,
suggestions, and constructive criticism.*

September, 2005

Preface

And it came to pass... the sons of the Strong-Ones saw that the daughters of men were very fair... AM said: "My Ruach will not always strive with men..." There were Nefillim in the earth in those days... (Earth) was corrupt and... filled with violence... And the Strong-Ones said to Zisudra: "The end of all things is before me..."
 Torah. Ancient Book of Beginnings.

"As with the days of Noach, so shall the coming of the Human One."
Words of Jeshua.

Prologue: The Me*

Aarda, my sister, my spouse, I shall not soon forget thee... thou whose love excels the rarest of wines... How fondly recall I nights shared upon beds of spices 'twixt scented sheets of finest silk, secrets too wonderful for words... and now thou art not... So bid I thee, dearest Aarda, dearest friend, adieu...
    (Day 39. Lord H'rshag's final love poem to Lady Aarda. Translated and edited, British Museum, version 3.2; 1981.)

* * * * *

"I'm here to see prisoner 1102." He spoke in a broad, California western accent. He showed his credentials, a pass and business card, to the dour-looking desk officer.

She glanced over the top of wire spectacles. Without getting up, she leaned her ample bosom over her desk. The badge and buckle of her Sam Browne belt clanked against the glass top as she reached out her hand.

"Are you Mr. Ladd?" she asked in a brittle voice.

"I'm her attorney," he volunteered. Looking to be in his early thirties, he studied the six-foot, broad-shouldered figure in the full-length mirror on the opposite wall. *After ten years, only twenty-five pounds over my playing weight*, he thought. *Not bad.*

---

*Pronounced "May."

The band-aid on his cheek felt particularly conspicuous. He flicked lint off the sleeve of his navy-colored business suit. His square jaw tensed and his thick neck reddened slightly as his dark blue eyes watched the officer slide ponderously toward the intercom.

"A Mr. Ladd is here to see prisoner 1102," she announced in a voice that quickly echoed a garbled feedback over the intercom static. "He says he's her attorney."

The intercom crackled "That's right," or words to that effect. Her graying black head bent closer to the speaker in an attempt to catch the rest of the equally garbled message.

The officer flipped another switch. "Send a matron out to the desk room," she ordered as she kept a steady gaze at the attorney.

With his free hand he reached into his pocket for a neatly pressed handkerchief and wiped his forehead and dark, closely cropped hair.

Another uniformed female appeared in the doorway, also gray-haired and bespectacled. Unlike the desk officer, she was slight of build.

"Mr. Ladd?" she said in a thin, impassive voice. "This way, please."

Fighting a recurring pain in his knees, he limped as he followed the matron down a dimly lit corridor.

"Wait here." She gestured to a casually furnished visiting room. *Minimum security*, thought the attorney as he observed the folding chairs and card tables.

Shortly she returned with a brunette looking to be in her early forties.

"Fifteen minutes," announced the matron before she left.

The woman inmate stood alone in the doorway. She wore her hair simply but neatly trimmed, just touching her white blouse collar. Above a breast pocket a patch bore the words: "Traceville Woman's facility." Over her cotton blouse she wore a navy blue cardigan. Her gray, pegged jeans gathered at the waist without a belt.

Eyes of deepest indigo locked in eye contact with his. They set beneath a high, well-rounded forehead. Gone now was the usual vivacious and animated expression. She searched his face with an expression of pained urgency.

Tension lined pink lips unadorned by lipstick.

The words "Oh, Huck" choked in her throat as she started for him. *Thank God you're finally here*, she thought.

He laid his attaché case on a nearby table. The unreality hit him: his professor and internationally renowned scholar, his lover, now a prison inmate. He tried to overlook the pallor of a normally peach-colored complexion.

THE DELUGE SCROLLS

"Artie," he whispered as he held her to his chest.

Amid sighs of soft passion, they pressed in a kiss.

"Darling," she said, "we were so foolish to quarrel."

"Just damn foolishness on my part," he insisted.

She looked at him. "It's been a living hell without you," she said, fondling his coat lapel. "How could I not forgive?" She spoke in low voice; her diction fast paced but well modulated. Past friends had said her diction reminded them of Katherine Hepburn's.

"To think," he said, shaking his head, "how I almost blew it."

"Don't do that to yourself," she said. "What's done is done. We've got to put it behind us."

He again pressed his lips to her forehead. "How have you been?" he said, changing the subject. "Are you all right?"

Her eyes searched his. "Yes," she said. "I'm treated well."

The smell of Lysol caught his nostrils. Could be better, he thought. "We haven't much time," he said, pulling out a chair.

As she seated herself, he flipped the attaché case around and opened the lid. After pulling up his own chair, he studied the contents.

She eyed him inquisitively. "Any new developments?"

Ironic, she thought. When she was first incarcerated on charges of contempt of court, offers came pouring in from all over the country of financial, legal, moral, and PR support. As time went on, however, the stream of well-wishers gradually reduced to a trickle and eventually dried up completely.

She then became engulfed by feelings of loneliness, isolation, and total helplessness.

He took out a yellow legal pad and a sheaf of official-looking documents. "Maybe" was all he said.

Artie stiffened. "Oh, come on," she demanded. "Can't you give me anything better than that?"

"That depends," he shrugged.

"Depends on what for God's sake?" She shook her head in disbelief. "Come on, quit sounding like a lawyer."

"I wish I could tell you what you want to hear," he sighed. "However, I think there is some movement from George."

A pause. "Tell me," he went on, "if they were to drop the charges, let you keep your notes, but give up the scrolls, would you consider a deal?"

She leaned forward. "Come again?"

He began writing on a legal pad. "George and I had a little chat up at school over lunch." *Funny*, he thought, *how people change.*

She continued to study him. "By the way," she said, "what happened to your eye?"

Reaching up, he gingerly touched the band-aid that stretched across the cheekbone under one eye. Just beyond it spread a fringe of discolored skin. "Oh, this?"

"Were you in a fight?"

He shrugged. "I'm not going to lie to you. Yes, I was in a fight. The inside of my mouth feels like shredded wheat."

She shook her head. "You could have lost your eyesight," she said, jaw beginning to tense, "to say nothing of your possibly being disbarred."

"It was nothing."

He didn't mention Snake.

Her expression darkened. "Don't say that. I'm sick of hearing it. Was it while you were up at school?"

"Matter of fact it was—"

She continued a level gaze at him. "You were going to the Matador's—for old time's sake. Right?"

"Right."

"And you found it wasn't there anymore. You found an establishment known as 'Osiris Club,' right?"

He nodded.

She shook her head. "Why?" She stretched out the word in exasperation.

Huck glanced away for a moment. "I don't know," he sighed. "Seems like a crazy idea even to me now that I think about it."

Her eyes softened a little. "Promise me you won't go there again." *Dear, foolish boy*, she thought, *you know how I worry.*

In the ensuing silence Artie reflected again on her present predicament. Had she loosed upon the world forbidden information? To Inanna, ancient Sumerian goddess of love and life, was entrusted the secrets of Me—an unwritten body of divine decrees as binding in the realm of the spirit as was the law of gravity and mathematics in the physical. When Inanna was seduced into disclosing its secrets to unworthy persons, she was banished from the Sumerian Pantheon and the Me was lost to the world.

Did Artie experience such an epiphany a week ago right here in the prison? Would word of her interest in things occult—such as that interview with the inmate clairvoyant—finally get out? And that at a most inopportune time?

Her thoughts went in retrospect to that scene a week earlier in the prison library...

...She had entered the day room. Thinking herself alone, she rummaged through the magazine rack disgustedly looking among ancient, dog-eared copies. On impulse, she glanced over her shoulder.

The petite blond by the window—like the woman—wore regulation gray slacks and navy blue cardigan.

Artie stared in surprise. "Oh, excuse me," she said. "I didn't see you come in."

The face had a soft, round contour, like that of a young girl, perhaps in her mid-teens. From the inmate's neck hung a golden necklace.

Such a pretty thing, thought Artie. She had the air of childlike innocence that reminded Artie of her six-year-old self, dressed in angel costume as she sung her solo in that long-ago Sunday school Christmas pageant.

She marveled that the girl had none of the hard, street-smart demeanor of the other youthful inmates. Probably just a frightened, little runaway, she concluded.

A thought brought her up short. The murdered child! The resemblance to that child found in Peppi's beach house a decade previous was so striking it left Artie in momentary shock.

It couldn't be, she thought. *It just couldn't be!*

The girl gestured to Artie and then pointed to the window. Lines of concern began to crease the smooth forehead.

As Artie was about to start toward the girl, she heard a clatter. Behind her the inmate librarian had entered, pushing a magazine cart.

"I've got some new issues here," she said.

"Oh, good," said Artie. She paused and turned again toward the window. "What was it that you wanted?"

"Who were you talking to?" asked the librarian. Artie looked at the librarian and then back to where the childlike figure had stood. "Uh—nothing," she said in embarrassment. "Thank you."

The librarian took the magazines from the cart and put them on the rack and left. Artie looked again to the spot by the window. On the floor lay the necklace.

She walked over and picked it up. It must have been religious of some kind; otherwise prison regulations would forbid wearing it. Yet it was not a religious symbol with which she was familiar; certainly not the cross nor the Star of

David. At the base of the necklace hung an equilateral triangle, point side up, within a circle.

As she studied it more closely, she noticed something unusual. The corners of the triangle extended beyond the circle. Its lines intersected with the circumference and neither geometric figure looked placed on top of the other. Rather, their lines intertwined with each other so that they appeared linked together like a puzzle.

She slipped the necklace into her jeans pocket…

…"Like I said," Huck's words snapped her thoughts. "George and I had an interesting chat over lunch."

Artie looked at him. "And?"

"He said they'd be willing to drop the contempt charges and let you keep your notes if you would give up the scrolls."

"So I keep my notes," she said, folding her arms, "then what? What about the provost? What about my suspension?"

"I honestly don't know," he said. "I realize that there are still a lot of 'ifs.'"

Seconds seemed to drag on as the silence lengthened. *A lot of "ifs" is right,* she thought. *My release would still leave a lot unresolved, not the least of which is that encounter weekend.*

I never did claim that those scrolls were a record of Lost Atlantis, she reflected further. She realized that they did contain much that was controversial, but she never thought it would come to this. Had she realized the publicity and firestorm of conflict, she probably never would have gone to Iraq.

Or at least she would never have dug past the lowest level of Neolithic culture.

"So what do you suggest?" she said, studying him.

"That's the whole point of my visit." He slid his chair closer and began writing the date, April 23, 1989, on the legal pad. "Do you want to accept George's offer, or do you want to see what the court decides?"

"Half a loaf now or double or nothing later. Is that it?"

They both sat motionless for an indeterminate period of time. He glanced at his watch. "Our time's nearly up," he said, leaning toward her. "I need your answer."

Another pause. When Inanna allowed herself to be seduced into betraying the Me did she let loose forces that not only caused the disappearance of the Me's golden tablets but also caused her own destruction in the earthquake?

Artie turned toward him. "No way," she said, drawing her arms tighter. "I'll stay here until hell freezes over, but you tell them 'no way.'"

Chapter 1

"Any attempt to spirit her away by stealth is doomed to fail. Thus shall you affect the rescue of the Lady Aarda: In full light of day at high forenoon... you shall with all boldness escort her out the front gate... for with furtiveness of manner would you surely invite suspicion. You would surely be caught and severely punished... Ariel, the Watcher, will attend to her needs... The Grand Vizier is old and full of days. Methinks he will soon go the way of all flesh."
(Day 26, T'rani-akhmen's counsel to Lord H'rshag and Shumrag. Trans. and ed. Brit. Mus. vers. 1.5; 1981.)

* * * * *

"Time's up, Mr. Ladd." The matron reappeared in the doorway.

Huck rose from the table and quickly stuffed the legal pad and other documents back into the attaché case. As he latched the case shut, Artie also stood to her feet.

"When will I see you again?" she said, searching his face.

He grasped the case and let it fall to his side. "I'll be up next weekend," he said. He slipped his free hand around her shoulder. "Good-bye, darling."

Gripping his upper arm, she returned his kiss. "It's hard saying good-bye," she whispered.

He cast a quick glance toward the doorway. "Take care of yourself," he said as he stepped away from her. She followed, stood beside the matron and watched him start down the corridor.

Five minutes later an olive-colored Mercedes roared up to the front exit of the prison. A security guard stepped from a small house to open a wire gate bearing the words: "Tracerville Women's Facility." A cyclone fence enclosed canary yellow cinder-block buildings. The Mercedes moved out into street traffic, leaving the gate to swing shut behind it.

Beads of perspiration formed on Huck's face as he negotiated his car through dust-choked traffic. Foliage of curbside palm trees hung limp. The crowded landscape of squat, stucco houses gave way to burnt, brown hills pockmarked with hard, spiny vegetation.

Reaching for the air condition button, he sat back and pushed on through the thickening Los Angeles traffic.

As the car sped along a narrow canyon, he reached for a dashboard telephone. "Angie? Huck. I'm coming in. No need to stick around. I've got an all-nighter. Order yourself a pizza and put what's left in the fridge. See you Monday."

An hour later he eased the Mercedes into a subterranean parking garage adjacent a complex of glass-covered professional buildings. He edged his car into a shadowy parking slot, climbed out, and started for the elevator. It shunted him swiftly to one of the top floors. The door slid open, revealing a corridor of cool colors of gray and green. Huge, frameless paintings of acrylic, done in the modern abstract school, hung along the wall. The door of the end office bore the words: "Garrick, Lloyd, Egan, Ladd and Travis, P.C. Attorneys-at-Law."

When he inserted a key into the lock and opened the door, he saw a picture window that revealed the Los Angeles skyline, glistening in the sunset and the golden, shimmering Pacific beyond. Slipping past the secretary's desk, he headed for an inner office. Flinging his suit coat over the leather arm of an easy chair, he pulled several law volumes from a shelf and carried them to a richly textured couch adjacent another window. He switched on a lamp, opened one of the volumes, and studied its contents in the lamp's soft glow.

He began jotting notes on a legal pad. After a few moments, he paused and looked out at the fading afterglow. The western horizon still glowed an orange and pale blue. As lights sparkled like diamonds in nearby buildings, he reflected on that corridor scene ten years before...

THE DELUGE SCROLLS

* * * * *

…Clad in jeans and T-shirt, a younger, longer-haired version of the attorney saw a black student approaching.

"Huck, don't tell me you're in this class, too?" The student's sweatshirt, cut short at the sleeves, bore the Cortez Pacific Athletic Department logo. A large, muscular hand gripped a notebook.

"George!" Huck gestured toward the classroom. "How's this teacher going to handle two rowdies?"

The two athletes gazed through the doorway at the students in their chairs. The corridor now echoed with an emptiness void of all other traffic. They peered into the classroom at an intense young woman pacing behind the instructor's desk.

"This class is Archeology 101," she announced to the earnest young faces in front of her. "You will be expected to come to class prepared."

Her dark hair hung in gentle waves well past her shoulders. She attired her slim figure in a dark, mini-skirted suit, bordered about the neck with a wide, lacy lapel.

Huck studied the shapely legs in pale gray hose as she continued pacing across the front of the room. *If you got it, flaunt it,* he thought, reflecting a popular cliché of the day.

Serious-looking blue eyes behind dark, shell-rimmed glasses swept the classroom. She glimpsed the two husky youths still standing in the hallway.

"You will each be given a syllabus," she said, again turning to face the class.

Huck gave George a nudge. "Sounds like she's really got her tit in a ringer," he whispered.

"Hey, hey, what're you guys looking at?"

The words startled him. From seemingly nowhere, Mike Travis, the varsity defensive linebacker, breezed past.

Recovering from the surprise encounter, he reached for the door. The instructor broke off mid-sentence as the two athletes tiptoed into the room. All eyes followed them in their attempt to gracefully slink to the rear of the room.

The woman glared at them. "You two can sit there." She gestured stiffly to a back worktable. They continued shuffling along a chalkboard wall when a crash shattered the tranquility of the room.

Huck had failed to notice the pile of protruding books extending out in the aisle immediately in his way that sat atop a girl student's desk. He glanced down to see the obstruction too late to keep the books from cascading to the floor. He could feel the color rising in his neck as he bent to pick them up.

"Nice move, Ex-Lax," the girl whispered.

Huck studied her a moment. Pale blue eyes from behind round, wire-rimmed glasses glared back. Wiry auburn hair bordered a freckled face and hung down over a brightly colored granny dress.

"Don't mention it, bow-wow," he retorted as he straightened up.

A tittering spread through the class. The instructor planted herself behind her desk, arms folded. With a humorless face, she continued watching the conversationalists at the back of the room.

"Another thing," she continued in a brittle voice. "I'm a stickler for punctuality. You would do well to remember that."

She eyed the two newcomers now stretched out in a more relaxed position at the back worktable. "I will now hand out the syllabuses," she said, biting her lower lip.

"Is it syllabuses or syllabi?" whispered Huck

"Sh-sh!" admonished George. "I think we're in enough trouble."

The student whose books Huck had knocked to the floor now approached with an armload of stapled booklets. He reached for one in the middle of the stack. "I want that one."

"Get lost," she hissed, trying to whirl away from him. She tripped over a foot that he had extended out into the aisle. As she fought to keep balance, several top copies spilled onto the floor. This time he made no move to help her.

A rustling emanated from the rear of the classroom. "Can we have everyone's attention?" said the instructor in an edgy voice. She fidgeted with a pencil, waiting for the noise to subside.

"Turn to page one," she said finally. "You will notice the first topic is your required text."

"*Civilizations and Cultures of the Past*," whispered Huck, "sounds like exciting shit."

"C'mon, man," pleaded George, "knock it off."

"Look who the author is: Ardith Mason-Rodgers, Ph. D."

"There will also be extensive collateral reading," the instructor went on. "You will find a bibliography in the back."

Huck pointed to the chalkboard bearing the words: "Archeology 101. Dr. Mason-Rodgers."

"Quantity copies of the text are available at the Union bookstore," continued Dr. Mason-Rodgers, talking rapidly and glancing at the back of the room. Her face turned taut as she spotted an upraised hand. "Yes—you in the back, do you have a question?"

"The name's Ladd," announced Huck. "Can you get it in paperback?"

Dr. Mason-Rodgers stood rigid, arms folded. "No, Mr. Ladd," she said, smiling a tight smile, "you'll have to buy the hardcover edition—and pay the full price like everybody else."

"I think I'll wait for the movie to come out," he whispered, this time loud enough for the back two rows to hear.

George slid his chair away. "I'm movin' to a different spot tomorrow."

"You will notice item two on the front page," the instructor said, struggling to maintain composure, "is your next assignment. Again, I strongly urge you to come to class prepared."

"She wrote her own textbook," said Huck. "Talk about greed and conceit."

The instructor continued. *I must slow down*, she thought.

"And get that hyphenated last name." Huck nudged his companion, who was painfully trying to ignore him.

"You will notice Chapter One is entitled: 'Ancient Egypt—The Cradle of Civilization.'" The instructor held up the syllabus, "—And then, Chapter Two entitled: 'Sumer—Civilization's Beginnings in the Fertile Crescent.' Yes—what is it now?" she asked with rising irritation in her voice.

Huck had again raised his hand. "What about Atlantis?"

This time the laughter was less restrained.

"No, I'm serious," he insisted. "What about Atlantis? I was reading this book: *Search for Lost Empires*—"

Dismissal time.

Lines of tension melted from Dr. Mason-Rodger's face. The students continued laughing as they filed out. "Hey, Angie, is this class a hoot, or what?" someone called out to the girl whose books Huck had knocked to the floor.

Angie stalked out of the room. "That pig!" she fumed.

Back at the worktable George began picking up his syllabus and notebook. "C'mon, guy," he shouted to Huck above the tumult of the exiting students. "We got full-contact scrimmage today."

Huck gathered his material. "Hey, wait a sec," he said, knocking over his chair as he rushed to George's side. "I want to talk with this prof a minute."

"See you at practice," returned George as Huck watched his bobbing Afro fade into the disappearing crowd of classmates.

Stillness settled over the scene. A solitary Huck stood in the center of the room searching vainly for the instructor.

He did not see her retreat to her office, eyes glaring.

* * * * *

...Outside the window, darkness had fallen over the city. Hundreds of tiny lights sparkled in the inky void. He glanced at his legal pad. *It's a wonder she even spoke to me after that,* he thought.

Reaching deeper into his attaché case for a sheaf of Xeroxed pages, he eyed the top of the title page, *The Deluge Scrolls:*

'Akir-Ema is fallen!
'Alas, my people! In a moment, gone is your glory, your beauty.
'How well I remember you as singers, dancers, musicians, and revelers sang in your streets as on holiday the throngs in bright, festal garments and festooned with garlands marched in holy processional. How I remember the celebrants crowding the portico of Lemekh's holy temple around the massive, marbled, gilded, and bejeweled temple columns that supported roofs and balconies ornate with frieze and mural. How the acolytes and choristers began ceremonies of singing, chanting, praying, and lifting of holy hands to our god, Lemekh the Great, in anticipation of hearing the spoken prophecy.
'How the people trusted, living confidently for generations under his care and now are not.' (Day 1. Lord H'rshag's Lament for Akir-Ema. Trans. and ed. Brit. Mus. Vers. 1.65; 1981.)

His watch said almost eleven. He recalled knocking on her office the next day...

* * * * *

... "Come in," called out a female voice.

Dr. Mason-Rodgers sat behind a desk in an office cluttered with bookshelves and filing cabinets. Today she wore her hair back exposing small, delicately shaped ears.

Without waiting for an invitation, he slipped into a chair.

Her face hardened. "Make yourself at home," she said in a voice edged with sarcasm. "Am I about to be treated to an encore?"

THE DELUGE SCROLLS

"Encore?"

She pushed her chair back. "That was some performance yesterday," she said. "Am I to look forward to your entertaining the class like that every day?"

"Oh, that," he said, smiling sheepishly. "Sorry about that. It won't happen again."

Dr. Mason-Rodgers rested her chin against her folded hands. "So, what brings you here, then?"

He fidgeted in his chair. One hand gripped a loose-leaf binder and a book entitled *Search for Lost Empires*. "I wanted to see you yesterday after class."

"About what?" she sighed.

"About ancient civilizations and stuff."

She tilted her head and looked off into space. "Ancient civilizations and stuff," she said, mocking his words, "is what this class is all about. What about ancient civilizations and stuff?"

"Well—you might also like to know I read tomorrow's assignment already and—"

"Yippee," she said in mock enthusiasm, as she made small circling motions with her forefinger.

"No, I mean," he stammered, "I read this stuff about Ancient Egypt and Babylon, but I was just wondering—"

"Wondering about what?" she said, folding her hands again. "Could we make this brief?"

"I was wondering about—well, about Atlantis, for instance."

Her hands dropped to the desk. "Atlantis?"

"Yeah." He held up his copy of *Search for Lost Empires*.

"Oh, help," she sighed. "Mr. Ladd, Archeology 101 is a class devoted to serious scientific study."

"I understand that."

She went on, "Ditto this department. Ditto this university. We haven't time for that sort of thing."

"But I've been reading up on this stuff," he countered. "Take Easter Island, for instance. Take Stonehenge. Take that airstrip down in Peru. Why doesn't somebody do research on that stuff?"

"Mr. Ladd," she said, leaning forward slightly. "Do you think I'd risk my professional reputation going after that kind of nonsense?"

She stood up and started for the door. "I've a departmental meeting in twenty minutes," she announced briskly, "and I've a lot of work to do."

He took the hint and followed her to the door. "Yeah, I suppose," he said. "Well, anyway, thanks for your time."

"You're quite welcome," she said with stiff formality. "Stop by anytime. My office is always open to my students."

When he had left, she shook her head and cursed softly to herself as she went back to her desk. *Probably on an athletic scholarship*, she thought. How ironic. She had always considered the term "athletic scholarship" an oxymoron. Like many administrators, Dr. Faasendeck had justified this on the grounds that a winning sports program meant more alumni donations for academic programs. This, in turn, forced other schools competing in their league to beef up their athletics as well, thus forcing an upward money spiral in ever-widening proportions. The pressure, also, increased on faculty members to see to it that these athletic stars stayed eligible.

She sighed as she sifted through papers that lay on her desk.

She could not shake the image of the tapered male figure walking down the hallway from her office.

Lost Atlantis, she thought. *Now I've heard everything.*

She spotted an envelope with the words "The National Geographic Society" on its letterhead. She tore open the flap and started to read:

Dear Dr. Mason-Rodgers:

... in response to your previous correspondence regarding the archeological expedition to Iraq that the Society is contemplating for next year. After reviewing your credentials, the committee has decided to extend to you an invitation to join the expedition...

The dream of a lifetime, she thought. To actually study the Ancient Sumerians on site. No more secondhand information out of books and museums.

Expert in cuneiform though she was, she had one regret: that she had never heard the language spoken.

She reflected on the ancient Sumerian Me, a system of universal decrees of divine authority. To hear and learn the spoken language, she felt, would certainly be an instance of such an epiphany.

She sat back and pondered the matter further.

Babylon.

One of the greatest world empires of antiquity: wealthy, prosperous, despotic, cruel; condemned in the Apocalypse as the Mother of Harlots, prophetically doomed in the Torah to soon be overthrown never to rise again and to forever after stand desolate, bereft of human habitation. Why had scientists not already tapped into the site of Babylon proper when it promised to be such a potentially rich archeological find?

As she reached in the narrow drawer under the desktop to withdraw some personal stationery, she paused. She looked across her office to a small bookcase. On the top shelf stood a figurine about half a foot high. It was in the shape of an ancient female deity standing bare-breasted and holding a pair of serpents twisting around her outstretched arms. Can a modern woman of science actually worship an ancient pagan deity?

She wondered.

At the upper right hand corner of the sheet, she started writing in a small, neat hand:

September 8, 1979

Dearest Peppi:

I finally did it! That invitation from The National Geographic Society has finally come through! If I can get a sabbatical next year, I'm out of here! No more classes—no more oversexed, overbearing, underachieving adolescent jocks for one whole year.

Speaking of which: I think I've met the biggest jerk of all. Came into my class yesterday. You guessed it. He put on quite a show. Hate to admit it, Peppi, but I almost lost it.

And now, in a more somber vein: Lester and I are still in a deadlock on this matter of divorce. He's being very difficult to deal with. Maybe I can go into detail when next we see each other.

Hate to end this epistle on this note, but, I guess c'est le vie. Anyway, I'm bound and determined to put it behind me and get on with my life.

In the meantime, Peppi, dearest, stay sweet.

Love
Artie

Her mention of Lester brought up another disturbing memory: that disastrous encounter weekend.

She thrust the envelope into a small, brown purse that lay on the desk. *Another dreadful faculty meeting,* she thought with a sigh.

As she neared the door, she realized she could still detect the woodsy scent of his aftershave. She paused briefly in the doorway. Was it the impish grin, or the expression of wide-eyed confidence set below a broad forehead? Or was it the chiseled, jaunty profile?

She slipped out the door and closed it behind her.

The crisp staccato of her heels echoed through the corridor as she walked down the hall toward a distant amphitheater.

Chapter 2

'Twas there also grew I to a youth—tall, strong, and stout. Vigorously in pursuit was I in many games with Ulki and Wolki, my companions by. We raced. We strove (wrestled.) We played at squamish, and at quoits... Learned we the finer and precise arts (science) till at the last were we allowed to sit at the feet of doctors wise. (Day 3. Lord H'rshag's early memoirs. Trans. and ed. Brit. Mus. vers. 1.5; 1981.)

* * * * *

"If you're going to foul up the air," Dr. Mason-Rodgers warned, "I'm leaving."

Dr. Berthold, head of the history department, inserted an ornately carved meerschaum between his teeth. "They got blowers on." He spoke in a deep, stentorian voice. "You won't even notice." He pointed to a sign that read, "Smoking Permitted."

"Is this a habit, or a hobby?" She cast him a sidelong glance. He began ritualistically scraping his pipe bowl. A balding, bear of a man with a gray goatee, he wore a rumpled tweed blazer, corduroy slacks, and shoes with no socks.

"I can't get through this meeting without my pacifier," he said, sucking the stem. "You know that."

Artie spotted a tall man striding toward the front of the amphitheater. He bounced on the balls of his feet in a mincing gait and his head wobbled uncontrollably. He squirmed slightly in his ill-fitting, double-breasted gray suit as he stepped up to the platform. The face was framed by cheeks still round with baby fat. Full, red lips puckered as though having just tasted something sour. Colorless eyes squinted behind rimless glasses. Gray, wavy hair swept back in a pompadour. Artie contemplated his wide, undulating posterior: odd body shape for a man when one stops to think about it.

She recalled Huck's exit from her office: the broad shoulders, the triangle taper, and finally the compact glutei muscles under the tight slacks.

"Let the good times roll," she had commented when Dr. Purvis Lester Rodgers, her estranged husband, turned on an overhead.

"Fie," said Dr. Berthold, flipping his tobacco pouch.

She shot him a wry smile. He was a confidant privy to the ugliness that had happened during an encounter weekend gone sour. He had often expressed impatience with her reluctance to press charges.

With long, delicate hands, Dr. Rodgers gripped the sides of the lectern and looked out at the audience without making eye contact. "I will first pass out some handouts," he announced in a tense, high-pitched voice. "Could we have a couple of volunteers?"

A chubby man with a small moustache and an untidy comb-over stood up; followed by a slender, cigar-smoking woman with long, gray hair. "Les's stooges," commented Dr. Mason-Rodgers.

"We have a long agenda," said Dr. Rodgers, clearing his throat. "But first, the minutes of the last meeting."

"I can't believe this," sighed Dr. Mason-Rodgers. "We've got everything right here in front of us. Why doesn't he just give us a couple of minutes to read them over and then ask for their approval?"

Voices droning and papers shuffling dulled her attention. Her reverie was cut short, however, by the following words: "Next on the agenda we have the following: recent university directives and guidelines pursuant to human rights and affirmative action."

Dr. Berthold sat upright, taking long puffs on his pipe.

"Item number one," Dr. Rodgers went on, "pursuant to the request by the department of archeology and anthropology for the creation of a department head: The University Provost has determined that only members of certain qualified minorities be considered; and that should qualified candidates be not forthcoming, the position of said department head remain unfilled. Be it further recommended that, in the interim, the department remain under the jurisdiction of the College of Arts and Sciences."

"Way to keep everybody under your thumb," whispered Artie.

Dr. Rodgers' voice droned on, "Item two," he intoned, "the Sabbatical Review Board has also decided to give minorities preferential consideration in the granting of sabbaticals..."

She straightened to upright position. "This may what I've been waiting for."

"What about him?" Dr. Berthold gestured toward the lectern.

"Going before the Sabbatical Review Committee," she said, standing up, "he wouldn't dare try anything."

She stepped to the aisle. "I've gotten all I want out of this meeting."

Dr. Berthold also rose to his feet. "Let's say good-bye to all this," he said, slipping his pipe into his coat pocket...

* * * * *

... Huck flipped open a voluminous tome that lay on the couch beside him. He then began jotting on a yellow legal pad beside it. He paused and again let his mind return in retrospect to the Cortez Pacific University campus of a decade before.

He recalled the factions that had divided the student body in those days. At the pinnacle stood the Greeks: sons and daughters of the socially prominent who organized themselves into Greek letter fraternities and sororities. These, in turn, derisively labeled the lesser affluent non-members geeks, or barbarians. Bearded, unwashed radicals, noisily disdaining both groups, formed a fringe of activists that championed the various social, economic, and ideological issues of the day.

A less boisterous group was the divinity students. Even though historically a private, church-related school, Cortez Pacific's vast secularly minded majority scorned this latter group as outcasts.

The jocks separated themselves into their own world of the athletically elite. The dislike of these groups for one another often erupted into violence, with the Matador—a favorite off-campus hangout—as the vortex.

The management, as a consequence, maintained a telephone hotline with the nearest precinct station...

* * * * *

...The Matador's interior reverberated with a hubbub of laughter, smoke, and youthful humanity. Murals of bullfighting scenes and dancing senoritas decorated stucco walls. Flickering candles in glazed pots at dark, oaken tables gave a dim light to the room. A trio of musicians in native costumes strummed on flamenco guitars, trying to cut through the crowd noise with melancholy chords of Spanish folk music. A contralto vocalist accompanied herself with finger castanets.

George Bouknight made his way to a remote table and joined other students from the archeology class. He set a beer mug down and pulled his chair up close.

A slim, bearded youth made room. "I'm Paul," he announced. He introduced Chris, a heavy-set, older-looking woman and Jacki, a sweatshirt-and-jeans-clad blond. As George took her hand, he noticed an almond-shaped eye tattooed on the back. Beside her sat Angie, the student whose books Huck had knocked to the floor.

"George," said Paul, "—Angie."

The Matador customarily crowded to capacity this time of evening with students coming in for their after-library mixer. Above the hubbub, those interested in eavesdropping could catch snippets of campus gossip floating through laughing and clinking of glasses.

(Ever hear the real reason why Doc Mason-Rodgers split from her old man?)

(Does Doc Mason-Rodgers have the hots for jocks more than she lets on?)

(Is Dean Rodgers just your garden-variety weirdo, or is he into kinky? Or maybe even flat-out scary?)

"We need to form a study group," Paul suggested.

The crowd of students pouring into the taproom forced George to stand and search the bobbing sea of heads. He caught a glimpse of Huck's dark hair and massive shoulders. When Huck finally spotted his wave, he began forcing his way toward their table.

Angie pulled away. "Watch your drinks, everybody." *I thought athletes were more adroit on their feet,* she thought.

Huck stole a chair from another table and slid it back first into their circle. He set his beer mug on the tabletop and sat down. "I won't bite," he said to her.

"What are they doing, cleaning out your cage?"

THE DELUGE SCROLLS

He studied her a moment. "Just got my distemper shot."
Paul again suggested they form a study group.
Huck eyed Angie. "I'd like that."
"You can read of course?" she said with a tight smile.
"No." He edged closer. "You're going to have to do it for me."
George suggested that Huck and he get the next round. As they moved toward the bar, he shouted in Huck's ear, "At least try to be nice, okay?"...

* * * * *

...Huck fought an impulse to doze. He stretched out on the couch and surveyed the pile of opened law books. He again began jotting on his legal pad. He glanced at the ship's clock on his desk. Midnight already.

The phone startled him and he jumped to his feet. Picking up the receiver, he sat on the corner of his desk

"Hello?" His voice was husky with fatigue. As he stood up, he favored a lame knee. "George? How did you know where I—? No, don't worry about the hour. You want to see me? Tomorrow?"

He leaned back over the desktop again. He absentmindedly stared at a pencil sketch of Abraham Lincoln hanging from a far wall. Below it read the caption, "A Lawyer's Stock in Trade is his Time and Advice."

As he bent slightly toward the phone, he could feel his mid-section roll over his belt. Once you stop training, he acknowledged, it shows.

"What time? Seven? I know a great little grill around the corner. Right. Seven."

He hung up the phone. If he thought he won the round the first day, he realized the second day had to have gone to her...

* * * * *

..."Mr. Ladd—" Dr. Mason-Rodgers' voice startled him. He looked up in a daze. George smiled at his discomfiture.

"Yes, ma'am," he said, struggling to maintain his composure.

"Mr. Ladd," Dr. Mason-Rodgers said again as she stood erect behind her desk. Blue eyes, framed by shell-rimmed glasses, zeroed in on him. "What is the name of the tablet discovered in 1799 by Napoleon's officers in the Nile Delta that enabled us to decipher ancient Egyptian hieroglyphics?"

George's face revealed nothing. Huck could feel the eyes of the class. "Could you repeat the question?"

"What is the name of the tablet," she repeated, using the same words and the same voice inflection, "discovered in 1799 by Napoleon's officers in the Nile Delta that enabled us to decipher ancient Egyptian hieroglyphics?"

He took a deep breath. "Good question." Silence began to weigh heavily in the classroom.

"Did you read the assignment?"

He looked straight at her. "Yes, ma'am, I did."

She began tapping a pencil. "In that case, I can't understand your inability to answer my question."

She folded her arms and turned toward the window. "The tablet in question is called the Rosetta Stone. Now do you recall reading it?"

Perspiration formed on the palm of his hands. "Yes, ma'am, I guess I just temporarily forgot."

She turned from the window. "You may recall my suggesting that you come to class prepared."

He tore a sheet from his notebook and wadded it up.

"You're going to find," she went on, "that merely reading the chapter is not going to be sufficient. You are going to have to outline it and then study it so that instead of temporarily forgetting, you will permanently remember."

"What's her problem anyway?" he whispered to George. He threw his wadded paper across the tabletop to the floor.

His attention again wandered until he heard her words: "Your first term paper will be due in six weeks."

"The shit has hit the fan," he said to George, again in a whisper.

"I have a list of books that I have set aside on reserve at the library," said Dr. Mason-Rodgers. "Remember that there will be others who will want to use them, too."

Huck nudged George. "I hate writing."

George passed him a note: "waiting till our senior year to fulfill a science requirement—stupid."

Huck looked at a chart showing a timetable tracking ancient civilizations. Dr. Mason-Rodgers droned on about the term paper.

Suddenly dismissal.

As the students gathered their books and started to leave, Huck got up out of his seat more slowly than usual.

That evening, the study group again assembled at the Matador. Amid the rising noise level, they found conversation becoming increasingly difficult. This, however, did not daunt their efforts. Huck remained the lone exception. Leaning against the back of his chair, he stared into his untouched mug, nursing both beer and sulk. He mused darkly on his altercation with Dr. Mason-Rodgers. He pondered the high, well-rounded forehead and oval face. He could still visualize the sensitive, articulate-looking mouth and the even, white teeth.

How can she such a bitch and fox at the same time?

Angie noticed his mood. "What's the matter, beer gone stale?" she said, pulling a cigarette from a package that lay on the table.

"Term papers." Huck shook his head. "I hate 'em."

Angie lit her cigarette. "You're serious, aren't you?"

"Damn right I'm serious."

"What did you do about term papers before?"

"I bought 'em," he admitted, "but they didn't have any for archeo. 101."

She shook her head. "So now you got to do this one on your own, right?" she laughed. "Serves you right."

"You're about as sympathetic as a barracuda."

"You should have majored in English."

He wadded up a cocktail napkin. "Okay," he said, "so who do you know that's an English major?"

Angie bent her head close so he could hear. "Me."

He paused. "Yeah," he said finally. "That's the ticket. You're going to help me."

"I am?"

He turned to her. "C'mon. You gotta. It's my only chance."

Angie sat silent. Paul gave her a nudge. "We need to talk." He gestured toward the exit.

She turned to follow him out into the foyer away from the din of the taproom. As they passed a cigarette machine, he gestured toward a men's room. "Be back in a sec."

The men's room door closed behind him and Angie began to discern individual voices from the all-encompassing rumblings just beyond the taproom doorway. She thought she heard Huck's voice from just around the corner: "So what's your problem, Mike?"

Above the crowd laughter, she heard another voice: "I need a place to crash for a few days."

She recognized it to be that of Mike Travis, one of Huck's teammates.

"No problem," said Huck. "Mind if I ask why?"

Another pause. Finally Mike again spoke. "Marge and I got problems. She thinks I've been runnin' around."

"Have you?"

"That," Mike's voice took a hard edge, "is beside the point. The point is that she is always jealous as hell. What she needs is to be shown who's boss. Know what I mean?"

"No, I don't," Huck's voice hardened as well. "Suppose you tell me."

"So," said Mike, ignoring Huck's remark, "how about it?"

Another pause. "On one condition," said Huck finally, "if I so much hear of you hittin' any woman, your suitcase is gonna wind up on my doorstep."

Angie felt a presence behind her.

"What are you doing, eavesdropping?"

Paul had just exited from the lavatory. "We need to talk," he said again.

Angie leaned against the cigarette machine.

"So talk." He eyed her. "Are you going to do it?"

She folded her arms and leaned away. "I don't know," she sighed. "Part of me wants to say 'yes' and part of me wants to say 'no way.'"

"Lemekh wills it." Paul edged closer. "This may be the lost priest of Lemur."

Angie brushed away. "He doesn't act very priestly to me."

"Appearances can be deceiving."

He turned to her. "Besides," he continued, "the tutoring experience could be valuable to you."

Angie shrugged and followed him back into the taproom just as they saw Huck and George about ready to leave.

Huck eyed her questioningly. "Big confab?"

She stood beside their table, arms folded.

"Be in the library," she said finally, "tomorrow at one."

Chapter 3

Learned we vigorously many sports such as fencing... Learned we poetry from bards of old. Learned we of the finer arts of music... and mysteries of the precise arts (sciences)... Learned we intricacies of rhetoric (composition) of ballad and rhyme...
(Day 3. Lord H'rshag's memoirs of his early years. Trans. and ed. Brit. Mus.; vers. 1.5; 1981.)

* * * * *

Huck paced the floor in front of the main desk of the Lemuel Adler Memorial Library and looked at his watch. Five minutes to one.

"Can I help you?"

The pale, bespectacled youth behind the desk looked up from his pile of books. He parted his hair in the middle and wore a stubble of a moustache.

Huck shook his head. "I'm waiting for somebody." He spotted Angie outside and almost collided with the door when it didn't open.

"Wrong way." The youth pointed to a door that said "exit." He continued stamping books with ill-concealed mirth.

When Huck finally found the exit, the door refused to open. "I'll have to buzz you out," said the thin voice from behind the desk.

Once out the exit, his footsteps reverberated against the marbled walls and floor of the lobby. He saw Angie waiting at the top of the stairway. "I can't believe this place," he fumed.

"Obviously you haven't spent much time in there," she said.

Upon reentering the library, Angie cast a knowing glance at the librarian. "Sow the wind."

"Reap the whirlwind," he replied. "Watch out for Snake."

She extended her thumb and index finger. "Blessed be—"

"What the devil was that all about?" Huck whispered as they headed for a conference room.

Angie laughed briefly. "Oh, nothing."

He tried to dismiss his misgivings as they seated themselves at the table. Later, they returned from the stacks with several heavily bound volumes from the reserve shelf.

He opened his packet of note cards. "Where do we start?"

"First thing," she said, pulling out a sheaf of typewritten sheets, "is that you've got to pick a topic."

He stared at the list in front of him:

- *Social Classes of Ancient Egypt Middle Kingdom Examined.*
- *Civil Law of Ancient Babylon and Egypt Compared.*
- *Religion of Babylon and Egypt Compared.*

"How do I make a choice?" he said with a wry smile.

Angie cast a sidelong glance. "Actually you don't have much of a choice. Most of the subjects have been picked."

Huck's shoulders sagged. "So what do I do?"

Angie ran her finger down the page. "Right here," she said. "This is about the only one left."

He took the list. "Good Lord, how am I ever going to write on *The Evolution and Development of Cuneiform?*"

Angie laughed briefly. "Actually you're in luck. Dr. Mason-Rodgers just happens to be an internationally recognized authority."

He surveyed the stark, tan-colored walls of the conference room. "How do you figure that to be an advantage?"

"Go to her for help," said Angie. "She's the best."

He looked through the door that provided the only visual outlet to the world beyond. He spotted a teammate headed for the exit with an arm around a shorts-clad blond. "I'd rather stick my head in a lion's mouth."

"Dummy. Get back in her good graces; whatever it takes."

Angie paused and studied him a moment. "I can see you still don't get it," she said finally. "When it comes to linguistics, the woman is sheer genius. She can read Cuneiform like you and I can read a newspaper. The top experts from all around the world look up to her. Also, they can't understand why she bothers teaching 101-level courses."

Huck reflected on that first class. *Probably not the smartest thing I ever did,* he concluded.

"Look," Angie's words brought him back to reality. "I'll help you with grammar and she can help you with content."

Huck sat back, idly flipping the pages of the topic list.

Angie pushed a book toward him. "Come on, get to work," she said. "I'm not going to do your research for you."

Huck began laboriously to write on the note cards.

After an hour, he turned to her. "Got to get to practice," he said, "but hey, I appreciate this." He scooped up the books. "Let's see if Doofus will let us out of here."

"His name is Wally."

"Right."

He followed her and piled the books on the desk. Satisfied with the count, the librarian reached for the buzzer.

"'Bye, Wally," said Angie as they started for the door.

"'Bye, Wally," said Huck, imitating Angie's voice.

* * * * *

...Huck stopped writing on the legal pad. His watch said one o'clock. *If weren't for the both of them,* he acknowledged, *I wouldn't even be here.*

He recalled a phone conversation Artie had told him about in later years...

* * * * *

...Her eyes narrowed as she heard the voice from the other end.

"Lester, whatever is this nonsense about the high priest of Rok? If this call is about school business, let's talk. Otherwise just hang up, okay? Yes, I have a Hershel Ladd in one of my classes."...

... At the other end of the line, Dr. Rodgers held the phone to his ear with one hand as he studied a document that lay on his desk:

Dossier on student Hershel Ladd, senior, physical education major. Grandfather—the Rev. Waldemars Ladovicius b. Riga, Latvia 1875.
  m. Isle Veciedins 1898.
  1. Waldemars Jr. b. 1900, 2. Jens b. 1902, 3. Joosip b. 1904, 4. Karl b. 1908, 5.Joris b. 1909, 6.Sjoren b. 1911, 7.Maris b. 1913, 8. Hilda b. 1915, 9. Marika b. 1917.
  Father—the Rev. Maris Ladovicius b. 1913
  m. Lisa Saarinen 1935.
  1. Gottfried b. 1937, 2. Petrus b. 1939, 3. Karl Willems b. 1941, 4. Rurik b. 1943, 5. Ingeborg b. 1949, 6. Arnoldis b.1951, 7. Vist b 1953, 8.Hershel b. 1955, 9. Dorit b. 1957....

...A pause. "What kind of student is he?" Artie said. "Well—I haven't had him in class all that long, but I will say this: he hasn't made a very good impression on me so far."

She glanced at her watch. She expected him momentarily...

...While she waited for Dr. Rodgers to continue, he glanced at the dossier. *That's it,* he thought, *the seventh son of a seventh son. Just as I suspected...*

...Artie shook her head with incredulity. "His English? Oral? Average, except that he uses it entirely too freely. Written? In a word, atrocious. How's he going to do a research paper? I don't even want to think about it. Do I expect to give him any help? That's going to be up to him."

Her expression darkened.

"I'm not to give him extra help?" she said, casting a sidelong glance at the phone. "You've got to be kidding! As an educator, what kind of counsel is that? What novice priest of Lemur? Whatever are you talking about? Oh, I get it, more of your weird games. Now you listen and listen good. Any subsequent calls you make are going to be recorded and that's a promise. I suggest you not call this number again for any reason. Good-bye, Lester."

She hung up just as Huck entered. As he sat across from her, she again caught the leathern scent of his cologne.

She began examining his note cards. "Young man," she said, eyeing the cards critically, "you're really going to have to work."

"Well," he shrugged, "Angie Morgenstern is helping me with the grammar. We were wondering if you'd be willing to help with content and research."

Dr. Mason-Rodgers resumed her examination of his note cards. "Yes, we definitely need to do that..."

THE DELUGE SCROLLS

* * * * *

...The timer gave a ring. Huck opened the microwave door and took out the pizza. Intensive tutoring from both women helped him not only with the paper but also, by the end of six weeks, in eliminating his grammatical deficiencies as well. He recalled sessions with Angie in that library conference room...

...He sensed the bare, tan walls closing in him. In one hour he would have to leave for football practice. The time for his release couldn't come fast enough. Words came to him as in a dream.

"Look." It was Angie's voice. "The subject and direct object of the verb have to agree."

He could feel sweat under his T-shirt.

"In number, gender, and tense," she continued...

He also recalled sitting in Dr. Mason-Rodgers' office...

...The scent of her perfume subtly wafted across her desk as she leaned toward him. She held a chart for him to look at. "This is the symbol for 'man,'" she said pointing to a three-stroke stick figure.

"I add this stroke," she continued, "and it becomes a woman."

She paused as he studied the figures in question.

"Now let's see your current draft," she said after a short silence.

She took the paper and examined it briefly. Then she laid it down on her desktop and took a red pencil. She began to cover the paper with scribbling until it looked to him as though she had written more on that paper than he.

Despite his sinking spirits, he noticed her smile.

"Don't be so discouraged," she said with a slight laugh.

Damn her, anyway, he thought. *She's playing with me.*

"Actually I see an improvement, believe or not."

As he sat dejectedly studying his paper, Dr. Mason-Rodgers leveled a gaze at him.

"Mr. Ladd," she added, lowering her voice, "don't give up. You are making progress. You really are."

She studied his still worried look. She felt her previous disdain for athletes and athletic scholarships wearing thin.

"After all," she added, "we've got to see to it that you stay eligible."

To his surprise, she followed her remark with a wink...

* * * * *

...After a girl student handed back his paper, wet hands picked up a corner of the front page. He spotted the red-penciled words "see me."

After dismissal he shuffled across the hall to her office. He cleared his throat. "You wanted to see me?"

"Oh, yes." She gestured to a chair. "Please sit down."

As he settled in his chair, she propped her elbows on her desktop and eyed him quizzically. "Huck, you amaze me."

This was the first time she had addressed him by his first name.

She took his paper and looked at it. "I purposely did not write a grade," she said, "because I wanted to have a conference with you about it."

She continued studying him. "What's the matter?" she teased.

"I don't know," he said, trying to sound non-committal. "Is something the matter?"

"Always have to play the hard guy," she said, shaking her head.

She watched him fidget in his chair as she let the conversation lapse. "You amaze me," she said again.

She took a red pencil and scrawled something across the cover page. He saw a large, red "A."

"I just wanted to congratulate you," she said, handing the paper back to him. "You are a quick study. We've found that out, haven't we? However, don't ever put things off to the last minute again."

"Point well taken," he sighed as he rose from his chair. "And thanks for your help."

He had almost reached the door when her next words caught him unprepared.

"How would you like to work for me?" she said. "I'm doing a post-doctoral dissertation on Sumerian culture. I'm going to need a research assistant. The work won't be all that hard and you can pretty much pick your own hours."

He hesitated briefly, and then answered. "Yeah," he said with a shrug. "I guess so."

"Good." She stood to her feet. "Start Monday?"

* * * * *

That next week Artie spotted a folded message tacked to the bulletin board just outside her office. She saw her name scrawled in large, masculine-looking handwriting:

THE DELUGE SCROLLS

22 October, 1979
Dear Dr. Mason-Rodgers,
Sorry I can't make it today. Something has come up. Something unavoidable. Will explain when I see you.

Sincerely,
Huck

She bit her lower lip. *Oh, dear God,* she thought, *now what?*

* * * * *

Huck and George stood outside an office door, studying the words on the frozen glass window:

George T. Sturgis, Ph. D., Athletic Director

He studied the note he held in his hand:

19 October, 1979

Mr. Ladd,

It is urgent that you report to my office Monday morning 22 October 1979, 9:00 AM sharp.

Sincerely,
Geo. T. Sturgis,
Athletic Dir.

They knocked. From inside a heavy voice bade them enter.
A white-haired man with a ruddy face looked up at them. A rumpled gray suit with narrow lapels draped loosely over a powerful-looking build.
The athletic director gestured to a couple of chairs. "Sit down, gentlemen."

Head varsity coach, Bob Schermerheim, sat beside the AD. Shorter but stockier, he looked to be in his early fifties. A square-shaped head set solidly on a thick neck was crowned with thinning, sandy-colored hair. Rimless glasses framed steely blue eyes. A hawk-like nose and jutting jaw framed a puckish mouth.

"Do you gentlemen have any idea what this is all about?" asked the AD.

"No, sir," said Huck. As he waited for the AD to explain, he studied the wall opposite. Cortez Pacific athletic squads from seasons past covered it from one end to the other. A younger version of the AD sat in one of the photos, front row center. The football he held had the number "39" painted across it. The faces bore the expression of naïve confidence. Hairstyles looked quaint—cropped short, shaved high on the side, and parted in the middle, or on the side, or swept straight back. Thin, leather helmets lined the grass in front and thin-looking shoulder pads protruded slightly under heavy woolen jerseys. Crudely stitched numerals spread across their chests. Bulky pants extended wing-like above their waists. They covered their muscular calves with knitted stockings tucked into ankle-length shoes with heavy cleats.

He marveled at how scrawny they looked in comparison to the thick-necked and heavily bicepped athletes of today. Better training methods and better diet, he concluded.

The AD's voice cut short his thoughts. "We have a complaint from the dean's office," he said, picking up a letter from the Dean of the College of Arts and Sciences:

16 October, 1979

Complaint is hereby formally lodged against one Herschel P. Ladd and one George B. Bouknight relative to an incident alleged to have occurred on or about Saturday 9:00 AM, 13 October 1979 in the men's rest room of the Lemuel Adler Memorial Library. The offense was alleged to have been committed against the person of one Walden T. Brookes. According to the victim's own sworn testimony, the incident occurred as follows: Messrs Ladd and Bouknight approached the victim in the abovementioned washroom. After engaging the victim in a brief conversation, the alleged assailants, Messrs. Ladd and Bouknight, seized Mr. Brookes in a violent and potentially injurious manner, held him aloft while rendering him immobile by holding his arms and legs tight against his body, did with all malice and intent, force the victim's head down into the bowl of one of the commodes. Whereupon the alleged assailants then flushed same, causing great amounts of water to flow over the victim's head and then fled scene of the crime on foot.

The AD laid the paper aside and looked at the two youths a moment. "Fellows," he said, "what's this all about?"
"That was Wally," answered Huck, "student librarian."
The AD glared at him. "What gives you gentlemen the right to pick on student librarians?"
"Well, you see it was this way, sir," Huck began. "We ran into him in the library john on the Saturday of Homecoming. When we got talking with him, we found that not only was he not planning on going to the game, he didn't even know who it was we were playing."
"We felt obligated to teach him a lesson in school spirit," said George, "by giving him a 'swirlee.'"
"We grabbed him and stuck his head down one of the toilets," added Huck, "then gave it a flush."
The AD eyed him with incredulity. "That's it?"
"Yes, sir."
"Get out of here," growled the AD.
After they left, Coach glanced at the letter. "What a crock," he snorted in disgust.
Five minutes later, Huck knocked on Dr. Mason-Rodgers' office door. "Got through sooner than expected."
She was seated at her desk. She put aside her pen. "Oh, good," she said, studying him as he pulled up a chair across from her.
She sat silent a moment. "I heard about your altercation with the student librarian," she said at last.
Taken aback, he was finally able to mutter, "No big deal. It's done and over with—I think." He saw her features soften.
"I'm glad," she said with a smile. "I don't like it when one of my students gets into trouble."
Heart racing, he rubbed sweaty palms on his pant legs.
"Especially when I need him to work for me," she added.

What's with this sudden chummy small talk? he wondered.

He noticed the figurine atop her bookcase. "Hey," he said airily, "sexy lady."

She briefly appeared flustered. "Just a memento," she said. "Let's get to it, shall we?"

She stood up and scooped a bundle of periodicals from atop the filing cabinet. "Let's go across the hall," she said as she staggered toward the door.

Huck likewise wrapped his arms around a pile of slick-covered magazines. Despite his attempt to maintain a neat armload, some of the issues slipped until they protruded at precariously awkward angles as he followed her to the classroom.

Plopping her load down on the worktable, she had to struggle to keep the periodicals from spilling onto the floor. As Huck scrambled to help, he felt off balance himself. He fell against her, knocking her against the wall. He reached out to help her to stay on her feet.

He caught a whiff of her perfume. "You okay?"

She reached down with her free hand to make secure one of her shoes that had slipped off her foot. She stood up, still gripping his sleeve. He thought he could see color rising in her face. She turned abruptly to the periodicals that were strewn over the tabletop and floor.

When they bent down to pick up the journals that lay on the floor, he noticed that her short, tight skirt exposed an ample portion of a well-shaped thigh. Freshly painted lips broke into a smile. "Aren't we a team?" she laughed as she stood to her feet.

The moment that elapsed couldn't have lasted more than mere seconds. Yet for the both of them the universe of time seemed suspended. With emotions swirling in turmoil, Huck licked dry lips and struggled to find words. However, it was left to Artie to break the tension by reaching for her research notes.

She showed him a typed sheet. "This is the list of subtopics," she said, forcing calmness into her voice. "Go through these magazines and categorize the articles that I've marked."

He looked at the list. "This stuff gets pretty intense. Now I know what they mean."

She looked at him. "Whatever are you talking about?"

"When they refer to you as an international authority."

She began fumbling through some of the magazines. "The truth of the matter is that we have just scratched the surface. We only know how to decipher a few characters on some clay tablets. We know nothing, for example, of the spoken language that these characters represent. I would not be able to understand a syllable of that language were I to hear someone to speak it today. I sometimes wish if only I could go back in time or perhaps resurrect someone who could speak that language."

She leveled a steady gaze at him as she wrote on a blank note card. "Keep track of your time," she said, smiling. "I usually take a half hour for lunch."

He studied the time sheet a moment. He had noticed her looking at him in class a lot lately.

Again, the moment seemed frozen in time.

"Well," she said at last as she scooped up some papers. "I've got to go."

He thought he detected a note of coquetry in her voice as she added, "See you later."

After she left, Huck began poring through periodicals, skimming through articles, and jotting on note cards. As he sifted through the list of subheadings, one in particular caught his eye: "The Me of Ancient Sumer." *Me*, he thought, *what the hell's that?*

Finally, he glanced at his watch. *Guess I'll find George and have lunch,* he decided. *Then I can get back the book he borrowed.*

Later, while seated with George in the Union cafeteria, he noticed him rushing down his sandwich. "What's your hurry?" he said.

George's lunch break doubled as an errand. He was to pick up a sandwich for his boss, Dr. Purvis Lester Rodgers, Dr. Mason-Rodgers' estranged husband.

Huck followed him as he ordered from the lunch counter. "One hamburger, plain—and a Diet Pepsi."

Huck was still following when they headed for Dr. Rodgers' office.

"Well," said the dean squinting over his rimless glasses. "It's about time."

George set the lunch bag on the desk beside Dr. Rodgers' elbow. The dean carefully took out the neatly wrapped hamburger and then the Diet Pepsi. He flicked narrow fingertips as if trying to shake off something dirty.

A single item lay on his desk blotter: a business card reading "Atlantis Films, Inc."

"Did you tell them I wanted it plain?"

With deliberation he unwrapped the hamburger and began taking dainty nibbles. "The meat is too rare," he complained. "Didn't you tell those people to prepare my hamburger well done?"

"Excuse me, sir, but you didn't ask me to."

He looked across the desk at Huck and George. Even when he looked directly at someone, his eyes had a strange, blank stare. It was as though he didn't want to acknowledge the reality of whatever it was that he was looking at. A deep crease ran along a crazy angle from the bridge of his nose to well up on his forehead.

"I was hoping you'd think to do that."

"There's a microwave in the staff lounge," suggested George.

Dr. Rodgers held the hamburger by the wrapper. "Don't bother now," he said. "I want you to get back to work."

As George stepped to a worktable, he handed Huck his copy of *Search for Lost Empires*.

Huck took the book. "I'd better be going," he said as he turned toward the door.

He stepped into the hall, glanced back briefly, and then walked away shaking his head.

Probably orders his pizza crust only, he thought.

As he neared the exit, he recalled Dr. Rodgers' mannerism of squirming as if wearing an ill-fitting suit.

Never have I met a guy, he reflected, *so obviously uncomfortable inside his own skin*.

As Huck continued down the corridor, he recalled a photo hanging from the wall behind the dean's desk. It portrayed a black-belted Korean assuming a combatitive stance. The bottom of the picture bore the following handwritten message:

To my good friend and pupil, Dr. Lester Rodgers,
Kim Sun Lee.

Chapter 4

I, H'rshag, being the seventh son of a seventh son, was at birth gi'en (given) to the priesthood of Akir-Ema. Cherished I joyous memories of ... careless (carefree) hours, quite free from anxious thought ... 'Twas there also I grew to a youth—tall, strong, and stout...
(Day 3. Lord H'rshag's memoirs of his early years. Trans. and ed. Brit. Mus., vers. 1.5; 1981.)

* * * * *

"Landlord, fill the flowing bowl,
And let us have another...
...Our lives will ever mer-rye be:
Tomorrow, we'll be sober!"

The Matador's interior came alive with the usual writhing and jostling of young bodies. In a remote corner sat the study group, tonight augmented by several members of the varsity. Well-muscled young giants in jeans and T-shirts had, with chairs purloined from other tables, wedged themselves into the booth. With Thanksgiving a mere week away, only a final victory stood between them and a bowl bid. Tonight they were celebrating early as they drowned out all other crowd noises with their singing.

Walden T. Brookes tried to ignore the nearby revelry. With him sat Randall E. Durwin, president of the Student Democratic Front. Looking older and huskier of build, Durwin observed the singers with dark, brooding eyes. The massive head, crowned with bushy, raven hair, lowered in disgust. A rough-looking hand stroked an unshaven chin. Beside him sat Jack Springfield, a tall, spare fellow with long auburn hair tied in a ponytail. Small, narrow eyes that were severely crossed looked askance at the revelers.

"Damn jocks," Randall shouted, "can't hear yourself think."

Later Wally, returning from the men's room, passed Huck's table. A shrill whistle penetrated the din of the taproom as Huck briefly goosed him. Wally's arms shot overhead as he began to do a little dance.

"Oh shit!" he shouted loud enough to shock the taproom into silence. The crowd watched an embarrassed Wally rejoin his table, eyes glaring.

Huck, in the meantime, gave George a nudge indicating their turn to go for drinks. As they returned, they passed Wally's table. When members of the festive crowd jostled him from the rear, his tray spilled onto Wally's party.

"Watch it, you oaf," screamed Wally, jumping to his feet.

Huck tried to mumble an apology but Randall also jumped to his feet shouting "Clumsy bastard."

"These are the guys who gave me the swirlee," Wally shouted in Randall's ear.

Randall moved his face in close to Huck's. "Why don't you pick on somebody your own size?"

Huck didn't budge. "Like who, for instance?" was his rejoinder.

George attempted to pull him away. "C'mon, we got that game Saturday."

His attempt at peacemaking, however, came too late. Sympathizers for Wally and Randall came surging from their tables. The occupants of Huck's booth, in the meantime, had also emptied it and rushed into the aisle. The pushing and jostling had already begun.

George continued pulling. "C'mon, we don't need this."

"Hey, I'm talkin' to you." Randall pressed in close to Huck. Suddenly he swung, missing Huck by inches. The momentum of his swing threw him stumbling over a chair.

"Let's go," shouted George. They joined Paul in heading for the exit to the back parking lot where Paul had parked his ancient compact.

The tavern's interior resounded to a crescendo of angry shouting, breaking of glass, and falling of furniture. As the back door slammed shut, a strange quiet settled over the parking lot. The three hurried toward Paul's car. Paul

THE DELUGE SCROLLS

slipped into the driver's seat with George beside him. Huck sprawled across the back. Overhead, stars shone like sparklers against slate-colored sky.

In the distance, they heard the faint wail of a police siren. After some coaxing, the engine sputtered nervously. Paul pressed the clutch and threw the gearshift into low with a grinding sound. The car lurched out of the driveway exit and into the street. They saw the sudden appearance of flashing red and blue lights. The continued shriek of a siren whizzed past them and into the Matador parking lot.

They sat in silence as their car sped through darkened streets. Paul inserted a tape into a cassette player. Sounds of Richard Strauss' *Till Eulenspiegel* filled the car's interior.

Paul, a music major, had been principal horn player for the university symphony orchestra. The tape was a solo passage he took in the opening section. He explained to his two passengers how a symphonic poem, through orchestral music, told a story.

"So what kind of story does 'Till What's-His-Face' tell?" said Huck.

The piece told a story from medieval Germany about a student named Till Eulenspiegel who enjoyed playing pranks on the university authorities. His harmless pranks, however, quickly degenerate into a power struggle with the establishment. In the end, Till loses and is subsequently hanged.

After another silence, Huck glanced out the window. "Cajon Boulevard up ahead."

Paul headed into a parking lot surrounded on three sides by apartment buildings. He pushed open his door and stepped to the pavement. "You'll never guess who else lives here."

Dr. Mason-Rodgers, it turned out, lived across the court from Paul's building. He pointed to a ground-floor window.

No shit, thought Huck. Among athletes, the one prof they considered to be the faculty centerfold.

Paul started toward his building entrance. "C'mon up and I'll show you something cool."

They followed him up to a second-floor efficiency apartment. When Paul turned on a small desk lamp, he gestured toward his bed that had been pushed tight against a window.

"Lay across the bed and don't be too conspicuous looking out," he said as he switched off the desk lamp. When he threw himself down beside Huck and George, he pointed to the darkness outside. They noticed that the Venetian blinds in the window across the court had been tilted at enough of an angle to give them almost unobstructed vision down into the bedroom.

"Is that her place?" said Huck.

"That's her place."

"No shit," laughed Huck. "How often do you do this?"

"Put it this way," he said wryly, "I just like to keep my eye on things."

In the darkness three faces pressed tight against the glass pane.

"Think we'll see anything?" said Huck after long moments of silence.

"Sometimes you gotta wait."

Presently a female figure, fully dressed in blouse and slacks, darted into sight. The figure paused and then began to unbutton the blouse.

Clouds of vapor formed on Paul's window as they watched her slip out of her slacks.

"No shit," someone whispered in a bated breath, "look at that!"

"C'mon." Huck nudged George with his elbow. "Quit shoving."

"You quit shoving," he retorted. "She's movin' away. There's nothin' to see."

The undies-clad female had slipped out of sight.

C'mon, baby, come on back!

Please, God, let her come back!

After ten minutes of high expectation, they watched as blackness swallowed the scene.

"Shit!" they exclaimed in a whispered unison.

* * * * *

"Mind if I join you?"

The noise of jostling crowds filled the Student Union Cafeteria.

The scent of her perfume announced her approach. Huck looked up to see the white collar and gray business suit. Fresh lipstick accentuated her smile.

He felt a secret embarrassment over his voyeuristic adventure of the night before.

Artie placed her tray opposite and took a seat. On her tray lay a morning paper. She pulled her chair to the table and glanced at the headlines: "Students Arrested in Campus Disturbance."

"Do you know anything about this?"

Huck glanced at the headline. "They gotta be kidding."

She continued looking at him. "Were you there?"

"Where do they get that 'campus disturbance' bit," he said. "The Matador is off campus."

"That's beside the point," she insisted. "Were you part of this?"

"I'm not going to lie to you," he said. "I was there, and yes—me and another guy had a little argument."

She shook her head. "You're going to have to be more careful. I need you. This research is part of an exhaustive study of ancient Sumerian civilization. I can't risk losing you."

Huck eyed her for a moment. "You're really into this, aren't you?"

She didn't answer right away. "When I was a young girl," she said finally, "I was always fascinated by things old." She related how her parents, as antique aficionados, had filled their home with artifacts until it resembled a museum. Artie, as a consequence, knew the history, the dynasty, and even the reign of the many bric-a-bracs, vases, and statuary that filled their home. Her thoughts flashed in retrospect to her earliest childhood…

…When only weeks old, her mind raced like quicksilver as she reached out to the figurines, votive murals, rings, bracelets, necklaces, and vases that lavishly furnished her parents' home. The shapes, the colors, the tactile sense of touch elicited a fascination. She felt a connectedness that made Inanna real to her even then…

…She went on to relate how her childhood playmates wearied of her fondness for games of fantasy involving the pharaohs, Queen Neferteti, and other characters of antiquity.

"I was pretty much of a loner most of the time as a result," she said. "But I really didn't care. I was more at home with the people of Second Dynasty Egypt than I was with school kids of twentieth-century America."

The front hall display case of her elementary school still contained a cutaway model of an Egyptian pyramid she made for a social studies project in the sixth grade.

"—In high school," she went on, "I did a term paper for an eleventh-grade English class on ancient Babylonian cuneiform that is still in our high school library today."…

* * * * *

…Huck returned to his private office. Pushing aside the law volumes and a legal pad that lay on the couch, he again flipped to a page in *The Deluge Scrolls*:

Mid tender youth scarce twice ten high-suns (twenty years of age—ed.) was I taken of my father on journey to the distant city, Akir-Ema, for reason of business and for the purpose of my continued schooling at the temple tutor-palace (Seminary –ed.) Sent we servants with all manner of beasties of burthen: auroch (oxen), dromedary, and asses laden with all manner of goods. So sent we them three weeks beyond (in advance) of our departure.

(Day 4. H'rshag's first trip to Akir-Ema. Trans. and ed. Brit. Mus. Vers. 1.75; 1981.)

A realization came to him. His athletic ability, his knack for getting by in school with minimal effort, and his subsequent willingness to milk the system for all it was worth as it were, all came back to haunt his memory. In subsequent days, however, all that had caught up with him. In her class as he studied the whole new scientific field of archeology, he acknowledged that he could no longer bluff his way through. Since meeting her, he would, for the first time in his life, have to knuckle down and do hard, honest effort.

Why had he previously been able to dog it, as they say? Had the gods smiled on him and gifted him as a strong, handsome athlete, quick of body, quick of mind? Had the Fates destined him to be blest as a demigod beyond that of mere mortals, even as they did Hercules?

Gods? Fates? What kind of pagan thinking was this for a child of the baptismal covenant? What kind of thinking was this for a catechist born into a family of Christian clerics?

No, he concluded, things before had simply been too easy. From now on he would have to settle down and work. That had been true of Archeology 101. That had also been true of law school.

He now knew that Artie had impacted his life more ways than one. Not only was she his lover, she was also the first person to ever force him to stretch himself, to reach his potential.

I owe her, he thought...

* * * * *

..."When I was in the eleventh grade," Huck was saying, "I turned in a paper that never was."

"I don't understand."

THE DELUGE SCROLLS

"My English teacher kept rather sloppy records," he began. "One day during roll call she said to me: 'Hershel Ladd, I don't have your paper.' 'Oh yes,' I said, 'I handed it in last week. You said I got "B" on it.' 'Oh yes,' she said, 'now I remember. I must have forgotten to record it.' 'When will I get it back?' I said. 'Let me get back to you,' she said. 'Okay,' I said."

Dr. Mason-Rodgers buried her face in the back of her hands. "I can't believe this," she said. "You ought to be shot."

He sat back. "By the way," he said, changing the subject, "based on the way I acted the first day, you must think I'm an awful jerk."

He took a couple of bites before realizing that she wasn't eating.

"I don't think you're a jerk," she said finally.

Another silence.

"This project," she said, returning to the original subject, "is very important to me. I've got a bid from the National Geographic Society to go on their archeological expedition to Iraq."

She took another sip of her coffee. "Enough about me," she said. "How about you? What exciting thing is going on in your life? How's that game going to go Saturday?"

"We're going to win." Huck observed the thinning crowd "We've got depth in every position that we haven't had in years."

Again, she studied him. "You really want that Yucca Bowl bid don't you?"

He leaned forward against the table. "Dr. Mason-Rodgers," he said, "I want that Yucca Bowl bid so bad I can taste it."

She stood up. "By the way," she said as she began collecting her dishes, "when it's just the two of us, it's all right to call me 'Artie.'"

Chapter 5

I (knew) not what happ'd next ...her gracious self stood before me, smiling ... "I have made decision," said she. "Tonight thou shalt join me in dance..."
(Day 6. Lord H'rshag's account of his first meeting with the Lady Aarda. Trans. and ed. Brit. Mus. vers. 1.5; 1981.)

* * * * *

"Whenever fighting Pumas hold the line,
They'll give their foemen a merry time ..."

The giant Greyhound sped along the desert highway rocking to the rhythm as some forty young male voices sung to the tune of *Washington and Lee Swing*. The day before, Cortez Pacific had beaten North Central Arizona 23-21. They had won by a last-minute field goal.

The singing and cheering had gone nonstop. "We cut the deck and drew an ace, the fighting Pumas set the pace!"

Huck watched the fleeting landscape change from open desert to urban congestion. His body seemed to groan in protest at the slightest movement...

...Two days before the game he sat in the lobby of his motel with a copy of the North Central Arizona campus paper in his lap. As he turned to its sports section, he knew he was in trouble. Beside an article featuring the school's star defensive linebacker, he saw a black, muscular behemoth seated at the edge of a weight bench. Directly behind set an Olympic-sized barbell suspended across a rack.

Eldred Mosley had just bench-pressed four hundred pounds.

The student journalist was interviewing him regarding the upcoming Yucca Bowl classic.

"'I got news for their quarterback, Mr. Ladd,'" the article quoted. "'I not only specialize in breakin' up plays, I specialize in breakin' up them that calls plays'"...

...Shortly after the opening kick-off, as he started to quarterback Cortez Pacific's initial offensive drive, he spotted the black giant lurking behind North Central Arizona's defensive line. Even before he called his team into their huddle, he could hear the taunts over the line of scrimmage: "Hey, Mr. Quarterback, I'm gonna disassemble you piece by piece."

At the snap, three hundred pounds of towering meanness came crashing through the Cortez Pacific line to deliver Huck his first sack of the afternoon. Third and long would take on a whole new meaning.

As he lay on the ground, ears ringing, he could hear: "Hey, Mr. Quarterback, how did you like that one?"

"I liked it fine." Huck slowly picked himself up from the trampled turf.

He tried rushing, short passes, long passes, options, and reverses. In all this, Eldred Mosley was not easily fooled. He could discern body language and direction of eye movements during the countdown. He would observe which section of the backfield seemed most tense and edgy. He would mentally check this with the down and number of yards to a first down and then call out the anticipated play.

Huck had tried, with minimal success, to evade the six-and-a-half-foot giant bearing down on him with the speed of a fast freight and thrusting hands the size of lunch plates in his face. George Bouknight's receiving his short, desperate passes over the line of scrimmage were what enabled Cortez Pacific to get on the scoreboard at all.

In the meantime, Mosley had made it a long afternoon for Huck, slamming him to the ground for a total of six disastrous sacks.

As Huck would crawl to his feet, he could hear Mosley's oily chuckle: "Hey, Mr. Quarterback, I'm havin' fun. How 'bout you?"

Late in the second quarter, Huck again struggled to his feet and found Cortez Pacific third and fourteen on its own three-yard line; score, North Central Arizona 7—Cortez Pacific 6.

"Hey, come on, guys," he said in the huddle. "That Mosley is killing me. If we don't stop him we're all dead in the water. I know he's big. I know he's fast. I know he's mean and I know he's tough. But, dammit, do what you gotta do to take him out. Two of you go after him if you have to and let your regular assignment go. I'll handle whoever he is. Whatever we do we gotta *shut him down!*"

He called for a quick kick. The kicker crouched down to receive the pass from center almost under his team's own goal post. The pass came too high and he had to jump to grab it. As he landed, Mosley came rushing close with two other defensive teammates right behind. A brush block thrown by Huck into Mosley's mid-section enabled the kicker to elude the defense by inches, putting the would-be tacklers in bad field position. In a fit of adrenal desperation, he burst toward the sideline, bringing the crowd immediately to its feet. With the sound of the frenzied roar in his ears, he broke into a foot race to the far endzone. The downfield dash finished with the nearest tackler a good five yards away.

Mosley narrowly missed blocking a conversion that sent Cortez Pacific to the half-time locker room leading 13-7.

During Cortez Pacific's first possession of the third quarter it happened. Third and nine, Huck faded back looking for a receiver. He poised for a throw to George when Mosley blindsided him with a hit at the knees and with a slam to the earth that momentarily jarred his senses. When his mind cleared, he saw a North Central Arizona defensive end streaking for Cortez Pacific's end zone with the ball.

When he tried getting up he felt a paralyzing numbness in his knees. He had to be carried off the field in time to see North Central Arizona up the score 14-13. He spent the greater part of the half on the sidelines with a trainer packing his injured joints. Strenuously trying to avoid a limp, he reentered the game late in the fourth quarter with North Central Arizona leading 21-20.

Cortez Pacific was third down and seven on its own forty. When Huck caught the snap, he saw George in the clear inside the North Central Arizona secondary. He barely managed to avoid another bone-jarring encounter with Mosley by quickly getting the ball off in George's direction. George, however, was stopped by the safety deep in North Central Arizona's own territory.

Less than a minute to go and three downs later, Cortez Pacific's offensive drive stalled on their opponent's twenty-yard line with no time-outs remaining. Catching a sign from Coach, Huck waited until the kicker came running onto the field.

Huck could see Mosley hunkered and ready to spring. At the snap, Huck braced for the onrushing blue jersey. His shoulder caught Mosely's midsection. Before being trampled to the ground for one last time, he heard the explosive sound of the kicker's boot.

The roar of the crowd told him the kick was good. Cortez Pacific had won: 23-21.

A vise-like grip jerked him to his feet. "Nice game, guy," said Mosley, slapping him on the butt ...

...The winter afternoon sun cast long shadows of palm trees and stucco houses across well-manicured lawns.

Huck rolled back his shirtsleeves and straightened his tie.

Dressing conservatively in dark-colored suits and ties was Coach Schermerheim's ironclad rule.

As the words: "We got system. We got class. We're the Pumas. We kick ass!" rang in his ears, Huck pulled from his shirt pocket a dog-eared paper and again read the small, neat handwriting:

> Has anyone ever told you that you are extremely attractive and sexy? Please destroy this note as soon as you have read it.
> Have a nice day.

The note had mysteriously appeared in his mailbox just before winter recess. Instead of a signature, the author had drawn a happy face. He slipped it back into his shirt pocket. Campus lay dead ahead.

Ten minutes later the team had disembarked from the bus—fully dressed in suits, shirts, and ties—in front of a hastily erected platform. Out front stood the marching band, one hundred strong and resplendent in orange and blue uniforms. The brass bells of their instruments glistened in the late-afternoon sun.

Student turnout, however, was a disappointment. George conjectured that it was due to the Christmas holidays. Huck, however, had other ideas. Many students still scorned as fascist anything as intensely competitive and authoritarian as intercollegiate football and military bands.

The team seated themselves in the front section and Dr. Sturgis blew into the microphone. A roar reverberated from speakers aimed toward the distant corners of "The Quad," a quadrangular-shaped greensward about the size of a football field surrounded by tan, stucco buildings.

"We are gathered here," said the AD, "to celebrate an historical event and to congratulate our boys and coaching staff for bringing back the 1979 Yucca Bowl trophy." The AD continued, "Having been a coach and a player myself, I can appreciate the hard work and dedication. Boys, you done good."

Scattered applause followed his words.

"And now," he added, "it gives me great pleasure to present our coach, Bob Schermerheim. Bob, why don't you share a few words with these folks?"

Coach Schermerheim sprang to the rostrum. "I don't need to say an awful lot." His gravelly voice echoed through the speakers. "'Cause these splendid guys said it so eloquently up at Kingman, right?"

Again, faint applause rippled throughout the Quad.

"I do want to say, however," he continued as he gripped the sides of the lectern, "something that I seldom say to the guys on the practice field but feel every day from the bottom of my heart."

He turned to the team. "Gosh, I'm proud of you guys."

Typical, thought Huck. Instead of being given to outright profanity, his "gosh, golly," and "dad-gummit" were legendary.

Coach's voice continued to boom into the mike: "I will now read the names of our 1979 roster. As I read each name, will the player please stand. I would request that you good folks withhold your applause until I have read the entire list."

Huck and George and their teammates in turn stood to their feet as Coach barked one more order into the mike: "Let's give our team another round of applause."

As they sat down, the AD again took to the rostrum and eyed the dwindling crowd. "And now," he announced, "it gives me great pleasure to introduce our beloved president, Dr. Harry E. Faasendeck."

The president, with deliberate stride, stepped to the rostrum. The short, pudgy man dressed himself in a black suit and clerical collar. Imitating Coach's mannerism, he gripped the sides of the lectern, thrust out a chubby chin, and looked resolutely out at the thinning crowd. Pale, blue eyes set in a cherubic face glanced over the audience. After adjusting rimless glasses, he took a handkerchief and wiped his forehead. He then passed it over hair neatly parted and unusually dark for a man in his early fifties. He cleared his throat and puckered his small mouth before beginning to speak.

"Mr. Athletic Director," he began with well-articulated accents, "Coach Schermerheim, team, members of the faculty, members of the staff, members of the student body, and friends: as Coach Schermerheim so aptly put it, there is hardly anything one can adequately say that would add to our fine team's accomplishment, however, permit this humble speaker to share a thought or two with you."

Humble? thought Huck as George gave him a nudge.

The president again cleared his throat. "I am reminded of a story: a man entered a restaurant and ordered lobster. Upon discovering that it had only one claw, he demanded an explanation. When told that it had been in a fight with another lobster, and that the other lobster had bitten off one of its claws, he handed his order to the waiter.

"'Take this one back,' he demanded, 'and bring me the winner.'"

He paused. "I—relate this story," he said, clearing his throat, "to illustrate the point that everybody loves a winner."

Dr. Faasendeck still had a few more words—and a few more words after that. At last, Huck heard, "And in conclusion, Coach, I would like to congratulate you and your fine team. Thank you."

The president sat down to the roaring of the wind into the mike. The AD stepped to the lectern. "We shall conclude by joining in the singing of our alma mater."

A drum roll preceded organ-like chords from the brass choir. The words, to the tune "Integer Vitae," floated faintly across the Quad:

"Eternal Spirit,
God of Truth and Virtue,
Bless now our school;
Beloved Alma Mater.
May her torch burn brightly
In darkness as in sunshine,
Now and forevermore. Amen."

As the last chords faded across the shadow-enshrouded campus, the AD announced, "This concludes our victory ceremonies. Thank you and have a happy holiday season."

When Huck stepped slowly down from the platform, he heard a female voice call out his name. "Huck? Over here!"

He spotted Dr. Mason-Rodgers rapidly walking toward him. She gripped his arm. "God, I'm proud of you guys."

He felt her arm entwine around his and caught a scent of perfume. The unexpected, intimate touch of a woman with whom he had been accustomed to sitting under her instruction set off a reaction both strange and immediate.

"Artie," he said in a surprised tone, (when it's just the two of us, it's okay to call me "Artie.") "Somehow I wasn't expecting to see you here."

"Are you kidding? I wouldn't miss this for anything."

She still held his arm as they walked toward the parking lot. "I watched the game on television," she said. "I thought you were taking an awful pounding."

"Hey, what can I say?" he shrugged. "That guy was good."

She recalled the sickening anxiety at the sight of his being carried off the field. When he went back in late in the fourth quarter, she shook her head in disbelief.

She eyed him with concern. "Do you hurt?"

"Just a little stiff. I'll get over it."

Still unconvinced, she shrugged and surveyed the parking lot. Aside from the few distant stragglers, they were alone.

"Tell me," she said, "do you plan on going home tonight?"

"Actually," he sighed, "I haven't even unpacked." He gestured to a solitary suitcase still on the parking lot.

"I would like to take you to dinner."

He felt his pulse begin to quicken. A cozy, little dinner with his prof? He dropped his arm. "I—I don't know what to say."

"Please," she said, "I insist. This is my own personal victory celebration. I want to do something—just the two of us."

"Let me take my suitcase to my car." He pointed to an ancient VW at the far end of the parking lot.

She pulled a card from her wallet. "Here's the restaurant's address. Meet me there as soon as you can."

The sun, having disappeared behind the horizon, cast a soft, golden afterglow behind the western mountains. Huck stopped momentarily beside his suitcase. He studied the trim figure walking briskly away from him and continued to watch as she disappeared into the shadows of the nearby buildings. He walked over to a street lamp and studied the card:

THE DELUGE SCROLLS

Flaming Embers Steak 'n' Lobster
14325 Pacific Av.
Santa Monica, CA 90403
1-310-945-2005

He realized that his close association with her during the tutoring sessions and in his work had all but obliterated the initial abrasiveness in their relationship, but a personal invitation to join her at dinner?

Why was she doing this?

He put the card into his shirt pocket and resumed his trek toward the ancient VW. Despite the pain in his knees, he quickened his pace.

Chapter 6

She look'd to me nonetheless fair. She appeared to me in festal robes. Again, made I bold to address her: "Mayhap I shall pay thee court, provided of course, I gain thy consent." ... I broke the seal and found the following message: "My consent, my lord, thou already hast."
(Day 7. Lord H'rshag's memoirs relating to his meeting the Lady Aarda at Ordination Festival. Trans. and ed. Brit. Mus. vers. 1.5; 1981.)

* * * * *

The neon sign "Flaming Embers" flashed an indelible brilliance against the California night sky. As his VW sputtered its way into the parking lot, he spotted Artie's foreign compact. He pulled beside it, locked his car, and headed toward the restaurant.

He pushed open the massive, ornately carved front door and pushed his way into the lobby and stood a moment to get his bearings. The amber light cast a dim glow over the crowd that thronged its interior. He spotted Artie beside the maitre d's desk. As they worked their way toward each other, their eyes met.

"I see you made it," she stiffly.

Huck nodded. "Yeah," he said, rubbing his neck.

Artie made a tight, little gesture toward the maitre d's desk. "Let's see if they are ready for us."

"Mason-Rodgers, non-smoking for two?" the maitre d' was saying.

They followed him to a corner booth. Artie slid in behind the table. Huck pulled a chair from the aisle side.

"Don't be so formal," she said with a pained look. "Come sit here." She gestured to the empty seat around the table corner from her.

He shoved the chair back and slid into the space in question.

"Anything from the bar?" A waiter appeared with an order pad.

Huck was about to order a draft beer, but never got the chance. "We'll start with a bottle of your best Vin-Rose," Artie said as she studied the wine list.

She bent close. "Oh, do try some wine," she teased. "Vin-Rose is good with steak."

She moved her head closer still. "Trust me."

Had she done some of her waiting at the bar?

The waiter brought the Vin-Rose and two wine glasses. She took a sip thoughtfully. Finally she said, "That will be fine."

She set aside the goblet and turned to the menu. "Let's order their special." She pointed with her little finger. "New York cut steak."

Huck slid back a little. "Tell me," he said, "is this Dr. Mason-Rodgers who addresses me, or is it the Vin-Rose?"

She cast him a sidelong glance. "Aren't we perceptive?"

She planted her chin on the top of her folded hands. "So," she said, "tell me a little about yourself."

"Not much to tell," he sighed. He began fidgeting with the saltshaker.

"I'm from up in the San Joaquin Valley," he added finally.

Mostly farm country, he went on to explain; produce: cantaloupe, lettuce, and stuff like that.

She edged a little closer. She was curious to know if there was money in that. Huck had allowed that, although the farmers would never admit it, that yes, they did quite well.

He still said nothing about his family.

She studied him a moment. "What were you like in high school?" she said, changing the subject.

The persistent look in her eyes told him that she was not to be put off. "Were you a good student?"

He related how the little prophecy motto beside his yearbook picture said: "To get as far away from here as soon as I can before they find out what it is that I did." While their yearbook mock election voted the valedictorian as "Done the Most for our School," it voted him "Done our School for the Most."

After completion of commencement ceremonies, the principal shook his hand and announced, "Ladd—with you gone, I think I'm going back in my office and die of loneliness."

In high school, he was either in trouble, or was absent. In his senior year, he was absent fifty-seven days, or one day out of three.

"How ever did you manage to pass?" she replied.

He went on to explain how he never took a book home; seldom even took one to class. As long as he could borrow a book, pencil, and notebook paper from other students, he had it made.

"This is unreal," exclaimed Artie. "I can't believe it."

A sizzling sound interrupted their conversation. The waiter brought a platter with a metal dome covering. He reached for a nearby cart and picked up a wooden salad bowl and began grinding peppercorns from a tall, wooden cylinder. When he finished garnishing the salad he left with the cart. While waiting for him to return with the breadbasket, Artie drained her wineglass, studied the label on the bottle a moment and then poured the remaining Vin-Rose into Huck's.

The waiter placed the rolls basket besides them. "Enjoy."

Artie waved the empty wine bottle. "Oh, Garcon," she said, "another bottle of Vin-Rose, s'il vous plait."

Huck cringed. *Garcon*, he thought, *is she crocked or what?*

Again, her mood changed. "What about your family? Is yours a typical American success story: farm boy to football hero?"

His expression darkened. "My parents are not farmers."

Artie tilted her head back. "I knew I could get you to open up about your family," she laughed.

Huck glared at her. "There's something else you should know about my parents," he said. "If they could see me here tonight, they would not approve."

"Not approve?" she said in feigned surprise. "Oh dear, whatever for?"

"They would not approve of my going out with a married woman," he said. "My dad's a minister."

He went to explain in more detail. His family name originally was Ladovicious. His grandfather was a Lutheran minister from Latvia. The family escaped to Germany from the Soviet army in 1945. After living as displaced persons, they emigrated to the U.S. in 1948, settling in California. His father was ordained in 1955, the same year Huck was born.

She turned serious again. "Let me tell you a little of this married woman's story."

The waiter brought a second bottle of Vin-Rose. She left it untouched for the moment. "I'm from the Chicago area originally," she said. "Winnetka to be exact. I was an only child. I suppose we were religious in the genteel sense, attending one of the most fashionable churches in the area. When I was twelve our Sunday school had an attendance contest: come six months without an absence and win a Bible. With four Sundays to go, my parents took me up to our cottage in Wisconsin. So much for winning that Bible.

"It wasn't long after that I quit attending altogether."

He eyed her with curiosity. Attendance was never at issue while he was yet at home. "What did your parents say to that?"

She shrugged. "What could they say?"

Huck again fidgeted with the saltshaker. "Since we're on the subject, how would you describe your present persuasion?"

She sighed. "I guess you could call me a secularist."

"What's a secularist?"

"Put it this way," she continued, "an atheist says there is no God. An agnostic isn't sure. A secularist, however, says 'okay, maybe there is a God, but so what?'"

She went on. "With so many different religions, how is one to know who is right? I've now come to the conclusion that any God wise enough to create the universe could also figure out a way to make it easier for us to know—that is, if it was really all that important to him—or her—or it—how or what we believe. I also have concluded that any God big enough to create the universe is not going to have so fragile an ego as to get all bent out of shape over whether we believe in him, or her, or not."

He shook his head. "Do you believe in life after death?"

She eyed him. "Do I believe in life after birth?"

He paused and fidgeted with the saltshaker some more. "What about—Jesus Christ, for instance?"

She poured herself another glass of wine. "I think he was a nice guy."

He looked startled. "That's—it?"

"What more is there?"

He licked dry lips. "Don't you believe, for instance, that he died for our sins?"

"As a matter of fact I do." She took a sip of her wine. "It's like in school.

One 'A' student can make a class of 'C' and 'D' students look pretty bad. He or she can then draw to themselves a lot of resentment and hatred."

"But don't you believe," said Huck, wondering how far he dare push it, "that he rose from the dead?"

"I believe," she continued, again raising her glass, "that the literal Jesus of Nazareth is a pile of dust in some forgotten Palestinian tomb. Who knows, maybe I'll get lucky some day and discover his remains somewhere. God, wouldn't that be a find?"

She paused. "Talk about finding your historical Jesus," she laughed, in speech becoming increasingly slurred.

She lapsed into a thoughtful silence.

He wanted to mention the trip to the Holy Land by Bishop Pike of San Francisco. In his quest for the "historical Jesus," the bishop took a wrong turn in a desert wilderness. His body was found a week later in a kneeling position and leaning against the base of a cliff.

However, Huck said nothing.

"Let's see, where was I?" she said finally. "Oh yes, and so it follows that Jesus died for our sins. As they say: 'The good die young.' He was like me, I understand, only in his thirties. God, the irony of it. I don't intend to be such a goody-goody myself. So here's to the sins of our youth," she said, raising her glass, "and here's to the sins of our old age."

She struggled to keep him in focus. "May the Lord forgive the one as readily as he forgives the other."

Trying to suppress feelings of embarrassment, he touched her glass lightly to his...

* * * * *

...The stillness was punctuated only by a buzzing and gurgling sound of a dimly lit aquarium. Absentmindedly, he began thumbing through more pages of *The Deluge Scrolls*.

> *We were then bidden to the banquet hall where we were waited on by companies of temple slave maidens, clad in gown of near transparency with an opening cut at the side, and with wrists, neck, and forehead decorated with garlands of flowers.*
>
> (Day 6. Lord H'rshag's account of the Great Ordination Banquet. Trans. and ed. Brit. Mus. Vers. 1.75; 1981.)...

THE DELUGE SCROLLS

* * * * *

...She pulled back slightly and smiled. "I was a good girl," she said, picking up the thread of conversation. "You know, conformed to everybody's expectations?"

She had come out to California right after undergraduate days. She gave account of her early years. Life on the West Coast contrasted radically for her and her friend, Peppi, from the sheltered milieu of their upscale Chicago north shore suburbs and with their idyllic, undergrad life at Northwestern. They had come out just in time to get caught up in the student revolution.

She reached into her purse and pulled out a snapshot.

"This is me during that period."

He recognized the younger, more adolescent-looking version of Artie. The cheeks were rounder. The hair hung long and gently curled. She wore a blue, denim vest over a tie-dyed T-shirt. Faded jeans tucked down into brown, buckskin boots completed her attire. Beads of Indian wampum hung from her neck. Her wrists were weighted with Indian bracelets. Two fingers of her right hand were extended in a "peace" sign.

The picture was taken during a campus "sit-in."

"I remember saying to Peppi," she commented, "'I love this. It makes me feel so "anti".'"

Huck looked at her. "Anti-what?"

She smiled wistfully. "Just 'anti.'" She went on to disclose how she had dropped out of school shortly after that. It had become irrelevant, or so she thought. She also had run off to join a commune.

Earthnation, she said they called it.

There were some very sincere people at the beginning, she related. "We were going to create a whole new world: Peace, love, no more hypocrisy or disharmony. We would be totally accepting of everyone.

"That was before the rats came up out of the sewer," she added.

At first he didn't understand.

"They descended on us like the plague," she said. "Eventually they took over." Interesting mix, she reflected: naïve, well-meaning students barely out of adolescence, cohabiting with convicted, street-smart felons.

She bit her lip thoughtfully. *Was I really that flaky in those days?* she asked herself. Seeking an answer to that question, she realized that her own folly partially contributed to that weekend that turned so ugly.

For all her idealism, her fascination for the new, the novel, the bizarre, she wondered if even now she had been totally weaned away from the mystical, the occult, despite her scientific training.

Shortly thereafter she married Lester. However, even then she thought him a little weird.

"Why did you marry him then?"

"Actually, he can be quite charming," she confessed. "On occasion, such as at a party, he can be quite witty."

"What happened then?"

"Nothing."

Nothing? He let the impact of her words sink in.

Artie recalled, on their wedding night, of lying expectantly in bed beside him. Amid mounting dismay, she detected him to be in turmoil. What's wrong? she had asked. I don't think I can do it, he finally said in a voice fraught with anxiety. She tried to assure him. There'll be other times, she had tried to say convincingly.

However, what virginity that had remained coming into the marriage still was intact the day they had separated.

Huck thought a moment. "That's heavy."

Again her mood changed. "No more heavy," she whispered.

The waiter reappeared with the dessert menu. "We have an excellent selection. I'll give you a minute to decide."

Artie studied the menu. "What would you like for dessert?"

Huck shrugged. "I don't know," he sighed. "What would you want?"

Silence.

She fixed a long look at him. Did this sexy Greek god of an athlete present the one ray of sunshine in her life? Funny, she thought, while her meteoritic rise to international renown in the archeological community was rapidly approaching its zenith, not many people seemed aware of a dark side. She pondered the disastrous months at Earthnation, fear of being stalked by Snake, an abusive marriage to Lester, and the loss of both parents within a year and a half.

Am I not entitled to a little happiness?

He could feel the restaurant atmosphere getting steamy. The tip of her tongue made little daring movements over her upper lip. He could see color creeping into her face. He saw her hand slide across the white tablecloth until their fingertips touched. He felt the point of her toe pressing against his leg. He sensed a response as she gripped his fingers. The soft contour of her cheek blocked out the dining room as he felt the moist longing of her lips.

THE DELUGE SCROLLS

The faint scent of her lipstick made him giddy. As they embraced, she fell in his arms in soft submission.

Her lips broke away with a whispered "I love you."

He struggled with the words: "I love you, too."

She nipped his ear. "Let's have dessert at my place."

He released her, sat up, and rubbed sweaty palms against his pant legs. "Good idea," he managed to say.

She placed bills on a small dish that lay on a corner of the table.

"Excuse me," she said, patting his hand before heading for the ladies' room. "Gotta go potty."

Huck slumped back in the booth. He watched her walk away with an unsteady gait.

Maybe I'd better drive, he decided.

Chapter 7

Amid the deepening twilight, amid the singing of the night birds, amid the flower-scented breezes from the gardens, she invited me to her bed of perfumed sheets of coloured silk. There, upon mattresses of deepest down 'twas where I first knew my Aarda...
   (Day 13. Lord H'rshag's account of his courtship of the Lady Aarda. Trans. and ed. Brit. Mus. 2.5; 1981.)

* * * * *

Huck didn't have long to wait after his resolution to drive Artie home. He saw her reemerge from the ladies' room. He slipped out of the booth and stood beside it.
   She walked unsteadily as she came toward him. "Well, shall we go?" she said with slurred speech.
   He didn't move.
   She looked perturbed. "What's the matter? Y'got a problem?"
   He held out his hand. "How about letting me drive?"
   She grasped his had and headed toward the exit. "Gr-r-r-f!" she said in a mock growl. "Come into my parlor."
   "Come on, knock it off," he urged. "Give me the keys."

She pulled herself up close to him and gave him a quick peck on the cheek. "Okay, hard guy," she said, opening her purse. "You win."

She took his arm and started for the exit.

"What are we gonna do 'bout your car?" she said, as with wobbling gait, she tried to keep up with him.

"Don't worry about it," he said with an amused look. "We can come back for it tomorrow. Right now, we've got to get you home."

"Ri-i-i-ight!" she said, again with a mock growl.

Shortly, Huck guided her car through darkened streets in silence. He cracked the window open slightly to let the night air rush in.

She slid closer and let her head rest on his shoulder. "Awful nice of you t'do this for me," she mumbled.

He eyed the traffic. "No problem," he said with a brief smile.

Her eyes closed again and her breathing became deep and regular. *Is the party just beginning,* he asked himself, *or is it all over?* He felt the passion that raged within him back at the Flaming Embers start to wane. He decided he would just get her home and put her to bed and then leave in her car. In the morning he would re-pack his suitcase, stop back, and check in on her.

One secret that he had struggled to keep from the male adult world of the locker room was that he had never been with a woman. How could he explain to them his family's religious roots? Despite feelings of disappointment, he determined that his first experience would not be with an older woman who was piss-assed drunk. He wasn't that hard up.

He continued driving through darkened city streets and reflected on his younger days as an acolyte in front of a large church. He had just taken his confirmation vows. He remembered the pride that his family felt at the sight of him serving at the altar. *Funny,* he thought, *how quick you lose touch.* Despite his attempts to present a good old boy persona, he had unsuccessfully tried to avoid the campus label of "christer," a name given in derision to divinity students or to any others with any religious inclinations.

Artie's apartment building loomed just ahead. He pulled into the parking lot and brought the car to a stop. He shut off the engine and a silence came rushing in about his ears like sea surf.

She didn't move.

He got out and opened the door. She groaned feebly as he reached to help her out. "What—where are we?"

"Your place," he said, struggling to pull her to her feet.

"That's sweet of you to bring me home," she mumbled as he walked her through the building foyer. He stopped at her apartment door and fumbled for her key. Opening the door, he reached inside for a light switch. A dim glow revealed an Early American-style living room.

Midpoint toward a sofa, she stopped. "I think I'm gonna get sick."

He hustled her to the bathroom door. Pushing it aside, he again flipped a light. As he edged her toward the commode, she made gagging sounds.

However, nothing happened.

"Maybe I can't do it after all," she complained. "Could you fix us some coffee—please?"

Releasing her, he left her standing over the commode and found his way to the kitchen. He spotted a coffee maker on the counter. Suddenly he heard gagging sounds from the bathroom.

He let the coffee spoon drop to the counter top and rushed back into the bathroom to where she was bent over the commode convulsing violently. He embraced her and held her forehead. When the gagging subsided, he gently wiped her face with a wet washcloth. She began to whimper like a sick puppy.

"God, but I've made a fool of myself tonight," she sobbed.

"Don't say that," he said, throwing the damp washcloth into a laundry hamper.

She turned and embraced him. "Just hold me," she sobbed.

After a moment, she looked up at him. "I'll be all right now," she said. "I think I could use some of that coffee."

When he returned to the kitchen, he discovered a slight problem: having been accustomed to brewing instant coffee in his own apartment, he had to spend several minutes familiarizing himself with the mechanics of her coffee maker.

"How's it coming?" Her voice came from the bedroom.

"I'm trying to figure this thing out."

Finally he drew water from the tap and pressed the "on" button. More minutes passed as the coffee gurgled through the filter.

"Smells good." Artie's voice came from the direction of the doorway. He turned to see her leaning against the lintel freshly lipsticked and in a white silken house robe. "You can make coffee, can't you?"

She moved beside him. "Cups over here."

She gestured to the cupboard. She took down two and let Huck do the pouring. She then turned away and let Huck follow her to the living room.

When they settled in on the couch, she moved close beside him. "By the way," she said, taking a sip, "thanks for driving me home. I'm sorry I made such a fool of myself."

He studied her finely chiseled features. The incongruity of his classroom teacher apologizing for making a fool of herself in her own apartment living room bothered him. "I don't think you're a fool," he said. "Not at all."

He glanced at his watch. "I really must be going."

"Oh no," she objected. "It's so late. I can make up a bed for you right here on the couch. I'll sleep in the bedroom with my door closed."

Huck thought long and hard on that one. The hand that held his coffee cup began getting sweaty. As he struggled with it, he felt her move her fingers down his hand.

"Don't go," she pleaded.

He felt the pressure of her slippered toe against his ankle and her lips brushing against her cheek...

* * * * *

...Huck rose from his office couch and stretched. He went to a kitchen and splashed cold water on his face. Mental fatigue, for the moment, had been pushed aside. He strode back to the couch in his office and pulled out more documents from his nearby attaché case. His mind went again in retrospect to that evening in Artie's apartment.

He recalled the shock of unreality at what she said next...

..."Make love to me," she whispered. "Please make love to me."

Her words took him off guard despite her obvious come-on. They threw his thoughts into a maelstrom of confusion. How macho would it be for a jock varsity quarterback to be introduced to the rite of manhood at the instigation of an older woman? Though he, for all practical purposes, had not seriously practiced the religious traditions of his family in the past four years, he saw this as a moment of truth, fault line, as it were, of seismic proportions.

Also how could he, a neophyte, respond to an opportunity that had so suddenly presented itself? His years of forced celibacy had not precluded his fantasizing just what moves he would make when the time came. Now, however, he felt anxiety as to how he could he bring it off with finesse.

He then recalled his attention being diverted by the same ceramic figurine, or perhaps a replica, that he had seen on her office bookshelf. He guessed it to be a kind of ancient goddess. A tiara crowned a head of luxuriant black hair that tumbled down in tight curls well past her shoulders. She wore a bejeweled gown and extended her arms outward with a serpent coiled around each forearm and wrist. She gripped the serpents by their throats as they glared up at her, mouths agape and exposing their fangs. She, in turn, glanced down at them with an expression of subtle amusement.

She noticed his distracted gaze. "Meet Inanna," she said, "Sumerian goddess of love."

"Where did you get her?"

"My father got it from an archeologist friend of his."

He recalled feeling a surge of passion as she kissed him again.

The next few moments he would rather have erased from his memory. The encounter, for him, was a disappointment. He attributed it to nervousness and awkwardness on his part.

After the debacle and despite her reassurances, he felt despondent as he watched her climb out from underneath the bed covers, don a house robe, and head for the bathroom. The despondency deepened at the sound of water splashing in the shower.

Lying back against the pillow, he thought of something that brought him up short. In panic he jumped out of bed, still sans skivvies, and bolted for the window from an oblique direction. Trembling hands pulled at a cord, flipping the blinds at a different angle.

With a worried sigh, he climbed back into bed.

Long after she had returned, he lay beside her, now re-clad in jockey shorts, listening to the hum of the electric clock. As he continued to lie back staring up into the darkness, he recalled the story of Onan from Holy Writ.

His brother, Er, was so wicked that God struck him dead. His father, Judah, then instructed Onan to go into Tamar, Er's widow, and get her pregnant so that she could raise descendants in his brother's name. Knowing that he would father the children only as a surrogate, he refused. Instead, he spilled his seed on the ground. The thing, so said Holy Writ, displeased the Lord and he slew him also.

Did Onan commit masturbation, or preliminary withdrawal? Did the Almighty judge him because of sexual sin, or greed? Women were forbidden to own property in those days. Unless she had sons to care for her, Tamar faced destitution in her old age. Er's estate, also, would go to Onan.

Plain, old-fashioned lust had brought Huck to Artie's bed that night. Greed had nothing to do with it. However displeased the Almighty may have been with him, he had not struck him dead. Is this a boudoir, or a confessional? Again, realizing his lack of regular church attendance since going away to college, he recalled his youthful self at confirmation, kneeling at the altar rail...

...The bishop passed among the candidates as he blessed them. The young Huck could see the vestment-robed figure getting close. He spotted the gold chain and cross dangling from his neck. As the sainted figure stood directly before him, thin infirm hands pressed gently on the young boy's head. An old man's voice—deep and resonant—intoned with prophetic earnestness the following benediction: "Grant, O Lord, this thy child's entrance into thy everlasting kingdom, worlds without end: through Christ our Lord. Amen."

The sacredness of the moment brought tears to the young boy's eyes...

...The dresser clock's luminous dial read four-thirty. He caught the faint perfumed scent from her dresser powder jar. His prowess as yet could claim only one accomplishment: He had not only botched his first encounter, he had soiled a woman's body.

Again, his eyes darted toward the window. Maybe Paul wasn't home.

He crawled out of bed and began dressing himself.

Chapter 8

"I adjure you. Answer me plainly: had you ever occasion to know the Lady Aarda?"... "The Lady Aarda and I have taken knowledge of one another," confessed I... "This offense be worse than thought," said Second Magistrate ... "This causes great confusion and violation of things sacred," said Third Magistrate ... "So, you took your ordination oath as one of the lewd fellows of the street who defile themselves with women as a thirsty dog drinks water?"...

(Day 35. Lord H'rshag's cross-examination at his trial for treason. Trans. and ed. Brit. Mus. vers. 3.2: 1981.)

* * * * *

The angry whine of the VW engine assaulted Huck's ears as he floored the accelerator. The flat agricultural valley slid past him with its varied patchwork of fields under irrigation. The late-afternoon sun was sinking behind the western mountains faster than was his liking. He realized now that he would not reach home before nightfall.

He recalled lying in the darkness of her bedroom...

...He reluctantly left the warmth of her body from underneath the bed covers and stepped out onto the thick carpeting of her bedroom floor.

THE DELUGE SCROLLS

Shivering in the cold chill of the morning air he reached for the crumpled heap of polyester that was his slacks. He crept into the living room and picked up other items of his clothing, carried them into the bathroom, and shut the door. He turned on the light and finished dressing.

As he slipped from her apartment to the parking lot, he could see his breath. In the darkened early morning chill, resisting the ignition current, her sports car engine coughed and sputtered before settling down to an even idle. He gunned the engine and sped out into the empty streets.

Later, inside the familiar surroundings of his own apartment, he threw items of clothing and toilet articles into a suitcase and was gone again.

The night cold still gripped the silent streets. After twenty minutes of speeding on in search of an all-night diner, he finally perched atop a stool of a coffee shop, nursing a doughnut over a steaming mug of fragrant, black liquid. Headlines of the *Los Angeles Examiner* flashed the following words:

> Body of Child Found in Actress' Mansion.
>
> Actress Mara Turner, returning from a European vacation, found her West Hollywood home had been broken into. Although nothing to date has been reported stolen, the interior was left in extensive disarray.
> The downstairs bathroom revealed the nude body of a young girl, believed to be about eleven or twelve years old. Cabbalist signs and graffiti left on the living room walls and empty video cartridges lying around have led police to believe it to be the work of cultist ritual sex and murder.
> Police seek for questioning an individual known only as "Snake."

Huck stared out the front window of the diner into the abysmal darkness beyond. *Sure would like to get my hands on the bastards that did it,* he thought.

Dawn breaking over the eastern sky found him dialing from a pay phone. A gravelly voice demanded, "Who is it?"

"George?" said Huck tentatively.

"Huck?" the voice answered. "It ain't even eight."

"I thought maybe you'd like an early start to your grandmother's."

Driving through the near-empty Los Angeles streets, he savored the

73

ever-brightening sunrise. He looked around the interior of the car. Was the very fact that it was not his an indication of a threshold he had now crossed and, having crossed, passed the point of no return?

As soon as he met George in front of his apartment, Huck knew he had some explaining to do. "Look's like Dr. Mason-Rodgers' car," George had guessed. "You sly devil."

"This has got to be kept quiet," said Huck after an embarrassed silence, "or the shit could really hit the fan."

George began loading his luggage. "My lips are sealed."

The trip to the south Los Angeles area, even in morning traffic took a good forty minutes. Nine AM found Huck again in his own apartment dialing someone out of bed.

"Yes?" Artie's voice was thick with sleep.

"Artie?"

"Huck." Her voice sounded fully awake now. "Where are you? Oh, my heart, you don't know how I felt when I reached over and found you gone. I was afraid you were angry with me."

"Not a chance." *(She's gotta be kiddin.')*

She groped for words. "What are your plans?"

"We gotta go back to the Flaming Embers for my car."

"Of course," she replied. "Bring back my car right away."

An hour later, he eased her car back into the parking lot. When he rang her front door, she greeted him wearing fresh lipstick and in a cotton blouse and dark slacks.

"When I saw that you had gone," she said as she ushered him in, "I felt so alone."

He strode through the living room. "I couldn't sleep," he explained. "So I got up to go home and pack."

He felt her tug his arm. "I can't send you away hungry."

The sight of pastel linen covering the dining room table aborted his suggestion that they go to MacDonald's or someplace. The two place settings consisting of highly glazed china and gleaming silverware had caught him quite unprepared. He was still studying the long-stemmed champagne glasses and flowers in a bud vase when he caught the aroma of eggs laced with oregano.

"I'm fixing us some quiche," she announced.

What's that, a fancy name for scrambled eggs? he almost said. Then he saw her look. "That's great," he said instead.

He took his place at the table as she brought over the still-sizzling skillet. "I made it with spinach and mushrooms," she said.

He began tasting the quiche—gingerly at first.

He looked up from his plate. Directly ahead of him atop the buffet stood the figurine.

Again, Artie's eyes followed the direction of his gaze. "I hope you don't mind Inanna joining us," she said.

He felt the beginnings of anxiety that the first real love of his life was going weird on him. "You refer to a clay figurine by name?"

During the lapse in the conversation, Huck cut some of the quiche with his fork. She continued staring at him. "Do you think this is superstition?" she said at last.

"You said it, not me."

More silence. Artie appeared to be groping for words. "Actually," she said thoughtfully, "this may not be as ridiculous as it sounds. There is a group of women right here on campus that would like me to use that figurine to help them reinvent ancient Sumerian goddess worship."

Huck took a sip of coffee. He knew well the women she was alluding to. They recently had assembled themselves in small groups among a grove of trees, a park, or perhaps a formal garden somewhere. They had tried, with special garb, ritual, and recitation of near-unintelligible incantation to recreate ancient pagan religions.

What would have been dismissed as mere nitwittery just a few years ago, now was taken seriously and welcomed as an alternative new faith.

"I know," he said. "What can I say? This is California."

Artie seemed deep in thought. "The thing is," she said, ignoring his remark, "that even I know very little about all that those ancient religions entailed."

"Except that it was a lot of bull-hockey."

She cast him a sidelong glance with a darkened expression. "Don't judge those people too quickly," she said. "They were actually a very cultured and intelligent people."

Huck recalled an illustration from Artie's textbook of an ancient Sumerian mural depicting a naked priest copulating with a female worshipper while she bent over sipping sacramental beer from a vase in front of an altar. "They were also a bunch of swingers, I gather."

"The goddess Inanna was also the keeper of the Me," she said, again trying to ignore his remark.

"Me?" said Huck. "What the hell's that?"

"It's quite complicated. We'll have to discuss it when there's more time."

She got up from the table and headed for the buffet. She picked up a fruit bowl that sat beside the figurine.

She placed it on the table and went to the kitchen, opened the refrigerator door, and peered inside. "Chilled champagne," she said, holding out two bottles.

"White or pink?" she said, returning to the table.

"Let's try the white," he said as he finished the quiche.

"How was it?" she asked.

He eyed the plate. "Not bad."

"I'm not talking about the quiche."

He felt her hand slowly grip his fingertips. "I enjoyed last night," she whispered.

Are you kidding? he thought. *When everything that could have gone wrong did go wrong?*

She seemed to sense his misgivings. She moved her face in close. "I really did," she said softly. "Trust me."

He arose from the chair and they embraced. He caught the oily scent of her lipstick. "Must you go?" she said, eyeing him.

"Yes," he said. "I really do."

"Promise you'll call when you get back."

He felt her grip his arm a little tighter.

"I'll call you as soon as I'm back in town."

"No matter how late it is?"

"No matter how late it is."...

...He glanced out at the massive irrigation sprinklers hurling torrents of water out across broad acreages of lettuce. The green of the fields glistened with a shimmering gold sheen in the pale afternoon sunlight. They contrasted with a moist coolness with the parched rolling hills that lay on the horizon. Torrents of air rushed in around him from his sunroof as he sped northward.

First taste of honey at twenty-four, he thought, *how about that? Been a good boy for twenty-four years and nobody's pinned a good conduct medal on me yet.* He felt the cleansing effect of the warm air gush past him. How many guys were doing it even in high school? He recalled slamming one kid's head against a locker for calling him a fag.

Even George chided him for his forced celibacy. *By the time you get* around to gettin' yours, he had said, all the good ones will be gotten, and what's left will be rotten.

A thought brought him up short. He was going home a man of the world. He knew his parents to be very perceptive about such things. Would they notice—something perhaps in his demeanor? As the countryside began to look familiar, he could feel a sense of anxiety. Should he turn back, and, upon reaching his apartment, call long distance and feign an excuse? No. He determined to push on and face his parents.

Once he made his decision, he began to feel better. Despite the darkness now enveloping the valley, he knew where he was. He turned off the main highway and headed down the blacktop toward the solitary spire that thrust up above the low hilltop into the moonlit sky and the manse he knew to be beside it...

...The morning after New Year's Day, Huck sat at breakfast watching the early-morning sun filter through the kitchen curtains. He admired the verdant terrain outside. Since coming home, the winter rains finally turned the burnt brown hills to a freshened green.

As he sat in the large manse kitchen warming his hands around a mug of coffee, he saw her, a small woman looking to be in her sixties, walk in. Green eyes that seemed to miss nothing surveyed the room. The thin face and broad, thin mouth bore an intensity of expression. Prominent cheekbones accentuated the contour of her features. Her iron gray hair was cut into a wavy bob and she wore an apron over dark slacks.

She walked past without greeting him. "You'll want eggs?" she said stiffly. Her speech bore a trace of foreign accent. As she stood at the stove, back to him, he studied her with mounting dismay.

"If it's not too much trouble," he stammered.

"No trouble," she retorted. She busied herself with some kitchen utensils, making quick, deft movements. "That isn't the sort of thing we call trouble around here."

"I see."

"Some people cause trouble of a different sort."

He wanted to ask what the problem was. "Guess I'll skip the eggs," he said finally. "I want to get an early start."

"Ya," she said drawing water into a saucepan. "I imagine you do."

He stood up and pushed his chair back. "All right," he demanded. "What is it?"

She didn't answer right away. "When I was doing your laundry last night," she said deliberately, "I found this already."

She turned and handed him the happy face note.

"It's just a note," he said, looking at it.

"I can see that."

"Doesn't mean a thing," he insisted.

He shoved his chair under the table. "I don't even know who it's from. Besides, I really don't see where it's anybody's business."

"So I suppose this is nobody's business either." She handed him another note, written on pastel, scented stationery.

He could feel the color leave his face as he took it from her and started to read:

Dearest,

I'm taking the time to write this note before rejoining you. I don't want you to blame yourself for what happened. Young men often climax prematurely during their first experience. Please don't be alarmed or disappointed.

You will soon get the knack performing correctly. I know you will. Please be patient with yourself.

Also, don't worry about me. Being loved by you and being held by you is in itself satisfying to me. The rest will come in time.

In the meantime, know that I love you.

As ever,
Artie

The small, neat handwriting matched that on the happy-faced note. She must have written it and inserted it into his shirt pocket just after her shower. Why didn't he think to check that pocket before?

His mother returned to the kitchen sink. "You're a grown man," she said. "Nothing you do is anybody else's business anymore."

He started for his bedroom. "Guess I'll start packing."

Chapter 9

The next day the temple guards detachment returned for to escort me to the Early-Advanced Presentment (pre-trial indictment, or type of grand jury—ed.) Soon I stood before the grim-visaged magistrate at docket in the temple court. "This be but a preliminary hearing," announced he...

(Day 35. Lord H'rshag's pre-trial hearing following his arrest. Trans. and ed. Brit. Mus. vers. 3.2; 1981.)

* * * * *

Again, with a high, angry whine, the VW sped along the flat California highway, this time headed south. Huck still labored to recover from the altercation with his mother. With his suitcase jammed into the back seat and with jaw tensed, he gripped the wheel and stared straight ahead.

"Damn!" He slammed his fist against the steering wheel.

He rubbed his stinging hand against his leg in an attempt to make the pain go away. Finally, he resumed the two-handed grip and continued driving, eyes straight ahead. First experience with a woman. What's the big deal anyway? Especially on a southern California university campus where fornication is considered just good, clean fun?

"Damn!" he shouted again. "Why can't she just leave me alone?"

That was it. She was leaving him quite alone.

"Ye shall not die," said the serpent. The words from his parochial school religion class came rushing back into his memory. "Ye shall become as gods, knowing both and evil." Huck didn't feel very god-like with his newfound knowledge. What was sex apart from love anyway? Or love apart from sex? And why does the Bible refer to sex as knowledge rather than love? And what, indeed, did the more experienced practitioners of casual sex of the locker room really know of either?

With them, wasn't it all little more than just an erotic sneeze?

Did he really love her? He sensed brittleness in their new relationship. He again visualized her perky smile, her voice, her mannerisms, her attentions, her kisses, and her touch. He concluded that, yes, he did love her. He only wished, however, that he could express his love under less complicated conditions.

Leave it to backsliders to get philosophical, he thought.

Damn Paul, anyway.

* * * * *

First day after the holidays; just like starting all over, he thought as he eyed the doorway of Archeology 101.

George passed him in the hall. "C'mon, man, what are you waiting for?" George was right. What was there to be afraid of? After all, she had more to lose than he did.

Huck followed him through the door.

"Good morning, Huck." Her tone sounded decorous, professional.

"Morning," he mumbled without looking her way. Her cover-up was masterful, he thought. At dismissal he slipped past her, surrounded by a tight little knot of students.

His Student Union mailbox contained an envelope bearing the provost's office letterhead. The message inside required that he report to Dr. Vawter's office 9:00 AM sharp the following Monday.

George stopped by with a similar-looking envelope. "What do you think? Are we in trouble again?"

Huck studied the note as he walked away from the mailbox. He wondered at the portent of the summons. He hoped against hope that it was over something he didn't know about.

Yet he feared that he knew only too well what it was about.

THE DELUGE SCROLLS

The following Monday, they stood in a conference room adjacent the provost's office. The room was lined with dark wooden paneling. Three heavy wooden tables formed a "U" shape. Thickly upholstered chairs were pushed under the tables. Heavy beige curtains hung from the windows.

Pacing restlessly beside them was defensive linebacker Mike Travis, a surly blond-haired giant with a crew cut and sideburns. His thin lips curved downward, giving a hawklike expression. With him stood running back Emory Wilson, a black youth short and stocky of build.

The athletic director, Dean Rodgers, and Coach Schermerheim came in from another door. The door to the provost's office opened. A large man in a rumpled gray suit entered. Beneath the tousled white hair, Huck noticed red blotches across the cheeks and nose. Dark, bushy eyebrows and dark-rimmed glasses accentuated piercing blue eyes. As he bade everyone be seated, he reached for a pitcher of water and poured into a tumbler. He popped two pills into his mouth and washed them down with a single drought.

He viewed the assemblage a moment. "Well, well," he said in a heavy voice, "isn't this a pleasant little party?"

He shuffled some papers. "This is just a preliminary hearing," he said, removing his glasses briefly. "What I have here is a warrant for the arrest of one Herschel Ladd, one George Bouknight, one Mike Travis, and one Emory Wilson—each on grounds of third-degree criminal sexual misconduct."

He put his glasses back on and continued, "This warrant was issued by the Sheriff's Department, Mohave County, State of Arizona."

He laid the papers down, took off his glasses again and laid them on the table as well. He leaned back in his chair and rubbed his eyes thoughtfully. Heavy lips framed a broad mouth that curled back in a grimace, exposing what reminded Huck of horse's teeth. Then he lunged forward in his chair again and looked across the table at the others. He slid his glasses back on his forehead and again picked up a sheaf of papers.

The moves are deliberate, Huck realized in the silence pregnant with tension. *The guy is a master at intimidation.*

Dr. Vawter studied the page further. "Fellahs, it looks to me like there's some folks over there in Arizona that want to book you guys on a sexual misconduct charge. What do you think about that?"

Huck fidgeted and looked down into his lap.

Dr. Vawter went on, "Seems that the alleged offense took place December twenty-third. That must have been during the Yucca Bowl trip."

He cast a hard glance toward the AD and Coach.

The provost then looked back over at Huck and his companions. "It says here," he said, readjusting his glasses, "that the alleged offense was indecent exposure. What do you gentlemen have to say to that?"

Before Huck could answer, Dr. Rodgers cut in. "A pretty pass," he whined. "We send these fellows out to represent our school, and now this," he added, tossing his head in indignation.

Huck eyed the dean. He studied the puckered expression behind the rimless glasses. Rounded cheeks hung in bulbs of flaccid flesh. Colorless eyes squinted as if trying to pretend that the world they viewed really wasn't there. He also noticed crease lines running across the dean's face and forehead at a crazy angle such as he had never seen on another human being.

What kind of monkey rides his back? Huck wondered. *What kinds of demons lurk just beneath that effete, intellectual façade? Is it the Gaderene Legion that one sees deep in the pools of those blank, staring eyes? What powerful, sinister forces rage beneath the personality of this mincing, prancing dandy?*

It doesn't take a professional psychologist, he reflected, *to see that the guy is under a severe mental conflict. I wonder what his problem is?*

George gave Huck's ankle a kick under the table.

Dr. Vawter pulled off his glasses and sucked the tip of one his bows. "If it was up to me," he said, again glancing at Huck and his buddies, "I'd throw these clowns in the clink right here and now."

Huck's thoughts were interrupted by Coach's voice. "Why don't we hear what the boys have to say?"

Dr. Vawter gave a shrug in apparent disgust. "All right," he sighed. "Let's hear your side of the story."

Huck waited. His three teammates turned their heads toward him. He licked dry lips. "Well," he said, clearing his throat, "here is what happened, sir. On the day in question, we had light drill in the morning. That afternoon, the four of us rented a car and drove down to Lake Havasu City. We went down into the state park to a canoe livery. Then we went down Lake Mead and pulled ashore for lunch and climbed a bluff to watch some girls that were canoeing by."

Dr. Vawter slipped his glasses back on his head. "Then what happened?"

"We—yelled some things."

Dr. Vawter glanced at the page. "Report here," he said briskly, "has you guys saying 'show us your tits,' or words to that effect. Is that about right?"

"Yes, sir," said Huck solemnly.

"Then what happened?"

Huck took a deep breath. "Some of the girls," he continued, "would get mad and stare straight ahead."

Dr. Vawter's eyes narrowed. "Know what that's called these days?"

"No, sir."

"That's called sexual harassment and is now grounds for expulsion. Did you know that?"

"No, sir."

Dr. Vawter tapped a pencil on the tabletop. "All right," he sighed. "You said some of the girls—"

Huck could feel prickly heat break out on his face. "There were others who would—do it."

"Would do what?" Dr. Vawter wasn't letting them off the hook.

Huck shrugged. "They would—bare their breasts."

"Then what happened?"

"We would applaud," replied Huck.

"You would applaud," the provost repeated. "Anything else happen?"

Huck fidgeted with a pencil. "One canoe," he began, "shouted back at us."

"Shouted back at you?"

Huck glanced helplessly around to his three companions. They remained immobile. "They shouted 'show us your buns.'"

"Then what happened?"

"We had no choice but—to moon 'em."

Huck felt his table shake in a subtle quiver. Apparently one of his teammates was convulsing in a spasm of silent laughter. Dammit, he thought, knock it off. This isn't funny.

Dr. Vawter again glanced back at the page. "Report here," he said, "has you gentlemen dropping your trousers and baring your buttocks in public. Is this what you refer to as 'mooning 'em'?"

"Yes, sir," said Huck, swallowing hard. *You know damn well what that means*, he thought. *Just more mind games.*

Dr. Vawter again slipped off his glasses and laid them on the tabletop. "Mr. Ladd," he said finally, "a college man is supposed to be gentleman and a scholar, wouldn't you agree?"

"Yes, sir."

"Is this your idea of gentlemanly and scholarly behavior?"

"No, sir."

From across the table came a restlessness. "May I say something?" Coach's voice broke the tense silence.

A desperate sense of gratitude welled up in Huck's inner being. Could Coach be counted on to go to bat, as he had often promised, whenever any of his players got in trouble?

Dr. Vawter nodded. "Go ahead."

"I think," said Coach, choosing his words carefully, "that we need to put the whole thing in perspective." With his fingertips, he spun a glass ashtray. "I think we need to discern the difference between what is obviously an example of college boy high jinks—and this is by no means condoning what they did—and genuinely deviant behavior."

Dr. Vawter leaned back in his chair. "Perhaps," was all he said.

Huck wrung sweaty palms as he waited for Dr. Vawter's next salvo. *This guy is a master at jerkin' our chain*, he concluded wretchedly.

After a continued pause, Dr. Vawter again turned to Huck. "What do you think we ought to do with you guys?"

"I leave that to your discretion, sir."

"You want we should expel you?"

"I would prefer a less draconian penalty, sir."

Dr. Vawter again put his glasses back on and leaned forward. "The Board of Disciplinary Review will be hearing this case in a couple of weeks," he announced. "You will be notified at that time. This meeting is now adjourned."

Huck stood up and worked his shoulder blades to relieve the tension. He spotted Coach moving into his peripheral vision. Feelings of gratitude, however, dissipated when he saw Coach's face.

As Coach slipped past him, he heard "I'll have words with you later" whispered in a low growl.

He felt his heart skip a beat. He would gladly face anything from the Board of Disciplinary Review than to receive one tongue lashing from Coach.

As he stepped to the hall, he sensed the presence of Mike Travis standing next to him. "What do you think?" Mike asked.

Huck shrugged. "I don't know," he said in a worried sigh. "It doesn't look good."

Mike stooped to a nearby drinking fountain. "I wouldn't worry about it," he said, straightening up. He wiped his mouth with the back of his hand and looked down the hall to where George and Emory were walking alongside Coach and the AD.

"Those two are our safety net," he continued.

Huck watched the parties in question round a distant corner. "How do you figure that?"

Mike gestured with his head. "As long as those two are in this thing with us, nothing is going to happen. Otherwise, you can just bet your sweet bippy we'd be dead meat by now."

Mike thrust a thumbs-up. "Ciao, baby."

He turned and started down the hall in the opposite direction.

Chapter 10

"*The Grand Vizier... desired her for his own.*" "*We have already known one another as man and wife.*" *My mentor's countenance waxed affrighted.* "*Have a care,*" *said he,* "*that none find out. Thy life be in grave jeopardy should certain in high places be privy to this knowledge.*"...
    (Day 21. Shumrag's warning to Lord H'rshag. Trans. and ed. Brit. Mus. vers. 2.1; 1981.)

* * * * *

The blare of the jukebox permeated every remote corner of the Matador. Tonight, Mike Travis and Emory Wilson had also joined the study group. However, the usual after-library crowd had not yet shown, leaving the taproom strangely quiet and empty.
    The study group centered their discussion on the hearing that morning.
    "How did you guys make out?" Paul asked.
    "I don't know." George shook his head. "I'm worried."
    Mike glared at him. "You got nothin' to worry about."
    George looked at him puzzled. "What are you talkin' about, man?"
    Mike gripped his mug, raised it to his lips and took a draught. "You know damn well what I'm talkin' about—MAN!" he said as he slammed the mug down again.

Huck, who had been sitting through the conversation in unaccustomed introspection, suddenly sat up. "Hey, Mike," he said, "come with me a minute."

Mike sullenly got up from the table and followed Huck into the corridor. "What do you want?" he mumbled.

Huck gestured to a phone booth. "Can you lend me a quarter?"

Mike leveled a gaze at him. "What are you going to do, call Dean Rodgers' old lady?"

Huck turned his head lest his face give him away.

"Here," said Mike. "Go call his old lady—or whoever. I'm going back to the party." He then turned to rejoin the others.

Once inside the booth, Huck inserted the coin, cast a furtive glance out the window, and started dialing. He heard a ring—two rings—then a female voice.

He spoke softly into the phone. "Hello, Artie? Huck. How you doin'? Excuse me—? What do you mean, 'Huck who?' It's me. C'mon, what's goin' on, anyway?"

Lines creased his forehead. "You say someone near to you has hurt you very deeply? Now what's that supposed to mean?"

Again he waited. "When was I supposed to call you?" *Oh, my God,* he thought. *I was going to call her as soon as I got back from vacation.*

He took a deep breath. "Look—" he began, "when I drove from up home, I had things on my mind; like fights with my mother. She found your note. Yeah, I'm sorry, too. It's just something we're going to have to work through."

He pulled the phone away from his ear. "So you see how easy it was for me to forget? Doesn't really excuse it, I know. Listen, what I really wanted to call you about was this: can I see you tonight? I know a place down in Burbank. Here, I'll give you the address."

After he hung up and left the phone booth, he returned to his table. He found Mike sitting with an empty beer glass and still glaring at George and Emory.

Huck gave George a nudge. "Let's go. I got studying."

"Me, too," said George, still eyeing Mike.

They exited the taproom, climbed into the VW, and sped with squealing tires out of the parking lot. Huck dropped George off at his apartment and, with another roar of the engine and grinding of gears, did a U-turn, and headed for Burbank.

An hour later, he sat opposite Artie in a secluded booth in a small, side-street bistro called the Pirate's Cove. The wait staff's heads were wrapped in bandannas. They wore old-fashioned, loose-fitting blouses. Waiters wore wide trousers while the waitresses wore miniskirts with tattered hem and a slit high up the left thigh. Murals along the walls depicted characters and scenes from Stevenson's *Treasure Island*.

Long John Silver, with Captain Flint perched atop his shoulder cast a single evil eye down on Artie and Huck as they shared a carafe of wine by flickering candlelight.

"Short notice, I realize," Huck was saying.

Artie sat tight in her corner, somewhat aloof. She took a sip from her glass. "It's all right," she said in a voice void of expression.

He searched her face. "Still mad at me?"

She shook her head.

"But you're not happy about what happened?"

"I'll get over it."

He reached for her hand. It felt cold to the touch. "Want to order something?" he said.

"I'm not hungry," she said simply. She tightened her grip on his hand. "I need you." Her voice sounded surprisingly steady. "When you didn't call, I didn't know what to think."

Forget to make one phone call, he thought, *and it's like Armageddon.*

After another short pause, she slipped her hand over his arm. "Please forgive me for being so silly," she said.

She let more minutes slip. "It was hard," she said at last, "speaking so formally to you yesterday."

"Not exactly a thrill for me either," he said, patting her hand.

"We need to talk," she said after another brief pause. Although the sadness had gone from her eyes, her expression remained serious. "I heard about the inquiry."

Huck shrugged. "Big to-do over nothing."

"A warrant for your arrest is not nothing."

Huck shook his head. "Everybody's making it such a big deal."

"It is a big deal. You could go to jail."

"All we did was moon a bunch of girls from a river bank."

She sat back with arms folded. "I thought as much," she said, looking straight ahead. "Why do you guys do those things?"

"I don't know," he sighed. "Guys just don't think, I guess."

THE DELUGE SCROLLS

A small line of customers formed at the cash register.

"I guess it just comes down this," she said finally, "that there are just some things that—oh, my God!"

"What is it?" Huck looked in the direction of her gaze. At the cashier's station stood a slender woman in a long dress. Her graying hair hung straight down her back. From her lips she let hang a small, slim cigar.

Huck slid toward the aisle. "I'll duck into the men's room."

Artie grabbed his wrist. "Don't bother, she's leaving."

"But what if she's seen us?"

"My point exactly," said Artie with resignation. "She's gone now, so if she hasn't seen us, it's all right. If she has, it won't make any difference."

Again, he started for the aisle. "Let's get out of here."

Again, she grasped his forearm. "You'll do nothing of the sort. That would be the worst thing. She may still be out on the parking lot."

As he settled back into the booth, her mood began to brighten a little. "Let's have some more of that nice wine," she suggested.

*****

Later, in her apartment and clad in her house robe, she began typing the words:

January 7, 1980

Dearest Peppi,

Thought I'd send you a sequel to that little epistle I wrote you last September. Who would have thought it, Peppi, how one can so thoroughly change their mind about someone, but it's happened. I've done a complete about-face regarding that guy they stuck in my Archeology 101 class. To put it bluntly, he's delightful—simply delightful. And sexy. (Okay, Peppi, you might as well hear it from me before you hear it from somebody else: we're having an affair.)

Even though rules and taboos are falling constantly around here, fraternization between faculty and student is still a no-no.

The reality is that sooner or later, somebody is going to find out about us. This brings me to the point of my letter. What we need is a nice, cozy little hideaway. Guess what comes to mind? You guessed it—your darling little beachfront cottage. We will pay you: by the day or by the weekend, and we'll pay you well.

Please say you'll do it, for an old friend who needs a favor.

Let's hear from you soon on this.

As ever,
Artie

Chapter 11

Thy love... better than precious rubies; thy kisses better than rarest wine. The locks of thy head are like the scented breezes from the mountain of spices. Thy lips are like honey and myrrh... Thy shoulders were exquisitely fragile to my embrace. Thine arms, thin and delicate, yet with passion did embrace me... Thy breasts were as twin clusters of grapes, or like twain noble towers... Let me linger in memory of the nights of delight... My sister, my spouse, I shall not soon forget thee...
   (Day 38. Lord H'rshag's love poem to the Lady Aarda. Trans. and ed. Brit. Mus. vers. 3.5; 1981.)

* * * * *

Lolling in the comfort of her chaise lounge Artie looked out at the rolling surf. From about the distance of a football field it washed gently up on the mauve-colored sand and rolled back into the tide. A smile of contentment crossed her face as she lay back on her cushion. A cloud ceiling extended without a break until just above the horizon. The clear sky behind the break shone a pale blue. The water also reflected a lighter contrast from the dark, heaving waves nearer land. Reclining in her navy blue bikini, she could sense Huck's gaze.
   Foam-flecked swells gently washed kelp and other seaweed up on the

beach. Overhead, seagulls screamed in defiance against the ocean breeze. The fresh sea smell heightened her senses.

Huck released his grip on her hand and stood up. Minutes before, he had come back from a swim in the heavy surf. He felt the edge of his trunks. "Getting dry," he commented.

He sat back down. Neither said anything as they admired the seascape from the porch deck area of the beachfront cottage belonging to Peppi. Artie had set up housekeeping with Huck during spring break. A slight breeze rustled through the beach grass that grew just on the other side of the picket fence bordering the property. Bronze-colored wind chimes shaped like the sun, moon, and stars jangled in the onshore breeze, making a tinkling sound behind them.

What a delightful idea, she thought, *renting this place during spring break.* Another plan occurred to her. For some time she had wanted to do some massive redecorating in her own apartment. She could put much of her stuff in storage, move out here with the rest, and spend the balance of the summer here around her Iraqi schedule.

Artie reached for her wine glass, finished its maroon-colored contents and then stood up. "More vino, darling?"

Huck continued to lie back as he handed her his glass.

"Y'know," he said, "since I met you, I've become quite a wine-bibber."

She laughed. "I'll make you a connoisseur yet," she said, taking his glass, "and wean you from that awful old beer."

She sat back on the edge of her chaise lounge. "There is one more thing I would like to wean you away from," she said thoughtfully, "and that's your penchant for getting into trouble."

"Hah," he said, flicking grains of sand onto her, "I never did tell you about my tour-de-force."

He then related to her his encounter with Vinnie Roman. He was Huck's rival as the school's chief troublemaker with one notable difference. Whereas Huck's escapades were done in fun, Vinnie was mean and malicious. The overbearing, dark-haired youth led a band of teenaged hooligans that terrorized the valley.

He was the one who had needled Huck about his "virginity."

Huck slammed the kid's head into a locker only after repeated taunts in the hall between classes in front of the other students. A teacher who witnessed the altercation briskly hustled them down to the principal's office. Vinnie, already on probation, was expelled forthwith. Huck, however, was given two choices: either three days' suspension from school or four swats from the paddle.

Huck chose the swats.

"I can't believe this," said Artie. "Whatever for?"

He explained that the incident had taken place on a Thursday before a home football game. Had he taken the suspension, he would not have been allowed to play the next day; nor would he have been allowed to attend the post-game dance.

Artie by now had become visibly upset that he had deliberately chosen to subject himself to corporal punishment. "I can't believe this. Public schools still administering that kind of discipline in this day and age."

He added that the principal had him lean across his desk, or "assume the position" as they called it. He then gave Huck one swat and then had him report back between classes for the other three at one swat per visit.

Artie's eyes burned with indignation. "That is so totally sadistic. How could you not help but be left with deep psychological scars?"

"We had a system," Huck replied. "We would pad the seat of our pants with notebook paper. In addition, I also borrowed a buddy's army surplus field jacket to help absorb the blows."

Though the principal never caught on, he did get his revenge on Huck later. At the Friday night dance Vinnie, contrary to school rules for an expellee, showed up at the dance with several of his gang members. They harassed girls, bullied some of the smaller boys and openly consumed liquor and tobacco.

"Where were the chaperones?" Artie wanted to know.

"Standing on the sidelines; too intimidated, I guess."

"And the principal?"

"Hiding in his office."

A thought occurred to her. "Did you do anything?"

"I grabbed Vinnie and dragged him out to the parking lot and threw him into the dumpster."

He lay back and looked at the clouds overhead. "You know," he said, smiling, "it's hard to intimidate people when you smell of garbage."

Artie gave a brief chuckle. "I wish I could have seen it."

"Then I got some of the varsity guys to round up the rest of the gang," Huck continued. "We told them to get the hell off the premises and stay off."

Artie swung over toward him. "You mean to tell me that you and your buddies singlehandedly did what no else dared do, rid the school of a bunch of terrorizing hoodlums?"

"That's right," he said. He got up and stepped to the edge of the deck. He went on to relate that the principal, however, showed his gratitude by giving Huck three days' suspension for fighting on school property. Whereas Vinnie had merely terrorized everyone, Huck had embarrassed the administration when he took matters into his own hands.

Before Artie could reply, the faint sound of the phone came from inside the cottage. She ran past the porch's sliding doorway. Immediately before her stood a circular dining room table. A large, modern-looking lamp hung overhead. On the table lay an opened attaché case with some scattered papers.

She reached for a telephone that lay across the table from the attaché case. "Hello," she said, struggling to control her voice. "This is—"

She glanced out into the interior of the cottage. A planter divided the dining and living areas. Clean-lined contemporary-style furniture had been set about the sparsely furnished living room. In a far corner sat a fireplace of modern witch's hat design, with its wide-mouthed hearth. A large picture window looked out into a back yard and driveway. Off on the two sides, doorways led to the bedroom and kitchen respectively.

She saw a shadow fall across the portal. Huck stood in the doorway. She motioned him into the dining room. "Yes," she said, jotting on a note pad. "Thank you very much."

A shriek of delight startled Huck as female arms clamped a tight hold around his neck. He heard a shout "We got it!"

He was finally able to pull her arms away. "Got what?"

"The Levi Wiseman Foundation for Antique Studies has finally given us the grant."

She had forgotten that she had given them Peppi's number.

She pulled out a chair. "Sit down," she said, gesturing.

"They want us to submit an estimate of expenses. Where's the calculator?" she said as he reached into the attaché case. "I can hire your entire study group. I realize the pay may not be all that great, but think of the experience."

"I was just thinking," he said. "How was it that you got that sabbatical so easily?"

"It's quite simple," she shrugged. "They were trying to comply with government guidelines."

"Did this mean," said Huck, "they're passing over someone else who may have had more seniority?"

Artie folded her arms and looked smugly out into the dining room. "I think there was one other applicant: a Seymour Gould of the psychology department."

Huck looked serious. "I understand he's in pretty tight with your husband. Couldn't this create problems for you later?"

Artie laughed. "Not to worry, mon cher. I know how to handle Lester."

Huck studied the pile of papers on the table beside that attaché case. He looked up to see a wall bracket in the corner of the living room. On the top stood the figurine.

"Brought what's-her-name I see," he said, smiling wryly.

"The name is Inanna," said Artie, apparently not finding his remark funny.

"Okay, whatever," he said, trying to suppress a sense of irritation. A thought occurred to him. "Did you know that Abraham was originally from Ur of the Chaldees?"

He went on to explain an apocryphal account from the Talmudic tradition of Abraham's leaving Ur of the Chaldees for the Land of Canaan. According to the account, Abraham, his brothers, and Terah, their father, all belonged to a craft guild in the city that specialized in the making of idols.

Abram began to question the efficacy of blocks of wood, clay, and stone that he carved or shaped into idols day after day. He decided to put his skepticism to the test.

One evening, as it fell his turn to close the family shop for the day, he stepped to a shelf of newly finished images that were ready for customer pick-up the next day and threw one of them to the floor.

When his father and brothers arrived the next morning, they were horrified to find one of the idols lying on the floor in pieces. When they demanded from Abram an explanation, he replied that just before closing, two of the idols got into a fight and one threw the other off the shelf.

"That's ridiculous," said his father. "Images don't fight. They can't even move!"

"My point exactly," said Abram. "Why then do we worship them?"

Terah realized his son was right. However, in a city obsessed with idol worship, such candor could be dangerous.

Shortly thereafter, Abram and his family left town.

Huck glanced at Artie and noticed mounting irritation. He was about to mention the commandment about the making of graven images, but thought better of it. "In the meantime," he said, changing the subject, "what say we get to work?"

"Good idea." Artie turned to her notes. She was just beginning to realize the logistics involved in planning an archeological expedition. The matter of visas and passports was just for starters. She also faced the matter of drawing up an inventory of needed equipment—for the digging, sorting, cleaning, and packing of any artifacts their shovels might turn up. Also needed was special clothing—rugged and loose fitting—for the hot, dry climate. Additional necessities were tents, cots, sleeping bags, and finally, first-aid equipment.

Again, she reflected on the proposed site of next summer's expedition. Babylon: the city allegedly cursed by the Almighty to remain forever deserted, inhabited only by satyrs, cormorants, jackals, and "doleful creatures."

"Doleful creatures." The word stuck in her mind like a bad memory or an irritating little ditty that would not go away. The word, along with "satyr" puzzled her. She recalled how in the course of her graduate work, her scrutiny of ancient languages involved the study of Hebrew. When the linguists translated the Torah into English, did they use these words to denote the existence of mere terrestrial beings that occupied ruins emptied of all human habitation?

Or—did they could denote something different?

Was there another Dr. Mason-Rodgers, who vied with the scientist and who dabbled in the mystical, the occult, and who kept statues of ancient female deities? Did this second Ardith leave her open to the acceptance of something that natural science could never accept or explain? Something otherworldly?

Something sinister?

Was it just superstition that kept native Bedouins from camping overnight at the site? Surely it was just coincidence that the locale had not yet been explored by scientists of the spade. Surely people of science would not allow themselves to be deterred by an ancient curse.

Poring over the work sheets, Artie quoted Huck dollar estimate figures. As he punched numbers into the calculator, they lost all track of time.

Finally she stopped. "Do you have some totals for me?"

Huck punched out more numbers. "Well," he sighed, "like the monkey said when he peed into the cash register: 'This is running into money.'"

"That does it," she said standing to her feet. "Why don't you go back to the sun deck," she suggested as she started for the kitchen. "I'll get some more wine."

Returning to the sun deck, Huck noticed that the clouds had largely disappeared. The skies had cleared to an azure blue. The late-afternoon sun, however, had lost little of its southern California brilliance. He stretched out on his chaise lounge and savored the cool of the sea breeze.

Sandaled feet appeared on the whitened boards of the sun deck. "More vin, mon petit?" Artie's voice startled him. "Nicely chilled, too." With two goblets of the white bubbly, she joined him.

He reached for his glass to hers. "To us."

They could feel the concentration of the sun's heat. Artie reached beside her chair for a pair of sunglasses.

Huck watched her lying on her back. He noticed reddening begin to spread across her skin, just above her bra line, up toward her shoulders, and down her midriff and thighs.

"Hey, love," he said, alerting her. "Better turn over."

She sat up, pulled her eyeglasses up to her hairline and glanced down at herself. She handed him a plastic bottle. "Appliqué, si-vous-plait. Do the honors, please," she said as she turned on her stomach.

She laid her sunglasses back on the deck. "Come do me, mon petit," she pleaded. "Protectez moi from the nasty old sun."

He tipped a dollop of its contents into his cupped hand, and then started rubbing the lotion between her shoulders.

She writhed with a deepening sense of pleasure. "Ah, feels so good," she sighed, closing her eyes. "Quell Plaisr!"

He unfastened her bra and continued daubing, rubbing and massaging across her body: her shoulders, the small of her back, her thighs, her calves, and finally the soles of her feet. All the while, she responded with more sighs and exclamations of ecstasy. "Let's go inside," she whispered.

A daring impulse occurred to him. Despite his uneasiness over the possibility of Paul's seeing them that night in her apartment, the risk of possible exposure during their lovemaking had now somehow created a perverse sense of thrill.

He swallowed hard. "Why not right here?" he said, as he slid his hand under her bikini.

A thought, however, brought her up short.

The scarring. How could he not notice? How could he not guess the origin of the reminder of that encounter weekend gone awry; and this however faint the telltale marks remained after the plastic surgeon's skin grafting? How could he not surmise the perpetrator? Could this be sufficient to deflect his passion of the moment?

She tried to focus his thoughts away from any possible lust for revenge. "Inanna is with us," she said, again in a whisper.

Huck was about to ask where was Inanna during her life with Lester when he felt a shudder. He knew it wasn't his imagination when she, too, looked up.

It seemed to have started in the northernmost corner of the cottage and then rippled diagonally outward across the porch deck, to the beach and on out to the sea. It had the effect of a freight train passing close.

The wind chimes jerked and swung on their strings crazily. The whole phenomenon was over in a matter of seconds.

Artie retied her bra. "What was that?"

He stood up and cocked his head. Even the beach birds stopped singing. "Tremor," he said, picking up his beach towel.

She looked at him. "Tremor?"

"Earthquake," he said simply.

She began picking up her beach robe, towel, and lotion. She turned to him. "What does this mean?"

He stood thoughtfully a moment. "I don't know," he sighed. "Maybe nothing. Maybe that was the end of it."

"Do you think we should leave?"

"Nah."

Another shudder. It followed the same pattern. However it rumbled with greater severity, sending the wind chimes crashing to the deck.

"Let's get out of here," said Artie. He followed her into the beach house. Once in the bedroom, she frantically started packing her suitcase.

"Aren't we going to take time to change?" said Huck as he, too, started packing.

"No way," she insisted. "Let's get out of here."

She reached into her purse. "Here," she said, throwing him the keys. "You drive."

He looked at her. "I don't know why you're in such a panic, we're in no more danger here than anywhere else."

"Dummy," she snapped. "If there's a major disaster, I don't want us to be found here like this."

He still hesitated when a third shock hit. The draperies and curtains swung violently. He heard the sound of falling dishes from the kitchen. He saw Artie blanch as the figurine crashed to the floor.

Stunned, she stood frozen on the spot. He watched expressions of horror and disbelief convulse her features.

For herself, she felt torn between two equally crazy notions. One impulse was to try to scoop up the pieces with some vague, futile hope of mending it later. The other impulse to flee, however, won out.

Without another word, they bolted for the foreign compact in the driveway. They thrust their luggage into the back seat. Huck jumped behind the wheel and Artie quickly climbed into the passenger side. He gunned the engine, spun the car around, and shot out of the driveway, sending arcs of gravel in all directions.

Out on the highway, they continued speeding southward. Even in their car, they were on edge, expecting another shock.

Nothing more happened, however.

Grasping the top of the steering wheel with his left hand, Huck glanced over at her.

"Sorry about your figurine," he said at last.

At first she didn't say anything.

"The ones at my apartment and my office," she said finally, "were mere replicas I had made."

Again she paused. "This one," she said, "was the original."

For a long time she sat back against the seat saying nothing. The dark sunglasses contrasted with her facial pallor. Tense lines etched the corners of her mouth.

"It was at least 4,500 years old," she said in a flat tone of voice. "It was absolutely priceless."

They continued south on Highway 1 in further silence, the sea to their right and the mountains to their left.

Her already lowered spirits sank still further.

Gone.

Inanna, goddess of love and fertility at one time worshipped and served by whole nations and societies. However, long since fallen into disuse, it had become the object of bemused interest by antiquarians. She now lay in pieces in a California beachfront cottage.

From deep within her welled up thoughts and feelings that alarmed her. Just a clay figurine; what's the big deal?

It's a 4,500-year-old artifact is what's the big deal! It represented a religion that predated Christianity. It even predated Judaism. It must have predated the tablet of stone that bore the Ten Commandments by a good thousand years. And what did it represent? Only a depth of fervency and devotion of a whole civilization that was the bedrock of our Western culture is all. It represented a civilization that flourished before the Homeric epic of the Fall of Troy. It represented a time when the Greeks were still village-level farmers tending sheep on rocky Aegean hillsides; a time when Celtic tribes were worshipping at Stonehenge on the Isle of Britain; a time when illiterate waves of hunters and gatherers roamed the Eurasian land mass and the Western Hemisphere.

The saliva dried in the inside of her mouth. She felt a pressure against her chest and breathing became difficult.

As though that was not enough, what of her own attachment to it? Did she herself actually believe in the existence of a powerful spirit being who would use a ceramic female idol as point of contact with the world of mortals? If so, how would she now feel toward Artie's negligence? Would she forgive? Or would she be forever angry?

Yet why could she not have protected a clay model of herself? Did spirit forces more powerful than she affect its destruction? If she was that helpless against those forces was that Artie's problem?

The scientist within her screamed out against such superstitious nonsense. Yet what did Artie the scientist know? What did the entire world of science know?

Amid the conflicting ideas that raged within her, the despondency became so profound that she actually felt a burning sensation gnawing at her gut, as it were; a torment that defied relief. While yet in the land of the living, was she in hell? The biblical Gahanna? The ninth circle of Dante's Inferno?

No.

Freud, for instance, didn't even believe in the soul. Yet did not he and his colleagues name their disciplines psychology, psychiatry, and psychoanalysis? Was not the prefix "psyche" from the Greek word for "soul"?

How could she find relief from the Pit?

The Pit she was taught not to believe in?

Silence became oppressive. Her only physical sensation was of motion of wheels and the hum of the engine.

She shifted her position and cast Huck a quick, sidelong glance.

"I hate this," she said at last.

"Hate what?" he said, looking at her.

She folded her arms tighter and slouched further down in her seat. "I hate being so sneaky—about us."

He continued gripping the steering wheel with one hand. "I hear you," he said. "But just think, in another six weeks we can say 'screw you, world.'"

Chapter 12

...*Dawn's roseate glow gave us notice 'twas time of preparation for the ceremony of sacrifice and homage. Thus prepared we our garments of most solemn worship. We were clad in simple robes of white linen with broad cowling about the shoulders... Stood we full erect for (2 hours.) The ceremonies lasted the remainder of the day... until midnight whence came we to the great oracle. Thus mounted the Grand High Potentate to the podium... Raised he his hands and intoned: "O, mighty and gracious Lemeck, hear the cries of thy people."... Methought the (statue) verily did come to life... (and spoke)... "Hear me, my people," it said... "Serve me ... Show kindness to the weak and powerless... Shun those who practice the black arts."*

(Day 7. H'rshag's introduction to the Statue Lemekh's Oracle. Trans. and ed. Brit. Mus. Vers. 1.5; 1981.)

* * * * *

The lights in the university chapel dimmed. Illumination for the cavernous Gothic interior emanated from the chandeliers high above the chapel floor. The steep, pointed ceiling, supported by darkly stained arches of wood, suggested branches of a forest. The California sunshine filtered through multi-colored light into the sanctuary. The congregation, seated in straight-backed pews settled to a reverent hush as Dr. Mitchell, Professor of Organ, began the prelude.

Peals of rumblings reverberated throughout the long, narrow auditorium. As the echo of the final chord died away, the university chaplain mounted the pulpit.

"Let us pray." (A pause.) "We are gathered here, O God," he intoned with flawless diction, "to express gratitude for thy many benefits..." After the invocation, a graduate assistant from the School of Religion mounted the lectern for the Epistle lesson. When he finished, the organist struck a chord and the congregation burst into the singing of the "Gloria Patri":

"Glory be to the Father.
And to the Son, and to the Holy Ghost,
As it was in the beginning,
So now it ever shall be,
Worlds without end. Amen."

The chaplain remounted the pulpit. "Hear again the Voice of Our Lord as he admonishes us from the Book of Proverbs: 'Wisdom is the principal thing. Therefore get wisdom, and with thy getting, get understanding also.'"

He settled in a seat beside the pulpit. The Baccalaureate in the Year of Our Lord in 1980 had begun. Commencement was scheduled for the following day, Monday.

The divine liturgy of the Baccalaureate continued apace. The graduates, in caps and gowns, watched from front section center. Immediately behind, arrayed in academic regalia, sat the faculty and staff. Toward the back and along the sides were spread family and friends. The climax of the service was the homily; this year to be delivered by the president, Dr. Harry E. Faasendeck. He mounted the pulpit, Oxford don's cap atop his head, and a multi-colored stole with velvet robe flowing out behind.

Upon reaching the microphone, he paused—he always paused before speaking. He laid out his notes across the pulpit desktop, clasped his hands behind him, and looked out over the audience.

"Members of the faculty," he began, "staff—graduates—undergraduates—alumni—and friends." He again paused and nodded before going on, "I am reminded of a story. It seems that a lowly stonecutter once lived in the land of Japan who was barely able to eke out living for himself and his family. One day a genie miraculously appeared before him just as a nobleman who was being carried in a sedan chair by his servants passed by on a nearby road."

THE DELUGE SCROLLS

Dr. Faasendeck continued his story: The genie granted the stonecutter's wish to become a nobleman himself only shortly to be forced to dismount his sedan chair and bow before the emperor who just then passed by in a carriage drawn by a team of white horses.

No sooner had the genie granted the man's wish to become emperor than he found himself caught in a rainstorm that damaged his silk robes and paper parasol. The genie then granted him another wish: this time to be made the spirit who controls the rain. The newly metamorphosed stonecutter found, upon creating his first rainstorm, that he could not wash away a mountain.

Make me to be a mountain, he said to the genie.

No sooner had he become a mountain than he discovered at the foot of his mountain, a stonecutter chipping away at his base.

He then made his final wish: that he be made a stonecutter.

Dr. Faasendeck followed the story with a plethora of polysyllablisms rambling over the rhetorical landscape seemingly in search of a thought. Amid the staid, learned cadences, a nearby student handed Huck a note: "Matador Special today: Ruben sandwich."

"Is he delivering a twenty-minute homily," the student whispered, "or a one-minute homily twenty times?"

What a pathetic little man, thought Huck.

When the president finally finished and returned to his seat, Huck got up out of his pew. He took his place with the university men's glee club as they filed in the front of the sanctuary. The organ struck broad chords to the introduction to "Integer Vitae" and soon seventy-five young male voices led the congregation in the singing of the alma mater:

"Eternal Spirit,
God of Truth and Virtue,
Bless this our school,
Beloved Alma Mater.
May her crest shine brightly
In darkness as in sunshine.
Now and forevermore. Amen."

Participation in the glee club was the one extracurricular activity for which he found time outside of football. As Artie stood with the faculty and as the singing filled the chapel, she realized how he had risked his spot in the organization. During the days of their beach house tryst, he had absented himself from the group's spring tour.

When the director demanded a medical report, Huck's alibi of feigned illness almost gave away the secret of their relationship.

She reflected further. Tomorrow was Commencement. After that they could—in Huck's words—say "screw you, world." From Peppi's beachfront cottage each morning it would mean rising at 5:30 and facing the rush-hour hassle. However, she considered the idyllic existence with the blue sea, white sand, blowing beach grass, and screaming seagulls well worth it.

A thought occurred to her.

Should she continue living at the scene of Inanna's destruction? Could she be putting herself in harm's way of vengeful unseen entities?

Stop it!

She almost shouted the words audibly. *You are sitting in the midst of a solemn academic convocation,* she chided herself. *What place has superstitious garbage in an institution of higher learning such as this?*

The chaplain stepped to the lectern a final time and pronounced the benediction. The congregation filed out of the auditorium to the musical pyrotechnics of Bach's Toccata and Fugue in D Minor.

That afternoon, Huck and George squatted on the floor of Paul's apartment helping him pack four years of acquired possessions into trunks, boxes, and suitcases. "Amazing how much crap you can accumulate in four years," he commented.

"Funny you should mention that," said Huck.

"Mention what?" Paul looked puzzled.

Huck shrugged. "Up in the chancel," he said with a wry smile, "was a strong fecal odor. The whole glee club could smell it. I'll bet even Dr. Faasendeck could smell it."

Paul suddenly looked serious. Huck, in fact, thought he could detect a look of terror in his eyes. Paul, obviously, had sensed something far more sinister than a glee clubber's clandestine fart. He resumed packing sheet music in a knapsack with a feigned casualness.

"Snake was here," he said at last in a subdued tone.

George looked puzzled. "Who? What?" he said, shaking his head. "Who's Snake?"

Paul averted their continued gaze. "Nothing," he insisted. "Just something completely unrelated. Forget it."

Huck eyed him as he began wiping his instrument case with a cleaning cloth. "I'm going to miss playing in the orchestra," he said in an obviously clumsy attempt to change the subject.

THE DELUGE SCROLLS

A short but awkward pause ensued.

"I'm hungry," said George finally. "Let's go to the Matador's."

Later that evening, assembled in their accustomed booth, they devoured Ruben sandwiches and washed them down with draft light. *Place is unusually quiet,* thought Huck, *even for a Sunday evening.*

"So," Paul was saying, "you guys got your passports yet?"

For a moment nobody answered. Again, more awkward silence. Huck eyed him with unease. Was he or was he not at home that night? What did the voyeuristic little bastard see, if anything? What does he know?

Huck struggled with the notion of Paul's being privy to his and Artie's intimate moments. The thought filled him with disgust.

As the lapse became prolonged, the tension mounted.

Suddenly loud voices reverberated in the rear passage, accompanied by the sound of feet kicking against the walls, moving closer to the taproom.

Huck recognized the hoarse, slurred voice of Randall E. Durwin. A second later he stood in the doorway with Jack Springfield and a couple of denim-clad strangers.

"Hey, look!" Jack Springfield reached out toward the wall to steady his lanky frame. His narrow eyes crossed inward and had a glassy stare "The jocks have beat us here again. Wha' do you guys do, live here?"

"Hey," shouted Randall. "We're talkin' to you."

The four new arrivals continued to weave and stagger in the doorway. "All right," shouted Randall again, "if you're too good t'talk to us, the hell with you."

They found their way to the bar. "We wanna beer," shouted Randall, pounding his fist on the bar top.

"Stoned," whispered Paul.

Again Randall's voice rasped out. "What d'you mean you're not gonna wait on us? C'mon, we got rights."

The bartender pointed to a sign over the bar: "We reserve the right to refuse to serve anyone who is visibly under the influence of alcohol or narcotics."

"Screw the friggin' sign," shouted Randall as he threw a glass against the wall.

Huck jumped to his feet. Before George could restrain him, he had reached the bar. "Hey," he shouted. "Knock it off."

The bartender had, in the meantime, retreated to a distant office and was picking up a telephone.

Randall turned to face Huck. "You got a problem?"

Huck slowed his steps. "Looks like you guys have been having quite a night already," he said, forcing a laugh.

"What the hell's it to you?" Randall shot back.

"Yeah, right," replied Huck. "Look, why don't you guys just order something to eat? They got a terrific Ruben special."

"Screw you and your friggin' sandwich," Randall's mouth glistened with moisture. "You friggin' gigolo."

His remark caught Huck off guard. Before he could answer, he felt a tug on his sleeve.

"Come on," George pleaded. "Let's split. The bartender has already called the cops."

Distracted by George's words, Huck let Randall move out of his peripheral vision. The impact of Randall's fist jerked his head back, staggering him a couple steps. When his vision cleared, he found himself still on his feet. The inside of his mouth tasted blood.

"I'll give you that one," said Huck, gingerly touching his lower lip, "but don't do that again."

Randall's hoarse voice screaming an obscene epithet alerted Huck to the cocked fist. He caught it with his left forearm and followed with a right jab to his antagonist's mid-section. The blow doubled Randall over with a groan, setting him up for Huck's left uppercut. Randall's head shot upward with a snap, eyes glazed. Huck's right hook to the jaw sent Randall flying across a tabletop. Blood shot out from his mouth in a high arch. Rolling over onto the floor, he writhed feebly with a low moan.

From every entrance, police began pouring into the taproom.

Chapter 13

Saw we that it be no mean desert floor (not a natural terrain.) Rather evidenced we a pavement of flat stones so laid, said my mentor, by the Plain-Ones of Ym' mili highsuns (1000's of years) ago... "And where are they today?" said I. "They are not," my mentor's answer... I risked wearying my mentor by asking: "What has become of these people?"... "No enemy destroyed them, nor yet did any pestilence consume them. They wearied themselves in their worship of this unseen god, and came to worship no more. Their manner of worship was, in time, forgotten."...

(Day 22. H'rshag and his mentor upon discovering the site of an ancient, abandoned temple. Trans. and ed. Brit. Mus. vers 2.7; 1981.)

* * * * *

15 Aug., 1980. Weather hot. Humidity low. Temperature, present, 104. Yesterday 124. Time 1400. Work progressing well, nevertheless plan breaking camp 25 Aug. 1980.

Artie laid down her ballpoint and eyed her latest entry into her diary. A stiff desert wind roared through the tent, flapping the side flaps. The oily smell of the tent canvas caught her olfactory senses. She sat at her desk in an area that served as office and workroom. The tent was an army surplus four-man squad tent, held aloft by four-foot cedar posts. The side could either be rolled up or battened down to pallets that comprised the floor. Adjacent her work tent stood a platoon-sized mess tent doubling as a workshop. Here the crew brought artifacts thousands of years old. Here the crew examined, cleaned, and finally inventoried the ancient remains. The artifacts were then carefully packed away into wooden crates.

She recalled the sense of misgiving that assailed her immediately upon arriving at the site. To her right stretched an arid range of jagged cliff formations. To her left the landscape swept away to a sandy plain that merged into a network of shimmering salt marshes in the distance. Only near the horizon did she see any suggestion of vegetation. That this place once boasted of a major metropolitan area that was the capital of a world empire elicited within her some disturbing questions: Why did a militantly nationalist government grant them permission to dig here anyway? Why also had there not been a scientific exploration here before?

The initial diggings oftentimes produced only sand or rock. The slow, backbreaking work guaranteed nothing. The sites chosen were selected only after painstaking geological and historical research. The diggings began the after the most extensive preliminary interviewing of locals; all the way from professors of antiquities at the University of Baghdad to local Bedouins.

Determining the area meant only the beginning. Artie faced a labyrinth of legal red tape: permission to exit the USA, permission to enter Iraq, permission to enter the area, and finally permission from provincial and local officials. Dealing with local village governments provided the greatest frustration. This involved title searches, not of years, but often of generations to determine the rightful owner of barren wilderness.

She also discovered the greatest lubrication that set in motion the most creaking of legal machinery, namely, the bribe.

The hot desert wind fanned her face; her skin darkened by the relentless sun. Her lips unadorned by make-up had turned parched brown. Her face looked dry and wrinkled. She dressed herself for the arid climate appropriately enough: suntan army shirt and shorts, feet shod with olive drab socks and heavy hiking boots. On the desk beside her lay a tan-colored bush hat.

For the first ten days, they found nothing. They may as well have been digging a trench—or perhaps a basement—through rock, sand, and sun-baked clay.

THE DELUGE SCROLLS

The entire expedition, sponsored by the National Geographic Society, consisted of colleagues from universities from all over the world—many with their own crews of young people. Scores of local laborers also joined in the digging in her sector of the ziggurat, or mound.

One unexpected situation bothered her: hers was the only crew camping overnight directly over the ruins of ancient Babylon. Other scientific teams camped at digs well away from the area. Was it superstition even from people of science, or was it mere coincidence? The local workers, moreover, insisted on abandoning the site well before sundown.

One day George received a letter from his grandmother warning them not to stay overnight in the locale. She warned George of a passage from Isaiah in the Old Testament.

Something about a curse.

...George, honey, I know you're a full-grown man. I know you've done pretty much what you pleased since you was a young one. But please, listen to your poor old grandmother just this one more time.

Last Sunday, our preacher preached on Babylon. She's a whore, George. Leave her alone. She is the habitation of demons. She's the abode of every unclean and hateful bird. For your safety, honey, you tell that lady professor of yours and her students to get out of there and quick.

Artie dismissed it as so much superstition.

Meanwhile, workers of many nationalities searched with painstaking scrutiny every shovelful before pouring it into a large sieve for further sifting. When they had exhausted all possibility of finding even the smallest potsherd, the dirt was again sifted in a fabric bucket or "goofuh" and carried to a secluded dumping site.

Ten feet of depth produced nothing.

"Not even an old Coca-Cola bottle," quipped Paul.

As Artie began to despair of their finding anything, Jacki discovered a shard about the size of a quarter in her sifter screen. Forty minutes later, one of the local Bedouins found another shard about the size of a tea saucer.

The particles matched.

Excitement spread throughout the camp. Now nearly every shovelful produced something. The diggers began to detect different layers of civilization. The scientists from the National Geographic Society had determined that their first find revealed a Medo-Persian civilization from the days of Alexander the Great. A few feet lower, the artifacts revealed what must have been a Babylonian and Chaldean culture of Nebuchadnezzar. Then came the Sumerian culture and Ur of the Chaldees. After a few feet lower, the style of pottery and tablets appeared more primitive and less sophisticated. They reckoned now to have reached an early Ur dynasty.

The tools, kitchen utensils, and household furnishings appeared much cruder in workmanship. This was to be expected, Artie had told her students. As years passed, man had advanced in his knowledge, and in his sophistication. Ever onward and upward.

No surprises here.

One week before Artie's August 15th journal entry, however, the diggers were searching through the remains of a people that went back to civilization's earliest Neolithic village-level beginnings.

Suddenly they came to nothing; only mud or beach sand—or possibly silt or river bottom. The dig became suddenly bereft of all manmade artifacts. National Geographic Society scientists guessed the date of this dirt to be anywhere from 3,500 B.C. to 8,500 B.C., or earlier.

The area comprised the size of an average American living room.

What should we do? The students had asked. There's nothing here.

We keep digging, Artie had insisted. This project is definitely not finished. If not by us, then certainly by somebody else after us…

…Artie sat, arms folded. Her eyes closed; her head swirled. She opened her eyes again with a start; almost falling off her camp chair. Looking at her watch, she realized that she had slept two hours.

She got up and walked slowly over to the ice chest containing only water and canned pop. She opened a Coke and let the warm, sweet liquid gurgle down her throat. She then set the half-emptied can back on her desk and reached for a thin, blue envelope. Pulling out its contents, she again read Huck's most recent letter. She recalled that phone call at one in the morning, the day of Commencement. Huck and the other antagonists from the Matador fracas had all been arrested and taken into custody. After being booked and fingerprinted, they were each allowed to make one phone call.

I know this is a terrible imposition, Huck had called apologetically, but I'm in trouble. Please come down here as soon as you can. And bring your checkbook.

She had then dressed herself and raced to the downtown precinct. After going through complicated legal and police procedures, she finally posted bond, and walked out with him at 4:30 AM—six hours before Commencement; too short notice for the administration to prevent his attending the ceremonies.

She was grateful for that.

After the ceremonies, still clad in cap and gown, they embraced and kissed openly in the sight of the entire university community.

Charges against George and Paul were dropped immediately. Huck, however, was released under bond, and was thus not allowed to leave town...

...Artie started reading:

Dearest Artie,

Hi, it's me, your prodigal. I've got a job in a cemetery. Maintenance. So, greetings from one gravedigger to another (!) Seriously, it's a drag not being with you.

No word of my trial yet. It seems that I broke the guy's jaw and they were going to charge me with assault and battery. My lawyer says we can plead aggravated assault and self-defense. He's confident that we will not have any trouble getting an acquittal. The thing is, they're so damned slow about it. Not only did they screw up my chances for going to Iraq with you, they screwed up my chances for law school this fall as well. Now what do I do? Wait for another year and in the meantime continue being a caretaker?

I miss you.

Love,
Huck.

P.S. Stopped by Peppi's beachfront. Things seem O.K.

She placed the letter in her desk and pulled a sheet of stationery from her drawer. She began writing in reply:

Dearest Huck,

My poor, sweet darling, how I miss you. How I long to see you, to hold you, and be held by you. The fates have permitted me to fulfill the dream of a lifetime and then—oh, the irony of it—forced me to go on without the love of my life at my side. Quell unpenser, mon petit. How unthinkable. How cruel.

But—nothing lasts forever. Not even this. I am almost done here. Expect me home just before Labor Day.

In the meantime, darling, I kiss this page. Kiss it, and I kiss you. I love you so much.

As Ever,
Artie

She resealed the letter into a self-folding envelope. It should go out with tomorrow's mail, she thought. The next day to Baghdad, and then the next day by air to New York, and then to Los Angles.

Good.

She got up from her desk and walked to the edge of the tent. Feeling a hot blast of desert wind against her face, she looked toward the dig. As the landscape danced in shimmering heat waves, she could see only the tips of the ladder protruding above the pit edge. She could not hear a sign of life anywhere. In the oppressive stillness, she strained to hear the sounds of work: voices, clanking of tools, the creaking sound of cables—anything.

They're either goofing off, she decided, *or—they may have just discovered something—and are studying it.*

Returning to her desk, she took out another sheet of blue airmail stationery. She recalled another incident two weeks prior. Down at the level of Third Dynasty Ur, Jacki found a tablet about the size of a breadboard. Across the top stretched a mural depicting a female deity, crowned with a diadem and clothed in a garland-embellished full-length dress, seated on a throne. Two serpents stood in a column on either side of her. In her hand she held out a scepter to two mortal worshippers, first a female, and then behind her, a male, both naked. Below the mural, the tablet contained two columns of writing. The right column consisted of a text in cuneiform. The left column contained a strange set of markings that Artie had never seen before.

THE DELUGE SCROLLS

That evening, after cleaning the tablet thoroughly with a soft brush and cleaning cloth, she held the tablet in front of her. *Inanna lives!* she thought. Did she even survive that beachfront earth quake? ...
...In a small, neat hand, she began writing.

Dearest Peppi,

Sorry I haven't written. So busy of late. Just haven't had time. By busy, I mean 14-16 hours a day. This site has finally turned out to be a real treasure trove. Your old roommate, little Ardith Mason from New Trier High School in Winnetka, may be making archeological history. Right now things are awfully quiet out at the dig. The kids are down at the stone-age level, so I really don't know what else to anticipate. Dead people don't speak. (I wish they did. I wish that, for once, I could just hear one sentence or phrase, for example, in ancient Sumerian—so that I could not only read cuneiform, but also understand it were I to hear it spoken. Wouldn't that be an epiphany to end all?)

I heard from Huck yesterday, so just before writing you, I thought I'd better get busy and answer his letter. His not being with me is a disappointment. Why is he not here, you say? Need you ask? Honestly, Peppi, I don't know how I am going to love him and cope with his puerile behavior at the same time.

Why do I love him? The obvious answer, of course, is that he is very sexy, but I know there's more to it than that. I don't have to tell you what it means to be genuinely loved by someone (although I sometimes wonder what excites him more: the rush of whatever wiles that I can summon to stimulate his libido, or the rush of adrenalin that he must feel in gridiron combat.)

Also, he represents a refreshingly artless (perhaps a tad naïve) and candid approach to life. I don't think him capable of a single devious thought or motive. He knows little, if anything, of the bizarre labyrinth that we trafficked in at Earthnation.

God, how am I ever going to break free?

I'm sure Huck doesn't realize how fortunate he is not to be part of all that shit. (I don't mean to be vulgar, Peppi, but that's really all that it ever was.)

I worry that Huck will always be there. With both parents gone, here I am a liberated professional woman who still feels like a little girl lost. Sometimes I cry at night.

Well, I guess when I start to unburden myself I really get going. Hope I haven't bored you. Thanks for hearing me.

I see one of my students headed for the tent.

Guess I'd better sign off.

Love
Artie

P.S. I look forward to getting back to your beachfront to crash for a few days.

Again she pondered the destruction of the figurine during the earthquake at Peppi's beachfront cottage. The loss was irreplaceable. Of that she was convinced. Even if she were to dig out here the rest of her life would she ever uncover a duplicate?

"Dr. Mason-Rodgers?"

She barely heard the words.

Hardly likely, she thought in answer to her own question.

She suddenly realized the sound of a female voice calling her name.

Startled she looked up.

Angie stood in the tent doorway, face bronzed and freckled. She wore an Australian bush hat with shirt and shorts of heavy denim material and colored in desert camouflage. Dust coated heavily on her hiking boots.

"Dr. Mason-Rodgers," she repeated. "Would you come here, please?"

She gestured toward the dig.

"Yes, Angie, what is it?" Artie started for the tent door. She moved quickly to where Paul and Chris stood at the edge of the dig.

"Something's happened down there." Angie pointed toward the pit.

Artie peered down into the abyss. The pit formed narrowing concentric circles spiraling downward. The series of ledges connected to one another by ladders. She saw George and Jacki at the bottom—down about twenty feet.

Working her way carefully around the top of the ladder, she began climbing down. She reached the spot where Jacki and Paul stood, well below the last stratum of civilization's most primitive level.

THE DELUGE SCROLLS

Looking directly in front of her, she saw a layer of sand—clear of any debris—rather like river bottom. Though they were at a level that could be 6,000 years old or more, the sand looked freshly washed.

George gestured toward the pit wall. Despite the desert heat and low humidity on the surface, the air felt cool and had a musty smell.

"My shovel just struck something hard," he said.

With pulse racing, Artie looked at him. "Dig some more," she managed to say. Carefully, gingerly, he and Jacki began digging around an as yet unseen object. They threw the shovels aside and began wiping off the dirt.

They saw a highly refined ceramic material. The surface appeared glazed to the hardness of armor plate, shining a kind of black pearl. Gold and silver threads wound in a plaid-like design and sparkled in the sunlight.

As they cleared away more sand, it resembled in size and shape of an early-twentieth-century milk can. It also resembled an olive oil urn of ancient Greece. Around a circular lid appeared a soft, gray metallic seal...

* * * * *

...Huck jerked his head with a start. *Must have dozed off,* he concluded. He scanned the notes on the legal pad and turned again to the Xeroxed pages of *The Deluge Scrolls*:

> *Akir-Ema—the greatest of empires since the dawn of the Upright Ones. Sovereign of all within his illustrious gaze: from the Great Island in our Southern Sea (Indian Ocean), to the several and diverse islands, to the... isles of the inland sea of Mid-Earth (Mediterranean), to the islands of the Great Western Sea (Atlantic Ocean), to the very lands hard by the dreary land of Dh'ul (or Thule, hitherto the northernmost inhabited lands.) Akir-Ema—founded and established generations of yore, all the while holding unnumbered years of unblemished peace. The happy result of which, many merchants grew rich... Many and happy be the citizens among her verdant parks and boulevards...*
>
> (Day 14. Lord H'rshag's reflections during his ordination banquet. Trans. and ed. Brit. Mus. Vers. 1.6; 1981.)

He laid it aside and turned to one of the law volumes...

Chapter 14

To the east and west stood twain pillars mayhap a full, high-ceiled chamber tall (about one story high), fashioned on three sides and rising to a pique (a kind of obelisk—ed.). Engraved on three sides thereon were kabbalic signs of great mystery. So turned I again to my mentor: "My lord," said I, "what see these unworthy eyes? Be this no less than an account of the beginning of things?"

(Day 22. Lord H'rshag and Shumrag, his mentor, discover the obelisks of the deserted temple containing the text of an ancient creation hymn. Trans. and ed. Brit. Mus. vers. 2.75; 1981.)

* * * * *

Artie stared at the object. "No more digging," she said, heart racing.

"What do you suppose it is?" said Chris.

Artie continued to carefully caress the object. "I don't know," she said. "This is unlike anything I have ever seen."

She began pacing in front of her students, much like she did in the classroom back on campus. "This is going to be very important," she said. "I want all this kept secret, at least for now."

She turned to George. "I want you to see to it that the local workers are kept busy elsewhere: washing the vehicles, packing artifacts—anything."

She took a shovel and began throwing dirt back over the jar. "We'll have the scientists from the National Geographic Society see this in the morning."

After supper, she again met with her students down in the pit. "Tonight we post guards here. Angie, I'm posting you first relief. Paul, you and Chris get your sleeping bags and sleep up there." She pointed to the ledge immediately above. "We'll post you people two hours on and four hours off."

Posting guard, she thought. *How dumb, on the face of it, when your crew is the only one camping overnight here.* Yet, upon contemplating the potential import of the find, she dare not leave any precaution overlooked lest she jeopardize her discovery.

She glanced at her watch. Darkness comes quickly out here on the desert, she realized as she scanned the horizon

Later, as the sky overhead turned velvet blue with a golden glow fading in the west, she began a solitary stroll out into the broad wilderness. Behind her, about a quarter mile distant lay the gaping abyss that was their dig. To her right rose the rugged façade of stone cliffs pockmarked with a series of caves, some of which looked suspiciously manmade, all yawning with a haunting emptiness. To her left lay open wasteland and shallow salt lake marshes that stretched across the horizon.

As a gentle breeze that broke the stillness briefly fanned her face, she turned and looked about. For what or for whom she was looking, she wasn't sure.

"Inanna, can you hear me?" she called out hesitantly. Her voice reechoed against the distant cliffs. All she could hear in answer were the cries of the desert cormorant.

Inanna, can you hear me? Good grief, she thought, *how superstitious can we get? Who is in charge here? Is it Artie the post-modern mystic? Artie, the feminist neo-pagan worshipper of ancient female deities? Artie the commune fugitive? Or is it Dr. Mason-Rodgers the scientist, the skeptic: the one who confessed to Huck to being a secularist? (Maybe there is a God but he's no big deal. Why should he care how or what we believe? Isn't it how we live that counts?)*

And where does that six-year-old innocent who sang her solo in that Christmas pageant of so long ago figure in all this?

The hot winds of the day cease at sundown. She felt totally alone in the expanse of sky, sand, and rock. Was it the evening chill or the eerie stillness that made her shiver? She again tried to suppress her uneasiness over the warning from George's grandmother's letter:

And Babylon, glory of kingdoms,
The splendor and pride of the Chaldeans,
Will be like Sodom and Gomorrah
When God overthrew them.
It will never be inhabited
Or dwelt in for all generations.
No Arab will pitch his tent there,
No shepherds will make their flocks to lie down there,
But beasts will lie down there,
And its houses will be full of howling creatures;
The doleful creatures will dwell,
And Satyrs will dance.
Hyenas will cry it its towns and
Jackals in the pleasant palaces;
Its time is close at hand and
Its days will not be prolonged.

Why is this place so deserted? she wondered. What was it with these people and their superstitions? Why did George's grandmother's letter cause such uneasiness? Was Artie about to step into a world beyond the comfort zone of science and rationalism? Was this existential "leap of faith," as it were, a venture into the world of Me?

* * * * *

As darkness fell, Paul and Chris returned with flashlights and sleeping bags to the pit. Just below them, Angie could smell the moist sand just inches from her head. She could hear Paul and Chris turning in their cots on the sandy ledge barely a couple of feet away.

"What do you make of the jar?" she could hear Paul saying.

More shuffling in the darkness below. "Been a long time," Angie said after a pause. "Maybe this releases us from our labors."

"One condition," said Paul, "that the high priest does not learn of what we find here."

"I hate that creep," said Angie after an uncomfortable silence.

Chris stirred in her sleeping bag. "But he is powerful."

"Only if we let him be," said Angie.

"Maybe now we can break free," said Paul thoughtfully.

Angie folded her arms and leaned against the bank of sand. She stared off into the darkness. "I'll break free," she said. "I'll just quit the damned game."

"That might not be so easy," warned Paul. "Some don't consider it a game, especially the younger players."

"They can consider anything they want," insisted Angie, "but that's all that it ever was."

She stepped away from the sand bank. "It was fun for a while, but this is getting ridiculous."

"Including the high priest?" said Chris as she leaned over the edge.

"Especially the high priest," said Angie.

"He really does consider himself a high priest, you know."

"He can consider himself the high priest of the shit house," Angie said, pacing the bottom of the dig. "He doesn't scare me."

"You apparently don't know all that's been going on," said Paul, lowering his voice to a whisper. "Have you ever heard of a character named 'Springheel Jack'?"

"Just from the sound of it," said Angie, "I don't even want to hear of Jack What's-His-Name—"

Angie shined her flashlight at her watch. One hour before relief.

* * * * *

Artie tossed fitfully in her cot. The cold night air prompted her to pull the army surplus blanket up around her. A numbing breeze began blowing through the tent. Convinced that sleep for the nonce had left her, she stepped to the wooden floor; the coldness made her feet ache. She still could not get used to the contrast between daytime and night temperatures of the arid regions.

She staggered to a small, ancient dresser that she had bought at a flea market in Baghdad and stood shivering in her brief undies. She pulled open a drawer and reached for a fleece-lined sweat suit. She glanced at her luminous dresser clock.

Two-thirty.

She took her flashlight and examined the inside of her hiking boots for unwelcome night creatures. Pulling the top army blanket from her cot, she wrapped herself in it and stepped outside.

The barren, rocky landscape reflected black shadows and a silvery blue under a brilliant full moon. With a hollow moan, the night wind drove in a bank of clouds from the open desert to the southeast. As wisps of cloud rolled across the moon, she could see flashes of lightning from the southern horizon: from the direction of the Persian Gulf and Indian Ocean.

On impulse she started walking toward the dig. When she reached the edge, she peered into the abyss below. Beyond the shadows of the pit wall, she could see part of the pit floor bathed in the moonlight. She saw the solitary figure of one of her students pacing the area. *The kids are doing their job,* she thought. *Good.*

The night wind blew more clouds across the moon, causing the scene to grow darker. She turned from the dig and began another short stroll out into the desert. She reflected again on the quote from George's grandmother's letter. She heard no howling creatures. Only the wind. She stopped and eyed the cliff formation about a mile away. In the open desert, however, it seemed much closer. The moonlight and scudding clouds made shadows moving among the jagged rock formations appear as though they were something living.

Off to the south, more lightning flashed on the horizon.

* * * * *

As pink rays of dawn broke over the horizon, Chris, then on sentry, could hear voices from the ground above. Workers, scientists, and student assistants shouted in a multi-lingual cacophony.

Artie called down to her from up top. "We'll relieve you so you can have breakfast shortly," she said. "I have Dr. Messner here from the National Geographical Society."

She and Dr. Messner began climbing down.

Once at the bottom, the students began clearing away the dirt. Dr. Messner—a small, neat man in his early sixties—squinted critically at the hard, shiny surface.

"Incredible," he said as he looked at it with a collapsible magnifying glass. He folded the magnifying glass and returned it to his jacket pocket. "Don't touch anything until I get back."

An hour later, he returned with a team of scientists and camera people. Artie's crew stepped away from the spot. "We'd like your people to dig some more."

Artie's students resumed digging until the jar could be lifted out. Two handles equidistant from each other encircled the rim near the top. George and Paul started to lift.

"It's heavy," grunted George. "There's something inside."

It appeared to be the size of a five-gallon milk can. The lid seemed to be sealed with a soft metal. At the very top was a knob, about the size of a finger joint, of dull, metallic substance. Two inches from the rim was another knob that looked to be of copper.

As Paul and George continued to move the jar out into the sunlight, George accidentally touched both nodules. He jumped back.

For a moment they just stared at him. With a startled look, he began rubbing his fingers together. "That thing just gave me shock!"

Artie continued staring at him.

Shock?

Static electricity. It had to be.

She bit her lower lip. "Let's—just let down the rope and haul it up," she said, struggling to force calmness into her voice.

George continued rubbing his fingers. "Dr. Mason-Rodgers," he said, staring at her with a frown of intensity that could not be dismissed. "Didn't you hear me? I said that thing just gave me a shock!"

Overhead, with the help of derrick and pulleys local workers began lowering a large hook. As Artie reached to steady the descending tackle, she felt as though her brain would burst through her skull.

She continued fighting tension in her voice. "We'll get it up to the work tent and run some tests there."

With the use of a webbing strap, her students carefully wrapped the jar and prepared it to be hauled to the present-day surface. Artie watched as the laborers from above worked a crank. The derrick rope tightened. Slowly the jar began to rise into the air.

First time it's seen the light of day in who knows how many millennia, she thought. As the jar continued to rise past her, she studied the two nodules closely. Copper. The one near the rim had to be copper. And the other? The dull, leaden look mystified her. Was it silver? (No, badly tarnished silver turns black.) Could it, in fact, be lead? Or some other metal? Impossible, she concluded. That was the technology late-nineteenth and early-twentieth-century labs used in making dry cells.

How could peoples of prehistoric times—even allegedly civilized peoples—have even known about them?

She continued staring as the jar rose further into the air. The crew working the derrick and pulleys finally hoisted it to the surface. With the help of a wheelbarrow, they moved it to the work tent.

Minutes later up in that tent, Artie quickly put her students to work wiping the jar clean of all sand, dust, and rubble until it stood on the tent floor as immaculate as though it were in a show room.

("That thing gave me a shock!")

George's words continued to haunt her. Should she test it herself? Should she grab the two nodules herself? What if nothing happened? Could she handle the disappointment after all the time and money they spent to satisfy her scientific skepticism? Conversely, what if it *was* electrically charged? How powerful a charge would it be? What voltage, what amperage could it deliver? Could it pack a jolt powerful enough to throw her to the ground unconscious and not breathing?

Realizing the potential danger, she licked dry lips. "I've an idea," she said finally.

As scientists and media people watched, and at Artie's instructions, George hooked a copper wire to each module. With insulated pliers, he brought them slowly together. Not knowing what to expect, they watched.

Suddenly a flash of light and popping sound made them jump back.

"Good heavens," gasped Dr. Messner, "it *is* electrically charged!"

No mistaking now. It was more than just static electricity. That much was now obvious. But still—? Something this sophisticated embedded in plain silt or beach sand below the most primitive Neolithic village-level culture?

Impossible.

Down below, further digging produced two more jars. By late afternoon, they had all three jars cleaned and standing in the work tent. They had tried testing the other two jars for any sign of electrical charge.

The other jars produced nothing.

More questions. Why no charge from these other two? One live battery and two dead ones, as it were, buried in ancient silt. What did it all mean?

Presently one of the local workers approached the work tent. "Mademoiselle," he said, "one of the lorries will not start. I think it is the battery."

A dead truck battery? *That's it*, she thought, *pulse racing*. Was this a chance for her to conduct tests without jeopardizing her own personal safety?

She looked at George and Paul. "Let's put it back into the wheelbarrow," she said, pointing to the electrically charged jar. "We're going to conduct an experiment."

THE DELUGE SCROLLS

They wheeled the jar to the motor pool. One of the local drivers sat slouched behind the wheel of the disabled truck. "Get the cables," she said to George. *Experimenting with an artifact thousands of years old,* she thought. *This is crazy, but I've got to do it.*

Gingerly George clamped the jumper cables to the nodules. The other end of the cables he clamped to the truck's battery. He paused. Something could explode. Or, maybe nothing would happen at all.

He signaled the driver to press the starter. A slow, rhythmic whine sounded from under the hood. With a roar, the engine suddenly jumped to life.

That's it, she thought. *No mistaking.*

Yet, *how in the world could it keep such a fresh charge after thousands of years?* Should she push the research further, or—should she just return it, go home, and forget the whole thing? Should she just go ahead and write her little dissertation about the Babylonian dynasty as though this had never happened? Was she prepared to deal with the possible reaction from the academic world to a discovery that could potentially be so unsettling?

The notion of resolve fixed itself in her mind. She would follow through; damn the consequences.

They took the jar back to the work tent. There would be more tests back in the electronics lab on campus.

That night, despite the heat and exhaustion, sleep had left them.

Perplexities and questions of epochal implications began assailing her thoughts from multitudinous directions. Was this knowledge of electrical technology part of the Me? Was loss of this knowledge for millennia part of the judgment visited upon Inanna for sharing its secrets with unworthy persons?

On the final day of digging, after about another foot of sand, they began uncovering the remains of yet another lost civilization. The pottery, artifacts, and mosaic tiling in the floors, indicated a civilization the most advanced and sophisticated yet discovered.

That same day, local workers digging above in one of the Babylonian dynasties made yet another discovery. They found what looked rather like a workroom with stone tables and on the floor lay a plethora of clay tablets; some completely covered with cuneiform writing. Others appeared partially covered with cuneiform and partially written with mysterious markings that Artie had never seen before.

The room evidently served as some kind of scriptorium, or scholar's writing room—similar to those of the medieval monasteries of Europe.

Scattered about the tables and on the floor, lay styluses of different shapes and sizes.

In the center of the room stood a fourth ceramic jar.

* * * * *

Late August an Al-Iraq Airline jet winged its way over rocky brown wilderness somewhere in the southwestern United States. A suntanned Artie, casually dressed in khakis, looked out her small, oval-shaped flight window. The skies around her shone a clear, hard-edged blue. To the south, a fluffy white cloud formation appeared. She could not tell whether her plane or the clouds themselves did the moving.

Four sealed ceramic jars, she thought. As she pondered their import, she wondered whether actually unearthing the bones of the historical Jesus from that forgotten Palestinian tomb would portend any less impact.

The jet touched down at the Los Angles International Airport and taxied to the terminal. Huck stood in the crowded receiving area, glancing anxiously at the sea of faces pouring into the walkway. He spotted a tanned figure in white blouse and suntan slacks.

He waved. "Artie, over here."

Her face brightened in recognition. "Oh, darling," she said, kissing him. "It's good to see you."

A pause.

"Let's get your luggage," he said finally, pulling her toward the claim area. "Sooner we get out of here, the better."

They endured the annoyance of recovering Artie's personal baggage and getting it through customs. Soon Huck's VW sputtered angrily through Los Angeles freeway traffic.

Artie fluffed up her hair and let it flow with the rushing wind. "I could use a good night's sleep."

"How about a nice, big, juicy steak first?" said Huck as they turned off the freeway and up a canyon boulevard. They pulled into the parking lot of a restaurant that fronted a marquee shaped like a giant longhorn steer and bearing the letters "Steer Haus" in sprawling script.

They entered the lobby, and were escorted to a secluded booth. "I've brought back cartons of artifacts," she said as they settled into the thick upholstering. "I don't know where I'm going to put it all. The archeology lab isn't all that big."

She scanned a large, ornate menu as she continued. "Actually, there are a few things I don't want on campus. When we're through here, I'm going to bed. The first thing tomorrow, you and I are going to look at some out-of-town real estate."

Their conversation during dinner centered on the little annoyance that, looking in retrospect, amused her. She related to Huck the superstition held by the local workers regarding a biblical curse on anyone spending the night at the site of the Babylonian ruins.

"All due respect," she said, starting her salad, "I still say it's nothing but superstition. We were there for weeks. Nothing happened."

Immediately she felt a sense of her own hypocrisy. Did not her own obsession with Sumerian mythology itself border on superstition?

She sat back against the luxurious softness of the vinyl upholstery. With a sigh, she thought of spending the next few days at Peppi's beachfront. The summer abroad had taken its toll. First of all, she had to contend with the dry summer climate. The searing desert heat could be brutal. Dealing with nationals different in language, culture, and religion, and not too friendly to outsiders, taxed her most adroit diplomatic expertise. Supervising a work crew of students and of those same nationals pressed her managerial skills even further. Keeping her own students' libido in check proved another challenge. She had to remind them that this was a scientific work project and not a coed frat party.

With the actual unearthing of artifacts, she found her real challenge just beginning. With every piece of pottery and tablet, she had to determine the era, meaning, and historical significance with as much on-the-spot accuracy as she could command.

The drain on her physical, mental, and emotional energy continued unrelenting until she took off aboard the Al Iraq airline flight from the Baghdad Airport.

She closed her eyes and savored the prospect of relaxation at the beach house.

Huck could only shrug. The Iraqi government had sent out inspectors to their find. They demanded a complete inventory of artifacts that the teams had unearthed. They demanded that some of the relics be turned over to the Baghdad museum. Along with some bribery the archeologists were then granted permission to keep pieces of antiquity that were duplicates in that institution.

As for the mysterious jars, they seemed to show a strange lack of interest. Huck recalled, moreover, from reading her last letter that the superstition about the Babylonian curse was the only reason that the Iraqi government had allowed them to take out anything at all.

Chapter 15

Anarchy and lawlessness would result... life would be intolerable. They know only destruction. They would be in direct communication with the Angry Things. There would be no shame. There would be no end of shame. Our choicest damsels—before the eyes of all—would be ritually molested, tortured, dismembered, and offered sacrificially. No man's life, Liberty, property, nor family would be safe... Ponder this and be wise.

(Day 35. Chief Magistrate's description of life should the Akiri society collapse, as part of his summary address during Lord H'rshag's trial for treason. Trans. and ed. Brit. Mus. vers. 3.5; 1981.)

* * * * *

Three hours later Huck still paced the floor of his cluttered apartment, throwing soiled clothing into a laundry bag. During her sojourn overseas, Artie had kept her car in his parking lot. She had now left with it a good two hours ago, but not before she had a chance to see his living quarters. It's a mess, she had chided him. Embarrassed, he had to agree. Next week he would have to start to organize things, he decided.

He picked up a light windbreaker jacket when an envelope fell out of a pocket and onto the floor. He stared at it a moment before dropping the laundry bag to pick it up. Pulling out the contents, he reread the following:

June 22, 1980

Dear Son:

It is not with the greatest of pleasure that I write this letter. I deliberately waited to give myself time to assess the situation with any degree of objectivity before writing you.

I have no doubt that Dr. Mason-Rodgers is an otherwise very good person and I have no reason to personally harbor her any ill will.

I say this to say that the fact remains that the life you now live and your present relationship with her is simply not right.

Please mark what I say as from a loving mother's heart.

Again, it is not Dr. Mason-Rodgers. It's the moral principle at stake. You are dangerously close to throwing your life away.

My hope and prayer, dear son, is that the day does not come when you have to look back on your life with regret.

Love,
Mother

He studied the letter at length. How could he have quite forgotten it? After a good two months, why was he still keeping it? He gave a sigh and slipped it into a desk drawer. He grabbed the mouth of the laundry bag and resumed picking up soiled clothing.

The phone.

Annoyed, he again let the mouth of the laundry bag fall to the floor. *Damn the phone, anyway,* he thought.

The voice sounded vaguely like Artie's. "Huck," she said in a timorous whisper. "Please come over, right away."

"Why?" He stared down at the phone with a blank expression. "What's the matter?"

"Something terrible." Her voice became brittle. "I'm at Peppi's. Please come out."

In a tone verging on hysteria, she added, "And hurry!"

"Be right out." He slammed down the phone and hurried out the door. On reaching the parking lot, he jumped into his VW and roared out onto the street. He felt his stomach tighten. Wordless thoughts of premonition seemed to slam into his brain like a malevolent brick wall. The fragility and the panic in Artie's voice sent shock waves of anxiety through his being.

What the hell is going on anyway?

The thought screamed in his mind with unrelenting dread.

Fleeting notions of evil sent floaters spinning and darting across his eyes. His mouth and lips defied all attempts to moisten them.

The mundane flow of traffic took on an ominous surrealism.

With face creased with tension, he goaded his ancient Beetle through city traffic until he reached Highway 1. This he followed on out past Malibu to just within a mile from the county line.

A cordon of police cars blocked the entry to the beach house driveway with lights flashing. Cars and vans from local TV stations also sprawled about the premises.

The unreality of the scene before him sent shock waves of disbelief through his brain. *What the hell is this?* he asked himself again when his stunned mind could finally articulate rational thought.

He found a parking lot about a block away. Without bothering to lock his car, he ran back to the cottage.

A yellow plastic tape with the words "Police Area" stretched across the entrance.

His anxiety heightened at the sight of a police ambulance pulling away from the driveway.

He found himself confronted by a burly figure in a three-piece suit. "Can't come in here, sir." The man's speech betrayed his Lower East Side New York origin with every syllable.

There was something vaguely menacing about the man's whole demeanor. Tiny black eyes stared coldly at him from a broad, beefy face. Lines along the corners of his mouth etched a hardness of a Roman gladiator.

Huck stared in bewilderment. "Say what?"

The man gestured to the tape. "Like it says: 'Police area.'"

Huck felt intimidated and angered at the same time. He stood with fists jammed into his sides. "Who are you?"

The man pulled out a wallet and showed Huck his badge. "Lieutenant Chevojka, Los Angeles Police."

Huck could feel color leave his face.

"May I ask who you are?" the man asked.

"I'm a friend of Dr. Mason-Rodgers."

The dark eyes set in the thick face intensified their menacing glare. "I didn't ask you who your friends were. What is your name?"

"My name," said Huck with deliberate sarcasm, "is Hershel Ladd. What's this all about?"

The detective's eyes narrowed. "I'll ask the questions." He pulled out a notebook and began thumbing through it.

"Huck!" Artie's voice came from a distance up the boardwalk. "Thank God you're here."

She came running toward him. The pallor of her tense face alarmed him further. She grabbed his shoulders and pressed her face against his chest. He held her for a moment. Her slender shoulders felt frail and vulnerable. She reminded him of a sparrow fleeing a predator.

"Take me away from here," she whispered.

Huck continued to hold her as he started for his car. More wordless questions assailed his thoughts as his feet crunched sand into the boardwalk slats that led to the roadside shoulder.

A thick hand blocked his departure. "Hold it," demanded the lieutenant. "Dr. Mason-Rodgers, we're gonna want you for more questioning."

Artie looked up at Huck, her face the color of chalk. "I've already told them everything I know."

He looked out across the property. The onshore breeze bent the beach grass into dancing waves of green. The heavy dark surf rolled in on high tide, spraying foam and seaweed well up on the sand. Seagulls circled over the cottage and screamed with portentous belligerence.

He turned to the detective. "I'm only going to take her to my place. It's not more than forty minutes from downtown."

Figures in blue moved toward them from newly arrived patrol cars.

"Step aside," ordered the detective. "You're blocking the way."

Huck stepped aside to let the uniformed officers past. "So why not let us leave? That way we won't be in your way."

The detective took out a ballpoint. "I'll need your name, address and phone number."

As Huck started reciting his address, the detective cut him off. "Your driver's license. I need to see your driver's license."

With a sigh, Huck released Artie and reached for his wallet. "Have you got everything you need?" he asked. He felt a rising resentment against this police bureaucracy as he fumbled in his pocket. He finally found his wallet and handed it to the detective.

Again he turned to her. "Will they let you back into the house?"

"No one goes in or out of there until we say so," said the detective as he copied Huck's address.

She looked at Huck. "My suitcase is still in my car."

"Can we go now?" he said, eyeing the detective.

The detective handed back Huck's wallet. "Be where we can get hold of you."

Huck embraced her shoulders and started walking her to her car. A thought occurred to him. "What about Peppi?"

Peppi! She had quite forgotten about her lifelong friend. How is she going to take all this? Artie looked at the ground beneath her feet.

"She's in Europe," she whispered, "on business."

Huck reached into the car for her suitcase. "Can we get in touch with her?"

Artie still couldn't come to grips with breaking the news to Peppi. How could she broach the subject to her dear friend, her successful businesswoman friend who had everything: a chic little dress shop in Beverly Hills and a breezy, oceanfront cottage?

"I suppose," she said with a tremor in her voice. "I just can't handle it right now."

Huck looked back at the cottage. The plastic stripping fluttered in the breeze. Apparently the police and TV people were all now inside. Around the yard and police cars, he saw no signs of life. "We're going to have to get you to a doctor."

He slipped her into the passenger side of his car and then climbed in behind the wheel. "Can you give me directions?"

Staring straight ahead, she simply nodded.

After his ancient VW beetle shot out on the highway and put distance between them and the scene of whatever crime had taken place back there at the cottage, he again studied her distraught features. *How deep is her sense of shock?* he asked himself.

She guided him to the doctor's office with hand directions. When they reached their destination, he helped her out of the car and into the building. When he finally convinced the receptionist that Artie had to see a Dr. Lee, she rang a little buzzer on her desk. A bespectacled oriental woman in pastel blue appeared. "Dr. Mason-Rodgers? Come this way, please."

The doctor turned to Huck. "Dr. Mason-Rodgers shouldn't be long." She gestured toward the waiting room. "You can wait out there."

Forty-five minutes later, a woman in white guided Artie back out into the waiting room. "Dr. Mason-Rodgers is under heavy sedation," she said. "She shouldn't be driving."

"I'm driving," said Huck simply. *Not be long,* he thought.

The woman in white handed Huck a bottle of pills. "She should take this as prescribed on the label," she said, "at least for the next twenty-four hours. She shouldn't be seeing anyone, unless it's absolutely necessary, and she should be kept quiet."

He took Artie by the arm. *Will I ever see her normal self again?* he wondered. "I'll see to that; and thank you."

He took her to the car and drove her back to his place. While guiding her from the car and up to his door, he remembered a similar incident: the Flaming Embers. This afternoon she felt different; she did not stagger nor hang on him. She walked slowly as if in a trance. Her grip felt weak and fragile. She replied to his remarks, not in the slurred accent of a drunk, but rather in barely audible monosyllables.

With the suitcase in one hand, he guided her into his cramped studio apartment and thought it serendipitous that he had tidied up the place. He set her gently down in a recliner. He tried not to let her expression upset him as he began unfolding the couch into a daybed.

"Ready for bed?" he asked as he helped her to her feet.

She nodded.

"Just lie back and relax," he said with feigned cheerfulness as he eased her onto the daybed. He eyed her as she stretched out.

"Comfortable?" he said finally.

He bent down, unbuttoned her jacket, and slid off her shoes. He returned to her jacket and slipped it off from her. Feebly, she moved her body in compliance. He unbuttoned her white cotton blouse and slipped it off as well. Again, she moved her body to enable him to complete the undressing. He tried to neatly drape her clothing over a straight-backed chair beside his desk.

Gently, he pulled the covers over her and closed the blinds. He sat back in the recliner and studied her. As the hours slipped by, her face began to look more relaxed and her breathing came deep and regular.

A thought came to him.

He still did not know the nature of the crime.

He got up out of his recliner and turned on the small television set on his study desk. Perhaps he could learn something from the late news.

The late news mentioned nothing of the crime. Had he missed something? He began turning the dial. *Gotta be something somewhere about it,* he thought. *What is this, some sort of gag order?*

THE DELUGE SCROLLS

Questions surged through his mind. What kind of weird goings-on is this? Why couldn't he find anything out? Why did he get this feeling that he was up against some unseen, demonic force that he couldn't reach out and touch, but was there anyway?

Would there ever be any answers?

With mounting inner turmoil, he continued watching the flickering tube. After Johnny Carson and the late, late movie, fatigue finally overcame his sense of alarm. His head nodded and sunk to his chest. Artie's deep, regular breathing was joined as in a duet by Huck's snoring. On the television screen, a dim holding pattern occupied the picture tube.

* * * * *

Slanting rays of dawn filtered through the rattan blinds. Artie stirred feebly and stared up into the semi-darkness. She became aware of her unclad body under the woolen blanket. Wide-eyed, she pulled the sheet about her shoulders and looked at the awakening Huck.

The sprawling figure in the recliner shifted position. "Artie?"

He struggled out his chair and staggered to the bathroom.

Still grunting in a somnambulant stupor, he reached for a water glass and turned on the tap. As the water gushed into the sink, he fumbled through the medicine cabinet and pulled out a pill bottle. He flipped two capsules into his hand and then shut off the faucet.

She saw him return with a tumbler of water and something in his hand.

"What's this?" she asked dully as he held the contents of his hand and the water glass up to her mouth.

"Medication," he said. "Your doctor said you were to continue the same dosage at least until today."

She looked puzzled. "Did we go to my doctor yesterday?"

He set the glass on a coffee table. "Don't you remember?" he asked in slight amusement.

She stared at him in bewilderment as he grabbed a house robe from the closet and threw it to her. "Here, why don't you shower while I go out to the car and get your suitcase?"

She let the sheet fall to the bed, exposing her shoulders. She tried to pull the robe around her as she struggled to her feet.

Stopping by the door, he turned to her. "Can you manage?"

"I—I think so," she replied.

A sudden ring of the phone all but buried her words.

The ring jarred his already frayed nerves. He fought an impulse to throw the phone through the wall. Regaining a degree of composure, he reached for it.

"Yes?"

A pause. Then: "Yes, Dr. Mason-Rodgers is with me now. You want the both of us?" His face darkened a little. "Well, can you give us little time? Dr. Mason-Rodgers is under heavy sedation. Nine-thirty? Yes, I think we can make it. Good-bye."

He slammed the phone back on its hook. His mouth twisted in disgust. "Lieutenant Chevojka," he announced. "He wants us down at the station for more questioning."

He heard a crash form the other end of the room. Artie lay sprawled over the coffee table. The house robe spread over one end and onto the floor. "I'm being clumsy," she said slowly.

He turned to her. "Are you hurt?" he said helping her to her feet.

"'M all right," she mumbled as she held onto him.

He started to ease her to the bathroom. "Well, then, let's get that little old shower going, shall we?"

Her face froze into a study of terror. "No," she said, shaking her head, "not in there."

Huck glanced into the bathroom of gleaming tile and then again at her. "Why not?" he said, puzzled. "What's the matter?"

"Can't go in there." She waved her hand in a fluttered little gesture of panic. He felt her body, drugged though it was, stiffen. She held out her free hand as if trying to push the whole scene away.

A thought occurred to him. "Something to do with yesterday?"

She nodded. "Horrible."

He continued holding her by the shoulders. Her body felt frail and delicate in his grip. "Want me to go in with you?"

Again, she nodded.

Slowly, he began edging her toward the bathroom. He kicked off his loafers. With his free hand he pulled off his socks and unbuckled his jeans.

He let them fall to the white tile at his feet. "You're going to have to hold on to me while I finish getting undressed."

Trance-like, she laid her hand on his shoulder. Awkwardly, he pulled off his T-shirt and slipped out of his skivvies. As he struggled to unfasten her bra, she gingerly reached for the faucet handle. Water began gushing from the showerhead. As she stepped out of her panties, she savored the feel of warm water over her body.

She put her hands to her face, wiping the water from her eyes. In a sweeping gesture, she brushed back her hair. As Huck began to lather her body, she turned and embraced him.

"Just hold me a minute," she pleaded.

He laid the soap onto a soap dish and grasped the wall bar. "Whatever happened yesterday?" he asked, looking down into her face.

Amid the cascading water he held her close. The sensuous warmth made them loath to leave the cocoon-like security of the narrow stall. Her body felt tenderly vulnerable. He kissed her forehead. "We've got to get going," he whispered.

She reached for the faucet handle, turned off the water, and took from him a towel. "Let's go down to the police station," she said stepping onto the bath mat. "We can talk about it there."

Shortly before nine-thirty, she and Huck sat opposite Lieutenant Chevojka in the precinct outer office. The large room seethed with the activity of uniformed officers rushing about and with the clacking of typewriters. Lieutenant Chevojka gestured to a nearby office. "Let's go in there."

As Huck got up from his chair, the lieutenant studied Artie a moment. "I think Dr. Mason-Rodgers can stay out here," he said. "You and I need to talk alone."

Once inside his office, Huck took a seat.

"Do you know what happened?" said the detective.

Huck said nothing. The detective slipped behind a heavy metal desk. "I have some pictures," he said. Without taking his eyes off Huck, he pulled a large, brown envelope from a side drawer. The lieutenant pulled a colored glossy out of the envelope. "I think these are in sequence." He flipped the photo onto the desktop.

"This isn't going to be pretty," he warned.

It showed the beach house living room with clothing and household articles strewn about in disarray. Huck studied the picture in bewilderment.

"Burglary?" As soon as he said it, he realized that that was not it.

"I wish," said the detective, reaching into the envelope for another photo. With rising consternation, Huck studied the second picture: one of the living room walls covered with lettering or graffiti. He tried to decipher the brown, crudely drawn letters:

"Take that, bitch.
Yer(sic) ass is had it.
You aint(sic) seen
The last of us."

The detective pointed to the lettering with his little finger. "Know what that's written in? Blood."

For a moment the detective sat back in his swivel chair. "Ready for the good part?" he said finally.

Good part? Huck could only continue to stare at the detective. Breathing became difficult as he awaited the next disclosure.

Lieutenant Chevojka again reached into the envelope. This time he pulled the picture out more slowly. "Brace yourself."

Brace myself? thought Huck. *Against what? Against who? How do I go about bracing myself?*

The picture showed a living room wall adjacent the bathroom and the slightly ajar bathroom door smeared with more brown stains.

Some were in the shape of handprints.

The lieutenant laid another photo on the desk: one of the bathroom's interior. The stains continued, soiling the wall, faucet handles, commode, and shower curtain.

His expression hardened further as he again reached into the envelope. "Now for the kicker," he said. "This is the kind of stuff we never get used to."

Huck stared in horror and disbelief at a picture of the bathtub. In supine position lay the nude, bloodstained body of a young girl—possibly eleven or twelve—mutilated about the throat.

Benumbed, he continued to stare at the grotesque savagery.

Curiosity overpowered the horror as he noticed the head and face. Her face bore an expression that was angelic and serene; her eyes closed as though in deep repose. The shoulder-length blond hair lay strung out neat and free of dishevelment.

Never could he have imagined such a horrific, vivid depiction of good and evil juxtaposed in a single photograph.

The lieutenant pulled two final objects from the desk drawer. One was a plastic bag containing a videocassette. Seconds seemed like an eternity.

The other plastic bag contained a small gold necklace with an equilateral triangle enclosed in a circle.

The silence became oppressive. "What do you make of all this?" the lieutenant said finally.

Huck sat still in his chair. His exterior immobility contrasted with the jagged shards of shock that jabbed at his psyche. *What do I make of all this?* he reflected. *Is he kidding? How can any sane person make anything out of something like this?*

Sick is too tame a word, he concluded.

The detective continued to study Huck for a moment. "Bathroom to your right," he said, gesturing to a nearby door.

Huck got up out of his chair and bolted for the bathroom. Long minutes later, he and the detective again stood beside the desk where Artie still sat waiting.

The detective eyed Huck's face. "You okay?"

"I think so."

The detective gestured to Artie. "I think this is enough for now," he said. "I suggest you get her back to her doctor today. Oh, and another thing, I suggest you both go in for counseling."

Right, thought Huck. Get counseling.

The lack of anything in the news still bothered him.

Some other things didn't add up as well. He wondered if those counselors could figure out how it was that a bunch of weirdos would single out Peppi's cottage right while Artie was renting it, break in, carry out their thing at the height of the summer season without the neighbors knowing, and leave Artie a personal note to boot.

Chapter 16

Priest: *From the fury of the Nefillim.*
People: *Lemekh, deliver us.*
P.: *From the destruction that wastes at noonday.*
V.: *Lemekh, deliver us.*
P.: *From the sackers of cities, the plunderers of fields, the pillagers of temples, the ravagers of women, the despoilers of infants.*
V.: *Lemekh, deliver us.*
P.: *From those who drink violence as a thirsty dog drinks water.*
V.: *Lemekh, deliver us.*
P.: *From those who scorn all laws of gods and men.*
V.: *Lemekh, deliver us.*
(Day 19. Akiri Litany to Lemekh for deliverance from the Nefillim. Trans. and ed. Brit. Mus. Vers. 2.3; 1981.)

* * * * *

...Huck threw his legal pad to the couch beside him and stretched. He recalled how the seventy-two hours that followed took on the surrealism of a dream...

...Stunned to numbness, Artie stared in horrified unbelief at the sadistic intruders' handiwork lying lifeless in the bathtub. Initially the sight of so bizarre an atrocity had paralyzed her into stony incomprehension. She felt her heart pounding in her throat as her rational self struggled to grope its way back to appropriate action.
Call the police or call Huck first?
Amid seconds frozen into eternity, she fumbled for the phone...

...Southwesterly winds blew clouds across the moon in the sky outside. He cast a furtive glance at the dwindling number of lights in the surrounding buildings. He flipped to another page of *The Deluge Scrolls*:

> *Three terrors beset Akir-Ema sore. Would to Lemekh they plagued us no more: terrors of the forest, terrors of the fields, terrors of city streets. There is no escape.*
>
> *In the forest Nefillim lurk. In the fields Ogoru curse. In city streets, mayhap e'en worse, the Hudishi run their wretched course.*
>
> *The Nefillim, bestial race of freaks, offspring of the Angry Things, give mighty shrieks in forest deep and mountain top and thus give notice they be destructive lot.*
>
> *Ogoru (Possible origin of Ogre—ed.), in turn, are Nefilli's seed with other mortal women who give not heed to sound counsel, but instead seek strange pleasures with Nefill's evil streak. Ogoru oppress those who toil in field and orchard and plow the soil. 'Pon all such exact they tribute sore and from lonely castles great riches store.*
>
> *Hudishi are but mortal youth: lewd fellows base, uncouth. Seek they Nefillim and Ogoru to emulate. Thus become they the burger's (city dwellers—ed.) fate.*
>
> *(Day 18. Trans. and ed. Brit. Mus. vers. 2.65; v 1981.)*

He laid aside the page and resumed writing his brief...

* * * * *

...They followed the detective's advice and sought counseling. Nobody came forward to claim the body. The Bureau of Missing Persons knew nothing of anyone of her description. Artie had confided to her counselor that, absent anyone's claiming the child, she would like to give her a decent burial.

Good idea, agreed the counselor. Good therapy. Good closure. Good way to release it and put it behind you.

Artie had found that obtaining the child's body did not turn out to be all that easy. She found reluctance on the part of the police morgue to give it up. Forensic examiners wanted to conduct more tests. Unsolved Cases Department questioned her motive for wanting the body of a child unrelated to her. Was she trying to cover up something? She found that getting Huck released on bail a few months previous involved less red tape than getting the custody of a corpse.

Once having obtained that custody, however, Artie and Huck also found making funeral arrangements to be no less difficult. The funeral director wanted money up front. Also, as neither of them had any religious ties in the Los Angeles area, getting a member of the clergy to officiate the funeral, they again faced problems. Like the officials at the morgue, they found clerics uniformly suspicious of their motives for wanting a Christian burial for an urchin who was a total stranger. Why also for one who died under such bizarre circumstances?

They finally did find a cleric who billed himself as a renegade priest who agreed to do the service.

On a day unusually clear for smog-laden Los Angles, three lonely figures stood in a remote corner of Gethsemane Memorial Gardens. Before them beside an opened grave and atop a blanket-covered frame, perched a small, flower-strewn casket.

"'Suffer the children to come unto me,'" intoned a bearded young man in a light blue suit and surplice and collar, "'and forbid them not, for of such is the Kingdom of Heaven.'"

He took a handful of dirt and sprinkled it over the casket. "'That which is sown in corruption,'" he went on, "'will be raised in incorruption at the last day.'"

He shook holy water over the casket. "We commit this earthen vessel whose name shall forever remain anonymous, save only to God, and her spirit to God who gave it. Shall we pray?"

Slanting rays of the afternoon sun filtered through the trees.

Artie tearfully contemplated the small casket that lay across the standard covered with artificial grass. Inside lay the remains of a young child she never knew in life. *What a beautiful-looking face,* she reflected. Beautiful even in death. Even in the terrible death that she suffered. How unspeakably gruesome must have been her last moments.

"'Grant, O Lord,'" he began, "'entrance of Jane Doe, thy child, into thine everlasting kingdom through Christ, Our Lord, to Whom be Honor, Power, Glory, and Majesty Forever, worlds without end, Amen.'"

A breeze, rustling through the leaves, punctuated the silence.

Jane Doe, reflected Artie. *What a horribly nameless anonymity to give to one so young; so innocent. Could we not have had one person come forward and reveal her true identity? How tragic that she could not have been buried with her real name. Now she must enter into eternity as a non-entity. There has to be a God,* she concluded, *to keep track of these unknown little lambs.*

In Pace Requiescat, little darling, she thought, staring groundward.

"I think this was a good thing you did today," he said, turning to Artie.

"Thank you," she said in an expressionless voice. *Good therapy,* she recalled her counselor saying. *An appropriate way to deal with a trauma.*

She took Huck's arm. "Let's go home."

Two hours later, they sat at a small kitchen table in Huck's apartment.

Good therapy, Artie reflected again. A gesture designed supposedly to give closure to such a horrendous experience somehow did little to lift the profound despondency that seemed to drag her spirits down into the depths of hell itself.

"How're you doing on the medication?" he said.

"She told me to take it only as I need it; only if things started getting rough."

They lapsed into another silence.

Evil is merely the absence of good. Many of her graduate school classes had been taught from that premise. Either that or merely a lack of the right kind of education. Now she realized what a cruel joke, what a cruel deception that all was.

"That picture," said Artie, changing the subject, "you know, the one I showed you at the Flaming Embers? I keep that as a reminder of what I almost became. At the commune, drugs flowed like water."

Huck leaned forward against the table. "Were you ever addicted?"

She shook her head. "I think I came awfully close."

He sat silent.

He recalled her telling him how the Earthnation members all but insisted on group drug orgies. They would sit on the filthy, worn living room carpet around a coffee table upon which was set a large, wooden salad bowl. In it was filled a good supply of pills and capsules of every imaginable size, shape, and color. Without knowing what any of the pills were, their possible side effects, or their purity, each member scooped up and ingested a handful.

Fruit salad, she had said they called the unholy concoction.

"I was literally teetering," she said, "on the brink of hell."

He eyed her. "You don't mean that literally, do you?"

Artie closed her eyes momentarily. "Don't try to tell me what I mean, or don't mean," she said, shaking her head. "I was there."

He paused. Then, "If the whole experience scared you enough to cure you, maybe it wasn't such a bad thing after all."

"You can't imagine how badly I wanted out of the whole lifestyle."

"So," said Huck, shrugging his shoulders, "you got out."

"It wasn't all that easy."

He studied her curiously. "Why not?"

"They weren't about to let me go."

She recalled the hairy, bearded scarecrow of a self-appointed guru confronting her. Don't even think of leaving, he had said, eyeing her behind thick, bottle-cap glasses. She recalled the tattooed giant, Snake, also confronting her. There's only one way you can leave, he had said, and that's out of here feet first.

His curiosity heightened. "Who wasn't about to let you go?"

"The people at the commune. They insisted I had made a pact with the devil. However, I think the real reason was that they suspected that I knew too much."

He shook his head. "This is crazy," he said after another pause. "Totally bizarre. Did they restrain you physically?"

"They tried. Talk about threats. You wouldn't believe."

Again, he shook his head. "Surely you don't take threats from a bunch of weirdoes seriously, do you?"

"You don't know those people."

He waited for her to go on.

She closed her eyes momentarily. She could again hear the screams of someone locked in a bedroom especially designed for confining those freaking out on a bad overdose.

"In fact—" She bit her lower lip a moment. Her eyes darted to a far corner of the room. "I have a strong suspicion that some of those people may have had something to do with the break-in."

He gripped her hand. "No kidding? Could you prove it? Couldn't it be some local sickos, maybe even some kids on a wild trip?"

Again Artie shook her head. "Maybe kids were involved, but I think they had to have had some adult leadership."

"Can you name names?"

She shrugged. "As I've said before, much of that period of my life was pretty much of a blur. While I was there, we had quite a turnover. I must have encountered dozens of very strange people. Remembering names would be impossible."

Again, she sat silent for an indeterminate period of time.

Every time she tried to sort out some semblance of order—chronological or otherwise—of her sojourn at the commune, her memory could only swirl in a psychedelic kaleidoscope of disjointed images.

"There was some awful riff-raff," she said at last. "Psychotics, convicted felons, even escapees and parole violators, but we didn't care. We considered them political prisoners: victims of an oppressive, fascist society."

Huck caressed her forearm. "At least you're free from all that stuff now."

Another silence; this time more prolonged. The sound of the faint rustling of leaves just outside the kitchen window and the hum of the air conditioner softly floated across the room.

He still wondered about the lack of coverage in the news. Had there, in fact, been a deliberate news blackout? He struggled to share his misgivings with her, but somehow could not find the words to leave his lips.

Meanwhile, she writhed in inner turmoil. First it was Earthnation. Then Snake. Then Lester. Then Dochen Estate, the scene of the nightmare of that encounter weekend.

At last she spoke. "How I wish."

In the further silence, Huck recalled an incident during his freshman year. One early morning first of November, George and he were taking a shortcut across campus. The Matador's had just closed and they were headed for their dorms across the darkened Quad. Rounding a corner of the administration building, they stopped short of stepping from its shadows out into the glow of a streetlamp. They heard voices from a lighted second-story window chanting as if in a kind of litany and response:

Damn the Jews! (Damn the Jews!)
Damn the Catholics! (Damn the Catholics!)
Damn the Niggers! (Damn the Niggers!)

Hail Victory! (Hail Victory!)

Hail Light-bearer! (Hail Light-bearer!)

Neither Huck nor George had ever mentioned the incident to anyone.

He pushed a plate of toast toward her. She picked up a half slice. "Thank you."

"Not to change the subject," he said, "but before all this happened, you said something about looking for out-of-town real estate."

She laid the toast back on the plate. "First thing in the morning. I'm convinced now more than ever that it's the thing to do."

She paused; then added, "One more thing—I've sent a cablegram to Peppi."

"You mean you didn't call her?"

Dark, dark, dark, she thought.

"Black as the pit from pole to pole." Words from Henley's *Invictus* came seeping into her mind.

Depression like a thick blanket settled over her with a sense of smothering that felt physical. Continued despondency pulled at her spirit as if trying to drag her with Jane Doe down into the grave.

Were recent events repercussions of that figurine's destruction at the beach house? Was the goddess Inanna completely unforgiving of Artie for being so careless?

It wasn't my fault, she almost caught herself thinking.

No, her rational self countered. *That's superstition. Don't even go there.*

Emotions like shards of broken glass tore at her inside.

She sighed. "I couldn't trust myself to keep my composure. I explained as much in the cablegram. I know she'll understand. I don't how she'll feel about wanting to continue owning it, but I do know this: no way am I ever going back there."

Chapter 17

Come twilight stood we at threshold of our ancestral Akiri villa, our slaves somewhat (several) sabbats (weeks) prior, having cleaned, unpacked, repaired, refurbished, and thus made ready our arrival. My father, having entrusted the family key to our chief steward, knocked at the great gate (of the estate.) Our chief steward, satisfied that it indeed be us, did forthwith open the same to us.

Entered we thus into an inner courtyard, the which be surrounded by vine-covered walls. Before us stood the great house (main mansion.) Thrice chamber-ceil (3 stories) high and fronted by a grand portico and sturdy columns, embellished on upper ceils (stories) by graceful balconies, each leading off to a goodly number of chambers, each elegantly fashioned by all manner of cunning design; our courtyard and villa grounds all carefully kept and pruned by gardeners diligently and industriously dressing and trimming all manner of shrubs and flowers. Above, on ornate pedestal, stood all manner of statuary in stone; all manner of fountains of flowing waters; all manner of hanging gardens (probably planters—ed.) ...

(Day 5. H'rshag opens the family villa in the city of Akir-Ema proper. Trans. and ed. Brit. Mus. vers. 1.75; 1981.)

* * * * *

The flat countryside of the south-central California agricultural valley sped past the driver's window of Artie's foreign compact. Huck, behind the wheel, continued to hurl it ever northward. Artie, in dark glasses, slouched down in the seat beside him.

Two days had passed since the incident.

"I was wondering," she said after a long silence. "I don't recall finding anything about this in the paper, or on television."

Huck shook his head. He felt relieved that she was the one who brought it up. "Be grateful," he said, trying to sound noncommittal. "You definitely don't need the publicity."

"Another thing," she said, ignoring his remark, "what about her clothing?"

All the police found was a Members Only jacket that was not the girl's size.

Artie had bought the child a special white communion dress for burial. Contrary the counselor's prediction, after viewing the child dressed in the white dress, the slash wounds across her throat covered, and the girl herself lying as in repose in the casket, the whole gesture did little to assuage the anguish she felt toward the little victim of such an atrocity.

"There was not one item of her clothing found in the apartment," she added, fighting a mounting anger that mixed with her grief and lingering sense of shock.

* * * * *

Three hours later, they emerged from the real estate office on the main street of a tiny mountain town.

They climbed into her car, this time with Artie behind the wheel. She handed Huck a real estate catalog. "Here," she said, wondering if she had even now sufficiently recovered to attempt such a thing, "I'll drive; you navigate."

With a burst of the engine, the car shot off down the short main street and headed out toward a winding mountain blacktop. Steep, rocky incline and giant evergreens sped by them. Her eyes watched the road as they twisted through solid forest. Huck carefully studied pictures of properties in the catalog all the while juggling a map and looking at properties throughout the Sequoia National Forest area. Artie thought the bewildering array of properties either too expensive, too small, not laid out right, or not secluded enough.

"Well, what do you want?" Huck finally asked in exasperation.

"I'll know it when I see it," she said.

As the afternoon sun cast pale light against the distant mountains, they pulled up into the yard of a well-weathered log cabin; its windows shuttered and a "for sale" sign in the yard.

"Looks like it hasn't been occupied in years," commented Huck.

"But I just love the way it's backed against that canyon," countered Artie. "Let's take a look."

They got out and started walking around it. "Look how the back yard slopes away from the house," she continued. "And it's got a walk-in basement. I just love it."

"Needs work."

They continued surveying the back. "It looks so roomy," she said. "Enough for living quarters and lab as well."

Huck shook his head. "It's getting dark."

"We'll come back in daylight," she decided, "when we can have the real estate agent to take us through. Let's get back to the motel."

Forest shadows lengthened in the deepening twilight as they climbed back into the car and headed for town.

The next morning, they returned with a real estate agent. She showed them through a musty-smelling interior festooned with spider webs.

"Wiring looks old," said Huck.

Artie turned to the agent. "I'll take it."

By noon they had returned to the real estate office. Artie signed a purchase agreement and made out a check for the earnest money deposit. "There," she said as they headed out the door. "We now have our own private laboratory."

The wisdom of setting up a private laboratory in a remote section of the Sequoia National Forest grew on her. Even at this early juncture in her research, she entertained a vague premonition that there would be people in positions of power that would like to sabotage their efforts, should they prematurely learn of what she was about.

* * * * *

The agent rejoined them out in front of the office. "Will nine o'clock Monday morning be all right?" she asked. "I don't think I can get the present owner up here any sooner than that."

Artie nodded as she opened her car door. "That would be fine."

Later that afternoon, with Huck at the wheel, they headed back to Los Angeles.

"This is going to work out just right," Artie said thoughtfully. "It'll give us time to move some stuff up here and set up housekeeping."

"Housekeeping?"

"Yes, I thought that since you can't get into law school this fall anyway, I could hire you as my caretaker. Since I'm going to have to divide my time between here and on campus, I'm going to want somebody on the premises full-time."

A full hour lapsed before either said anything further. As their car sped through the flat agricultural valley, Artie folded her arms and leaned back against the seat. It was the first time since the break-in he had seen her smile.

"Do you like it?" she asked.

* * * * *

The following Monday, Huck pulled a rental truck close behind Artie's sports car in front of the real estate office. They had both driven up, laden with household goods, to a motel the previous Sunday afternoon.

Nine AM, the real estate agent assembled all parties: Artie, Huck, the owner, and two attorneys. She read a few clauses, asked a few questions, and then handed copies of a multi-paged legal form to each party. After a cursory reading of the contracts, they each signed the other's copy and then returned them to their respective owners. Artie handed the agent a certified check for the down payment. The agent then handed it to the seller. At the close, all stood and shook hands. The down payment had taken a substantial chunk out of Artie's savings; nevertheless she felt elated as she stepped out the door of the real estate office.

That afternoon they again pulled into the dead-end driveway. As they entered the cabin, Artie thrust her arms into the air.

"Ours," she exclaimed.

"Still needs work," grunted Huck. "Let's get unloaded."

They spent the next three hours cleaning the cabin and moving in a multitude of packing cartons. The last rays of evening sunset filtered through the trees by the time they finished unloading the two vehicles. When Huck finally placed the last of the cardboard cartons down on the living room floor, he straightened up, rubbed the small of his back and eyed the fireplace.

"Bet there hasn't been a fire in there in years," he said. "I spotted a cord of logs out behind the shed. What say we get a fire going?"

"Good idea." Artie had just finished unpacking some older dishes in the kitchen. Five minutes later, Huck had returned with a bushel basket of logs.

He threw a couple on the hearth and began to coax them into a blaze. Artie reached into a grocery sack and pulled out a bottle of wine. She took two long-stemmed goblets from their newspaper wrappings and started for the living room.

They sat on the floor with backs propped against wooden crates and sipped from the goblets. The dancing flames reflected against the rounded, wine-colored glass.

A large sliding door led to a veranda and on out to branches of nearby trees that sloped away from the cabin. Beyond the trees lay a deep canyon and distant rocky peaks that reflected in the soft, golden glow of afternoon sunlight. In the yard outside, shadows had already deepened as darkness enveloped the forest.

For a long time they just sat in front of the hearth. They savored the warmth, the crackling, the hissing, and spitting from the burning logs. As the last of the dim sunlight faded from the mountains, they began to pick up on the night sounds from wooded acres nearby. From a tree just outside their window, they heard a hoot owl.

Artie fixed a hypnotic gaze on the dying embers. "Did you ever fantasize making love in front of an open fire?" she said softly.

Huck reached out and touched her hand.

"Oh, I don't mean tonight," she said quickly. She fought to suppress a yawn. "I'm much too tired tonight. But surely you must admit by now that this place has possibilities."

Huck reached his arm around her. "At least give me a good night kiss."

* * * * *

...Huck jerked his head up with a start. He rubbed his eyes and tried to focus on the yellow pad. *This isn't going well*, he thought as he absentmindedly glanced again at the Xeroxed pages:

> *This being Day 3 since the amazing and distressing sight of the destruction of my beloved homeland, Akir-Ema (Atlantis?—ed.) in so cruel, so frighting (frightening) a manner, I, Lord H'rshag, minded to yet more (again) take quill in hand to leave to whate'er posterity All-That-Is Good may yet deign allow to inhabit this orb (planet) a final tale and testimony of a glorious land and people who, for generations, flourished and are no more.*

(Day 3. Lord H'rshag continues his 40 day log as a final account of his homeland. Trans. and ed. Brit. Mus. vers. 1.75; 1981.)...

* * * * *

..."Mail call." Huck's voice echoed throughout the cabin living room. He dumped the morning mail onto the dining room table.

"I'm in the shower," announced Artie, struggling to be heard above the sound of splashing water. Late September 1980 and Artie had busied herself that morning with the last-minute cleanup in preparation for setting up their lab.

Huck heard Artie's voice above the scurrying sounds from the bathroom. "Anything important?"

He continued sifting through the thick bundle. "Mostly junk mail, and some bills. It doesn't take long, does it?"

He paused; then: "What's this? An envelope with a P.I.E.—Pacific Inter Mountain Express—letterhead?"

Artie emerged quickly from the bathroom, wearing jeans and a blouse. Her hair wrapped in a towel. She took the envelope and studied it a moment. With a letter opener, she tore open the flap and pulled out the contents.

"The stuff from Iraq is here," she announced. "It's in their Los Angeles terminal."

She dialed the phone and was finally able to get in touch with the warehouse manager. She spoke briefly, tersely—struggling to maintain composure. With hands wet with perspiration, she hung up.

"Let's get packed," she said, hurrying for the bedroom.

The next day she and Huck stood near the delivery entrance at the rear of the science building waiting for the P.I.E. truck to back up to the loading dock. The driver jumped out with a clipboard bearing a sheaf of papers. Artie stood at the edge of the dock with a clipboard of her own while Huck, George, and Paul unloaded the truck. Shortly, a half dozen wooden crates were transferred to the archeology lab and storeroom. Artie made one last-minute check with her copy of the manifest papers. Satisfied with the tally, she signed the driver's copy and handed it back to him as he climbed up into his cab.

As the truck roared its exit, she turned to four wooden boxes the size of orange crates still on the dock.

* * * * *

Two days later, with the crates safely stored in the cabin basement, Artie and Huck sat on a couple of battered kitchen chairs and pondered the import of their contents.

They were about to uncover possible documentary records that have not seen the light of day in millennia. Did they have before them artifacts that governments, universities, science foundations, private collectors, or museums would fight—even kill—to get their hands on?

The moment of truth had come.

Huck took hammer and chisel and carefully tapped a wedge under the top of one of the crates. He then inserted a crowbar underneath. Nails squeaked in protest as he pried the lid further. He removed it and pulled out the Styrofoam packing to reveal a black ceramic jar.

"Look at that," she whispered as Huck carefully pried away one of the sides of the crate and lifted the jar out onto the basement floor.

"I guess if we're ever going to learn the contents," she said after another pause, "we're going to have to break the seal."

She gestured to a dull, metallic-looking sealant that encircled the lid.

Huck began digging with a screwdriver into the soft metal. He continued to scrape until he saw a line following the jar top. Beads of perspiration formed on his forehead as he continued scraping. At last he exposed the entire circumference of the jar lid.

She got up from her chair and stood beside him. "Lift up the lid," she said, heart pounding. She felt perspiration running down her back. Would this be sort of like letting the genie out of the bottle?

The lid didn't move.

Immediately she felt her spirits plummet in profound disappointment that bordered on panic. Had she gone to all the trouble to wrangle a sabbatical, organize an archeological expedition, spend weeks in searing desert heat in a foreign country digging in sandy waste just to end in failure?

"Maybe it's screwed on." He tried turning it. It still didn't move.

He turned to Artie. "Now what?"

She continued struggling with feelings of rage, panic, disappointment, and frustration. They mounted like a dark wall in her inner being.

Suddenly she realized that most modern jars screw on clockwise. "Try turning it to the right."

Huck pushed the lid to the right. Slowly, heavily, it started to move. It felt to be locked in a groove. After a half-turn, he felt the lid break free.

Her feelings of disappointment gave way to a rush of impatience that strained her nerves almost to the breaking point.

"Well, lift it," she said, her voice barely audible.

She felt herself beginning to tremble. *Dammit,* she thought, *hurry up!*

He set the lid on a workbench and studied the jar's edge. It appeared to be layered with more ceramic material interspersed with sheets of tissue-thin gold and silver foil. Flush against the jar top was wedged a tightly stuffed linen cloth. With great effort they began pulling it out. The buff-colored fabric looked to be a woman's garment; a kind of cross between a modern Western-style dress and an ancient Greek tunic.

She stared at it in disbelief. Here at last was her first connection with people who very likely predated ancient Egypt and ancient Sumer. Yet, based on the style of this dress, they very obviously were a people a lot like us.

Artie held it in front of her and found it atypical of full-length women's skirts down through the ages. She felt she could wear it through the streets of downtown Los Angeles without attracting undue attention. The dress also had an overlay about the shoulders and a cape down the back. Intricate designs of gold and silver thread had been embroidered into the cape hem.

"I have never seen anything so beautiful," she said. "On today's market, this would be priceless."

No evolutionary throwbacks here, she thought. Biologically and genetically they were us. Compared to three and half billion years of the existence of life forms on this planet, was the ten, twenty, or even fifty thousand years enough to show any significant organic change in our species?

No, any circumstantial evidence of evolutionary change would require far longer than fifty millennia.

She laid it across a kitchenette table. A stillness void of all sound except for the hum of the electric clock settled in.

Huck reached down into the jar again. "There's something else—a kind of scroll."

He grasped it by a handle and carried it to the workbench. Taking the screwdriver again, he shaved away the waxen seal. Then, after turning on an overhead fluorescent lamp, he began to unroll it.

After carefully opening the scroll about a foot, he paused.

The light of the fluorescent lamp revealed strange-looking markings.

Artie examined the scroll closely. "Strange, it looks very much like papyrus, which is Egyptian. Sumerian records have always been on clay tablets."

The material also had the consistency and toughness of modern window shade.

Huck unrolled the scroll across their makeshift bench.

"Look at that," whispered Artie as strange markings began to appear. "Open it up some more."

He unrolled it further. Before them lay the cryptic symbols.

She studied the markings intently. She recognized the markings to be similar to those on the tablet from Iraq.

Immediately questions occurred to her. Did the markings move from right to left like Hebrew or did they read from left to right like modern English? Did these obviously linguistic markings represent a pictographic or word-picture system? Or were they logographic, representing mere sounds? Did each stoke of the stylus represent complete words or just syllables? Did they represent consonants only with vowels implied? Or was it a complete alphabet system that included vowel sounds? Did the system have its own solid base of logic, or was it an amalgam of systems borrowed from other cultures each with their own peculiar inconsistencies, like our own English?

Brilliant linguist that she was, she realized that cracking the code would tax her intellectual prowess and expertise to the limit.

She flattened down the edges of the scroll with books from a nearby bookshelf. She took a camera from another overhead shelf and began taking flash pictures. As Huck unrolled and rerolled the scroll, she continued taking more pictures.

"We're going to have to put this stuff back in the jar," she said as she exhausted the film. "This stuff is remarkably well preserved, but as old as these items are, we don't want to risk rapid deterioration because of overexposure to air and light."

She handed him a tape measure. *How in the world am I ever going to make any sense of those markings?* she thought. Their linguistic character was obvious to her, but right now she could not think of anything in her knowledge of ancient alphabet systems to which she could even remotely relate.

"Mark how far we unrolled the scroll," she said, trying to quell her misgivings, "put it and the dress back into the jar and reseal it. We can't take any chances."

Chapter 18

My love is like a blooming flower;
    Her fragrance graces shady bowers.
    Her petals gilded by sunshine bright
    Gives me source of great delight.

My love is like a blooming flower;
    Gleefully sing ei—a, ei—a.
    Gleefully sing ei—a!
    (Akiri exclamation of ejaculatory ecstasy, not unlike "hubba-hubba," or "va-va-voom" of more recent times—ed.)

O noonday heat, do not wither;
O scorching wind and droughtish weather
Forbear, lest thou love's blossom wilt
And cause it fall to rotting silt.

My love is like, etc.

Let sunshine change to warmish rain
And quench love's thirst. So freely

THE DELUGE SCROLLS

Drink, my rose, love's pleasant showers.
Thus while we away the summer hours.

My love is like, etc.

(Akiri love song. Trans. and ed. Brit. Mus. 3.5; 1981.)

* * * * *

"Your pictures are back."
Huck sat at the upstairs kitchen table with the telephone extension chord across the counter top. Monday evening and Artie had just that morning gone back to her new city apartment.
"Those markings came out real clear," he continued. "I got prints made of the whole set."
He studied the mid-October darkness outside. Already chirping night sounds were beginning to fill the forest.
"You're coming up tomorrow?" he continued. "Of course I'm glad, but I'm thinking of you. You just started your lab work today. See you when? Tomorrow night? I love you, too. 'Bye."
Next evening Artie, having just driven up from campus, sat beside Huck atop a stool in the basement lab. A complete set of Artie's snapshots of the scroll's markings spread across a door improvised as tabletop in front of them. The fluorescent light overhead turned to bright as she looked over the photos with a magnifying glass.
"What do you make of it?" said Huck.
"I don't know." Artie shook her head. "All I can say is that it's unlike anything I have ever seen: not hieroglyphics, not Sanskrit, not cuneiform. I'm stumped."
She put a set of the prints into a thick, reinforced manila envelope. "I'm mailing prints to Dr. Messner of the National Geographic Society and also to Sir Wilfred Woolsey of the British Museum. It will be interesting to see what they make of all this."
Later that night, Artie sat leaning thoughtfully over the kitchen table. An untouched cup of cocoa that sat in front of her had already turned cold. Presently Huck emerged from the bedroom, tying a house robe over his skivvies.
"Lord sake," he said, "what time is it?"

The kitchen clock said two-thirty.

He pulled up a chair beside her. "Going back in the morning?"

"Have to."

"And you're coming back Friday?"

She turned to him. "I've a lot of equipment ordered for our lab," she said. "We'll have our work cut out for us this weekend just setting up."

In the stillness, they could hear the hum of the electric clock. Other sounds ceased and silence pressed in heavily upon them. It was as though time itself had stopped and the entire cabin had become a tomb. Outside in the darkness the thick pine branches hung low and still in a blackened void that made their presence felt rather than seen. The entire forest beyond their window lay silent.

"Aren't you coming to bed?" Huck asked finally.

"I wouldn't be able to sleep." She shrugged.

She again examined a snapshot of the scroll with a magnifying glass. "Those markings," she said, "represent a whole new system of alphabet; one up to now totally unknown to archeological science. They show a definite linguistic pattern."

Huck marveled at what he was hearing. As he observed her narrow shoulders hunched over the photos and the refined-looking features intently concentrated on the scroll's markings, he recalled Angie's comment. She was right about Dr. Mason-Rodgers. Huck sensed a mind racing like quicksilver as she studied the mystery.

He reflected again on the chain of events that brought them together. Huck Ladd, varsity quarterback for Cortez Pacific University and four-year letterman, postponing the fulfilling of his undergrad science requirement until his senior year. Something counselors would not allow non-athletes. Finally to graduate, he allowed himself to be assigned to a section of freshman archeology, of all places! Then he had the stupid audacity to start off his first day in that all-important required course with a confrontation with a world-renowned scholar in antiquities.

It was crazy, he realized. *What was I thinking of?*

More minutes buzzed away on the electric clock.

Finally he spoke. "I'm gong to bed," he yawned.

Long after he left for the bedroom, she continued to sit at the table, staring into her cup of cocoa. The jars. The clothing. The scrolls. Discovered in a layer of silt or river mud below the most primitive Neolithic village level of agricultural civilization and above a still-older ceramic flooring of extremely intricate and sophisticated design. What did it all mean?

THE DELUGE SCROLLS

As the light began in the eastern sky, she walked to the bedroom and started to shower. After being too keyed up to sleep and after spending a sleepless night pondering the new revelations, her body clock began to deliver messages of profound fatigue. The cascade of warm water began to have a soothing effect on tired muscles and frayed nerves. *A good, warm shower is worth half a night's sleep anytime,* she thought.

She peeked out into the bedroom at the deeply snoring Huck. She briefly studied his broad, muscular form sprawled across the bed. The skivvies-clad hunk lay with blankets entangled at his feet. *He could sleep through a volcano,* she thought.

Twenty minutes later, she scurried around the dining room in her city clothing and grabbed her attaché case. She went to the kitchen table, scribbled a note, and stalked briskly out the door to her car.

* * * * *

The following Friday turned out to be another bright autumn day as Huck again guided a rented van down toward the walkout area of the cabin's basement level. Jumping out of the vehicle, he quickly pushed open the sliding glass entryway, and then returned to the rear door of the van, eyeing its contents. Some of the cartons contained component parts of a computer. Huck was impressed at the way Artie had jumped on the innovation of using a personal computer set-up in language translation. Another example of her genius, he reflected, staying ahead of her colleagues in using state-of-the-art technology.

One carton contained an especially designed case that Artie had contracted to be made at a scientific supply house to her specifications: wooden but reinforced with metal and with a glass top. Two rotating handles projecting out the ends and connected to two rods inside the interior, rather like two barbecue spits. Keeping the scrolls sealed and under glass reduced the risk of air damage. A canvas cover kept over the glass when not in use provided further protection from light damage. The inside edges were also lined with narrow fluorescent bulbs.

Another case contained components of an electrical exhaust pump. This way the scrolls could be observed while kept in a partial vacuum, thus reducing further any possible air damage. As Huck wheeled the cartons into the basement, he heard Artie's car pull into the front yard.

"Hello," she called, "anybody home?"

"In back," he shouted.

She approached the van as he finished the last of the unloading. "Oh, good," she said.

They busied themselves that afternoon, evening, and all day Saturday. Sunday afternoon saw the lab equipment finally installed, including, at Huck's insistence, a fire extinguisher.

When he finished the final cleanup, he collapsed into a chair. "Looks like we're finally operational," he sighed as he reached for a can of Coke on the countertop. As the lukewarm liquid caffeine trickled down his throat, his eyes followed the ancient time-frayed wires that strung above him, stapled to the ceiling studs. He still wondered how the cabin's antiquated wiring would handle all the electronic gadgetry.

Artie took a chair beside him. "Looks impressive," she said.

Apparently oblivious to his concern, she turned to the sliding glass panel. In the waning sunlight she could see the yellow of the poplars shimmering among the evergreens. Beyond the depths of this autumnal Eden, the western sky radiated a soft, golden hue.

"You know," she said, "I've never noticed how beautiful the trees are at this elevation in the fall."

She leaned back against the workbench a moment with arms folded. "Let's have early supper," she suggested, "and go for a walk."

Later, wearing sweaters to shield them from the autumn chill, and as the afternoon sun rays filtered through the forest foliage, they strolled hand in hand down a mountain path, sensing only the sound of the wind rustling in the trees.

She studied him a moment. "You seem quiet this evening."

He didn't answer right away. A breeze stirred in the branches above them. Again, the aspen leaves fluttered nervously. He took a deep breath. How should he go about broaching the subject to her?

"Heard from another mistress last week," he said finally.

"Whatever are you talking about?"

"The church," he said. He could feel his pulse quicken.

She turned and looked straight ahead without answering. After several seconds of continued walking, she still didn't know what to say. Finally she, too, took a deep breath before saying the obvious. "Okay," she began, "what about the church?"

"They sent me a letter."

"And—?"

Huck swallowed. "They want to know where I stand with them, or maybe where they stand with me. I'm really not sure."

Again she searched his face. "I don't understand."

He released her from his embrace, tore a twig from a nearby tree, and began stripping away the leaves. "Now that I'm out of school, they want to know if I intend to continue my membership in my parents' church or transfer to another congregation."

"That's it?" Why is that such a big deal, she was about say. However, she hesitated. She noticed a look in his eyes. "You're concerned about this, aren't you?"

"Yes," he said, "as a matter of fact, I am."

Another pause. "So what are you going to do?"

"What do you mean what am I going to do?"

"Are you going to continue membership in your parents' church," she said in exasperation, "or are you going to transfer?"

He shrugged. "I don't know."

"What do you mean you don't know?" she said, shaking her head. "What's the problem?"

"Us."

Lines around her mouth hardened. "What about—us?"

"We're living in sin."

"You've got to be kidding," she retorted. "Us—living in sin?"

Huck appeared flustered. "Under our present relationship," he said after breaking another twig. "I couldn't go back to being a full-fledged member in any case."

"Living in sin?" she repeated, almost laughing. "I thought this was the twentieth century. What kind of church are you from anyway?"

Huck threw away the twig and thrust his hands into his pockets. "Our synod," he explained, "still concerns itself with such things."

She gave a shrug. "Since when do we need the church's permission to live together anyway?"

Silence lengthened as they turned and headed back toward the cabin. The setting sun cast a pink glow on the snow of the mountain peaks. During all her childhood days in her parents' church back in Winnetka, she had never heard of such a thing. As far she had been able to ascertain, their church was little more than a religious social club. That anyone would take such disturbing moral and ethical issues all that seriously was quite foreign to her.

For his part, Huck continued to wrestle with her last remark. Did her insistence that she was a secularist speak not only for herself but our entire generation? Are we living a heroic lifestyle Wagnerian in scope?

Or are we living in a fool's paradise; a Greek tragedy whose end will be downright classical? Will our own lives be a replay of drama similar to Oedipus, Macbeth, or Faust? Will we yet witness our own twilight of the gods? Our own downfall?

Upon leaving the forest, she looked at him. "I'm sorry I'm creating problems for you."

"You've given me your love. What can I say?"

When he pushed open the front door, she pulled him to a stop. "Let's build a fire," she whispered.

He followed her in and kneeled in front of the hearth. When the blaze finally crackled and hissed with a full start, he stood to his feet. "I'm going out to move the van."

He left her heading for the bedroom as he started down the basement steps to the backyard walkout. Sliding open the doors he moved on out to the parked van. After reparking it up in the front yard, he reached into the glove compartment. He spent the next few minutes filling out rental agreement forms affixed to a clipboard. Then he copied some numbers from the odometer.

He finally flipped the clipboard shut and threw it back into the glove compartment. When he reentered the cabin, he saw Artie emerge from the bedroom, clad in a maroon house robe. In her hands she held two snifters of brandy.

She leveled a steady gaze at him. "I'm going over to the fireplace," she said, "if you care to join me."

He stepped into the bedroom and quickly changed into a matching house robe. He joined her at the hearth as she stretched herself out on a bearskin rug. "Isn't this cozy?" she said as he lay beside her. The dancing flames cast a flickering glow about the living room. He slid along the bearskin rug beside her and savored the warmth of the fire.

She handed him a brandy. "You were mentioning something about your church," she said as their fingers interlocked.

He took his glass from her. "I can't remember," he said.

She took a sip of her brandy. "God, how delightfully pagan," she said staring into the fire.

On the mantelpiece sat the clay tablet with the love goddess mural and the bilingual text. They both looked up at it at the same time. Though the ancient text still remained a mystery, the illustration made the text's meaning clear enough. Artie slid over closer to him.

"Just like living in a cave," she whispered.

Huck tipped the rounded glass to his lips. He savored the warmth of the liquid as it trickled down his throat. He felt its effects as it filtered down into his bowels. He felt its soothing numbness radiate out to his limbs. He felt giddiness. He saw the living room take on an aura of mellowness. He turned to her and kissed her.

"Oh, mon infant," she sighed as she returned his kiss.

He moved away and studied her. "You're becoming like your old self," he observed. "You're beginning to show a little color."

He slid back toward her. "How are you doing with your medication?"

She stretched her legs out on the rug. "Getting along pretty much without it," she said, staring thoughtfully into her glass. "My counselor thinks I'm making good progress."

Lingering moments of silence settled in about the cabin. She no sooner had said those words then she realized them not quite true. She could not get the girl out of her mind. She tried to visualize the girl alive and carefree, as a child's life should be. Certainly as were her own sheltered, growing-up years. She realized that only when she came out West to graduate school and hobnobbed with revolutionary wannabes that she became confronted with the dark side of human experience; her own traumatic weekend at Dochen Estate a case in point

"By the way," she said finally. "Have you been to see your counselor lately?"

"Nah."

She looked irritated. "Well," she sighed, "I guess it's really a case of your own mental health. If you aren't concerned, I guess there's no point in my worrying."

"Okay, let me tell you what happened," he said, defending himself. "I went to her the first time and we had our little talk. At the end of the hour, she tells me: 'You've been through a great trauma.' Well, hell, I knew that even before I went to see her. Why should I pay to hear something I already know? So screw it, I never went back."

"Maybe you don't need it much as I," she said, edging away from him. "After all, it was my friend's beach house that was broken into. The feeling as though I've been violated is hard to shake. Then there's the heinousness of the crime. Never in my worst nightmares could I have envisioned such a thing ever happening."

He reached and pulled her back toward him. "Hey, don't be so defensive," he said, kissing her on the forehead. "I want you to be okay; whatever it takes. Have you been having any problems?"

She sat thoughtful a moment. "Maybe Dr. Lambert was right. Maybe our giving that child a decent funeral was good therapy for us."

She took another sip of her brandy. "I've been having flashbacks."

He looked puzzled. He wondered if the fact it was never in the news caused her concern. That they never found any television or newspaper account of the crime certainly gave him concern enough. How could it not affect her at least as much, if not more?

"Actually they're quite benign," she said. "Not scary or frightening. I'll give you an example."

She moved to a more upright position. "When we were first looking at property, as we approached the turn-off from the highway, I saw the child."

"Maybe you saw someone who looked like her."

"No," she insisted, "I saw her standing by the mail boxes."

"Well," he said with a wry smile, "what was she doing?"

"She was gesturing to me. She was pointing to the turn-off."

She looked at him with a pained expression of her face. "Please don't look at me that way. This is hard enough."

He gave her shoulders a squeeze. "Sorry. Go on with your story."

"She was wearing the communion dress," Artie continued. "The one we bought for her to wear while in the casket."

Huck paused again. "Okay," he said finally. "Now suppose, for instance—for discussion's sake—that she may have been a neighbor girl that looked like her?"

"I thought of that. So I checked with some of the neighbors. Nobody has a girl answering that description."

Huck shook his head, but said nothing. "I guess you do need therapy," he said at last.

Before she could give him a dirty look, he bent over close. "Let me be your therapist," he whispered.

She caressed his face and kissed long and passionately. "Let's not think of unpleasant things," she whispered as she let her robe fall away.

He felt the passion within him rise. The memory of their first encounter floated into his consciousness. One discordant recollection distracted him from his focus on this tender moment. His mind suddenly again fixed on Paul. Was he, in fact, home that night? Huck wondered if he should actually confront Paul. Would he ever admit to Huck of getting his jollies watching their first intimacy? Huck realized the irrationality of his animosity, but somehow he didn't care.

Damn that spying little weasel anyway.

Inanna be praised, Artie was about to say, again glancing up at Huck. She caught the words in her throat as she began to detect in him a growing discomfort over the subject.

The phone's ring shattered the moment

Cursing softly, Artie jumped up in a dazed fury and ran to the phone, pulling on her robe as she did so.

She grabbed the receiver. "Hello?" she demanded. "George? For heaven's sake, it's ten o'clock Sunday night. Whatever is the matter? Say that again. Where are you now? The science building? You've already called the police? Good. I'll be there in about three hours."

When she hung up, her face took on a tense pallor.

"That was George. Somebody's broken into the lab," she said, biting her lower lip.

She rushed back into the bedroom and reemerged fully dressed with a small suitcase in her hand. "I'll call as soon as I know something."

After she dashed out the front door, he could hear her gun her engine. He heard her spin gravel as she roared out of the driveway. Then all was quiet.

What would she find when she got to Los Angeles, he wondered? What clues would the broken-in archeology lab turn up? Why would anybody be that interested in an otherwise boring place as an archeology lab? Did somebody see an artifact that might be of priceless value? If so, who and which one? If not monetary value, what else would prompt someone to break into the place? How many people even knew about the recent additions to the lab?

He continued to lie back against the couch, looking into the fire. He wrapped the folds of his robe about him. He sipped thoughtfully at his brandy. Watching the dying flames, he sat upright and put down his drink. He reached over to a nearby planter and picked up a woodchip that lay at its base. He studied the woodchip, turning it over slowly in his hand. The soft crackling of the embers punctuated the silence.

"Damn," he said finally as he threw the woodchip into the fire.

Chapter 19

"There would be those who accuse us priests of fraud.
"We did traffick in much delusion to give the populace something to believe in when, at a time, they believed in nothing. We priests are the real Lemekh. Although we may have resorted to many tricks, we did it to keep the unity; a unity which we believe in very much."
(Day 35. The Chief Magistrate's rebuttal during Lord H'rshag's trial for treason. Trans. and ed. Brit. Mus. vers. 3.5. 1981.)

* * * * *

The University Club in downtown Los Angeles bustled with activity on a weekday afternoon in late November 1980. The wait staff was carefully laying fresh linen over the dining tables in preparation for the dinner hour. The maitre d' escorted Drs. Faasendeck and Rodgers to a remote table.

The educators seated themselves. As Dr. Faasendeck picked up a large, tousled menu, he looked across the table at Dr. Rodgers. "Do you have the correct time?"

Dr. Rodgers glanced quickly at his watch. "It's four-fifty."

Dr. Faasendeck took off his watch and studied the rich paneling of an interior illuminated by glittering crystal chandeliers. "My watch has been acting up of late," he said. "I imagine Dr. Vawter will be here right at five."

"I look forward to these meetings like having a root canal," nodded Dr. Rodgers.

Dr. Faasendeck reinserted his watch back on his wrist. "I know what you mean."

Dr. Rodgers eyed his menu. "I don't think I'll order."

Dr. Faasendeck studied him. "Are you not hungry?"

Dr. Rodgers squirmed in his seat and glanced over the top of his bifocals. "I have a chronic nervous stomach."

Dr. Faasendeck picked up his silverware and began wiping it with his napkin. "To be in delicate health must be a trial," he said, searching the dining room. "Until one loses one's health, one has a tendency to not appreciate being healthy and normal."

"Normal," said Dr. Rodgers with a smirk. "How God-awful boring." He gazed pensively toward the ceiling. *As Edna St. Vincent-Millay once said,* he thought:

"I burn my candle at both ends.
It will not last the night.
But oh, my foes and oh, my friends,
It gives such a lovely light."

He glanced toward the entrance. "I wish Dr. Vawter would get here," he sighed. "I say the sooner we get this over, the better."

Dr. Vawter's appointment as provost came under rather unusual circumstances during the seventies when dissidents had seized control and occupied the Administration Building...

...From a small room off the faculty dining room in the Student Union two mature-looking men paced the floor and eyed one another. A spare, somberly dressed gentleman with white hair stopped.

"Dammit, Harry." Gray, bespectacled eyes looked grimly from a narrow face toward the president. "They're nothing but a bunch of semi-literate, unwashed Jacobins. Bolsheviks. A bunch of hooligans."

"Now, Karl," interrupted the president.

"No," shouted the then provost. "Don't 'now Karl' me. Listen to me for once. Get the police. If you don't have them run off the campus, know assuredly that they'll soon run us off."

Dr. Faasendeck tried to adopt a conciliatory attitude toward them. He refused at the then-provost's behest, to call the police. Instead, he sent up a pitcher of lemonade to the dissidents as a gesture of good will only to have them smash it on the corridor wall. They then presented him a list of nineteen non-negotiable demands. Suppose, for the sake of discussion, Dr. Faasendeck had said, that we give in to your demands. In that case, the spokesman had told him, we would probably come up with another list of nineteen non-negotiable demands.

The dissidents had given Dr. Faasendeck a deadline. Meet these demands, they had said, or we cannot guarantee that we can control our people. We represent the voice of moderation. Deal with us. Or deal with those more extreme than us.

Then it happened.

Smoke began curling up along the rooftop gables. Don't call the police, the protesters had warned. Don't even call the fire department.

The then-provost was about to countermand the president. People's safety and university property were at stake. As the pall of smoke over the ad building thickened, however, Dr. Faaasendeck gave in to their demands.

They then gave him permission to call the fire department.

One of the demands was that Henry I. Vawter, Litt.D., be appointed immediately as provost.

Shortly the then-provost was given early retirement.

Henry I. Vawter, Litt.D., had established a colorful record as a freelance writer, expatriate, soldier of fortune, and general champion of radical causes. As a teenager, he left home to fight with the Abraham Lincoln brigade in the Spanish Civil War. In 1940, he demonstrated against President Roosevelt's new draft. His attitude, however, took an about-face June 22, 1941, when Hitler attacked the Soviet Union. In his newfound enthusiasm for the war, he did not wait for the Japanese attack on Pearl Harbor. While it was yet summer of that year, he enlisted in the army.

To his credit, he had served his country well throughout World War II—in North Africa, Italy, and later in England and Europe—all the while earning the Purple Heart (with a couple of oak leaf clusters) and several other citations. He then reenlisted in the Regular Army, finally taking his discharge at Camp Kilmer, New Jersey, in July of 1948.

The Cold War had by then begun in earnest. From the separation center, he took a cheap apartment in New York's lower East Side. The first night in his new apartment, he threw his war medals into a trashcan.

He took work as a busboy in a Manhattan automat and enrolled in a couple of classes at City College of New York. He divided his days between working, studying, radical activism, and writing—always writing. By 1950 he had divorced his first wife and published his first novel. *West Indies Passage* was published, printed, promoted, and distributed by an underground publisher. Radical organizations that had circulated it secretly from campus to campus were unanimous in their critical acclaim. "Here is one dirty book worth reading." 1952 saw the sequel *East Indies Passage* even more successful. During the early fifties he left for Hollywood and obtained employment as scriptwriter. His career entered an eclipse during the McCarthy hearings. The late fifties also saw an end to his second marriage. He spent time in Latin America: Mexico, Bolivia, and Guatemala, eventually ending up in Cuba. He marched with Fidel Castro's Barbudos into Havana New Year's Day, 1959.

He returned to this country in 1960 and got a job with a newspaper that sent him to cover the Congo Independence. He became friends with Patrice Lumumba shortly before that Congolese leader was captured by his enemies and killed. In 1961, he came back to the U.S. and spent the next few years as a vagabond, part-time student, and habitué of off-campus coffee houses and bars. Nineteen sixty-four saw him at Berkeley University in time to witness the birth of the student revolution. He wrote speeches for its early leaders. Whenever and wherever campus unrest erupted in those days, he was always at the forefront.

When the disturbances rocked the Cortez Pacific University campus in the seventies, the rebel leaders demanded that Harry I. Vawter be installed as provost forthwith. Only he understood today's student, they had said. He was the one authority figure whom the radical leaders and their followers could relate to or trust. They wanted him as provost, even if it meant firing the present one. As billows of smoke rose over the roof of the Administration Building, Dr. Faasendeck gave in to their demands...

..."Here comes Dr. Vawter now." Dr. Faasendeck caught a glimpse of the imposing figure in a rumpled white suit.

As he pulled up a chair, Dr. Vawter nodded to the other two occupants. "Harry—Lester—"

Dr. Faasendeck forced a smile. "Dr. Vawter, it's good to see you."

Dr. Vawter glanced at his watch. "I'm on a tight schedule."

Dr. Faasendeck cleared his throat. "Yes, of course." He produced a sheaf of notes. "Before we meet with the Board of Regents next week, we have an extensive agenda to cover."

"I'll bet," said Dr. Vawter, lighting a cigarette.

He studied Dr. Faasendeck. A timid, frightened little man, he concluded. A fat, soft Pillsbury doughboy in a round collar. Typical of so many prelates he had seen over the years. He compared them with himself and others like him. Bold, daring, decisive, and committed. Hard-core revolutionaries who are reckless, relentless, ruthless, remorseless. *The world is ours,* he thought. *The future belongs to us, not the pudgy, little kewpie-doll types in clerical dress.*

No wonder Christianity has a bad name.
And Dr. Rodgers. What a pathetic bundle of neuroses! His prune face and perpetual squirming is enough to give me the heebie-jeebies if I hung around him long enough.
No wonder this university is such a screwed-up mess: run by Dr. Kewpie-Doll and Dr. Puckerpuss.

"A big item," said Dr. Faasendeck, shuffling his papers, "is a review of our policy regarding religious organizations."

"About time," said Dr. Vawter, puffing deeply on his cigarette.

Dr. Faasendeck eyed him nervously. "As you know, the university has traditionally been a religiously affiliated institution."

"I don't care what the traditional affiliation has been," Dr. Vawter ground his half-smoked cigarette into the ashtray.

Dr. Faasendeck looked puzzled. "I beg your pardon."

"Those religious clubs," he said. "This is the last year we're having them on campus."

Dr. Faasendeck made nervous, little popping sounds with his lips. "I beg your pardon," he said again. "We can't do that."

His small fists clenched as he rested them on the white linen tablecloth. "Are you forgetting, sir, that this is, after all a private institution?"

Dr. Vawter lit another cigarette. "I forget nothing. Our school is the beneficiary of all kinds of grants funded with monies from the federal government. We've got hundreds of students here on government grants, loans, and scholarships. Wherever we turn around, we're taking money from the public till."

Dr. Faasendeck shook his head. "But I still don't understand. No one's complained. I just don't understand your concern."

For a moment Dr. Vawter puffed on his cigarette thoughtfully. "My concern is this," he said at last. "I'm not about to sit around waiting for litigation for something I already believe in."

THE DELUGE SCROLLS

Again Dr. Faasendeck shook his head. "Your point is well taken, but what about freedom of religious expression?"

"What about freedom from religious expression?"

Dr. Faasendeck tried to clear his throat of hoarseness. "What about the alumni? Many of them contribute heavily."

"You're the PR expert." Dr. Vawter lit another cigarette, despite an already burning butt wedged in the ashtray. "I'll let you figure that one out."

Dr. Faasendeck sighed. "That won't be easy."

"So, what's next on your little old agenda?"

Dr. Rodgers cleared his throat. "I have a young man who has applied for graduate study in the archeology department. He has also applied for an assistantship."

"I know him; black kid." Dr. Vawter inhaled thoughtfully on his cigarette. "I would very much like to see him get that appointment."

"Well," sighed Dr. Rodgers, "that may not be easy. His undergraduate record shows some glaring deficiencies."

"Is that right?" Dr. Vawter eyed Dr. Rodgers. "Like I said, I would very much like to see him get that appointment, even if it means forgiving the damned deficiencies."

Dr. Rodgers twitched in his chair but said nothing.

Dr. Faasendeck crept tentatively back into the conversation. "I appreciate your concern for a sufficiently secular academic atmosphere, but aren't we forgetting that I, for instance, am myself an ordained clergyman?"

"Really?" said Dr. Vawter. "You're a cleric in name only. You're just as secular as I am. Right?"

Dr. Faasendeck said nothing.

Dr. Vawter pointed with his cigarette for emphasis. "I want this school to be on the cutting edge of a new, truly revolutionary educational movement."

Silence hung heavy. "Are you not forgetting, sir," said Dr. Faasendeck, clinging desperately to the hope of some semblance of concession, "that we live in a pluralistic society?"

"As I've said before, I forget nothing."

Dr. Faasendeck heaved a sigh. "Is it not true, then, that in a pluralistic society there is room for many diverse—even conflicting points of view to coexist side by side."

Dr. Vawter again puffed deeply on his cigarette. "Not true."

"I beg your pardon?"

Dr. Vawter laughed. "What's the matter?" he said. "You got to have everything in duplicate? I said 'not true.'"

Dr. Faasendeck's neck reddened. "I understand the concept of a pluralistic society very well," he insisted.

"You understand only half the equation," retorted Dr. Vawter. "You were right about a pluralistic society as being a society with diverse, even diametrically opposing value systems coexisting, but what you don't get, however, is this: A pluralistic society is also a society that is in a period of transition, i.e. it is a social order that is jettisoning one value system even as it embraces a newer one. Sort of like a snake shedding its skin, as it were."

Dr. Faasendeck sat silent.

"The old values served humanity well in their day," continued Dr. Vawter, "but their demise is long overdue. As I see it, we need to hasten that demise with all possible speed. It's high time we slammed down the coffin lid once and for all, and started nailing it shut. Wouldn't you agree?"

Again Dr. Faasendeck tugged at his collar. "I—don't know if I'd go so far as to say that."

"Really?" Dr. Vawter leaned back in his chair and glared at him. For a long time, he just continued puffing on his cigarette.

"And just how far would you go?" he said finally.

Chapter 20

*"Who be you?" he demanded... "Tell me truthfully!" "I am called H'rshag,"
answered I... "I am a priest of the Empire of Akir-Ema... "I, being left to languish
in this gruesome dungeon fast (almost) twenty years, heard the door-bolt sliding
across. Was I to be released?... "Your days of captivity are ended," she added...*
 (Days 31 and 33; Lord H'rshag's account of his imprisonment by the
Ogoru and of his subsequent escape. Trans. and ed. Brit. Mus. Vers. 3.4;
1982.)

* * * * *

Huck glanced out of the window at the fresh-fallen snow. *Winter comes early in the higher elevations,* he thought as he pulled the knit cap over his head and drew a pile jacket over his red shirt. Last day before the 1980 winter recess and Artie would be starting north. He decided that he had better plow out the driveway one more time before her arrival. He opened the front door and began tramping through the snow toward the shed.

He mounted the snowplow on the front of the tractor. He then climbed up into the seat and coaxed the engine into coughing and idling. He spent the next three hours pushing piles of snow from the driveway as he worked his way down the quarter mile to the county blacktop.

From down the mountain, he could see car lights reflecting off the snow. He waved to Artie as her car sped by. Grinding the tractor in gear, he followed her.

She pulled her car up to the house then opened her trunk. "Could you give me a hand?" she called out to him, "I've groceries in the trunk."

He struggled with the grocery sacks into the house, set them on the kitchen countertop and then pulled her into an embrace. "Welcome home," he said with a kiss.

That evening, before a crackling fire, she sorted through the mail. Huck stretched out on the couch beside her, getting sensuous delight rubbing his stocking feet into the thick, bearskin rug. Outside the window, icicles hung from the eaves.

Artie held up a large manila envelope. "It's from Dr. Messner. I've been waiting to hear from him."

She tore open the edge and pulled out the contents. She saw that he had sent her a report from a linguistic expert in ancient languages. The break-in at the archeology lab back in October proved a blessing in disguise. During the inventory to determine losses, they had discovered another bilingual tablet. This one, however, had turned up in the last layer of civilization below the stratum of sand and silt. The cuneiform was identical to that on the love goddess tablet. However, across the top, instead of a mural was stamped a signet: an equilateral triangle enclosed in a circle…

…One question puzzled her: did the mysterious markings say the same thing as the cuneiform, only with different characters? If this were, in fact, a translation of alphabet, but not the language, she would have a chance in deciphering the markings.

When she shared her dilemma with Huck, he had told her of a Bible lesson from his parochial school days how, at one time, the entire human race spoke one language.

The Bible? She had replied. Surely you don't expect me to seriously incorporate something from religious writings in what has been systematic scientific research? (All due respect, of course.)

He shrugged. What have you got to lose? he had reminded her.

Good point, she had acknowledged.

Taking his advice, she had set herself to first studying the tablets, and then the scrolls.

As she studied the markings, a thought occurred to her. She recalled from her own school days how that, in certain classes in English grammar, she was required to diagram sentences. She now saw in each one of these characters a kind of word cluster diagram.

She also recalled that when she was a young child her mother had taught commercial and business classes at Northwestern. As an intellectual exercise, her mother tutored her in Gregg shorthand. While her classmates were struggling with *Dick and Jane*, she worked at learning the mysterious symbols of that now-antiquated method of commercial dictation.

With this new flash of insight, she again rushed to break the lock of mystery. Further perusal revealed that the markings went from left to right.

She carefully analyzed each stroke of stylus and quill. She coded and systematized these markings in volumes of spiral-bound notebooks. She kept reference books at her desk. She checked and rechecked esoteric volumes on cuneiform vocabulary and syntax. She checked a special dictionary for the deciphering of knotty idiomatic expressions. Yes, she thought—her mind racing like a cheetah—*it all fits*. She saw the beginnings of genuinely modern human speech. From imitation of animal sounds and infant babblings to more stylized words and phrases, to the precise syllables of trade and commerce, and on to the more abstract philosophical concepts of hoary sages. It's all here. One thing, however, still bothered her.

She would still be unable to recognize the spoken language.

To know the spoken language. To hear voices actually communicate. To hear the subtle little nuances. To hear the melody, the rhythm, the pace of sounds and words, the rising and falling of accented syllables, and the voice inflections. *Oh*, she thought, *if only*.

Oh? In our own language how many different ways are there to say "Oh?" Finally she fed the data into her computer...

...She had logged her knowledge of Sumerian vocabulary into the computer as well. Shortly before the Thanksgiving holidays, she had sent her latest printouts via overnight express to the National Geographic Society and the British Museum for confirmation. She now held in her hand Dr. Messner's report.

Was this, in fact, a translation of Lingua Prima? Hands wet with perspiration held the English words before her:

> I, Xisusthrus, being approach the six hundredth year of my life, did take brief respite from my labours on the giant vessel. I with my sons: Ithemsthrus (Shem?—ed.), Ahamaru (Ham), and Iafet' (Japheth) did take

cease from such labours for the nonce, the purpose of which to welcome the August party of strangers from the distant land of Lamekh.

Same distinguished strangers also having presented themselves at court in audience of my illustrious father, T'reni-Akhmen of Shurrupuk-Erdu.

After many days of feasting and celebration, I was minded to resume oversight of the vessel, I therefore did invoke the blessing of the Strong-Ones upon the Lemekhi and, after having presented them with many gifts, bade them go in peace.

I, being binden under grave (serious) constraint to accomplish the perfection (completion) of the great vessel, having been given vision by Am of impending amazement (disaster) that will shortly come to pass in which all flesh shall perish, save those safe within the vessel.

As I sought to warn my people of the destruction to come, I found their dullness of hearing the cause of much heaviness. They misconstrued me to be really bent on the conquest of some seaport city and the establishment of a great merchant fleet. They say that I intend the collection of animals to be used in trade with distant lands.

Also, they show no interest in the work that my sons and I are undertaking to draw seed (semen, and fertilized embryos) from these animals to take aboard the ark against the day our vessel again settles on dry ground to repopulate the earth. (Was the ark actually a kind of gigantic ancient artificial incubation lab?—ed.)

I pondered oft these sayings of the vision, looking hard as to their meaning. Yet, convinced was I as to their truth and solemnity, did set myself to the oversight of the building of the vessel.

Artie's heart raced as she studied the footnotes. Xisusthrus was believed to be a Babylonian name for the biblical Noah. Lemekh, Akir-Ema, or Lemur were names for a hitherto mythical lost continent referred to by Plato and other ancients as Atlantis. Shurrupuk was an ancient name for Babylon. The name T'reni-Akhmen, the colleague said, meant literally "Death-It-Shall-Be." According to ancient holy men, this was another name for the biblical Methuselah. His name was intended to be prophetic, portending the coming Deluge. According to biblical chronology, the year Methuselah died, at age nine hundred sixty-nine, was the year of the Flood.

Strong-Ones was a name of deity: a variation of the Hebrew "Elohim," or God. Am meant the Eternal One, who lives in the past, present, and future simultaneously, a concept similar to the Hebrew acrostic YHWH, or Jehovah.

The pounding in her temples almost caused her to black out with each heartbeat. Wet hands continued holding Dr. Woolsey's report as she again pondered the information before her. These echoes of an extremely ancient past seemed to reach out from the eons with an eerie connectedness. In her mind's ear, could she even now hear the walls of fixed opinion that separated myth from historic record, like the spiritual, to come tumbling down?

"This is dynamite," she whispered.

Long after Huck left for the bedroom, she got up and headed for the basement. Softly, she went over to one of the worktables, threw back the canvas that covered the glass case. She turned on the specially designed fluorescent lights along the sides of the case itself. There again lay before her the ancient scroll.

She picked up one of the notebooks that lay on her desk and studied notes and sketches she had previously made of the symbols. She studied reports from the National Geographic Society and the British Museum.

She sat down to the computer, pressed the power button and watched the soft green light jump to the screen. As the hours rolled by she worked, oblivious to the passing of time. She studied the screen and again saw the mysterious symbols. This time she saw also directly underneath equally mysterious syllables written in Latin alphabet:

Akir-Ema wah Nah-dah-een. Vay, Shtah-mah Kha-os-a weh Ma-zhe-dee.

* * * * *

Upstairs in the bedroom, as the time also ticked away in the darkness, Huck tossed and turned, reaching out in his sleep for the empty space beside him.

Sometime in the early morning, his repose came to an abrupt end. What was it that woke him just now? He glanced at the luminous dial of the nightstand clock. Five-thirty. Sensing something unsettling, he pulled on his house robe.

He went to the top of the basement stairway and saw a soft light glowing from downstairs. Did he actually hear Artie scream a moment ago, or had he merely dreamt it? When he reached the bottom of the stairway, he saw her sitting at the computer very still, holding both hands to her face.

He took a step toward her. "Are you all right?"

She didn't answer right way.

"Look." She pointed to the computer:

Akir-Ema is fallen! Alas (or woe), my people (race, stem, lineage, nation, or ancestry.) Gone (empty, void, or chaos,) is your glory (brilliance, sunburst, brightness, or glitter.)

Edging close, he saw the screen. "What is it?" he whispered.

"I did it," she said, struggling to maintain control.

"Did what?"

She stood up. "I cracked the code." She pressed the printout key. The buzzing and clicking began as a printed sheet in English came rolling into the hopper. Were these Latin characters in our own vernacular actually the voices of the long since deceased coming to life? *To paraphrase a proverb*, she thought, *do dead men tell tales after all?* What message do they now bring to us, the living?

Finally the printer stopped. "Look at that." She pointed to the following words:

Day 1. Lament for Akir-Ema.

Akir-Ema is fallen! Alas, my people, gone is your glory, your beauty… in a moment is not… How well I remember you… as musicians and revelers rang in your streets… on high holiday… clad in bright, festal garments… as we celebrated the benevolent shelter of Lemekh the Great…

Alas, the great city once clothed in linen of purple and scarlet… Merchants who waxed rich because of you will cast dust on their heads and howl: "Alas, that great city in one hour is made desolate."

None shall buy her merchandise any more: of gold, silver, or precious stone, of pearls, of fine purple and silk. All manner of wood: teak, mahogany, and acacia; all manner of ivory, bronze, iron, and marble. All manner of spices: cinnamon, frankincense, wine, and oil. All manner of cattle, sheep, horses, swine, goats, and apes. All manner of exotic birds: peacocks, cockatoos, and macaws. All manner of instruments of musick: the harp, kithara, flute, shawm, sackbut, cymbal, and drum.

Alas, that great city wherein many waxed rich trafficking in souls of men: of menservants, of maidservants, of slaves of burthen (labour), slaves of pleasure (concubines), of slaves skilled as tutors, as scholars, as scribes, as slaves skilled as troubadors and tellers of tales (storytellers—e.g. Aesop of Aesop's fables—ed.)

Alas, that great city wherein many waxed rich as artisans, skilled and cunning in all manner of workmanship. All this and more in one hour is not.

I, Lord H'rshag, by some strange quirk of fate was sent as envoy aboard a priestly barge on a diplomatic mission to Shurrupuk (antedeluvian name for Babylon—ed.) when calamity struck. The waters fall in sheets from heavens e'en as I sit at cabin. The storm waxes increasingly violent. Thunder rolls across the blacken'd heavens. Jagged forks of fire (lightning) shoot out from the roiling, black mass of sky-vapour (clouds). Ever present, the flickering glow of the mysterious sky-fire stretches over all. (Perhaps the author is an eyewitness to what we now call a "fire storm." Perhaps there was a greater concentration of hydrogen in the upper atmosphere than today. Perhaps it was the burning of that hydrogen that precipitated the catastrophic deluge— ed. Brit. Mus. 1980.)

The heaving, blacken'd seas threaten our fragile bark with tidal waves that rise higher than mountains e'en as I write.

Aarda, my beloved, my sweet thing, my sister, my spouse: we who have been through so much that would threaten us, when all seem'd serene and life at last promised sweet safety from all that would make us afraid, and now I am to see you no more, for you, too have perished with Akir-Ema, my beloved homeland.

Artie re-read the sheets and then slumped back into her chair, bathed in sweat. For long moments she hardly dared breathe, much less speak. "If there is such a thing as a religious experience," she whispered at last, "I'm sure that this is it."

She grasped Huck's hand. "Those poor people," she said. "Those poor, beautiful people."

The silence lengthened. Look, this stuff happened thousands of years ago, he was about to say. Her expression, however, prompted him to check his words. "Let's go upstairs and have some breakfast," he suggested instead.

As they sat across the kitchen table with plates of instant scrambled eggs, Huck studied her a moment. He perceived a haunted, far-away look that bothered him. Her stooped body posture made her look as though life had gone out of her. Her pale countenance, hollow-looking eyes and listless hair caused him concern.

"Know something?" he said at last. "You look terrible."

Suddenly a spark of indignation reanimated her expression. "Excuse me?"

"Look, you've been running on empty for days now, and it shows."

The scene at the breakfast table seemed to swirl before her eyes. She felt feverish, sluggish. She felt a headache coming on.

"You're right," she sighed. "I haven't slept for more than a couple of hours at a time for weeks. Come to think of it, I do feel extremely tired. I'm going to bed. Don't let me sleep much past noon, okay?"

"Then what?"

"Then it's back to work, of course."

"No," he said. "Come on, let's to something else this afternoon."

"Like what?" She shook her head in exasperation.

He looked out the window. The snow lay thick and wet amid relatively mild temperatures. "Let's do something stupid," he suggested tentatively, "like maybe, make a snowman."

Artie smiled as she stood up. For a moment she said nothing.

"Alright," she said with resignation "But first, as I said before, don't let me sleep much past noon."

She pushed her chair back under the table and walked slowly toward the bedroom. As she pushed the door open, Huck observed the window shades already tightly drawn, throwing the chamber into a Dantean-like gloom, despite the brightness of the outside.

Later that day, about one, he softly pushed open the bedroom door. He studied her as she struggled to awaken herself. Knowing her predilection for despondency, he hated seeing her envelop herself at naptime in such a stygian void.

He pulled open the shades as she struggled to her feet. Trying to shield her eyes, she pled with him not to let in so much light.

"It'll be a blinding glare only a moment," he said. "Time to expose yourself to the light of day."

They spent the next hour rolling wet snow in the yard and making it into a snowman. As she engaged herself in the finishing touches on the face, he hit her with a snowball. This brought retribution in the form of ice and snow down his collar.

In their frolic, however, he noticed nevertheless a detachment, as though she were still preoccupied. He wondered whether their little snowman project was just another dumb idea of his. Why, what with all the epochally significant research she's involved with? He had only wanted for her a little diversion to help her keep refreshed and her senses alert when she did get back to work.

He stopped and looked at her. "What's the matter?"

She eyed him quizzically. "Nothing. Why do you ask?"

"Your mind's not on the snowman is it?"

"You're right. I'd better get back to work."

Huck walked over to the snowman and put the finishing touches sculpting the face. Working on the snowman reminded him of a childhood escapade. When he was nine, his father had a church in a small northern California village. The children who lived next door to the manse had built a similar snowman. They finished off their masterpiece with a carrot for its nose. That evening, under the cover of the early darkness, he stole over into their front yard and inserted a second carrot into the snowman's lower anatomy, thus giving it a risqué appearance that caused quite a scandal in the neighborhood.

"Tell you what," he said. "Why don't you go back to the lab. I'll fix us some supper around six. After that, why don't we plan on a relaxing evening in front of the fireplace?"

As he started to the shed for more firewood, she returned to the basement. Throughout the afternoon, she busied herself at more translating. While she heard footsteps upstairs announcing his return to the cabin, she again punched the "print" button.

> Editor's note: Day 2 is Lord H'rshag's account of the geographic location of the alleged Atlantean empire referred to in the scrolls as "Akir-Ema." Apparently it was a sister island north of Madagascar, located somewhere off the horn of Africa. (i.e. Ethiopia or Eritrea) in the Indian Ocean. There were evidently colonies worldwide, especially in the Mediterranean Sea (giving rise to Greek legends of Lost Atlantis). Evidently there were also large island colonies (now long since vanished) in the Atlantic Ocean. There may have been continent-sized island that made the Atlantic of that time more like a large river, called Ossyanhu, or "Ocean."

Later that evening, after supper, while she sat on the living room couch, Huck started a fire in the hearth and then sat beside her. He put his arm around her and they admired the darkness outside where soft large flakes fell to the earth. After long moments, he released his embrace and put another log on the fire.

"It's almost like we're married, isn't it?" she said.

His reaction was immediate. With consternation he asked himself was it the loose ends of their relationship that bothered him? Fighting a vague sense of its going nowhere, he pondered his uneasiness.

She sensed his perplexity. *Ironic*, she reflected, *it's usually the guy who wants to stay footloose and fancy-free.*

He resumed his place on the couch and sat thoughtfully.

"That's just it," he said. "We're not."

She cast him a quizzical glance. "Still worried about living in sin?"

"I don't know," he sighed. "Being married would be nice."

Married. The word stuck in her mind. A normal life. With a man like Huck. How good it would be for her to finally extricate herself from the morass of surreal perversity and live a normal life. Was it too late for her? Was she herself damaged goods, as it were? Did she carry too much hurtful psychological baggage? Could all counseling in the world rid her of those emotional scars from that encounter weekend? Or were they like the physical scars something she would have live with the rest of her life? Apparently all the counselors could only enable her to tolerate the pain.

Tolerate. Interesting word. Tolerance. Always good people are expected to exercise tolerance.

Even with the intolerable.

She kissed him. "Couldn't we just pretend?"

He evidently didn't like pretending. As a little girl, she pretended to be Neffertetti, or Cleopatra, or some other heroine of antiquity. At the commune, she pretended to be a revolutionary. She realized that she would eventually have to quit pretending.

Minutes lengthened into hours. The flames died down to embers. The chill at their backs permeated the cabin. He finally took his arm from her shoulders. "Shall I throw on more wood?"

"Let's just let it die down," she whispered.

Huck stood up and yawned. "I'm going to bed."

He turned and sauntered off toward the bedroom. She could see the bedroom light flick on. She could hear a shuffling sound. *He's probably stripping down to his skivvies as he calls them*, she thought. He habitually slept in his underwear. *He's probably dropping his clothes on the floor*, she conjectured.

I don't think he has ever hung up anything in his life. She marveled at how comfortable she had become even with his foibles.

She watched as the light flicked off and the room became engulfed in a void. Frost now formed heavily outside the glass doors. The hard cold crept relentlessly around the cracks in the door and windowsills. No insulation no matter how tight could keep the cold out on a winter night such as this.

Shivering, she stood and crossed the now darkened living room. However, instead of going to the bedroom, she again headed for the basement stairs.

The early-morning hours saw Artie still in front of the computer. The clock on the desk said six. Huck had just come down bearing a breakfast tray and yesterday's mail.

"Sorry to interrupt," he said, putting pop tarts and coffee in front of her, "but I think you'd better eat."

She continued staring at the computer screen. "I think I'm about to crack more code."

More translation appeared on the soft, green screen.

Day 3. My earlye eyars.

(As has been previously stated, Lord H'rshag tells of his noble birth, his schooling and early years at the Akiri province of Basilea.)... My father, lord of lands and wealth, as one of the five sets of twin brothers that make up the ten princes of our empire, held no mean station within Basilea's gates... Learned we mysteries of the Precise Arts (science,) Erd' (earth—probably geography or navigation). We learned the precise measurements of land and sea. We learned how to perform on instruments of musick. We learned ballad and rhyme and construction of mural and cameo. (Possibly painting and the fine arts—ed.) Learned we the wise laws as inscribed on the golden tablets (possibly a written version of Me—ed.).

Huck studied the printout and then looked back at her. Did he even now appreciate the full significance of her findings?

He laid the mail on her desk.

"What's this?" asked Artie as she pointed to an official-looking envelope. "It's addressed to you."

The return address read: Prosecutor's Office, County of Los Angeles. He tore open the envelope, pulled out and examined the contents.

"They're dropping the assault and battery charges," he said, handing her the letter.

"About time," she said tersely. *Finally we get this dear boy out of trouble with the law*, she thought. *But for how long?*

He gave a sigh of relief. "Now maybe I can go ahead and apply for law school."

Chapter 21

I, H'rshag, being born of noble lineage, seventh son of a seventh son, was at birth given to the priesthood of Lemekh. Cherished I many joyous memories of childhood's carefree hours, quite spared from anxious thought. Learned we all manner of statecraft. Learned we the hallowed traditions of our belov'd Akir-Ema.

(Day 3. Lord H'rshag's memoirs of his early years. Trans. and ed. Brit. Mus. Vers. 1.65; 1980.)

* * * * *

The next few days were characterized by an almost ceaseless, 'round-the-clock routine of labor at the computer lab. Days melted into nights that again melted into days until Artie lost all track of time.

We've had our play, she had told Huck, and now I've got to get back to work. Huck, for his part, busied himself plowing out the driveway, carrying the chain saw into the forest after firewood, and driving to town on errands.

One morning shortly after sunup, with breakfast tray in hand, he descended the cellar stairs and could hear the computer keys clicking. He got to the bottom of the stairs and paused. Again he saw her sitting hunched over the keyboard. The intensity of her posture indicated a mindset oblivious to everything else. Dared he break the spell with so mundane a distraction as mealtime?

"Artie?" he said softly.

"Please—not now," she whispered. "I'm about to punch in another translation."

That was it. She lapsed back into her trance-like fixation of her work. Was she even in the world of the present? His world? Or was her soul transmigrated into another time; another place?

He came over closer and watched as the printout started rolling:

Day 4. I, H'rshag, prepare to Journey to the City of Akir-Ema.

...*Scarce earlye of a third day of our journey began we to approach the environs (suburbs) of Akir-Ema. Traveled we along the Highway of the Gods: the hard and smooth surface being made so by great stones laid flat and cunningly laid by multitudes of slaves (labourers) many generations of yore. Travel was thus made both safe and pleasant.*

As we neared the Akiri (suburbs), we were joined by others; merchants, pilgrims, pleasure seekers on high-holiday (vacation,) Soon we waxed numerous as we neared the city.

Pleasant country estates soon gave way to environ (suburban) villas and to sumptuous apartment dwellings, till at last approached we Akir-Ema's gates. Having stated our business to the warders of the gate, they bade us enter the illustrious city proper. The delightsome sights and sounds we evidenced till now were all but prologue.

Having crossed the outer canal (border or city limits; one of three concentric canals or waterways that ring the city) scarce prepared was I for the splendours of sight and sound that now awaited us.

Akir-Ema, most favoured city, brightest jewel of the Orb': streets cobbled or laid with slabs of granite rock (unlike small villages or even some provincial capitals that be laid out with streets of earth or dirt.) Streets thick with traffick—all manner of dunnumu-chariot (a kind of self-propelled conveyance, probably similar to the modern golf cart—ed.), all manner of wheel (bicycle—ed.); riders borne of one, two, or three (unicycle, bicycle, or tricycle.) Traffick of all manner of beasties of burthen, owners of which be bounden (required) to muzzle their horses and tiger-horses (zebras) with pouches of fodder (nose-bags) and pouches for dung (a type of "diaper" for the catching of animal droppings to prevent pollution of the streets—ed.)

Akir-Ema, home to souls one million by half, (500,000—ed.) city of lights, city of gardens, city of fountains.

THE DELUGE SCROLLS

Akir-Ema, city of trees: tall, lush, and verdant. All manner did grace thy streets and boulevards, and parks and villas. Trees—from lowly shrubs at out feet, to towering giants five-fold ten full cubit (eighteen inches) high (seventy-five feet.)

Akir-Ema, city of towers; some tall and delicate, others mighty and massive, reaching full toward the expanse (sky, or heavens) a full thrice-ten chamber-ceil (stories) save five (twenty-five stories.) (Akiri evidently used elevator systems involving mule-drawn winches and water bucket counterweights—ed.)

Akir-Ema, city of banners, flying from many-a-lofty staff and halyard; banners, bunting, and flags unfurling all manner of heraldry denoting craft guilds, mercantile houses, fraternal organizations, and prominent families. Their brilliance flying from houses, buttresses, towers, and parapets of many colours: soft pastel blue, pink, jade (pale green), desert (beige), all the while roofed with tile of red, black, slate, and gold.

Akir-Ema, teeming with life. Merchants busy with the busyness of buying and selling all manner of goods and dainties. Thin stalls did line thy shaded streets. Walking vendors did hawk their wares of all and sundry trinket and bauble. Household mistresses, household slaves (stewards) did jostle one another in thy market place.

Voices of children and tender youth did ring with laughter as they made run and shouted to one another on their way to their tutor-palaces (schools.)

Akir-Ema, gracious city, thus didst thou greet me for the first time with thy beauty and with thy grandeur.

Artie looked at the printout. For a long time she just sat, studying it. She could almost hear the streets of that long-since-vanished city come alive with sounds; sounds of vendors, sounds of pleasure seekers, sounds of lovers strolling along the boulevards; sounds of children racing along the pathways at play. She visualized the massive and stately buildings, the walls of brick and stone, all colored with the soft pastels of alabaster. She visualized the well-dressed citizens in their bright and luxurious costumes of silk, velvet, fur and linen.

"I almost feel as though I know those people," she said at last.

Huck leaned toward her. "Do you know what day this is?"

She sat back in her chair. "I'm tired." Her tone of voice indicated she didn't really care what day it was.

"It's Christmas Eve."

She took his hand and smiled. "I'm going to bed."

She rose slowly, took off her white laboratory smock and hung it on a nearby hall-tree. "Don't let me sleep past two, okay?"

She kissed him briefly. "'Night, darling."

He started up the stairs after her and tried to keep busy tidying the living room. After an hour of putzying he sat down on the couch and watched television—with the volume turned low. He could hear slow, measured breathing from the bedroom. Outside, the sky shone cobalt clear. The sun's rays reflected with dazzling brilliance off the thick, wet snow.

He got up and made a trip to the woodshed to bring in Christmas packages. Later he busied himself taping greeting cards around the cabin interior. As the afternoon sun began casting long shadows out in the yard, he returned to the couch to watch more television when he heard a stirring in the bedroom.

"Huck?" Artie stood yawning in the bedroom doorway. She was dressed in sweatshirt and jeans. He got up from the couch.

She staggered into the living room as if in a daze. Her hair resembled a squirrel's nest. Her pale face and puffy eyes more nearly portrayed a soul emerging from the grave rather than refreshing slumber.

"What's the matter," he said. "Didn't you sleep well?"

She continued a vacant stare. "I slept very well," she said. "In fact, I feel as though I had been drugged."

Another pause. "Yet I don't feel rested at all," she said. "As I say, I feel as though I had been drugged."

He continued studying her. "Did you have a bad dream?"

"I don't think I dreamt at all," she replied. "I just remember a kind of sinking off into oblivion."

He shrugged. "Sometimes daytime sleep can be that way. It's not always the most restful kind of sleep."

Artie still seemed not convinced. Somehow she could not bring herself to disclose to Huck that despite the assurances of her counselors, she was having residual flashbacks from that encounter weekend.

Closing her eyes momentarily, once again her mind's eye saw the darkened subterranean recreation room. Its strobe light flashed a hard glow, alternating between moments of total darkness. No medieval torture chamber could have filled her with more dread. Your memory of it will diminish in time, her counselor had assured her, and its trauma will gradually affect you less.

She was still waiting for time to heal the rawness of her psyche.

She looked out the window. The late-afternoon sun cast weak, slanted rays through the curtained windows. Outside, shadows fell long across the crusted snow. How faint, how distant the sun's life-giving rays seem during the long winter months.

Would the longed-for coming of spring with its promise of new life be sufficient to lift a spirit perhaps too accustomed to darkness?

He slipped his arms around her. "I've heated some soup," he said. "Maybe you'll feel better after you've had something to eat."

Later that evening and following a light supper, they repaired to the living room.

Huck plugged in the Christmas tree light cord and miniature lights glowed like tiny stars among the evergreen's branches, suggesting real stars looking down on a wintry landscape. He then flicked on the TV and settled back on the couch.

It was a time for dreaming, for reminiscing.

"Did your family open gifts Christmas Eve, or Christmas morning?" he was asking.

"Always Christmas morning," smiled Artie. Her mind went in retrospect to the Victorian mansion that was her parents' home. As an only child she had, by her own confession, been spoiled rotten by mommsie and poppsie. You never seemed spoiled to me, he had replied to her.

She could always count on the high tree set in the ornate, cavernous parlor to be well stocked with large, brightly wrapped packages—all for her, from mommsie and poppsie. Of course, when she got older and began to earn her own money, she would reciprocate.

She pulled another photo from her wallet. This one showed her at age six. Huck again recognized the eyes, the expression, the smile, despite the round, childlike features. Black, wavy locks tumbled about the shoulders. She was seated on an oriental rug in front of the massive, intensely decorated Christmas tree. The dark frock with white lace and white stockings had obviously been part of her Christmas gifts.

The Sunday before Christmas of that same year, she recalled being in a Sunday school pageant. She saw again her six-year-old self on the fellowship hall stage with her class singing "Away in a Manger". She had a solo on the last verse:

"Be near me, Lord Jesus.
I ask thee to stay

Close by me forever
And love me, I pray.
Bless all the dear children
In thy tender care
And take us to heaven
To live with thee there."

Huck recalled recent conversations with Peppi, who had known her since childhood. She had related to Huck that despite being a pampered only child of well-to-do parents, she had never been obnoxious or bratty. All who knew her from those days had known her to be a charming and winsome youngster.

He shrugged. For himself, he recalled as to how he and some of his school buddies would observe the approaching Christmas recess. During those final days, they would walk through the halls wearing sprigs of mistletoe hanging from their back belt loops.

"Did your family celebrate on Christmas Day?" Artie finally asked, trying to change the subject.

"We always had services on Christmas Eve," he said as he watched the flames dancing in the hearth. "There was a special candlelight service then we opened our presents first thing when we got home before going to bed."

Huck remembered his greedy restlessness as he sat through the reading of the lessons and the singing of the carols. He felt a little guilty over his youthful impatience with the spiritual and his enamorment of things material.

Again, silence settled in the cabin. He noticed a look of wistfulness cross her features. He finally managed courage to voice his observation. "You miss your parents, don't you?"

Outside fog settled in the forest.

Artie continued a contemplative stare into the tree lights.

"It's funny," she said at last.

"What's funny?"

"When I was at Northwestern," she began slowly, "I worried about how I would take care of them in their old age."

Huck looked at her with incredulity. "Even as well off as they were?"

"As I said, it's funny."

Gone, she thought. *They're both gone. Funny how even a grown woman—educated and professional—somehow never outlives her need for mommsie and poppsie.*

She folded her arms and slouched further down into the couch as the circle of shrinking embers faded to a dull red.

Chapter 22

Thus awaited we an evening of most pleasant amusements... having engaged all manner of clever entertainers. Thus rejoic'd we at the brilliant display of jugglers, dancers, mimes, maskers (actors,) musicians, and fools (comedians) till early twilight broke the easterly sky...

(Day 4. Lord H'rshag's account of a banquet at their townhouse villa, celebrating their arrival at Akir-Ema. Trans. and ed. Brit. Mus. Vers. 3.5; 1981.)

* * * * *

Christmas Day the skies shone with a hard brilliance. Artie and Huck spread out at opposite ends of the living room couch with their stocking feet propped up over one another's laps. Occasionally, they reached down to a wooden bowl of popcorn.

Bands, floats, and faces flashed in imagery on the TV screen as they watched a Santa Claus parade from a distant city. At the parade's finale, the screen segued to two jowly men in business suits carrying on staccato-like dialog about an upcoming football classic.

After sitting before the onslaught of athletic jargon for fifteen minutes, Artie glanced toward Huck. "Do we have to watch this?"

Huck shrugged. "You don't have to watch it if you don't want to."

"God help us." She sighed, swinging her legs onto the floor "You do your thing and I'll do mine."

She stood up and headed for the basement.

In the ensuing silence he could hear the clicking of keys. He turned his attention back to the big screen. He pushed aside the bowl of popcorn and swung into upright position. He sat hunched forward with fists clenched as he felt himself drawn into the intensity of primitive ritual male combat. The raw savagery of twenty-two padded giants slamming bodies over territorial rights of a green and white-striped gridiron sent him straining and sweating his way through a game from the East during the forenoon, a Midwestern contest in the afternoon, and finally sports highlights in the evening. He then searched the dial for more scores. After evening news, he turned off the set.

He stepped to the stairway and peered down into the lab below. He discerned only a dim light but no sounds.

He saw the slight figure in a white smock hunched over the glass vase. With a magnifying glass in one hand, she jotted in a notebook. Again, she seemed oblivious to all surroundings of the here and now. Her concentration on her worksheets created a trance-like stillness. A spell that Huck was loath to break.

Suddenly she turned her head his way. "What's the matter, no more football?"

Oh, God, please don't let her be mad at me.

She rolled the canvas back over the glass stop. "In case you're interested," she said, returning to the computer, "I'm about to punch in another translation."

He waited. She punched the "enter" key. Characters began popping up on the pale screen. As printed sheets rolled into the hopper, they read the following lines:

Day 5. I, Lord H'rshag, re-open our family villa in Akir-Ema.

Twilight stood we at threshold of our ancestral villa... (our slaves did ope the same to us.)... Entered we thus into the inner courtyard, the which be surrounded by vine-covered walls. Before us stood the greathouse (main mansion.) Thrice chamber-ceil high (3 stories) fronted by a grand portico and sturdy columns. The halls, pillars, arches, and lintels were cunningly wrought with murals and decorative frieze inlaid while marble, ivory, and gold. The floors of our great hall were of a mosaic of brilliantly coloured ceramic laid in intricate design by the cleverest of artisans... As darkness fell, repaired we to the great hall for a bit of supper and entertainment.

Our hall and villa grounds were well lit by hundreds of torches with fires of men and fires of gods (of electrical energy) cunningly lighted with (various) colours.

(H'rshag, his father, and their domestic staff celebrate their first evening in their Akiri villa banquet hall.)

Day 6. I, H'rshag, am made ready to be presented at court of priests and nobles.

My father, having duly arranged my enrollment at the temple tutor-palace (priestly seminary) expressed great burthen to have me presented at court of priests and nobles. Preparation and such presentation and attendant ceremonies of sacrifice, of worship, and feasting required weeks of planning with much aforetho't.

So summoned my father the most excellent tailors of all Akir-Ema, to fashion for us festal and ceremonial robes and uniforms, for balls, and receptions, all in readying for the great day.

Thus I was measured and fitted for my uniform of the officers for the military ball. The likes of which consisted of one maroon tunic, fastened high at the collar and trimmed at the edge with black velvet and golden thread, and bounden at the waist with broad, black leathern belt, 'Neath the hem of which I was attired in skin-tight (possibly a type of denim material) breeches. Shod was I with black leather'n (street shoes) with attendant black leather'n puttees of finest polish and quality.

Fitted o'er my shoulders and clasped about the breast (close) below the neck, wore I a cape of black satin and velvet and fur stole of finest silver fox. To complement mine attire, I was given a sabre encased in a bejeweled scabbard of finest gold. Across my breast lay a sash of lavender, bearing my family's crest.

My outfit was completed by a soft cap of black velvet ornamented with pearls and crowned with ostrich feathers.

My festal robes for worship, by contrast, were of plainest attire, bereft of insignia denoting rank, title, or station. The which being in keeping with our belief that Lemekh be no respecter of persons

My robe of finest linen had as its only embellishment, the Trident, ensign of our empire embossed o'er the heart.

Day 7. The Grand Festal Ball (Wherein I, Lord H'rshag, first met the Grand High Priestess, the Lady Aarda.)

'Twas of an even of most pleasantly fragrant night as the scent of perfume of manifold number of spices which grow in abundance throughout our fair city that my parents and I were transported over highly arched and elaborately fashioned bridges that crossed the network of canals and waterways that laced the thoroughfares of our metropolis and up to the mountain temple area high above the city to the great hall of the feasting there to be joined in high holiday and merriment with (hundreds) of others.

Transported were we by a most grand carriage through Akir-Ema's broad boulevards and up the mountain drive to the temple grounds. There we were to be escorted by footmen up (100) flight of steps to the great hall.

Priestly and noble caste and their families came to the festivities and solemn ceremonies all attendant with the inauguration of a new high priest and for the meeting of the ten elders of our empire that is held every five years.

The great hall supported stout columns of polished bronze ten arm-span (about 15 feet) thick and extended upward five (stories.) As we crossed the entrance, throngs of merry-makers greeted us.

First in order of ceremonies came the formal presentation. Here I was a-thrilled at being presented to and, in turn, had presented to me, all the great and near great of our empire. At first, I was a-thrilled at being presented to the elders and their families, all arrayed in the finest of silk, linen, and velvet robes coloured in scarlet, purple, blue, gold, silver, and jade. Gold and silver threads bordered their sleeves and hems of their garments. Crowns, amulets, and rings set with all manner of jewelry graced the heads and arms.

As formalities persisted, however, metho't these ceremonies waxed most tedious.

While standing in the receiving line, my father took me aside and pointed out to me certain among the priestly and noble class who were not to be trusted. He confided with me that the new Grand High Potentate must constantly be aware of the intrigues and conspiracies that swirl around him just below the surface in the affairs of state as they are held among the mighty at court and temple. Our glorious city in truth, he warned me, be a veritable nest of vipers.

Saw I fair how this played out when I begged leave for to retreat to the inner closet. (Evidently the Akiri civilization had inside plumbing—ed.) *Here amidst the marble pillars and Vespasian fountains, I caught the sight of two figures robed in royal crushed velvet with gold fringe. Them I knew instantly to be elder-princes of Ossyanh-u* (Ossian, an Akiri colony on a large but now-vanished island in the Atlantic Ocean—ed.) *and the elder-prince of h'Mnu* (a civilization predating the Minoan on the Island of Crete). *Without being seen, I watched them slip furtively into one of the cordoned stalls and engage in hushed conversation. I ascertained them bent on the following mischief:*

I overheard them desire our empire engage in military ambitions of conquest such as she had not done since the beginning days of our illustrious founder, Lemekh the Great. In addition they seemed desirous of our engaging in expeditions of conquest of Akh-aya (Achaia, or Greece?—ed.), *a group of small city-states on the Sea of Mid-Erd'* (Mediterranean?—ed.).

I realized this bit of skullduggery to be the latest in a long history of enmity that lay latent for generations between the people of Akh-aya. Back eons to the beginnings of things, our father Khai-nu (The Acquisitor, or Cain of Genesis—ed.) *slew Abv-el* (lit. Father-Strength, or Abel of Genesis - ed,) *during a quarrel over a proper offering to the Strong-Ones. Shortly before Khai-nu was driven out by Am, A-Than-Abv-el,* (Possibly later known as Athena in Greek mythology—ed.) *widow of Abv-el, fearing for her life and for those of her family, fled with her children to the eastern isles of the Sea of Mid-Erd'* (Mediterranean Sea i.e. islands of the Aegean Sea).

(Editor's note—According to the Plato's Atlantean legend one of the factors that led to the Atlantean downfall was the ongoing feud between the followers of Poseidon, or Atlanteans, and the followers of Athena, or Ancient Greeks.)

I left as quietly and as discreetly as I could and relayed what I had heard to my father. His reaction was strangely noncommittal, perhaps because he felt it dangerous to show any reaction whilst mingling in such an uncertain crowd.

I was glad to see the arduous ritual finally come to an end.

We, then, were bidden to the banquet hall, it being a large, delicately designed hall with walls, pillars, and ceiling of creamy white porcelain decorated with frieze of and mural of red and blue. Garlands of flowers and ivy did drape colonnades that lined the sides of the chamber. Here were we confronted at table with all manner of sumptuous viands and delicacies.

Companies of most comely temple slave maidens—clad but in filmiest of gown which were gathered at the waist with a bright-coloured scarf and adorned about the forehead, wrist, and ankle with garlands of flowers—did unceasingly run to and fro bearing trays laden with all manner of fruit; pomegranate, figs, apples, nuts, and apricot.

These same also bro't all manner of drink: wines, drink of apple, malten drink (beers, ales, bitters, etc.) plus fruit drink (non-alcoholic) of every variety. Also came they with trays laden with all manner of breads, cakes, and pastries.

At the last, since this be the time of high feasting, as the Grand High Potentate sat with his favourite pet leopard beside him, he commanded trays of flesh be brought. (Ed.—Akiri diet was believed to have consisted mostly of fruits and grains. They evidently confined the eating of meat only on high religious holidays, usually in connection with the sacrifices offered.). The temple servers, then, bro't all manner of flesh and meat—wild boar, venison, fish, and wild game of every species.

At finish were we served every kind of dessert: puddings, sugared fruits, plus we were treated to a delicacy of greatest rarity, namely milk of kine flavoured with extract of vanilla and mingled with crushed ice shipped down from mountain glaciers (probably a kind of a kind of ancient ice cream dessert—ed.) topped off by heated aromatic drink of rarest cacao nut drawn and distilled with great cunning of the brewer's art (a sort of coffee or cocoa drink laced with alcohol).

During the festivities we sat at long rows of couches and at tables of most dear (expensive) darkened and polished hardwoods. Murals curiously wrought with tapestries embossed with gold, silver, and multi-coloured threads depicting annals of our empire's glorious history festooned her walls.

High above, hung massive chandeliers of bronze and crystal, lighted with untold numbers of candles and fires of the gods. (Probably some form electric lights—ed.) Fronting us was set a mounting (stage of platform) whereupon during the dinner a company of musicians amused us with musick on all manner of instruments such as the viol, kithara, cymbal, *drum, shawm, and sackbut, delighting us with a multilplicity of melodies (possible a form of florid contrapuntal style—ed.) supported by a dazzling polyrhythmic accompaniment. Soloists demonstrated great skill in singing with multiple voices (possibly an extremely dexterous display of yodeling), alternating with a singing of simple monody (Possibly a type of chant or recitative—ed.) the words of our most popular love song:*

"My love is like a blooming flower;
Her fragrance graces shady bowers.
Her petals gilded by sunshine bright
Gives me source of great delight.

"My love is like a blooming flower;
Gleefully sing ei—a, ei—a."

Fast (immediately) after the feasting we were presented with all manner of our empire's finest acrobats, jugglers, dancers, maskers, and fools (comedians—ed.). In finale, moving to the (ballroom,) there rose to a platform his most excellency: the Grand High Potentate of all Akir-Ema for to bid us welcome and to announce the festivities to be transferred to the hall of dance. Amid gold and glitter and splendour were the young ladies and gentlemen so recently presented at court. As we mingled among ourselves across the dance floor, the older revelers soon joined us. As I participated in the many musical games and dances, I caught snippets of conspiratorial conversations among the merrymakers. I caught not all of each nefarious talk, nor did I know the various skulduggerers by name. I heard just enough to let it be an unsettling note to an otherwise enjoyable evening.

Fast (almost) the midnight hour, bade the master of ceremonies all music to cease.

So stopped all musick and merriment. Amid a trumpet fanfare entered the retinue of the High Priestess of the Vestal Virgins (a woman's monastic order similar in nature and in name to a much later order in the Roman Empire—ed.) arrayed in all manner of brilliantly coloured gowns and habit, followed by gorgeously plumaged male slave escorts, carrying a lengthy multi-coloured train. The great lady herself appeared arrayed in a long gown, cut low about the breasts, of deepest purple and spangled with all manner of costly jewels. Her fair countenance and raven-black hair be crowned with a gold and bejeweled tiara.

She and her retinue continued on procession until they stood before the high priest. The retinue then parted, forming a centre aisle. Two male slave escorts in grander plumage than their fellows advanced toward her, bearing on their shoulders two long staves of polished acacia wood. Between them, from the staves, was suspended a giant power jar fashioned of clear mica glass. Within lay a bottom covered with sand. From the which grew a short, stubbled network of shrubbery. In amongst the shrubbery crawled two deadliest of vipers. The male slaves set the jar on the marbled floor before the high priestess. They then removed the jar lid and retreated into the crowd.

The high priestess looked upon the deadly, crawling beasts and smiled. She appeared to address them briefly. Then she did a thing that did verily make the hairs stand on my head. She reached down into the jars. As they poised to strike, she quickly seized each of them by the throat. She withdrew them from the jars and held them aloft before the people. They immediately wrapped their writhing bodies about her wrists and forearms. They glared at her, mouths agape and fangs bared, while she again addressed them briefly. Before a throng enrapt with a horrified fascination, she then raised them, each in turn, to her lips.

"Kiss me, my precious ones," I heard her say.

In stunned silence those in the banquet hall watched as she then, with a snapping motion of her forearms, flung the serpents back into the jar, herself unharmed throughout the whole ritual.

My mentor explained: "Custom requires she do this on each festive occasion to demonstrate her worthiness to hold position of the most exalted female of the empire."

"Does not custom also require," asked I, "that the high priest also perform some similar deed of ordeal?"

"Hoosh!" whispered my mentor. He glanced furtively about. "You put both our lives in jeopardy with such a question."

I held my breath at such a beauteous sight of so fair and elegant a lady. By custom, the High Priestess doth select from among the young men of our company, one to be her escort to the dance. She, with graceful stride, glided across the highly polished floor her choice of male escort to make.

So scarce did I dare believe it true. Her gracious self, the Great High Priestess stood before me smiling. As she reached out toward me I observed her armlet in shape of a serpent (which we consider to the symbol of wisdom.)

"What a beautiful youth," exclaimed she. "Tell me, what be thy name?"

"I am called H'rshag," 'plied I.

... "I have made decision," said she. "Tonight... thou shalt... comfort me by joining me in dance."

Just as suddenly... found I myself in the arms of the lady fair...

"I am High Priestess..." quoth she ... "My name at the first was called Aarda."

We glided effortlessly across the marbled floor. I waxed bolder than was my good.

I asked: "Shall I see you again?"

Day 8. The Inaugural festivities continue.

So revel'd we right merrily till dawn's roseate glow... gave us notice of time to prepare for the solemn convocation and worship of our god, Lemekh.

Fast (almost) fainted I as I saw my first sight of the awesome statue. He stood (90 feet) high so cunningly wrought of the finest gold that he nearly blinded me as he glistened in the sun. He stood nearly naked, but dressed as a warrior. His noble head and face were all but completely covered with a battle helmet. His right hand, cocked at the shoulder, held a giant three-pronged spear. His loins were girded with a wide-buckled girdle bearing a broadsword. His left hand supported a great shield fronting the Akiri crest, the Trident. It also was held discreetly across the front, shielding his secret parts from shameful exposure lest lewd fellows of the street make sport of so sacred a place.

His feet were shod with warrior's sandals and wrapped by leggings up to his calves. The inside of each leg also bore a small dagger.

He stood in a chariot of finest gold, pulled by six giant, golden winged horses. Circumventing these were hundreds of statues of naked young sea nymphs arranged in three rows.

We stood in silence all that day and on into the even. Whilst we stood thus motionless and silent, our ten elders of the ten kingdoms of our empire, dressed in robes of crushed velvet and crowned with gold, met in secret. Such was their wont every five years to hold counsel within the temple's inner sanctuary, a beauteous edifice pinnacled with the giant likeness of a seahorse.

I was told that it was a place of dark, yet of indescribable beauty. Its walls and ceilings were paneled with mahogany, acacia, teak, and other priceless hardwoods. They were also overlaid with gold, silver, ivory, and burnished bronze that glistened with a fiery red in the glow of the dim oil lamps.

At one end of the sanctum, stood an imposing gold statue of Lemekh (Poseidon of Plato's Atlantis?—ed.). He stood on a golden chariot, wielding his trusty trident (three-pronged spear), and, as in the statue outside on the plaza; he drove a team of six winged horses through a turbulent sea. A team of dolphins ploughed the golden waves hard (Immediately) ahead of the horses. As before, scores of naked sea nymphs and mermaids also ran ahead of the chariot.

Inscribed on the bronze columns were ancient words denoting the precepts of Me. In the middle of the open floor lay a giant altar and bed of coals countersunk below the floor level. Here the priests and elders slew white male beeves in sacrifice: ten in all—one for each kingdom. Before their burning carcasses, the elders imbibed in a libation of part wine and part bulls' blood while they gathered in the encircling portico and discussed the weightier matters of the empire. When they reached agreement, they inscribed their deliberations on golden plates to be recorded with the empire's archives.

Out on the temple plaza, meanwhile, our vigil continued on until midnight from whence came the ceremonies of the Most Solemn Oracle. Thus mounted the Grand High Potentate to a podium... Raised his hands skyward and intoned: ... "Oh, Mighty Lemekh, hear thy people. Pray, give us counsel. What of the state of our empire? of our people? Speak, for thy people hear."

Raised we our ceremonial daggers (A short dagger with wavy blade—ed,) to the darkened skies. "Hail, all hail, Lemekh," shouted we as one with a mighty shout.

Then turned he to the worshippers. "Join me in the Litany to Lemekh for the Deliverance from the Nefillim—

"From the fury of the Nefillim," he began.
"Lemekh, deliver us," we responded in unison.

When we had finished, he commanded us: "Prepare and kneel, O faithful ones. Bow in obeisance before your mighty god, Lemekh. Behold, he speaketh!"

So sheathed we our daggers and pulled the cowling of our robes up and about our faces and prostrated ourselves before his statue on the glistening, marbled pavement.

We waited 'mid thundering of (100) drums a-rolling. The four giant torches, the which stood (60 feet) high at the four cornered base of the giant statue belched out flames of many colours. (The same torches belch out by day many-coloured smoke.) Thus blasted the torches with increasing force the multi-coloured flames as in a great forge, with a great hissing and a great roaring, till the very ground beneath us did tremble.

Flickering lights and shadows danced off his surface until methought the statue did verily be alive. The face, half hidden 'neath the helmet, fain would look at us as a visage that quickeneth (come to life) and ready to break forth into speaking:

"O, my people," it roared. "Be thou careful to serve me in sincerity all thy days.

"Show kindness to the weak and powerless. Show benevolence to the poor. Show gentleness to your slaves, forbearing threatening and cruelty. Keep to the high moral paths. Strengthen the hand of righteousness and justice. Remember your high station with meekness and humility; remembering 'tis but a blind throw of fate's lot that you are above the burghers (middle-class,) the merchants, the tradesmen, the plebeians (labouring class), and the slaves.

"Heed well to the wise laws inscribed on the golden tablets.

"Rule justly. Judge with equity and compassion. Heed the cries of the fatherless and widows."

The statue paused. He struck me paralyzed with dread. Yet so thrilled was I, my hairs stood on end.

The statue continued: "Shun those who practise the black arts: who consort with the Angry Things (demons); who cause issue of the dread Nefilli. Emulate them not lest they destroy you.

"I, Lemekh, have spoken."

As his words died away into the night, I lay as one dead.

Day 9. I, Lord H'rshag, again meet the Lady Aarda.

The Grand High Potentate turned to us and commanded: "My children, Lemekh bids you arise."

The speaking of these words gave me strength to rise. At the moment musicians struck solemn chords, sang we out nation's hymn:

"Almighty Lemekh:
Glorious is Thy Presence.
We adore the, and worship thee,

Humbly bow before thee.
Grant us long and peaceful reign,
The better thus to serve thee.
Now and forevermore. Thus ever be."
The Grand High Potentate again led us in the Litany for Deliverance from the Nefilli.

"*From the fury of the Nefilli,*" *he intoned.*
"*Lemekh deliver us,*" *we chanted in response.*

After we finished he raised his arms and bade us depart in peace. For the remainder the night repaired we to the outer courtyard for light refreshment of fruit, cakes, and wine, and lighthearted camaraderie. 'Twas there again encountered I the Lady Aarda… She looked nonetheless fair, dressed simply in her worship garment (plain linen robe with head cowling) than she appeared in festal robes. Again, made I boldness that bordered on the foolhardy. (Intimate relationships with the vestals outside of official festivals be forbidden on pain of death.)

I made bold to address her: "Mayhap, I shall have thy consent to stop by thy great-house," said I.

The great lady looked away, feigning deafness at my words. I looked to the opposite direction to certain in the crowd and perceived eavesdroppers to my words, their futile attempts to mask their nosiness notwithstanding. What had they heard? Thought I in terror for a moment. As I moved to another part of the hall, away from their prying eyes, a damsel, obviously a house slave, bearing a small scroll of note in her hands, approached me.

"*From my mistress,*" *she said before quickly running away. I broke the scroll's seal and read:*

"*Look well to what you say, with whom you speak, where you go. Certain powerful, dangerous people already notice you. I say this not to frighten you, but to put you on the alert.*

"*As to our previous conversation: my consent, my lord, thou already hast.*"

* * * * *

Artie laid the sheets on her desk. As she stepped back her shoulders sagged. Her sigh conveyed a tiredness of bone-deep profundity.

"Are you still mad at me?" said Huck.
"No, of course not." Her voice carried a strange tone of detachment.
"What are you going to do now?"
"I'm sending copies to the National Geographic Society and to the British Museum."
"Is it going to take long?" He hated the way this came out.
"It could," she replied. "You go on to bed. I'll be up later."
"Kiss?"
She gave him a quick peck on the lips. "Now go to bed, hear?"

* * * * *

After a brief four hour's sleep, Artie was up again the next morning. As Huck set himself to the routine of getting another breakfast of insta-waffles, syrup, and coffee, she continued with more translating. That evening, she punched out another translation.

> *Day 10. I, H'rshag, staff my villa with domesticks and begin my courtship of the Lady Aarda.*
>
> *After my father did bid me farewell to return to our native Basilea, I carried a purse full of gold to the slave brokerage for to purchase labourers for the maintenance of my villa.*
> *So brought forth the broker from the slave pens a goodly contingent of male and female domesticks to stand before me naked upon the auction block for examination and approval.*
> *As distasteful as haggling over souls like melons in the marketplace was to me, I now had appointed myself a full staff of servants for to maintain mine estate. I bought one single bondman to keep stewardship over all my goods: a man tall, clever, and quick of eye; one second only to me; one to stand at my elbow for my every beck and call; one who with but an eye blink, a clap of the hands, a gesture or a motion could command other domestics to spring into action. I secured a most commanding presence.*
> *Dhjek, called he himself by name*
> *Critics of our system complain that slaves have no life of their own, that our slaves are but brute beasts.*
> *Nothing could be further from the truth.*

To the contrary, many possess an intellectual prowess, a resourcefulness, and a shrewdness surpassing even that of their masters. The entire slave community forms a labyrinthine network of information and gossip about the empire's most powerful and wealthiest families that can be gotten from nowhere else. Wise indeed is the lord who curries favor with a trusted slave and uses his services as informant as to the real goings-on in the body politic.

Thus, having secured a goodly company of servants, I set myself to the courtship of the Lady Aarda.

Prepared I a message on papyrus scroll announcing my intent, to the which was sealed firmly a waxen seal with my family crest.

Having sent a courier on ahead I, of a pleasant, balmy evening, set out to call upon the great lady in person. I stopped by the gate of her villa and pulled a bell-cord. A butler answered and inquired as to my person and intent.

Upon hearing the nature of my business, he bade me enter and led me up a garden walk to the great house. He led me across the front portico and into the main hall and bade me wait.

After a moment which seemed an eternity, there appeared the great lady herself dressed in full formal gown of state, coloured gold and white, and studded with pearls covering her modestly from her neck to her ankles. Her bare arms were again enwrapped with the serpentine armlets.

"Waited you long?" she inquired.

"Truthfully," said I, "any wait is but an eye-blink at the prospect of meeting such a one as you."

"Shame," she chided me good-naturedly. "You fain would gain my favour with such shameless flattery?"

She escorted me to an intimate parlour where we spent the evening in light talk and refreshments.

This being the first evening of courtship, I did not stay overlong. Rather, excused I myself whilst it was yet earlye.

* * * * *

When she tore the printout sheets from the printer, she called to Huck, "I need your help."

As he approached the top of the stairs, she announced, "We're finished with one jar. We're ready to start on another one."

He came down and began to help her with the task of changing scrolls.

They slowly turned the valve that let the air back into the case, bringing it back to atmospheric pressure again. They carefully lifted the glass lid, and took out the scroll. Huck then carried it over to the safe and rolled out a second jar. He lifted the first scroll back into its jar, resealed it, and rolled it over into the safe.

He broke the seal on the second jar and laid it on the bench. From within the jar, he pulled out a plain linen garment with a trident embossed across the chest. Laying it also on the bench, he pulled out the second scroll. She inserted the scroll into the case and began turning the spit handles.

More markings appeared.

As she turned the scroll further, Huck struggled to suppress a yawn. Dare he make a suggestion at this critical moment?

"It's two in the morning."

"So?"

"Just thought you might like to know."

"Well," she sighed. "I am tired."

She rolled the canvas top back over the glass.

"Got another suggestion," he said as she hung up her smock. "If it's a clear day tomorrow, what say we take a hike in the mountains?"

She paused. *I am on the brink of the discovery of the millennium,* she thought, *and all he thinks about is hiking in the mountains. How clueless can we get?*

She turned to him. "Are you kidding? How can you can you even think of such a thing when we're in the middle of an historical breakthrough that is absolutely unprecedented?"

"Like you say: you're tired, and like I've said before, you've been running on empty for days now. If you don't take some time off, you'll get so punchy, you won't know what you're doing. Then what good will that do your research?"

She yawned and almost blacked out. Her head swirled as in a dark whirlpool of oblivion. The buzzing in her head seemed to carry her into an inner universe that rivaled outer space in its void. Even her feet seemed to lose the sensation of contact with the floor beneath her. She grabbed the corner of the desk to keep from falling over.

She realized Huck was right.

"All right," she said as her vision cleared, "if it's a nice day."

Chapter 23

They will indeed throw her over the (precipice.) But she will not fall into the (volcano.) She will be caught in a net. She will be rescued...
   (Day 20. Shumrag's counsel to Lord H'rshag as he prepares to witness the sacrifice of Lady Aarda to the volcano. Trans. and ed. Brit. Mus. vers. 2.75. 1981)

* * * * *

   Two days after Christmas saw another bright, wintry landscape in the High Sierras; the air just cold enough to be invigorating. Artie and Huck, each bearing a backpack, trudged through the deep snow as they followed the forest trail. Wet snow hung thick on the evergreen branches overhead. On either side of the trail lay sodden, gray snowdrifts two feet high.
   The sunny skies, however, began to cloud over with winds heavy with moisture driving leaden clouds in from the northwest.
   A break in the dense forest opened up a landscape of tundra and scrub brush.
   "Timberline just ahead." Huck pointed to the rise in elevation. Artie could see the tall timber beginning to give way to stunted pine growing sparsely over a broad meadow. Alpine grass showed in bare patches between

the drifts of snow. Beyond lay sheer rock coated with wind-driven drifts of snow and sheet ice.

"There's a ledge right over there," said Huck. "With a terrific view of the valley."

He pointed to an outcropping about a mile distant, just on the other side of the meadow. A ridgeline pointed jagged fingers of rock formations up against a racing cloud ceiling. Short stubbled alpine grass writhed before boisterous winds.

"We can stop there for lunch."

Twenty minutes later they came to the outcropping.

A level place in the rock formation opened to a gaping emptiness that stretched down into a canyon a good thousand feet below. Wedged at the bottom, white water twisted like a ribbon of silver between steep, rocky banks. Farther in the distance another mountain range covered with evergreens rose to meet a yet another range off on the horizon.

"It is beautiful." Artie's eyes swept the panorama.

Huck climbed to the top of a flat boulder and walked a dozen paces closer to the precipice. Among a sparse growth of knee-high evergreens, he stood in a wide stance in defiance of the elements.

Then he took a couple of steps closer to the edge.

"Don't, dummy," she shouted.

"Come on, get daring," he said. "Just sit down very carefully. Don't move around and you'll be all right. The view is really great."

Reluctantly she started across the rocky plane. Carefully picking her way among the black ice, she laid her pack on the flat surface and sat down on a clump of frozen moss. The stone beneath felt cold to the touch. Moisture from the ice began to soak through her woolen slacks. She looked down at the rugged drop that seemed to draw her into its nothingness. Juts of granite formations poking up from the canyon wall supported small clusters of saplings struggling for existence among the bare stone. The scene suggested the mouth of a giant beast with rows of rocky teeth.

The primeval wilderness below looked untouched by human intrusion. Perhaps not even hunter-gathers of millennia past ever ventured down there, she thought.

Huck wriggled to the edge and let his feet dangle over.

"Don't!" Her voice now had a tinge of anger. "You idiot!"

"It's all right," he laughed. "I'm not going any further."

They broke into their packs and began munching trail mix. He studied her face. The cold, bracing air brought out color to her cheeks. Mountain breezes fluffed out her thick brunette locks. He continued studying her profile, her high, rounded forehead and articulate-looking lips.

He reached into his knapsack and withdrew a thermos. He unscrewed the top and poured her some hot tea. She pulled off her gloves the better to hold the metal container. Small, delicate-looking hands turned blue with cold and sought to draw heat from the steaming cup.

Blowing gently into her drink, she noticed a mischievous look in his eye. He laid a hand on her knee.

"Remember what happened a year ago today?"

She took a sip of the nearly scalding liquid. She let its sensation trickle down her throat, warming her inner being.

"What happened a year ago today?" she said finally.

He slid back slightly. "My rite of passage."

She took the cup from her mouth and looked out into the emptiness. *What in the world are you driving at*, she wondered. "Rite of passage?"

"You deflowered me."

"Oh, stop it." A tiny fist hit him in mock anger.

They heard the distant scream of an osprey. Its call seemed to accentuate their aloneness in the mountain wilderness, giving them the illusion that they were the only inhabitants on the planet. They could have been a contemporary Adam and Eve, frolicking in a twentieth-century Eden, biting cold and barren though it may be.

He bent close. Her expression softened as she kissed him. As he pulled back, he could observe the wind-kissed color of her cheeks. He felt cold moisture from her nostrils even as he felt the soft warmth of her lips.

"Let's go back to the cabin," she whispered.

Heart racing, he stood up and reached for his knapsack.

As she stood up to join him, her scream shattered the air. Shock waves struck at his stomach, as she seemed to have vanished.

Ice underfoot had made standing treacherous.

Struggling with the unreality of what happened, he stood trance-like. Fighting a blinding disbelief, he peered over the edge. Not ten feet below, she lay dazed and bleeding on a narrow, rocky ledge. Inches from her shoulder the precipice stretched downward to the canyon floor.

His initial thought was to contact the County Rescue Helicopter Service. Disturbing realities began entering his mind. He would have to leave her lying down there alone. He would have to rush back to the cabin and phone emergency service. He would have to give them as accurate a description as to the location as he could. He would have to hope that they would be able to pinpoint the spot within a particular grid on their county map. He would then have to rush back to this scene.

Rush? Even that would take a good two hours each way. He would also have to bring stuff with him; stuff like extra blankets, more tea and trail mix. He would also have to bring smoke bombs and flares to signal the rescue helicopter when it did fly overhead.

And when would that happen? Even with flares, it could be a day or two before the rescuers found them.

She could die of hypothermia, shock, or exposure by then.

He could feel color leave his face. He would try to get her out himself. "Don't move," he managed to say. "I've got a rope."

A throbbing panic welled up in his throat as he rummaged through his knapsack.

He heard a weak voice from below. "I think my leg is broken."

After frantic fumbling through his pack he found the rope. He tied one end of it around one of the larger tree stumps. He tied a loop with a bowline at the other end. He searched through his jacket pocket for a pair of leather work gloves. Tying a second loop around his waist, he carefully slid back to the precipice.

"Here it comes," he said, forcing calmness in his voice. "Don't move until I get it to you. Then wait until I tell you what to do."

"Please hurry," she urged. "It's starting to hurt."

Please, not like this, he thought as the rope finally reached her. *Get us out of here and I'll do whatever it takes to make that sonofabitch give her her freedom and marry her, okay?*

"Slip it over your head," he shouted. "Easy."

He listened for movement from below. As the wind picked up, it made a whistling sound, making hearing anything from the ledge difficult.

He paused. "Got it?"

"Got it."

Now what, he thought. Would this even work? One slipup, one miscalculation could send a badly injured Artie plummeting down a thousand feet into the narrow canyon.

Even a helicopter could not get her body out.

He waited. Then: "Get the rope up under your armpits. Reach your hands up around from the inside. Loop them around the rope again and fold your arms in and lock them together."

He again waited briefly.

"I'm going to start pulling—slowly."

God, don't let anything go wrong!

"It's going to be a little scary, so don't panic. If you don't loosen your grip, you're not going to go anywhere. Push your good foot against the side of the cliff as you come up. Keep the injured leg out away from everything. It might hurt, so try to be brave."

He could now hear a soft sobbing. *This is crazy,* he thought. *On the way up she could crash into the side of the cliff. She could wrack herself up real bad.*

What else could he do, he wondered as he called out. "Ready?"

"Ready."

He started pulling. "Whatever you do, don't look down."

As he started to pull, he felt the weight heavier than he had anticipated. Out of shape as he was could he even do it?

Another grim possibility occurred to him. What if worst came to worst and she slipped and fell to her death?

First of all, just the idea of losing her was itself unthinkable, but other ramifications, like dark titan demons besieged his mind, remorseless as a juggernaut.

Would the Sheriff's Department believe that it was an accident or would they suspect foul play? After all, Artie and he by now were married all but in name. Some months previous she had designated him beneficiary not only to the mountain property, her still-ample investment portfolio, but her late parents' estate back in Chicago as well. Only in a joint venture with her estranged husband in an establishment called Atlantis Studios was he not included.

If the law suspected the worst, how could he defend himself?

Don't even go there, he thought.

He could feel the rope start to sway.

He braced his foot against the base of the boulder for more power. He could feel the rope develop a tendency to slip in his gloved hand. Perspiration formed on his forehead as he gave one last burst of reserve. He felt himself beginning to shake from exhaustion.

This is a crazy idea, he thought. *Should have called the helicopter.*

Too late now.

He saw the top of her head; then a face, smudged and bloody, appeared over the rock. He saw her reach for a higher hold on the rope. He grabbed her jeans with his free hand. Trying to ignore a sudden shriek of pain, he pulled her the rest of the way onto the flat surface.

With the both of them gasping for breath, he tried to pull her gingerly away from the cliff's edge.

"Oh, honey," he said, holding her. "Thank God you're safe."

Long moments he continued to sit holding her close. Gradually their breathing resumed a semblance of normal.

She gripped his sleeve. "It's all right," she whispered.

The wind began to turn icy. Despite winter clothing, it cut through like a knife. He felt her start to shiver. *I've got to get her out of here*, he thought, *and fast.*

He again reached for her knapsack and placed it under her head for a pillow. He took out the thermos and poured more tea. Raising her head slightly, he held the cup to her lips. "Try to drink some of this."

She began swallowing little gulps. "Please take me out of here."

"I'm going to have to make a splint first," he said. He cursed inwardly the fact they were above the timberline. No wood for a splint. He took off his pile jacket and rolled it carefully around her injured leg. Then he used his belt to strap it on. Gingerly, he started to pull her to her good foot.

"Can you hobble?"

"I think so," she replied. They started back down the trail, but the progress seemed maddeningly slow. She groaned softly with each feeble hop.

He eyed their packs that lay a short distance back toward the cliff. "Forget the knapsacks," he said. "I'll come back for them later."

The trip back to the timberline seemed an eternity. In the forest, amid the deepening snow, the going would even get even more difficult.

The skies began to clear, revealing a sun sinking ever lower behind the trees of the timberline. Long shadows stretched across the tundra meadow, lengthening by the minute.

Looking back in the forest, he saw shadows growing even darker.

"I can't do it," she said, gasping. "I just can't do it."

He paused and eyed the snowfields that reflected pink from the setting sun. Vapor from their breath began hanging low in the air. He crouched down and carefully hoisted her onto his back in a piggyback position. He could feel the air getting colder by the minute. Again, they struggled on through the snow.

If we don't make it back before dark, he thought, *we're in trouble.*

As they got closer to the forest, they found it afforded some protection from the evening chill. However, the closer the trail approached the forest, the slipperier it became underfoot. Finally they reached the forest edge and Huck continued to cautiously carry her under the snow-laden canopy.

Suddenly she leaned to one side. "Put me down. I think I'm going to get sick."

His first thought was to carry a vomiting Artie through the woods, ignoring the mess that would cover the both of them.

"It's all right, honey," he panted as he continued to struggle through the snow. *We've got to make it back before dark*, he thought. No two ways about it. "Just let it go."

"No," she insisted. "Put me down. Please."

He again gingerly set her on her good foot and let her lean against a tree. Her body convulsed. With deep growling and gurgling sounds, she splashed the contents of her stomach out across the snow.

He studied the yellowish bilious liquid that lay in a Rorschach-like splatter. At first steam began rolling up, but soon the lower temperatures froze it into a solid crust.

He could feel her start to shiver.

Shock.

The word stuck in his mind as he lifted her back up into piggyback position. He stumbled on through the gathering darkness as she continued shaking. She breathed in shallow, irregular gasps. Her speech was becoming increasingly incoherent.

He noticed, however, that she was no longer sobbing. The pain is probably unbearable, he thought. She's a gutsy little lady.

The Yucca Bowl injury was beginning to assail his knees. Stabbing pains increased in intensity with each step.

In the distance, amid the gathering dusk, he spotted the cabin.

He tried pushing against his shortening breath to hurry up a slight rise, through the wet, slippery snow without dropping her. *Only one year off training*, he thought, *and I'm this out of shape.*

Fixing his eyes on the cabin, he became aware only of his own heavy breathing. At this juncture, she could be nothing more than a heavy field pack.

He finally made it to the cabin and kicked open the door. Once inside, he changed her to a cradle position and carried her to the living room couch. Gently he pulled a blanket over her.

When he stepped to the kitchen, he kept studying her. She lay on the couch in supine position. Her face looked pale as a bed sheet. Her breathing continued shallow and irregular.

He dropped a couple of tea bags into a small ceramic pot and turned on the heat underneath. While the teakettle simmered, he slipped over to the countertop. Picking up the telephone, he began dialing the hospital.

"I'm going to get the VW ready," he said after hanging up the phone. "You're going for a ride."

She barely acknowledged his words as he strode across the living room. He left the cabin entrance ajar and headed outside and backed the VW up close. He collapsed the rear seat and folded the front passenger seat forward. Leaving the door on the rider's side swinging open, he scurried back inside and brought her out. Carefully, he placed her in a lying position and covered her over with an army blanket.

He climbed in on the driver's side and started the engine. When they started down the highway, new snow began falling. He looked in the rearview mirror and saw her face ashen gray—even her lips. He pushed the accelerator and felt the car skid. *Can't chance it,* he realized.

Fortunately, he encountered no oncoming traffic. As he pulled up to the emergency entrance of the small county hospital, he beeped his horn and medical personnel came rushing out, wheeling a stretcher.

He followed while they whisked her into the building and down a short corridor to the emergency area. They nodded for Huck to step back out into the hallway. Then they pulled a linen screen and began cutting away her jeans. After giving her a sedative, they pulled off the rest of her clothes and got her into a hospital gown. Back on the gurney again with a bottle of liquid suspended overhead, she was wheeled into the X-ray lab for an examination of her leg.

At the behest of a supervisor, Huck found his way to a visitor's lounge. After thumbing through a couple of well-worn magazines, he gave up on it and began pacing the floor. As the adrenaline rush of the last few hours began to wear off, he began to feel shakiness in his inner being. Anxiety and despondency compounded his discomfiture.

Two hours later, he saw them wheel her out of emergency and into a regular hospital room. He followed them as they lifted her onto the bed and tucked wool blankets around her.

She pulled her hand out from under the blanket. He held it and kissed her forehead.

"You'll have to come down to the admitting room," the nurse was saying to Huck. "We'll need you to fill out some forms."

Artie gave his hand a squeeze. "Some performance out there," she said, smiling between dried lips. "What do we do for an encore?"

He gave her hand a kiss and stepped again into the corridor.

The hospital found complications attendant to her fall. They found her suffering from low body temperature and hypothermia. They found her in a state of deep shock. They also found severe frostbite in her extremities beginning to set in. The disturbing reality that he almost lost her out there in the wilderness continued to press in on him with dark thoughts of how close things could have turned out badly.

Very badly.

Needle-like sensations jabbed his knees with each step. Had she known the pain he was in, he knew that despite her own injury, she would be upset if he did not himself check into emergency.

He shrugged and headed for the exit.

Akiri Temple Area

Artie in a pensive mood

Nautulus Akiri symbol

Message markings on Akiri scrolls

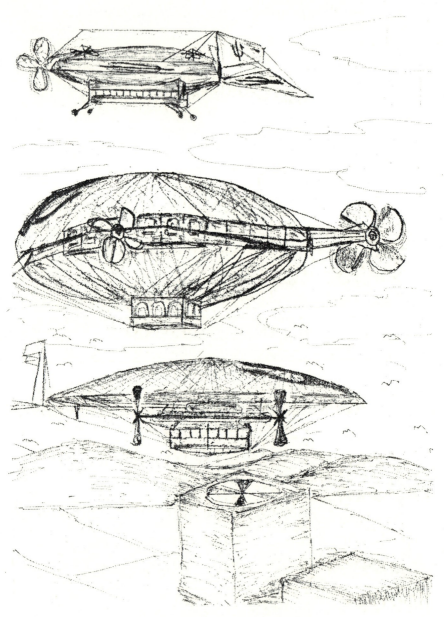

Ancient Akiri air transport

Neffilim—Evil, misbegotten creatures

The Demon Springheel Jack

The Lady Aarda

Trident—the Akiri logo

Chapter 24

"Most noble H'rshag," it began. "I bring you tidings of the Lady Aarda. She sends her love. All is well. E'en though recent events be attendant by anxious moments, not a few..."
(Day 39. Shumrag's final carrier pigeon message to Lord H'rshag. Trans. and ed. Brit. Mus. vers. 3.2; 1981.)

* * * * *

"If you will fill out these forms," the clerk said. "We'll get Dr. Mason-Rodgers ready to be discharged."

Had Artie been admitted for a mere leg fracture, she would have been discharged as an outpatient; however, the hospital had kept her longer due to severe bruises, abrasions, and for the effects of exposure.

They also wanted to check for internal injuries.

Four days after the accident, Huck, while waiting outside the hospital business office, watched staff personnel wheel Artie from her room.

They approached the wide, swinging entrance. An orderly helped her onto crutches. Huck hovered a slight distance while they assisted her through the doorway. "Careful," he said. "Can you keep your balance?"

"I'll be all right," said Artie. "Just get the car ready."

He rushed to the car, pulled the rider's door open, and then ran around to the driver's side, casting an anxious glance at hospital staffers lifting her into the lowered rider's seat.

"Let's get home," she said as they placed the crutches beside her. "I've a lot of work to do."

Shortly, Artie's car started down the driveway toward the street.

Snow banks edging the sides of the village main street glistened with a dazzling brilliance under a clear, sunny sky. Balminess hung in the air just cold enough to be invigorating.

"Happy New Year, darling," she said as they followed the winding road. "It'll be good to get home."

He drove slowly to avoid jarring her. They finally pulled into the driveway and he helped her out of the car and into the house. He eased her onto the couch in front of the fireplace. With crutches on the floor beside her, she would spend the afternoon watching the flames and absorbing the warmth. It felt good against the throbbing.

Outside the picture window the snow hung thick on the tree branches, again reflecting the sun's brilliance.

She motioned for the phone. George could be put in charge of the others in the inventorying and categorizing the remaining artifacts. Nothing major could or need be done until the doctor would put her leg in a lighter cast, enabling her to drive back to Los Angeles. In the meantime, she could concentrate her efforts translating the scrolls.

After she hung up the phone, Huck brought her a package from Sir Geoffrey Woolsey of the British Museum. It contained computer disks bearing a revised programming of the translation.

The antiquated language of the first version had bothered her. She had written Sir Geoffrey to ask whether it would be possible to reprogram the translation to more modern English.

Adjusting to get comfortable on the couch took a bit of doing. No matter the position, her leg still pained her. She watched a group of sparrows fluttering about a bird feeder just outside the window. Despite the sunny, wintry day, they looked desolate and forlorn. *I wonder if they are as miserable as I feel,* she thought.

Giving up on creature comforts while nursing a broken leg, she gestured to Huck. "Help me get to the basement."

When she reached the basement, she turned to him. "Please get me some pain killer," she said. "My leg is starting to hurt."

As he returned from the kitchen with a couple of capsules and a glass of water, she settled in the swivel chair beside her desk. "Maybe if I get to work, it'll help me forget about the pain."

"Don't overdo." He started for the stairs. After returning her water glass to the kitchen, he again retreated to the living room. *Wonder what's on the tube*, he thought as he stretched on the couch.

He flicked the dial in a futile search to escape the inanity that played out before him. Mindless chatter, self-pitying losers parading their dismal lives before a national audience on the talk shows. Vacuous sit-coms on other channels.

Early evening darkness had not cast shadows from the kitchen for long when Artie called from the basement. "Please help me upstairs."

Huck looked from the bluish, glowing square and saw a dark spot before his eyes where they had focused on the screen. He stood up and tried to accustom himself to the living room twilight. Finally he picked his way to the top of the stairs and descended to the basement. He saw Artie seated at her computer desk. Her pale face had a pinched, pained look. He stood beside her, helped her to her feet and then handed her the crutches.

As she reached the top of the stairs, she paused.

"I don't know what's the matter with me," she sighed. "I was just so tired I had to stop."

"First day out of the hospital," suggested Huck. "Or it also could be the medication."

He helped her into the bedroom and onto the bed. Taking special care when slipping her pant leg over her cast, he helped her off with her slacks and blouse.

He then pulled the sheet and blanket over her.

"I was about to punch in another readout," she said. "I'll get at it in the morning."

Huck decided to sleep on the couch for a few nights lest he risk bumping into her. He spread bedding out and the leaned back. Nine o'clock saw him still sitting: a solitary figure watching revelers from New York City mill about Times Square.

"Happy 1981," shouted the announcer as the lighted ball slid down its cable.

* * * * *

New Year's Day Artrie again sat in front of the computer, crutches on the floor beside her. Words in English appeared on the screen:

Day 11: I, Lord H'rshag Continue to Court the Lady Aarda.

Thereafter saw I the Lady Aarda often. She gave me consent to escort her incognito to all manner of public places: to theatre, to the dance, to the concert, to public banquetings (restaurants –ed.) We strolled often through the many verdant parks that graced our fair city. We amused ourselves with street entertainers, fools (comedians) on stilts, and those with trained animals. We attended many fashionable masquerade balls.

With disguise of wigs and dress in the manner of ordinary well-born ladies, plus often exotic costumes, the Lady Aarda escaped recognition as the High Priestess.

She finally bade me be entertained as her houseguest. She appeared before me arrayed in a mesh gown of hemp netting that left her arms bared, generously exposing her flesh. The mesh hung more loosely knit along her sides than in front and back. Golden serpentine bracelets graced her wrists and ankles. Around her neck she wore a golden brooch bearing an eyeball-sized sapphire with a signet of her order.

She ordered her cooks to prepare us the most delightsome delicacies. Then, whilst reclining on silken couches and sipping the rarest of wines, we amused ourselves with her household entertainers. Dancer slaves arrayed in little or no costume did dance most provocatively while singing:

"My love is like a blooming flower.
Gleefully sing ei—a, ei—a,"

Amid deepening twilight, the Lady Aarda, finally having dismissed the entertainers, and servants, did embrace me most fervently, and kiss'd me most passionately, and confessed her sickness of love. So fill'd were we together with love's longing, that presently she ushered me to her bedchamber.

Amid the singing of the night birds; and flower-scented breezes from the gardens, she invited me to her bed of perfumed sheets, of coloured silk. 'Twas upon mattress of softest down that I first knew the Lady Aarda.

Day 12: I, H'rshag, Learn from Lady Aarda the Secrets of Me.

Again, of an evening, made I my way through Akir-Ema's sylvan boulevards to the villa of the Lady Aarda. As soon as she greeted me in the receiving parlour of her great house, I knew this even would be different. I first perceived this by her dress. She wore neither her purple festal gown, nor yet her provocative fishnet attire. She, rather, had modestly clothed herself in the habit of her order. From the neck down, she wore a shimmering silken white gown with full-length sleeves. She gathered the gown about the waist with a wide girdle of gold and silver thread cunningly woven in an intricate design. Across her breast she wore a broad plate containing a series of precious stones (viz. beryl, opal, amethyst, emerald, ruby, jade, jasper, sapphire, chrysolite, and pearl) each bearing a signet representative of the ten principalities of our empire. About her forehead she wore a gold chain headband with a medallion consisting of a triangle within a circle. She covered her head with a blue, silken shawl.

Her otherwise radiantly beautiful countenance also looked pale and drawn. Her appearance and demeanor alarmed me.

"I have something to show you," she said, sensing my discomfiture. "Come with me."

She took me through the great house back into a remote section of her estate where grew a thicket of gnarled bramble bushes. "I have now fasted seven days in preparation for this," she said, explaining her pallor.

We made our way through the thicket until we came to an outer wall where stood a small temple fronted by round columns and covered with vines of ivy. She led me through a low arched doorway covered with a heavy, gilt-edged curtain of purple. Fast (immediately) faced we a foyer with a second curtain of like appearance. We pushed our way into an inner chamber. Immediately smoke from incense burned my nostrils. From a gold chain fastened at the ceiling hung a small lamp that provided the only light in the murky, perfumed interior.

"We keep this flame perpetually burning," she said.

The lamp cast its dim light on a floor-level pool bordered in bronze and stone. A frieze of pomegranates encircled it at the brim. Scenes of women dressed in vestal habit in various attitudes of prayer and other sacred exercises were engraved about the pool. Circumscribing the pool just outside the rim were the following words:

"As in water, face answers to face, so mind answers to mind."

"This basin is a well," she said, "one that has no bottom."

Skeptical, I stepped to the basin's brim and peered down. The surface lay as still as glass. From the depths, I saw light from the lamp reflected against the stone sides spiraling ever downward into oblivion.

"This shrine," she continued, "is known only to those within the order. You are now the only outsider privy to its existence. Herein is located the secret site of the Me oracles."

She stepped forward and stood beside me. She also peered down into the well's depths. "Many years past," she said, "our founder paid a pilgrimage to the land of Shurrupuk. There she gained audience with the righteous patriarch, En-okh, before his mysterious disappearance. He directed her to this well that was then in a wilderness. She oversaw the construction of this shrine. As the environs of Akir-Ema spread to this site, we of the order kept watch over the Me.

"Me embodies eternal, unwritten truth and wisdom kept by us in secret. Part of their wisdom had been written down on the golden tablets kept by the priesthood. Alas, in recent days they have gone increasingly unheeded."

I pondered her saying as she again glanced down into the water. "Is it well with Akir-Ema?" she said, addressing the water.

The water remained as a mirror.

She turned to me. "The stillness in the water is a 'no' answer," she said, pointing to the pool's mirror-like surface.

She again addressed the water. "Are perilous times upon us?"

This time ripples radiated from the center of pool and spread outward to the rim. The light reflected from the lamp overhead broke into many irregular shapes in the disturbed waters.

"That's a 'yes,'" she said.

"Has the inauguration of Pyl as Grand High Potentate finally brought to rest the instability that threatens us?" (Stillness returned to the water.)

"Does His Eminence need to be watchful?" (Ripples.)

"Are the dark women (daughters of Gjn-eth or Gwinneth of Celtic mythology—ed.) among us?" (Ripples.)

"Do they still produce their evil offspring, the dreaded Nefilim?" (Heb. for "giants," or "fallen-ones."—ed.) (Ripples.)

"Is there any way to shield ourselves from this danger?" (Stillness.)

She hesitated. She seemed in much troubled of spirit. "Is it safe to bring Lord H'rshag here?" she said at last. (Stillness.)

Again, she turned to me with a look of much weariness. "We mustn't stay," she sighed. "To others, all this may not appear very tiring, however, I am now nearly drained of all strength. The uninitiated do not realize how wearing is this exercise."

Foreboding descended over me as we turned toward the entrance. I caught the earthy smell of rotting vegetation as she pulled aside the curtain and we stepped back outside.

Dark clouds stretched across the evening sky enshrouding the whole of heaven save for a thin line of sunset's pale glow strung along the horizon. A slight breeze stirred the withered branches of the bramble bushes.

The air felt thin and cold.

"It has been revealed to me," she continued, "that not only are the days of Akir-Ema numbered, but our entire epoch. In the future, this will be called the Age of Gold. An epoch of inferior empires will follow in an Age of Silver. These will, in turn, follow in grosser epoch of peoples in an Age of Bronze. A powerful but barbaric people will follow in an Age of Iron. A vastly inferior Age of Lead follows this. The end of all things will come in an Age of Clay followed by an Age of Fire.

"You have a trusted friend in Lord Shumrag," she said as she stood beside me. "I hope someday you can entreat him to take you on the journey of mysteries to a deserted temple in a wilderness country. There you will learn much. More, I cannot say now."

My heart grew heavier still as I saw tears well up in her eyes. "We must go now," she said, kissing my cheek. "Meeting with you is becoming increasingly difficult and dangerous. Do not call me again. When it is safe to do so, I will contact you.

"Farewell, my dearest Lord H'rshag."

I left her standing by the temple among the bramble bushes as I found my way out the front gate.

Day 13: I, H'rshag, am Ordained.

I, being duly prepared and educated, was finally ready for ordination into the holy priesthood of Akir-Ema. After many days of preparation of sacrificing and ceremony, I was subject to the most rigorous of examinations as touching my character and knowledge sacred to the holy worship of the god Lemekh. Upon satisfying the doctors' hard questionings, I was made ready for the final initiation. So began I in all-night vigil, kneeling in prayer beside the altar of my order in a perfumed, private chapel inlaid by gold and ivory, hard by the temple plaza.

I was greeted at dawn by my brother initiates. The day consisted of visits by family and loved ones. Ceremonies then, commenced at twilight. Stood we before the Grand High Potentate. With gravity of mien, he led us thru the ordination oath:

"I do solemnly swear, to the willing forfeiture of even life itself: to zealously and unreservedly discharge my holy duties to the Akiri people, and to the great god, Lemekh, or may this oath by my destruction. So help me, mighty Lemekh."

Lemekh exhorted us: "Sons of the priesthood: eschew those who traffick with the three terrors of Akir-Ema: the Nefilli, the Orgoru, and the Hudishi. Resist them to the death."

In response, then, the Grand High Potentate presented to each of us our priestly medallion and signet and then led us in the recitation of the Litany for Deliverance from the Nefillim.

"From the fury of the Nefillim,"
"Lemekh deliver us."

This was followed by the presentation of sacrifices: flesh of animals, all manner of fruits, grains, and wineskins before Lemekh for him to consume and to thus obtain his blessing.

Family, friends, and general populace were then bidden to depart. Thus we were brought into the hall for the ordination banquet. So sat we at table as female temple slaves brought us the most sumptuous of dainties. Amid the savory aroma of meats and gravies, we dined and drank merrily and without stint.

A female temple slave brought me a plate of dates. She surreptitiously whispered, "Lady Aarda sends her love." Then she added, "Look well to what you eat."

I noticed something amiss. Our servers were bringing us food from off the sacrificial altar. "My lord," said I to my mentor, "what see these unworthy eyes? I perceive that the servers bring us victuals offered in sacrifice to Lemekh."

"Quite true, my son," he said. "We all be partakers of the sacrifice."

In horror I spat out my morsel. "Say not so, my lord," I pled. "I will not be party to such sacrilege."

"*Trouble not your mind, my son,*" *urged my mentor.* "*Lemekh is but a statue, incapable of consuming food and drink.*"

Benumbed, I stood to my feet. "*But the people offer the sacrifices to Lemekh,*" *said I,* "*not to the priests.*"

"*All one and the same, my son,*" *he said.* "*We are the real Lemekh the Great. We perpetuate the memory of the once mighty chieftain who founded our empire long ago, and long ago fell at the hands of the minions of the nefarious Nefillim. It is we who perpetuate the faith that unites the people.*"

"*But does not the statue come to life?*" *I asked with deep dismay.* "*Heard I not the Oracle speak with my own ears?*"

"*The voice, my son, is but a priest speaking in an echo chamber deep below the feet and is amplified up through the hollow statue. By the time it comes forth from the mouth, to the worshippers, it is truly the voice of a god.*"

"'*Tis fraud,*" *cried I with more audacity than wisdom.* "*I will expose the lot of you to the people.*"

To my surprise, he made no move to restrain me. "*Go ahead,*" *said he.* "*Destroy their faith. What would you fain give them in return?*"

He glanced at me with a smirk. "*Disillusion the people and they will rebel.*"

His words struck me like a thunderclap. They pierced my heart like the fire of the gods (lightning); like the hammer of Moloch (God of the forge; prehistoric equivalent of Haephestos or Vulcan of the later Greek and Roman mythology—ed.) Rebellion? Impossible. Akir-Ema, the greatest of empires? Certainly greater far then the primordial empire Ym'; (Oldest of all mythical civilizations, predating even Lost Atlantis; sometimes referred to by antiquarians as Mu.—ed.) Certainly greater far then the petty fiefdoms of Shurrupuk that waste their time and substance bickering over their inconsequential quarrels.

Akir-Ema, the greatest of empires since the dawn of the upright ones; sovereign of all within his illustrious gaze: from the Great Island in our Southern Sea (Indian Ocean,) to the isles of the several and divers (other) coasts of remotest barbarism; to the isles of the great inland sea of Middle Earth (Mediterranean); to the islands of the Great Western Sea (Atlantic); to the very lands that touch hard by the dreary lands of Dhul' (Thule—mythical northernmost lands of human habitation) itself.

Akir-Ema: founded and established generations of yore all the while, holding forth unnumbered high-suns (years) of unblemished peace. The happy result being that many merchants wax exceedingly rich because of her. Many and happy be the citizens who stroll without fear through her verdant parks and boulevards.

Yet, recall I how at a time, when it was not so. The land lay rent and prostrate by petty tribal chieftains warring over many an inconsequential jealousy and grievance, real and imagined. Life itself was cheap.

For good reason he made no move to restrain me.

"What you need, my young friend, is to now go out and perform a few weddings. It is time for you to enjoy our custom that allows the presiding priest the choicest of all privileges, that of spending the wedding night with the new bride."

(Akiri tradition held that the bride spending her wedding night with the priest instead of with her husband guaranteed her a fruitful womb and prosperity to her family—ed.)

"I have always loathed that custom," I said. "It smells of downwind of a goat."

"Love it or loathe it, then," laughed my mentor. "It changes nothing. Furthermore, you yourself have now eaten of the sacrificial food."

Greatly disturbed was I at the truth of what he said that I sat in silent turmoil.

He plunged his dagger into a roast quail that lay on a nearby platter all dripping with the scented juice of spiced flesh. "Take and eat, my young friend," said he. "Trouble yourself no longer with dark thoughts. This is the time for merriment."

As I raised the quail to my mouth, he smiled.

"Welcome to the priesthood," he said.

Day 14: Akiri Geneologies.

I spent the days that followed under intense grilling by Shumrag, my mentor, regarding my people's history. I was minded to commit the following genealogy to memory:

Year 1: Akiri reckoning dates its years from the settling of Kha-inu (biblical Cain), his wife and children in the land of Ehrets-Nodh (biblical land of Nod.) Ehrets-Nodh (lit. "wandering") was so called because it had been hitherto peopled by nomadic herdsmen.

65. Kha-inu, sons, and armed servants drive out nomadic peoples of Ehrets-Nodh and begin building a city.

THE DELUGE SCROLLS

120. Kha-inu dedicates completed city and names it for his son, En-okh.
135. En-okh begets I-radh.
234. I-radh begets Methu-Sheal
344. Methu-Sheal begets Lemekh.
390. Lemekh begets Tubal-Kha-Inu by wife, Zyl'. Tibal-Kha-inu develops city of En-okh into a highly sophisticated society of craftsmen and metal smiths.
402. Lemekh begets Jabal by wife, Adah. Jabal develops a highly elegant society of culture and musicians.
412 En-okh assassinated by followers of Nefillim.
652. Kha-inu dies.
659. I-radh assassinated by followers of Nefillim.
660. Methu-Sheal assassinated by unknown assailant
661. Lemekh renames city of En-okh, Lemekh, or Akir-Ema, after himself. He begins a series of wars to unite the land of Ehrets-Nodh into an empire.
704. Lemekh declares establishment of Akiri Empire.
732. Lemekh begets Shyrug.
807. Lemekh slays Nefilli warrior; only mortal ever to do so. He binds his wives and children to an oath of vengeance regarding any attempt of the Nefilli or their minions seek retaliation: "If my father Kha-inu be avenged sevenfold, let me be avenged seventy and sevenfold."
811. Shyrug begets 'No-Stradh.
819. Lemekh assassinated by followers of Nefillim.
834. Shyrug sets on conquest of islands of Mid-Erd (area of Mediterranean Sea.)
929. 'No-Stradh begets Kha-inu-Stradh.
931. 'No-Stradh assassinated by followers of Nefillim.
973. Kha-innu-Stradh begins conquest of islands of Great Western Sea (Atlantic Ocean.)
992. Kha-inu-Stradh begets Rha-ul.
1057. Rha-ul begets Dummuz.
1107. Kha-inu-Stadh assassinated.
1140. Dummuz begets Magog.
1180. Dummuz assassinated.
1184. Magog begets Tubal II.
1198. Magog assassinated.

1212. Tubal II begets Pyl.
1237. Shumrag assumes regency pending Pyl's coming of age.
1256. Pyl is installed as Grand High Potentate.
1352. H'rshag is ordained.

Day 15: Wherein I, Lord H'rshag, am taken by my mentor to the Pit of Terrors. (An ancient nuclear reactor?—ed.)

Then came to pass that of a day in course of my long tutelage that Shumrag, my beloved mentor, took me on most awesome journey deep within the bowels of Earth; deep below our city Akir-Ema.
Entered we into a chamber, tightly darkened, seal-ed chamber. Straight and swiftly sped we downward. (Possibly a sort of elevator—ed.) Sudden came we to a standstill. So ended 'bruptly our trip downward Came we to the nethermost station; Station Z its appellation. (Station - Z, a loose translation with the last character of the Akiri alphabet—ed.)
As our chamber doors did open, temple guards full armed did greet us. Heav'ly armed, did none-less greet us; yet most cordially bade us enter.
Entered we a high-ceiled chamber; portentous, fearsome place of danger. So said I: "Beloved mentor, need we go here any further? This place fills me with foreboding. Must I learn its evil intent?"
"My son," said he, "you are most favour'd. Secrets you shall see today be greatly hid to but a few. 'Tis rarest sights you're privy to."
So donned we then the strangest raiment: suits with plates of leaden armour, helmets with formica visor thus to give protected vision. O'erhead were lighted high-ceiled chambers with flickering flames of blue and amber, contained and sealed in lamps of crystal: quartz refined to finest crystal.
At motion from our travel guide, climbed we aboard for chariot ride, a dunnumu-chariot* to journey downward to long tunnels dank. (* Dunnumu-chariot—A self-propelled vehicle, powered by giant electric dry cells. Dunnumu: from Greek "dunnumos," or dynamic –ed.)
So sped we along down narrow passage full four runner's league still pressed we onward. (10 miles—ed.)
Stopped we hard (close) by terminal chamber, well within the outer tunnel. Our guide showed a widened panel set within a metal chamber. Showed he us the row of levers: secret source of greatest power.
Moved he then one single lever till it pressed 'gainst plates of copper. Anon heard we distant rumble causing now the ground to tremble; a

roaring from the tunnel distance. The mica-lamps (electric lanterns) then grew dim as 'mid the tunnel there 'ppeared a glow.

The glow began soft, unearthly violet, which soon commenced to grow much brighter, as within the deep came full-bellied rumbling and a pulsating roar.

Sounded still more fearsome tumult, a deafening, strident, lamenting whine, more shrill than ever wild Banshee's shriek. As louder grew the hellish din, frighted was I. I soon grew faint, when one more terror dwarfed all before.

I shook till I could take no more when suddenly 'midst the tunnel's roar a deafening hiss and darting flame with haste now through the tunnel came. A blue-green streak o' fire bright vanished, leaving behind a darken'd night. Anon, shot another fast (immediately) follow'd the first.

With terror methought my bowels would burst. To stay or run, I neither durst. At last cried I: "Belov'd Mentor, let us flee this place of terror."

Then thrust the guide the lever backward. The tunnel was still and dark once more. Then took he us to hidden chamber set well beneath the earth.

Showed he us an inner chamber sealed with crystal windows round. The chamber was barren of all and sundry save one small rock on plain pedestal.

Threw he again a metal lever. The chamber glow'd; began to quiver. "This stone," said he: "'Philosopher's Stone.' Its hard, smooth surface contains power unmeasur'd, far exceeding all previous power."

A high arc of purpled flame played 'round the stone as our guide spake. And again the ground beneath did quake. "Our wizard-priests," (scientists—ed.) said our guide, "must take greatest care when this power is tried. (Experimented with—ed.)

"Should fall these stations to unskilled hands, 'twould cause destruction upon our land. 'Twould bring to end of life now known. And thus would end our ancestral home."

This solemn warning took I heed. Thus we left the evil place. Forget not ought I saw that day. Its fearsome meaning went not away.

Thought I oft forever after as Akiri lived 'mid mirth and laughter quite ignorant of the pit of terror hard (immediately) beneath their city fair, where lurks great powers of destruction there.

Day 16: Wherein I, Lord H'rshag, first sight the dread Nefillim.

I, H'rshag, betook myself to forest on holiday with Ulki, loyal friend of my youth. Hied we to forest not three day's journey from Basilea, ancient provincial capital, for to do some sport of hunting of boar and deer. Came we at last to a forest deep, dark, and primeval. Pine, spruce, and fir extended well upward of (two hundred feet) above us. Hoary, moist strands of moss hung heavy from every branch, some a good (six feet) or more. Every tree trunk and every rock was alike covered with a soft, mossy green blanket. Gigantic ferns of every variety grew in abundance. Sunlight penetrated only in patches of golden sheen. Wet, moist surfaces pressed in around us hushing our footsteps and voices, as did the musty smell of rotting vegetation. Truly, it was a place of foreboding and mystery.

Deep within the forest builded we our booth (lean-to, lodge, or camp—ed.) of sturdy pine bough.

"Wolki, my kinsman," said my companion, "would have loved such a venture as this."

"Why did he not join us?" I asked.

"He is not," said my companion with a voice suddenly sad.

"You mean dead?" said I with want of discretion.

"Worse," said he. His face invited no further discussion.

As nightfall pressed in upon us, I quite forgot misgivings engendered by the conversation as we fell to sweet and soothing slumber within its cozy shelter. Resting in the assurance that our blazing campfire be sufficient to ward off all beasts of prey.

For reason unknown, rudely woke I to dark of night save for silv'ry moon. With foreboding I descried our fire to be but embers. As I moved to awaken my companion, unaware was I of greater danger still; the like of which wolves and pumas are but house pets when compared to this greatest dread.

I first discerned an o'erpowering stench; fouler far than polecat's scent or refuse from a mortal man. I wakened my companion. We fled our booth, hid ourselves in the forest, and listened. The night birds sang not. Nor yet any forest creature stirred. We cocked our ears and heard nothing.

Suddenly the night was rent by a scream that caused the blood run cold. Was it a man? Or beast? Or Angry Thing? (demon) Or something part all three? It pierced the ears. It echoed thru the forest. It reverberated from the distant mountains and then, with wave, after wave, it finally died away.

We looked at one another, but could not speak. Anon, wetted I my lips and spoke: "Nefilli," said I. We stood as stone for the space of (one hour) or thereabout.

On distant mountain top, on bare outcropping of rock glowed a light, lighting up the sky. "Let us go and see," said I, as our youthful curiosity waxed stronger than fear.

Thus trudged we off thru thicket and fen (swamp) twice a league; half a league (about ten miles) toward the light of distant fire. We neared as we dared, still half a league off. Heard we now the crackling logs of yon blazing fire.

Saw we figure of a man. Naked, yet full covered with hair from head to foot. Stood he taller by half than ordinary mortal man. Nails sharp as eagle claws protruded from his fingers and toes, looking capable disemboweling a mortal man with one swipe. A single eye had he that glowed like coals of hell as threw he yet more logs to fire. Logs say I? Nay, more like whole trees threw he them like mere twigs into the blaze.

He was joined by yet another: one fully clothed with cape and widened leathern girdle. About the waist did hang a sword; a fearsome blade, wide and curved and the which be as tall as mortal man's shoulder. The handle had a length twice as a man's handgrip. Horned headgear crowned his head.

"O mighty Grenzlbl," (probably the Grendel of the Danish saga, Beowulf—ed.) let the ceremonies begin," said the fire-builder to the leader. Grenzlbl seized a gemsen horn hanging from his shoulder broad and blew a blast that reechoed o'er woodland and hill.

Died away the fearsome blast; silence for the nonce at last. Silence say I? Nay, silence save for low voices chanting:

"Ave, Lucanu. Ave, Lucanu," (lit. "Light bearer."—ed.)

From deep within the forest appeared, marching single file as in processional, up toward mountain summit full twelve by count others of their kind, chanting as they marched. They carried a shield of gigantic proportion, upon which was laid one of their own; perhaps a fallen warrior.

Continued they their chant lament as they laid their slain companion on blazing logs. Flames mounted higher as sparks showered the heavens in dazzling display, consuming to ashes the evil creature's remains.

Grenzlbl sniffed the air. "I smell mortals," he said, pounding his mace to the rock beneath his feet.

In fright Ulki and I took flight. Rushed we headlong into the night. In hot pursuit the wretches came. At last we reached our go-cart (A vehicle similar to the modern golf-cart—ed.) parked by our campsite and in great terror fled we the scene.

That night's terror holds me still. I've ne'er 'gain gone near the hill. 'Tis evil place wherein there dwells the race of monsters call'd Nefill.

Day 17. (H'rshag and Shumrag, while on a similar fishing trip deep in a remote forest, discover the origin of the Nefillim: A votive stone around which cultic women (dark women) with naked bodies rubbed with scented oil, danced by full moon and, in ritual, mated with embodied demon spirits—ed.)

Day 18. The Three Terrors of Akir-Ema.

'So returned my mentor and I to our hunting lodge in forest deep. Brake we tidings of our newest finding to our genial host. His jaw grew slack. His countenance blanched.

"'Tis much amiss that comes to pass in these forests and mountain waste. Invoke we oft Great Lemekh's arm to shield us from untoward harm.

"Three terrors beset Akir-Ema sore. Would to Lemekh they plagued us no more: terrors of the forest, terrors of the fields, and terrors of the cities. There is no escape.

"In the forest, the Nefillim lurk. In the fields the Ogoru curse. In city streets mayhap e'en worse, the Hudishi do run their course. The Nefillim, bestial race of freaks offspring of Angry Things, with mighty shrieks in forest deep and mountain top, give warning they be destructive lot.

"Ogoru, (possibly the origin of ogre—ed.) in turn are Nefilli's seed with still other mortal women who give not heed to sound words, but rather seek strange pleasures with Nefilli's evil streak. Ogoru would oppress those who toil in field and orchard and plow the soil. 'Pon all such exact they tribute sore and from lonely castles, great riches store.

"Hudishi are but mortal youth: lewd fellows, brutish, base, uncouth, seek Nefilli and Ogoru emulate. Thus be they burgher's fate. (*Burgher—city dweller.) They dress themselves with clothing strange—as women, as apes, as parrots, as wildcats, or some dress as Angry Things: bodies of men; legs and horns of goat. Others dress themselves not at all; but run naked, sometimes with bodies painted, through city streets. Unashamed, they relieve themselves in publick fountains; openly cohabit with young women—or worse, peradventure with their own kind in publick parks.

"Anger'd without cause, befogg'd by lotus and (hashish—ed.) They *harass, attack, assault innocent passers-by. Thus in mischief and idleness, they waste away their days a-bye."*

Day 19: Litany: For Deliverance from the Nefillim.

Priest: From the fury of the Nefillim.
People: O, Lemekh, deliver us...,
... V: From those who scorn all laws; and all things sacred, of gods and men.
R: O, Lemekh, deliver us.
V: From those who hold secret hellish ritual atop evil mountains of a midnight at fullness of moon, and spend wild orgy baying at the moon like dogs; and drink their soul-damning drink of wine, mixture of pharmacopoeia (drugs—ed.) and men's issue, and blood of woman's uncleanness, and dung of sheep.
R: O, Lemekh deliver us.
V: From those who hunt mortal men as one hunts fox and elk.
R: O, Lemekh, deliver us.
V: From those who devour their victims whilst they yet live.
R: O, Lemekh, deliver us.
V: Preserve thy people, thy treasured people. Preserve thy people. Preserve this illustrious land of Akir-Ema for thy name's sake.
R: O, mighty and merciful Lemekh, deliver us.

The sound of a footfall on the cellar stairs startled her. She looked at the clock on the shelf. Eleven thirty-five P.M. She had been at the computer since early that morning, completely oblivious of the time. She turned around to see Huck standing behind her.

The room lapsed in silence.

He studied her for a moment. He marveled at the petite figure in the white smock sitting at the computer. Her face still looked pale to him. Was it still the result of the injury, or was it from overwork? He thought further. No. He thought he began to realize what had largely escaped him much of the time: the import of her finding. Before them lay the translation of historic revelation that predated the pyramids or the primitive cuneiform tablets of Mesopotamia.

Was this a written record of events that reached well back into the primordial mists of myth and legend?

"What's the matter?" he said softly.

She shook her head. "It's all right," she sighed. "Just tired."

"That stuff's getting to you, isn't it?"

"A little, I suppose."

Another pause.

Was the intensity of her involvement in the scrolls raising a temptation to lose her scholar's sense of objectivity?

"Come on to bed," he whispered at last.

He helped her to her feet. At the bottom step, she stopped. "Please," she said. "Get me a pain pill. I'm starting to hurt again."

He hurried to the downstairs bathroom for her pill and a tumbler of water. When he returned, she took the pill and emptied the tumbler of half its contents. He placed it on the desk and started helping her up the basement stairs. After ushering her to the bedroom door, he walked pensively to the living room couch. He lay back, trying to breathe in the heavy smell of dampness. Unable to sleep, he studied the icicles hanging from the eaves just outside the sliding glass door and the blackened void of night just beyond.

Two break-ins, a murder, a fall from a precipice: What's going on? he thought. If the stuff from the scrolls was getting to her, recent events were beginning to get to him. Was all this a cosmic omen to which he should be paying attention? Or was it just coincidence?

Six the next morning a clicking sound wakened him and he headed for the basement. There he saw her studying the following words on the computer screen:

Day 20: I, H'rshag, learn that Lady Aarda is to be offered in sacrifice to the god Lemekh.

Came a day when my mentor bore the following tidings: "Lady Aarda, by dint of her beauty and virtue has been selected as offering to Lemekh's spirit that dwells in the sacred fiery mountain."

Grieved, I left not my house one full week. I sat among the deep ashen heap in stinking sack cloths of mourning. I took no food and precious little drink. Refused I song of pipe or harp, nor yet betook I any merriment. Finally entered I into my own private chapel to hold vigil before my own altar.

The days of mourning passed, I rose to bathe, to shave, to adorn again clean raiment, to anoint my body with scented oil, and finally to partake of food.

On the appointed day, great multitudes of us followed to the holy mountain. Guards halted all but the sacrificial party who marched on to the summit to all manner of solemn musick.

"Why this fraudulent folly?" I asked my mentor. "Why this taking of an innocent human life in the name of a cause we know is a lie?"

He replied: "Your beloved will not die."

"You are mad," I said.

He explained: "The priest will indeed march her up to the (volcano's edge,) and throw her over the precipice. However, she will fall into a net just below the inside edge of the crater. From there she will be escorted to a commodiously furnished apartment carved into the mountain.

"There, her every want, save you, O H'rshag, will be met until time of next year's sacrifice. The Lady Aarda will subsequently be moved to live forever afterward in the Forbidden Garden adjacent the temple.

"Once there, you may go and see her. You and she may be joined in secret marriage. You, as a priest, will appear before the people. She, however, will remain cloistered behind the garden walls."

Day 21: Wherein I seek after Aarda in the Forbidden Garden to take her to wife, only to discover that she is betrothed to another.

One (year) later I approached my mentor to announce my intention of taking my Aarda to wife.

He bore me the most unwelcome tidings: "Thine Aarda is given to another."

"To whom, pray tell?" queried I.

"To the Grand Vizier," gave my mentor answer. "First Council Chamberlain to the Most High Grand Potentate. Short space ago he laid eyes on her and desired her for his own."

"But we have already given ourselves in pledge to one another," said I. "In secret ceremony long ere I came to serve at the temple have we done this. We have already known each other as man and wife."

My mentor's countenance waxed pale. "Beware," he warned. "Not only thy life, but hers also be in great peril should certain persons in high places be privy to this."

On the morrow, I stood upon the pavement of the now deserted temple plaza. I caught the smell of fresh wind blowing across the open area.

"Hear me, god of Akir-Ema," shouted I. "O, god who hath eyes but can see not; who hath ears but can hear not; who hath legs but art incapable of running to anyone's aid, let us see if thou art powerful enough to prevent the self-inflicted taking of an innocent life!"

So saying, I drew my sword and forthwith prepared to plunge the same into my bowels.

"My son, hold!" shouted a voice behind me. "Do yourself no harm. Mayhap I can show you a better way."

I turned to see my mentor rapidly approaching.

"I have friends in high places," announced he. "Mayhap we can engineer a rescue. However, the risks be great. Be you willing?"

"Plague take the risks," I shouted. "No risk be e'er so great as to daunt my determination to rescue my beloved."

"Tonight then," said he, "you must prepare yourself. On the morrow we shall embark on a long journey."

Day 22: I, H'rshag, am taken on a Journey of Mysteries by Shumrag, my mentor.

In that time when saw I five tens of summers, purposed Shumrag, my wise and benevolent mentor, to take me on the secret journey of mysteries. This journey sanctioned by neither Grand High Potentate nor Grand Vizier, nor yet by any of the priestly order of high degree, was then prepared and done in secret.

Most noble Shumrag and I betook three day's journey to ancient provincial capital, Basilea, my ancestral home.

My father greeted me at his estate portals. "So," said he, "how are things in the viper's nest?"

"You mean the temple court?"

"Precisely."

I tried not to let my misgivings sully the prospects of the bright nature of my visit here among the old, the familiar. So spent we nevertheless many (weeks) with friends and loved ones reliving days of (carefree) childhood and youth.

From thence went we many days' journey beyond to a wilderness country: a lonely, rocky place far from civilization's haunts; an empty place where none was wont to dwell.

Anon came we to hill country too rocky for dunnumu-chariot. Forced were we then, to proceed on foot, yet three more day's journey. At dawn of the third day, then, came we to a summit o'erlooking a plain place (Plain, valley, depression, or hollow,) the which lay below us of a great distance. With much (effort) descended we down a path exceedingly steep and stony till gat we level with the plain place.

I perceived it not larger by half than our own temple plaza (probably about the size of a modern football stadium—ed.) To the southernmost end stood circles of pillars each inside the other. (Probably a petroglyph formation similar to those in the British Isles and Northern Europe, such as Stonehenge—ed.) Stood the pillars two-fold the height of a man or better (12-15 ft.—ed.) Stood they each twain topped by a third, looking very like a votive sanctuary or perhaps a site of an oracle.

To the northernmost I noticed (a type of stage) reached only by steps of unhewn stone. At top center stood a sacred heap (cairn) or altar likewise of unhewn stone bearing a blacken'd surface as if of old, sacred fires burned thereon.

At either side stood twain pillars (about 1 story high—ed.) fashioned on three sides and rising to a pique (a kind of obelisk—ed) On the sides thereon were engraved well-worn cabbalist inscriptions of great mystery.

My mentor opined: "These inscriptions appear to be text of a hymn of great antiquity."

* * * * *

Artie stared at the soft-glowing screen. After pressing the space bar she watched the preceding words come up.

She pushed the print button and tore off the sheet. She then hobbled over to the desk, and began to study it. Turning around, she found that Huck had returned from upstairs with a breakfast tray.

She felt a surge of fatigue that weighed at her like an anchor. Her head swirling with the fresh discoveries of a world unknown for thousands of years had left her drained of all emotion.

"What a place to stop the translation," she said. At Huck's urging, she stopped for breakfast.

Huck placed the tray on the desk beside her computer.

He eyed her lined face with concern. "You okay?"

She reached for her coffee. "I really don't know," she sighed. "I've stopped trying to figure that one out about five thousand years ago."

They nibbled at the muffins and sipped their coffee in silence.

In ancient Greece Plato wrote of it. He, in turn, got it from Solon who predated even him. Solon learned it from an unknown Egyptian priest to whom it was already ancient history.

When Huck took the tray she started punching more keys. She heard him mounting the stairs as the printer again began clicking.

Day 23: The Creation Hymn.

Leader: At the first: the Strong-Ones.
Small Chorus: He spoke. And the expanse (heavens) and erd' (earth) were. (Ed. Comment: —Here we are confronted with an interesting concept. Back in the 17th Century, Archbishop James Ussher calculated the date of creation to be 4,004 B.C. At present, astronomers estimate the "Big Bang" to have taken place approximately 12 to 15 billion years ago. Recent Mayan translations have reckoned the date of creation as having occurred some 45—followed by 27 zeroes—years ago. Or, in other terms—some 3 sextillion times our own 15 billion years estimate.

(Also, both the Ym'ian and Akiri calendars show an interesting—and a very modern scientific concept, namely: the difference between the solar year, the cosmic year, and the galactic year. The solar year, of course, takes 364.25 days, or the time that the earth takes to make a complete orbit around the sun. The cosmic year, then, is the length of time it takes our entire solar system to complete one orbit around our galaxy. The galactic year, in turn, represents the length of time our galaxy takes to make one orbit around a hitherto undetermined center of our galactic cluster.

(By Akiri and Ym'ian reckoning, creation began some 45 plus 27 zeroes ago in terms of solar years, 15 billion cosmic years, and approximately 6,000 galactic years ago.)
People: Erd' was dark and formless. Khaos (chaos) ruled the deep.
Leader: The Strong-Ones breathed a mist; and he brooded over the waters.
Sm. Cho.: Strong-Ones said: "Let light appear."
People: Light appeared.
Leader: Strong-Ones proclaimed it good.
Sm.Cho.: Thus divided he light from Khaos (darkness).
People: Strong-Ones called the light "day"; Khaos called he "night."

Sm.Cho.: *Thus even and morn; Day the First.*

All: *At the first: Eternal Mind. He, who is always present with the Strong-Ones. Worthy, O Keeper of Life, are you to receive glory and honour, and power. For thy good pleasure spoke thou all things into being. Sing we U-sanh-u. Sing we Three-fold U-le-lu.*

Leader: Strong-Ones spoke: "Let expanse be in the midst of the waters 'neath the greater expanse above the waters."

Sm. Cho.: *It was done.*

People: *It was done.*

Leader: Divided he the expanse in twain; layer of ether above and layer of air below.

Sm. Cho.: *Thus even and morn; Day the Second.*

All: *The expanse declares Strong-One's glory. Layer of air and layers of ether declares his craftsmanship. Sing we U-sanh-u. To thee, sing we Three-Fold U-le-lu.*

Leader: Strong-Ones spoke: "Let the waters under the expanse gather together in one place. Let clay emerge and dry."

Sm. Cho.: *It was done.*

People: *It was done.*

Leader: Strong-Ones called clay Erd'; heap'd (condensed—ed.) waters called he sea.

All: *Strong-Ones called them good.*

Leader: Strong-Ones spoke: "Let Erd' bring forth grass and herb yielding seed, and fruit-tree yielding fruit whose life is in its seed, each after their stem (race, kind, lineage, or manner.)"

Sm.Cho.: *It was done.*

People: *It was done.*

Leader: Strong-Ones declared it all good.

Sm. Cho.: *Thus even and morn; Day the Thrice.*

All: *Let the floods clap their hands. Let the hills be joyful together. To Am give glory, laud, and honour. Sing we U-sanh-u.*

To him sing Three-Fold U-le-lu.

Leader: Strong-Ones spoke: "Let lights rule in the expanse; to divide day from night; to be for signs, and for seasons; and for years. Let them be for lights in the expanse of the expanse to Erd' her light also."

Sm.Cho.: *It was done.*

People: *It was done.*

Leader: Thus commanded Strong-Ones two great lights; the greater to rule day; the lesser to rule night.

All: Declared Strong-Ones them good.

Leader: Thus even and morn; Day the Fourth.

All: Am reigns supreme. Let Erd' rejoice. Let all rejoice. Sing we U-sanh-u. To Am sing we Thee-Fold U-le-lu.

Leader: Thus spake the Strong-Ones: "Let the waters produce in abundance—all manner of living creature with life. Let winged fowl fly in my expanse above Erd'."

Sm. Cho.: Thus the Strong-Ones bro't into being: great sea leviathan, ev'ry living, moving thing from the waters.

People: So came they forth in abundance; after their seed (or stem, lineage, race, descendency, manner, or kind—ed.). So came winged fowl (Pterodactyl?—ed.) in abundance after its (manner.)

All: Declared the Strong-Ones them good.

Leader: So blessed the Strong-Ones he them, saying: "Be fruitful and multiply."

Sm. Cho.: Let the seas and erd' be filled with your offspring.

Leader: Thus even and morn: Day the Fifth.

All: Am reigns supreme. He is enthroned between the kharu-bvim and reigns high above all. Sing we U-sanh-u. Sing we Three-Fold U-le-lu.

Leader: Strong-Ones spoke: "Erd', bring forth ev'ry living creature in abundance: cattle, creeping things, beasties of the field—all after their (manner)."

Sm. Cho.: It was done.

People: It was done.

Leader: Strong-Ones said: "Let there be beasties of the field, things that creep, and cattle—all after their (manner)."

All: Declared the Strong-Ones them good.

Leader: So said Strong-Ones: "Let us make one like unto us; in our (stamp, reflection, likeness, image—ed.) as a mirror reflection of ourselves. Give them dominion over all our works."

Sm.Cho.: It was done.

People: It was done.

Leader: Strong-Ones said: "Be fruitful. Multiply. All Erd' lies before you. Be her master. Eat the fruit thereof."

Sm. Cho.: It was done.

People: It was done.

Leader: So declared the Strong-Ones them good.

Sm. Cho.: So declared all that he had made good

People: Thus even and morn: Day the Sixth.

As the clicking of the printer continued, she heard Huck again returning to the basement. She glanced up at him as he resumed his standing position behind her. Beyond him she could see the early-morning twilight outside the sliding doors. Tree branches overhead still bent heavily downward, laden with thick, wet snow. Sunlight began to penetrate the dusk of the murky forest.

The clicking continued.

All: Am reigneth. Am shall rejoice o'er all creation. Raise the tumultuous rejoicing. Publish his fame throughout the erd'. Praise Am with singing. Praise Am with harp and zither. Praise Am with timbrel and dance. Let all breath praise Am. Sang all U-sanh-u. Let all join in Seven-Fold U-le-lu. Let all join in Seven-Fold Let-Be!

Huck studied the printout in silence. He recalled Artie mentioning an opinion long held by scholars of antiquity of every persuasion, namely that the Genesis creation account had actually been incorporated from an even more ancient Babylonian creation hymn.

Could Artie be unearthing from these scrolls a creation account predating even ancient Babylon? Even more ancient than Lost Atlantis? Who were these "Plain-Ones"? How came they by this creation epic they celebrated in poetry, music, dance, and liturgical drama? Was it really myth handed down from the mists of a primordial past, or was it, in fact the oracle of Ruach-ha-khodosh? A part of the Me?

What was the jar containing this scroll doing in the Sumerian scriptorium? Were the ancient Sumerians themselves sufficiently curious about their past to become archeologists in their own right? Had they themselves discovered and translated the creation epic from sources of even more incredible antiquity?

He studied the slim figure hunched at the computer—his lover herself only a few years his senior—the internationally recognized genius who accomplished in months what might have well have taken her older male colleagues years.

Angie Morgenstern had it right.

The new sheet bore the following words:

Shumrag, my mentor, stepped to the westernmost stone. "There's more," he said.

"Thus it was," read the westernmost stone, "in the day that Am spoke into being That-which-was-not, placed he Red-One in Para-Dies; an expanse of park (reserve, or a kind of botanical garden—ed.) abundant in all kind of tree and vegetation, lying where in the great expanse where four rivers meet, beginning where twain rivers meet (Tigris and Euphrates Valley—ed.) extending southward well into the Great Western Continent (Africa—ed.)

Thus spake Am: "Here have we one cast in our (image) to keep, as caretakers, the garden. At last we have one to whom we will entrust that which the misbegotten fain would spoil."

* * * * *

Artie studied the printout. "Misbegotten—?" She pondered the words that coursed through her mind. Angry Things—Nefilli (or "fallen ones")—demons—malevolent thought or centers of energy—negative forces? Were they all words describing the same phenomena? What were these centers of negative energy? Were they, as some conservative scholars aver, disembodied members of a fallen, pre-Adamic race? Fallen angelic beings from extraterrestrial realms?

The printer continued.

* * * * *

When Red-One's members were yet unformed, declared Am: "I will cause Red-One to fall into deep sleep and while in such a state, I will draw from him one like unto him, to complement him. Thus shall I declare them: 'Red-One' (or 'clay creature'—ed.) and 'Wif-One' (or 'Helper-One'—ed.) Her, I will call Erdh' (or 'earth-mother'—ed.)."

Declared Red-One: "You are my own flesh and bones."

Am then said, "Multiply; dwell in the park. Eat from every tree save one: The Knowledge Tree. Whoso eats of that tree—dying, they will surely die. Hear me, my children, and heed my counsel."

Thus it was as Erdh' lingered hard by the forbidden tree, she heard a voice: *"Why behold you the tree's beauty and the beauty of its fruit? Come and eat."*

"I perceive this not to be my husband's voice," replied she. *"As for the fruit, Am forbids we even touch it, lest we die."*

"Discern you Am's oracle aright?" said the voice. *"Knowledge, not destruction, be the lot of those who partake of this fruit. You will become god-like, knowing evil as well as good."*

Erdh', looking longingly at the fruit, ate. Anon, gave she same to Red-One, her house-band (caretaker, or husband—ed.) who likewise ate. Erdh', reaching again up into the tree for more fruit to eat, was suddenly stricken by the Asp, most subtil of beasties, who by great stealth, lurked, hidden well within the tree's foliage.

She screamed. As she lay dying, Red-One felt new shame at their nakedness. So sewed he broad-leafed loincloths for to cover their shame. As Am sought them out in the cool of the day, they hid themselves. The voice of Am called out: *"Red-One, where are you?"* From behind a tree replied Red-One: *"We hid ourselves because we were naked."*

Replied Am: *"Who told you you were naked? Have you eaten of the forbidden tree?"*

Declared Am: *"Because you have disobeyed, I curse erd' with briars and weeds. Though your wife will recover from the venom, its pain will yet return to torment her when she bears her young. In toil and sweat shall you henceforth eat your bread until you return to the clay from whence you came.*

"As for the Asp: I will put hostility between your seed and that of the woman. Her seed shall crush your seed's head, albeit, your seed shall bruise his heel."

I, H'rshag, pondered the sayings of the obelisk.

Thus confesseth the Akri priesthood: At a time when nothing was, so assembled the gods for to decree the creation of all that now is. They then decreed the creation of one like unto them.

Yet they, having already given many graces and blessings to all other creatures had naught left to bestow on the Upright One.

Then determined one of the Sons of Light, Para-k'l-abv', to bestow on Upright One's brow a coal from off heaven's sacred altar. For this, he was banished from the presence of the gods.

Burned still the Sacred Fire within the upright one's bosom. At one time, life for the upright one was more pleasant than today. From our own illustrious Akir-Ema, we see marvels of the upright one's accomplishments.

We have houses for dwelling, for trade, for pleasure (brothels), for feasting (restaurants), for storage (warehouses), and for worship (temples.)

We see the accomplishment of roads, highways, ditches, and streets. We see aqueducts and canals; of craft, of all manner of (literature), of verse, and of musick. We see accomplishments of tillage; of the bringing forth from erd' all manner of fruit and grain, of milk, and the use of beasts for the easing of the upright one's burden.

At one time, he had as yet none of these, nor had he need of any: nor none of civilisation's amenities: nor needed he of any tillage. Upright One had only to reach up into the nearest tree to sate his hunger. He went about naked, needless of clothing to hide shame, nor yet to provide warmth.

Nor was fire needed to protect from the cold, nor yet to frighten away harmful beasts. In erd's paradies, civilised man's refinements were unknown and unnecessary.

Again the printer stopped. Beyond the glass patio doors, they could see the sun rising higher above the snow-capped peaks. For a moment they said nothing. She continued looking at the printout. She laid the paper aside.

Lost Atlantis, the Garden of Eden. Places long shrouded in the mists of myth and legend now came rolling off the printer from scrolls encrypted with mysterious, cabbalist symbols. Would such discovery beggar the credulity of the intellectual community to the point of summary rejection? Dare she even show it?

Slowly, painfully, she got up and limped to the computer. "I'm going to restructure the whole program."

"Language still too antiquated?"

"Yes."

A realization came to him. Their knapsacks still lay on the trail. He was tempted to just leave them to the elements. After all, were they perhaps already temping fate to the point of irresponsibility and recklessness? Perhaps unseen forces in expressing indignation at puny mortals challenging their power may yet have more unpleasant surprises in store.

Upon further reflection, he decided: No. He would do the heroic thing and defy whatever gods there be and go after the knapsacks.

Another thought brought him up short. What kind of pagan thinking was this for a child of the baptismal covenant? For the confirmed catechist? What claim did such heathen notions have on him? As he put on his jacket, Artie assured him that she would be all right.

He stepped from the cabin and savored the balmy air. Large chunks of heavy snow kept falling off the tree branches. Overhead the sky cleared to an indigo blue. Underfoot, the snow still lay deep and wet. The January thaw made going treacherous. He marveled at his ability to carry an injured Artie down that path a scant six days ago. For the next hour he continued stumbling through the forest before leaving the timberline and headed out over the open alpine tundra. A faint, balmy breeze fanned his face as he emerged from the dense, snow-covered forest. Once out from the heavy, wet canopy of evergreen, however, he felt the air grow raw and bitter. Breaths of pristine mountain air penetrated his nostrils, invigorating him and making him feel giddy at the same time.

He spent another hour hiking across an ice field and then onto bare rock. As the stony trail got rougher and steeper, his progress slowed more.

He paused and massaged knees that were beginning to pain him.

He tried to rub the circulation back into his injured joints. The trees back in the forest bent and writhed in the winds that buffeted the treetops.

The formations that stretched before him all had a certain sameness. Could he find that spot again? Gray cloudbanks began moving in across the blue skies overhead. The wind had now become a stiff, bracing force. How could an atmosphere that felt so mild and balmy back in the thick, dank forest suddenly change to such a numbing, frigid blast once he no longer enjoyed the shelter of the trees?

He stopped to blow on his stiffened hands. How could he have neglected to wear gloves? He spotted an eagle circling high above. As he watched, he noticed her soaring in wide, lazy arcs up against the tumultuous cloud formations. After a few minutes, she straightened out her circular flight pattern and flew in a northwesterly direction toward the horizon. She grew gradually smaller until she all but disappeared, becoming hardly more than a dot above the distant mountain range. For some unknown reason, he followed in the direction to which she had vanished.

He took his compass to make sure he kept going in the same direction. He didn't believe in portents, he tried to persuade himself; yet, absent any other guidelines, what did he have to lose?

He finally spotted an outcropping that looked familiar. As he trudged closer, he saw the knapsacks.

He stopped for a moment while yet a good quarter mile from the precipice and thought of what might have been had not that narrow ledge caught a severely injured Artie from plummeting a thousand feet or more. What if she had been injured so badly that he could not have moved her?

What if she had slipped from the rope as he strained to pull her up? What if darkness had fallen before they spotted the forest trail that led back to the cabin?

Clouds rolling high over the mountain range began picking up momentum. The wind created a whistling sound. The cold seemed to turn his face to granite. Slowly he resumed his trek to where the knapsacks lay. Slinging one over each shoulder, he started back, favoring his knees with each step.

A break in the clouds revealed an afternoon sun that had started to sink down behind the trees when he finally reached the timberline again. Looking deep into the forest he saw a figure standing in the path. There shouldn't be another human within miles.

As he got closer, he noticed that the figure looked like that of a young girl, probably in her early teens. She wore a knitted ski cap, pile jacket, and jeans; all quite appropriate for the winter mountain trail. The wind blew her long blond strands across her smooth face.

Even from the distance he could discern the delicate features. The resemblance they bore to the murdered child brought dark, wordless thoughts. It had to have been just a coincidence.

She gestured to him.

A gaze of fixed earnestness accompanied the gestures. How could a total stranger know who he was? Whatever was she trying to convey to him?

He hurried to get to the spot on the trail as quickly as the treacherous footpath would let him. His feet struggled in the wet, slippery snow and he found himself getting short of breath. *Not the lean, mean machine I was when I was playing,* he thought. *How quick you can get out of shape once those days are over.*

She now pointed toward the cabin.

This new turn in her behavior ratcheted up his sense of anxiety. What was going on anyway? When he arrived to where he thought she stood, he saw no one. Desperately fighting a sinking sensation he tried to ascertain whether or not he missed the trail somewhere.

The only tracks he could see were his own.

An inexplicable sense of alarm abruptly cut short any questions. What prompted him to start hurrying toward the cabin? He knew only that when the cabin came in sight, a premonition made him sense that something was wrong.

He stopped a moment along the trail. In the stillness, all seemed the same. The glow of the late-afternoon sun filtered through the heavy, snow-laden evergreen branches. The pale winter sun hung low on a horizon broken by dense bramble shrubbery. Weak shafts of light cast long shadows of naked aspen branches. The waning daylight and the oppressive silence precipitated dark thoughts.

Why this foreboding?

Suddenly he saw it.

Wisps of smoke rolling up along the eaves.

Seized with a fit of adrenal energy, he dropped the knapsacks and bolted up the trail toward the front door. Gray smoke billowed out as soon as he opened it. Choking, he pulled a handkerchief from his pocket and dipped it in the snow. Holding it over his face, he edged along the wall toward the kitchen.

The smoke seemed to roll up from the basement.

"Artie!" he called out in a voice muffled by the handkerchief.

No answer.

He turned and ran out the front door again. This time he raced around in back that led to the basement level. He slid open the door only to find smoke again pouring out. Just inside hung the fire extinguisher.

Thank God, he thought. He grabbed it and began spraying foaming effervescence into the smoke. In the dim, distant recesses of the basement he could now, through the smoke, see dull, red tongues of flame that hissed in protest as he squelched them with the white spray. Still coughing, he stalked the blackened basement in search of an electric fan. Upon finding it, he plugged it in, and let it begin blowing the smoky residue out the sliding glass door.

Once the basement had cleared, he tried to take a preliminary assessment of the damage. Charred papers lay everywhere. Filing cabinet and computer exteriors were blackened with ash, but the difficulty lay, on casual examination, in determining actual damage. Valuable stored information and priceless artifacts that were in jeopardy notwithstanding, one overriding anxiety now assailed him.

What about Artie?

He heard coughing from above.

Still holding his handkerchief to his face, he ran to the top of the stairs.

"I was tired," she explained, "very tired."

He pressed her close to him. "Never mind that now," he said. "Thank God you're safe."

He continued holding her for a moment. He savored the tenderness of her face and shoulders. He felt that she needed his protection. But, he wondered, could he protect her from everything? Are there forces against which even the brute force of a former football star is helpless?

He released her and again took a brief survey of the wreckage.

The fan had pretty much cleared the basement. He took it upstairs and proceeded to clear the living and dining area. It took some minutes before the house—upstairs and downstairs—had sufficiently cleared so that he could close the doors.

Arms folded, Artie stood shivering against the kitchen doorway. Huck studied her briefly. As he started loading logs onto the hearth, he also noticed the barn-like chill that pervaded the cabin's interior. Once he had a blaze crackling in the grate, he straightened up and looked outside. Darkness had already fallen in the yard and forest. He put the screen across the hearth and headed for the kitchen. A burnt smell still hung heavy in the cabin. He pulled a chair out from the kitchen table for her.

"Let's have something to eat," he suggested, "and then you can tell me what happened."

While preparing supper over the countertop, he studied her. He pondered misgivings that she occasionally shared with him about her premonition of a being a cosmic lightning rod. Question, she thought: where would the lightning strike next?

Over soup and sandwiches, she related how she had originally planned to skip lunch. Her leg pained her quite severely. Mid-morning, she took a pill. By afternoon, drowsiness had overcome her so that she could not continue.

She made her way upstairs to the bedroom intending to doze for fifteen minutes and then return to the basement. Her next recollection, however, was awakening out of a deep sleep to a house filled with smoke.

In panic, she struggled to the bedroom door. She heard him scurrying around in the basement, moving furniture and playing spray from the fire extinguisher into smoldering flames.

They tried to speculate as to the cause. As they rummaged through the basement wreckage, they concluded that it originated by the portable electric heater. They examined the spot where it stood and discovered that the intense heat had melted and fused much of the metal and rubber.

Artie struggled with the notion of the Babylonian curse. The more her rational mind tried to shout it down, the more intense became the conflict. Misgivings regarding the figurine also added to the turmoil.

Huck, for his part, felt he dare not mention the phrase "living in sin" to her again. After all, with a woman of her intellect and skepticism, it would be just too embarrassing.

THE DELUGE SCROLLS

Perhaps the claims adjuster from the insurance company could help.

The following days the claims people came out to examine the extent of the damage. That the insurance covered the computer and other office equipment came as good news. A cleaning company could get rid of smoke damage. The state of valuable records concerned them.

They found the exterior of the glass case holding the scrolls blackened by soot but undamaged. The computer had suffered heat damage and had to be replaced. Her software, filed away on shelves from the opposite end of the basement, might still be good. They would have to await the arrival of a computer replacement to know for sure. Once they had a new computer, things would again be back to normal.

Except for one detail.

Although the adjuster could not ascertain the cause of the fire, she did determine the heater to be the fire's origin despite its safety measures.

* * * * *

By February, with new and heavier wiring, Artie resumed working on her new programming amid a completely refurbished basement lab. She again tried running her new translation program through the computer.

One afternoon in early February, she looked out the glass patio door. The skies cleared to a brilliant blue. She could tell, however, from the hoarfrost on the tree branches that the weather had turned markedly colder. Was sending Huck out to cut firewood a good idea, she wondered? She felt the freezing air seep through into the basement lab despite a new portable heater turned up to high.

She pushed the "on" button and watched the screen. Before her appeared the following words:

Day 24: I, H'rshag and Shumrag my mentor, meet the Ancient Keeper and Ariel, the Watcher.

For a long moment Shumrag and I studied the words of the east obelisk. We suddenly realized that we were not alone. Over against the sand-brown cliffs at first appeared naught but bare, rocky emptiness. Then we saw at the mouth of the cave a man tall and lean of build. He appeared dressed in a long, woolen robe of coarse homespun. His skin looked sun-darkened. He was bald with a tight, curly beard, white as chalk. His eyes looked a near-transparent, light blue. His gesture of peace allayed our fears somewhat.

"Can I be of service?" His voice resonated surprisingly firm for one so old.

"We are priests of Akir-Ema," said my mentor.

"I know who you are," he announced.

"You have the advantage of us," said my mentor.

"I am called T'reni-akhmen. Keeper of this place for the Strong-Ones; a caretaker if you will."

"Do others here dwell with you?" asked my mentor.

"Save for a small remnant, for many years now," he replied, "I have dwelt here in solitude."

I then saw less than a dozen figures wrapped in homespun shyly peeking out from the mouth of a nearby cave.

"If I may be so bold, how old are you?"

"I am upwards of nine hundred years."

"Why do you stay here?"

"Many generations ago men from Ym', after long years of hardness of heart, began again to call upon the name of Am. I was appointed caretaker of these premises. The worshippers of Am established this spot as their sanctuary. Here they assembled once each year from all corners of the earth to worship Am and to celebrate his marvelous works of creation."

"Are the words of this worship," said my mentor, "on these two pillars?"

"They are the sacred words to our liturgy whereby we spent in celebration of a festival that lasted seven days. Each day was set aside in honour of a different day, or phase, of creation. We offered much sacrifices, much music, dancing, and drama—all depicting episodes of the Creation Epic. It was a time of great solemnity; yet a time of great celebration."

The caretaker suddenly seemed to wax much older than even his nine hundred plus years.

"Ah, the perverse heart of people," he sighed. "The Plain-Ones simply wearied themselves to worship in this manner. Gradually, year-by-year, the number who came dwindled until they ceased coming altogether."

"Why then do you remain?" I asked.

"Am placed me here," was the reply. "I should be obligated to remain until he removes me, perhaps in death."

"Are there none left now-a-days, that worship in the manner of the Plain-Ones?"

"None that I know of save my kinsman, Xisusthrus, a king; even as I am also an absentee king of a neighbouring city, in the land of Shurrupuk."

"And why does he not come?"

"I know not," said the venerable caretaker. "He spends all his time overseeing the building of a strange, sea-going craft, upon dry land, a great distance from any sea. Furthermore, for many years now he has been collecting and maintaining a vast menagerie of beasts; many and varied exotic species of every sort imaginable in a zoological park and a vast villa or game reserve. Why, I do not know."

I was startled by the appearance of another; a damsel who looked to be not yet twenty. A round face, smooth and fair looked upon me with eyes reflecting heaven's deepest blue. Hair the color of sunshine and the gold embossed robe waved gently in the mildly warm breeze. She stood dressed in a full-length linen robe. A bejeweled tiara of white gold and set with gems of every color crowned her head.

The caretaker sensed our puzzlement. "When I say we live in solitude," he explained, "I am honored on occasion by a visitor."

The damsel stepped forward. "I am Ariel." Her voice flowed in rhythmic flute-like syllables. "I am a Watcher."

My curiosity piqued to new heights. "A Watcher?" said I. "You are not mortal then?"

She smiled. "Once there were many of us who joined the terrestrials in their celebration here. On Day Seven, we joined the Plain-Ones in one final paean of praise. We formed as a choir over there."

She pointed toward the open stage area.

"It was a time," said the caretaker, "that the Morning Stars sang together and the Sons of God shouted for joy."

* * * * *

Day 25: Wherein T'reni-Akhmen gives account of Akir-Ema's origin.

Thus spoke T'reni-Akhmen: "Khai-nu, the Aquisitor (Cain –ed.) having slain his brother, Abv-el (lit.: Father—Strength, the Abel of Genesis—ed.) in a fit of jealousy was sent out by Am (The LORD) to a land east of Paradise: the Land of Ehrets-Nodh.

"Am's curse on Khai-nu was in the form of a second face that grew out of Khai-nu's forehead, smaller and having only one eye. Khai-nu, fearing that so fearful a disfigurement would make him so hated and scorned that he feared for his life. Am, out of compassion, then, assured Khai-nu that any who would harm him would pay seven-fold. Thus protected by Am, he settled here with his wife and little ones.

"Shortly, Khai-nu built a city and called it En-okh, named for his son. Four generations later there was begotten Lemekh (sometimes spelled 'Lamekh' or 'Lamech'—ed.), great-grandson of Khai-nu who renamed the city after himself. It was a time when this land was severely rent by warfare among petty chieftains. Lemekh, by military and diplomatic leadership together, was able to meld this entire fractious land into the illustrious Akiri Empire as we know it.

"And here is how he accomplished this: upon emerging victorious from battle, he would observe the defeated captives naked and in chains or shackled by fishhooks, being prepared for shameful exhibition. Such was the custom of victorious armies to parade their prisoners before the eyes of the civilian population. Immediately he flew into a wondrous rage.

"'I will not have this,' he thundered. 'Reclothe these men in their battle tunics; however, do not give them back their weapons. Do not parade them before me in disgraceful chains. Let them march before me in military formation as the honorable soldiers that they, in fact, are. Consign them, however, under armed escort not to slave dungeons, but rather to military barracks. Let them not spend their time in slavish servitude, but rather, continue to train them in warfare. Give them time to sufficiently grieve loss of nation, people, home, and loved ones. Then give them opportunity to make a choice; either bondage and servitude, or honorable military service in Akir-Ema's ranks.'

"Thus did the noble Lemekh deal kindly, wisely, and prudently with vanquished peoples. Thus did he win the hearts of many a rival clan until the Akiri Empire became as you see it today.

"Furthermore, Lemekh was such a mighty warrior that of all mortal men born of woman, he and he alone was ever able to kill a dreaded Nefilli warrior in mortal combat. Fearing vengeance from other Nefilli or their minions, he bound his family to the following oath:

"'Hear me, my wives and children: I slew one, not of hate nor malice, but rather of self-defense from one who intended to kill me. If my father, Khai-nu, would be avenged seven times, let me be avenged seventy times.'

"Alas, Lemekh's oath was never honored. One day, while he was at sea, a cowardly wretch struck him in the back, killing him. Then he threw him overboard. Instead of wreaking vengeance, his followers spread the story that he rose from the sea and returned to reside at the site of your temple."

Day 26. Wherein Shumrag follows up T'reni-Akhmen's discourse.

"The priests, fearful of what the people might do should they learn of Lemekh's death, erected the great statue of Lemekh and proclaimed him yet alive:

"'This, O People, is your god, Lemekh.
Bow in obeisance before him!
On pain of death, let none worship any
Save the great god, Lemekh!'"

Then T'reni-akhmen spoke: "I know of your mission. You desire to rescue the Lady Aarda from marriage to the Grand Vizier."
"You know this?" I gasped, astonished.
"It is the Me," he said. "By it I know many things."
"We plan," I said, "to enter the Forbidden Garden by stealth of night, subdue the small detail of guards who keep her under house arrest and spirit her off in the darkness."
"Such a scheme is doomed for failure," he warned. "It would be disastrous for all concerned. This is how you will rescue the Lady Aarda: to throw off suspicion, you will first arrange to have H'rshag out of the country. You will then wait until (Akiri version of Walpurgis Night—ed.) when the guards are well drunken. Next morning, when the guards are sufficiently hung over, you will instruct the Lady Aarda to dress in a coarse, homespun outer cloak of a female house slave, complete with hood and market basket. Escort her boldly. (For furtiveness of manner, you would readily give yourselves away.) Go three streets to a power-chariot previously made ready. Spirit her aboard the same and without delay bring her to this place. Here, I will be her guardian. Here, Ariel the Watcher will attend to her needs. Here she will remain until H'rshag returns from his foreign journey.

"The Grand Vizier is old and unwell. I think that he will soon go the way of all flesh."

Day 27: We take leave of the Keeper and the Watcher, leave the Temple of the Plain-Ones, and prepare for the diplomatic mission to the Kraaviki.

So spent we, then, many days in fellowship with our new-found friends. Many a night we sat around a camp fire listening to the patriarch and the Watcher tell of things of great mystery regarding the Me and of gods older than Lemekh; of the origin of the now deserted temple and of races of super beings from the realms beyond the pale of time and space: things which the gentle Ariel appeared wonderfully conversant. Our hearts burned within as we listened in wonder to these many strange and awe-inspiring tales of worlds beyond the heavens that shined above us.

We also learned of the Dark Side; of the origin of the Angry Things. We learned again of the Seven Ages prophesied in the Me tablets: the Age of Gold, the Age of Silver, the Age of Bronze, the Age of Iron, the Age of Lead, the Age of Clay, and finally the Age of Fire.

After many days, we took leave of our new-found friends: T'rani-akhmen, the venerable saint, his dwindling band of followers, and Ariel, the Watcher. With much heaviness embraced we the stalwart patriarch. Ariel, gentle pixie, reached out her hand and clasped mine. To the touch, despite the sorrow of parting, I felt a strange serenity. I saw in her eyes an earnestness too profound for words.

"Fear not, dearest H'rshag," she said. "All-That-Is-Good shall go with you."

A tear fell from her cheek to the ground. From the spot that absorbed the teardrop sprung up a Lilly-of-the-valley.

Lest night's darkness overtake us, we began our trek up the rocky trail laden with a generous supply of provisions, given through the liberality of our hosts. Nearly three days' hiking, then led us to where we left our power chariot. After an additional three days we finally again reached the provincial capitol of Basilea.

Here we feasted many more days at my father's home. Each morning as we would get ready to depart, our family would entreat us to stay yet another day. Come evening, we would vow that for sure on the morrow, we must be on our way. Again, in the morning, our family would persuade us to stay just one more day. Finally lest we wear out our welcome and become a burden, we set our foot down and insisted that tomorrow we would depart.

Our partying would definitely be at an end.

'On that particular day we rose early and once more set out for Akir-

Ema. While we were in the midst of bidding friends and loved ones goodbye, from out of the crowd a shockingly filthy little creature made his way straight toward me. His garment hung on his skinny body in tatters, barely covering his dirt-covered nakedness. His hair and beard hung about his head and shoulders impregnated with camel dung. As he approached me, I was barely able to breathe because of his stench.

His appearance bore all the marks of a shaman. As he neared me I stared in disbelief. Why must these so-called men of God feel the need to prove their piety by making their persons so repulsive?

Burning eyes shot through my being as his long, claw-like fingers reached for my silken mantle.

When the shaman seized my mantle he tore it two. Before I could demand an explanation, he held the pieces aloft.

"As this garment is torn asunder." His voice boomed out like a trumpet blast. "Just as surely will the owner be torn from his homeland."

Stunned, I remained rooted to the spot. What was this filthy little madman saying? Anger boiled up within me. I turned to my father and said: "Surely, good father, does Basilea so lack in lunatick asylums that raving creatures such as this pestilential fellow are allowed to run at large?"

My father and the others said nothing. They stood as pallid statues.

The shaman held up the pieces of my garment. "Doubt my word?" he cried. "You, a priest of all people? Yet you doubt my word?"

He threw the torn garment to the dust.

He shook his fist. "I have spoken," he shouted.

He then turned on his heel and walked away.

Trembling, I observed my father and the others, still standing with faces ashen gray.

Damnable little dung beetle anyway! How dare he and his ilk presume to speak on behalf of the Almighty? Are not we of the priesthood the proper spokesmen for Lemekh the Great?

Immediately my spirit became exceedingly troubled. Are not all citizens of Akir-Ema enjoined on pain of death to heed no other oracle than that of the statue that comes to life? Do not we priests hold exclusive prerogative to reveal divine truth to the people? How now do we allow these vermin-infested little vagabonds to usurp this office?

And yet, I also knew our empire's dirtiest little secret, namely that the whole system of divine oracles from a talking statue is but a fraud. Had this scurvy little maggot called our bluff? Is this shaman privy to the secret that haunts those of us in the priesthood?

Damnable, lying little flea-bitten weasels, thought I. They can't all be born seventh sons of seventh sons. Where then is their claim to prophethood?

Who speaks for God anyway?

Is it that the priest speaks to God on behalf of the people, and the prophet speaks to the people on the behalf of God?

How I longed to return to the great and sophisticated city of Akir-Ema and get away from this company of rustic bumpkins who with great superstition put such store in these ratty little fur-balls.

I wanted with dispatch to separate myself from their company, even though my father be among them. In great distress I picked up the remains of my expensive, silken mantle, now torn and dust trampled.

After more anxious moments, my party and I resumed our preparation for my long journey back to Akir-Ema.

No longer would I call Basilea my home.

Days later, when we finally arrived at the city gates, the keepers eyed us suspiciously.

"What is the problem?" we asked in great dismay. "We are priests who serve daily at the temple."

"You are spies," insisted the guard, "disguised as priests."

"Summon the Grand High Potentate," demanded my mentor. "Your commander will hear of this."

"We know you," said the guard disdainfully. "You have just come from the forbidden, desert temple of the Plain Ones."

A bolt of fear shot though me. Had we been followed? Something was wrong.

"Of a truth," said Shumrag, showing sudden boldness, "we did come from the Temple of the Plain-Ones. But what of that? Since when is it forbidden to visit a deserted temple while on furlough and not in neglect of our priestly duties? Since when is a sightseeing trip to a temple abandoned by a people long since vanished from the earth forbidden to priests of Lemekh?"

"The Grand High Potentate has so decreed," said the guard.

"Grand High Potentate Pyl?" my mentor asked in disbelief.

"Pyl is no longer Grand High Potentate," said the guard arrogantly.

"Impossible!" exclaimed my mentor.

"Rok had replaced him," sneered the guard.

"That scoundrel?" said my mentor, indignant. "Was he born or did his dad spend time wanking it out behind a cattle shed, leaving him as residue on a manure pile to be hatched out by the sun?"

"Have a care," warned the guard. "If you wish to keep your tongue, keep your tongue."

The loathsome sun-urchin (colloquial insult or put-down—ed.) then announced that we were under arrest. Shortly we were thrust into the Temple goal.

Day 28: I, H'rshag, and Shumrag are imprisoned.

So Shumrag and I were unceremoniously incarcerated in the temple gaol: no formal charge, hearing, benefit of counsel, or offer of bailments; because, near as I was able to perceive, a power struggle raged within the priestly hierarchy, and the new Grand High Potentate was a vile usurper; and that we had visited an ancient site of the Temple of the Plain Ones. This when we were not in active service at temple and thus could in no way be accused of neglecting our priestly duties. What foul conspiracy lurked behind all this concerned us sore. We, being locked in separate cells, were also cut off from communication with one another.

Our uncertainty was cut short, however, when one day the guards summoned us to have audience with the then Grand High Potentate, the High Priest Rok.

They led us into a palace foyer lined with a cordon of turbaned Numidian guards, black as soot and taller by a head than the average Akiri. They arrayed themselves in turbans and leopard skin battle tunics with wide leathern girdles. Each held a shield the height of my shoulder. They kept small bayonets or daggers strapped to each inner ankle with their sandals and leggings. Each also held at the ready a crossbow, battle-axe, or broadsword. The latter widened to the width of a man's thigh and had a blade honed keen enough to sever, while held stationary, a silken scarf floating downward past it through the air.

As the temple guards ushered us into the drawing room of the high priestly palace, we were treated to the sight of a man exceedingly fat, dressed, not in priestly habit, but in the gossamer film of a woman's garment. His face gave a bizarre appearance beneath a heavy layer of a woman's cosmetics, yet with massive jowls that looked three days unshaven. He, with eyes bloodshot and heavy with mascara, glanced at us with a jaundiced gaze. With dirty fingernails painted bright red, black hair in tight, little ringlets, and ears pierced with ornate golden earrings, he appeared before us a veritably repulsive mountain of a man, lolling about on a wide couch covered with overstuffed satin cushions.

"Good morrow, gentlemen," greeted he us as he passed a perfumed silken scarf under his nostrils.

He followed up his greeting with the command: "drop your breeches." (Begging your pardon, sire?)

"Since I am in such a foolishly generous mood," said he, "I will do what I seldom do, namely repeat my command. Gentlemen, drop your breeches." (We complied.)

"Now turn around." (We complied.)

"Now thrust up your tunics and bend over." (We complied.)

"From this degrading posture we could look back and see him fold his hands in complacency. "And now, gentlemen, state your business."

"What is the meaning of our incarceration?" demanded my mentor.

"Not so fast," replied the usurper. "I have questions to ask of you." So saying, he paused and dipped fingers thick as sausages into a goblet of water and rose petals.

"You must excuse the attire," he went on. "You see, I find it very relaxing when in the privacy of my own quarters and not having to wear the vestments of my office, to recline in the soft, comfortable clothing of a woman. Do not misconstrue this to mean that I am one of those deviant fellows who take delight in parading around in female disguise. I am, in fact, every whit as manly as any."

He took a pinch of dried lotus leaves from a small urn and sniffed them up his nostrils. "You demand to know of me the meaning of your arrest. Very well, I demand to know the meaning of your unauthorized trip to the forbidden temple."

"We thought no authorization necessary," replied my mentor. "We knew not that the Holy See deemed the abandoned site of an ancient temple in an uninhabited wilderness be so threatening to the mighty Lemekh that its visit be forbidden to his priests."

"It was once a place of worship to gods other than Lemekh. Therefore even the brief visitation to such a place cannot be allowed; not to any citizen of Arki-Ema and certainly not to his priests."

"I am well versed in priestly law," said Shumrag. "I know of no such proscription."

"Out of ignorance, then, shall we say? It is a factor in your favor. This gives me justification to grant the two of you clemency. Otherwise, you both could even now find yourselves being made ready for the rack."

He plucked a confectionary from a bowl of figs dipped in honey.

THE DELUGE SCROLLS

"Shumrag, you may redeem yourself. You will be given a chance to prove yourself yet loyal to the priesthood."

He picked up a fan of ostrich feathers. "Pyl, the former Grand High Potentate, is still at large. He must be hunted down and killed."

The usurper stopped, sat upright, and leveled a hard gaze at Shumrag. "And that is where you come in. Your mission is to hunt down and kill him. You are to make it look like an accident. If you fail, or refuse; it will be your life for his."

"Why must I seek the Grand High Potentate's death? I neither hate him, nor do I know his whereabouts."

Rok's puffy lips broke into a smile. "I am giving you this task precisely because you do not hate him," he said. "He considers you as friend. He trusts you. He no doubt will come to you for help. Again, I warn you, if you fail—"

The usurper paused and again shot us a hard look. "It is I who am now Grand High Potentate. Pyl is now nothing more than a common priest such as yourselves."

He then turned to me. "As for you, my young friend, since you are new to the inner workings of the priesthood, I will exercise the greatest of leniency. I am sending you on a diplomatic mission to the Kraaviki."

He paused; then went on. "How dare you stand before me in so disgraceful manner? Get yourselves dressed and turn and face me like men. You behave intolerably, like the male temple courtesans. For shame!" (We complied.)

"Now off with you! Leave before I decide that the headsman's axe has thirst in need of being slaked."

Day 29: Shumrag and I are released from prison.

Convinced with the futility of further discussion with this misbegotten pig (colloquialism for "bastard"—ed.), we made egress from his presence in much troublement of mind

"Somehow," said my mentor, "I know not how, but I am bounden determined not to carry out Rok's dastardly order."

"How came such swine to the priesthood anyway?"

"Ah, my young friend," said Shumrag. "That's another lesson in your priestly schooling. You are forced to learn the sad fact that there are many villains and rogues in our ranks. You, being born seventh son of a seventh son and of noble birth are eligible to become even Grand High Potentate someday. Unfortunately, others have purchased their way into the priesthood. Still others have stolen their office by craftiness or even by force.

"Say you, then, that the entire system be built on fraud?"

"To clean up the hierarchal order," said Shumrag, with resignation, "would be akin to wet-mopping a dirt floor."

He looked furtively around and then continued. "But soft, I would counsel discretion when discussing these things."

"I would sooner, even at peril of my life, declare myself a follower of Am."

"Don't waste your courage on lost causes," said my mentor with a smirk. "Ponder this: the Strong Ones counts among his followers one solitary old man and an eccentric king of a Shurrupuki puppet state who spends his time on such foolhardy ventures as the keeping of large game and animal refuges and the building, on dry land far from any water, a strange giant sailing vessel. Lemekh, however, counts his worshippers in the millions."

Knowing the truth of what he was saying, I held my counsel.

"'Twas providential, was it not," said I instead, "that this misbegotten son of a dung-beetle (i.e. bastard—ed.) did sentence me to go on diplomatic mission to the Kraaviki, the very thing that we ourselves did plan? Is not this the doing of All-That-Is-Good?"

"Perhaps," was all the answer I received.

We approached the temple plaza; much consternation filled our bosoms as we surveyed the sacred area. Everywhere, the hallowed stone pavements were covered and besmirched with filth and leakage of dogs and men. To add to this horror, we also discovered that gold leaf had been stripped from the statue of Lemekh himself.

"Methought the statue to be solid gold," said I. "Never did I imagine him to be but gold leaf."

Where the gold had been stripped, there exposed underneath, were baser metals: up about the head, silver. The chest and shoulders consisted of bronze. About the loins it was made of iron. The upper legs were of iron and the calves were of lead. The feet were of a mixture of iron mixed with clay. (Cast iron? –ed.)

"'Tis ugly," said I beholding the statue. "That which I have long considered a thing of beauty is actually ugly."

Shumrag looked about. "Watch your tongue, my son," he said. "Such is the talk of suicide.

"Tis the work of the temple slaves. They show themselves to be true sons of bastardy. I see now how they will be the destruction of us all."

We parted vowing to meet again to make final my plans for departure. As I walked through the streets of the once beautiful city, I was saddened by the shabby appearance of many streets, boulevards, and villas. Dismayed was I at the careless, unkempt appearance of the passersby. The Akiri were a people aforetime, of which, took great pride in their grooming and their dress.

As I contemplated their slovenly state, I encountered a most pitiable figure huddling in the doorway of an abandoned shop. I recognized him immediately as the kinsman of my boyhood friend, Uliki, even though as he appeared wizened, old beyond his years. His stance was stooped; his hair gray; his skin wrinkled as a prune. His glazed, feverish eyes looked at me with a fixed stare.

"Wolki," said I in surprise. "Be it really you?"

"Bak-shish," he said, barely above a whisper.

I took him to my own villa. There, having given him quarters among my own staff, and having him fed, bathed, and given change of raiment, I enquired as to how he came to this pass.

"In my early youth; in my tender childhood," he began, "I was pressed into service at the temple."

Astonied, I asked: "As an apprentice priest?" (No.)

"As a man-servant, then? How is it that I never saw you?"

"Nor yet as a man-servant. 'Tis shameful to relate," said he.

"You are speaking of temple service," said I. "How is it you can speak of such a glorious calling in such a manner?"

"I served as a catamite," (male cult prostitute—ed.) he said. "As a young boy, I was pressed into this service."

Rose I from my seat, too shocked to speak. "Never have I heard such outrage," said I, when at last I found my speech.

"There is a secret order among the priests that make it common practice to keep children as courtesans. I was cast deserted and destitute to the streets when they wearied of me."

"By All-That-Is-Good," swore I, "I will dedicate my life to the downfall of these misbegotten scoundrels. (i.e. bastards.)

"I am ill," he said, gasping. "I am afflicted with pestilence. My days grow short. See to yourself, my good friend. There is much evil coming upon the earth."

"In the days ahead," said I, "I will be gone much of the time. However,

I will instruct my staff to take care of you. You will remain here in my household to be given food, clothing, and shelter, and whatever medicines can still do you good. I will see you again when I return." So summoned I one of my servants to my library and instructed him to take Wolki to his quarters. Afterward, I again sought out Shumrag to complete my preparations for the diplomatic mission to the Kraaviki.

Day 30: I, H'rshag, go on a mission to the Kraaviki.

The day of my departure finally arrived. I took final leave of my staff, of Dhjek, my steward, and of Wolki, my houseguest.

"If I am still alive then," he said sadly.

As Shumrag shunted me aboard his power-chariot to Akir-Ema's outskirts to a wide, plain expanse-plaza (airfield,) he showed a sense of urgency that my mission get launched.

When I enquired, he gave a most shocking answer: "I fear that Rok may yet want you as his courtesan."

I stared at my mentor. Memory of that fat degenerate casting eyes at me filled me with renewed dread.

"Let us cast off with all possible speed," said I when at last I found power to speak.

We took a section wherein moored a fleet of expanse-vessels (airships) were being readied. Companies of porters busied themselves loading provisions for a journey lasting many days.

The (airships) consisted of a (cabin) with deck (or floor) of hardwood. These were borne on a superstructure (fuselage) of light basket-weave (wicker) material. Placed at the superior end (bow) set the captain's cabin. Placed at the nether end (stern) set, banded (together) a battery of (power) jars (giant dry-cell batteries.) These were fastened in a running manner to a rope and belt that extended well beyond the (stern) of the gondola—(sometimes) one, two, or three fly fans (propellers) of great size the which to propel the craft through the firmament (air.)

Above our heads, held fast by sturdy rope and cable, hung a bag of skins finely sewn and stretched taut, containing a great quantity of heated breath (hot air.) To the center of the gondola's (deck) stood an earthen oven, for to heat the (air) within the gigantic bag.

To either side and extending out beyond the (stern) hung sails suspended and trussed to long poles. To these were also attached manifold rope and cable to a control center near the (bow.)

(*This evidently served as a system of controls for steering the vessel; a system similar to the wings and tailpiece of our modern aircraft.—ed.*)

From the mainsail, flew the Akiri crest: the Trident.

I mounted into the lead vessel, whereupon my captain ordered his signalman to wave the flag. Straightway then, did the power crew engage the (propellers) and straightway did the ground crew cut away the moorings. We rose into the (air) as the landmarks of Akir-Ema and his environs dropped below and away from us, shrinking ever smaller 'til we reached the height thereof of fast (almost) 500 cubits (750 feet) wherein our commander gave command to our steer-man (helmsman) to set sail full speed north by northwest, straightway setting sail a good 20 knots (about 20 mph) on a steady course.

Full two weeks traveled we when we stopped by a colony on the Isle of M'no (possibly Minos or Crete.) to the delightsome topaz expanse of the Great Inland Sea of Middle Earth (Mediterranean,) set in its easterly position as a large emerald jewel. There we refreshed ourselves with much food and drink and much rest. There we refurbished our store with new provisions.

"We have stayed here long enough," said I finally to my pilot. "Let us be on our way."

Sumrag's warning regarding Rok's filthy designs against me haunted me still.

Again, set we steadfast north-by-northwest for to reach the Great Northern Continent (Europe.) So sailed we o'er the boot-shaped peninsula (Italy) 'til we reached Hylvisi (Switzerland,) a land of much high mountain. Thence proceeded we further north to a most rugged, desolate land: a land of mountains and forests; a land bereft of cites and villages; a land bereft of tillage.

Of a late afternoon twilight landed we gently atop a bluff overlooking the Great River Flowing Northward (Rhine River.) So set our skilled crew, our fleet of vessels.

"Here before you," said my fleet commander, "lies the land of the Kraaviki."

My commander replied, "The Kraaviki are a people exceedingly shy. Perhaps here you can learn their reason."

He raised a ram's horn to his lips and blew a great blast. The sound thereof echoed against the forests and mountains many seconds before dying away.

We stood in silence. Ere lapsed a runner's league (about 3 min.) there appeared on the forest edge a man.

Stood he tall of stature, I trow (guessed) 4 cubits (6 feet) from foot to head. His countenance was handsome, strong looking, and regular. His brow was bushy but finely shaped. His high forehead denoted great intellect. His reddish brown hair hung to the shoulders. His ruddy complexion framed eyes of deepest blue. (We Akiri, by contrast tend to be of dark complexion and olive-colored skin.) His well-formed, muscular frame denoted great strength. He wore an animal skin tied about the loins. He wrapped his feet with animal fur and thongs of sinew. The chipped point of his spear appeared surprisingly sharp for so crudely fashioned a weapon.

I faced him and removed my helmet, slapped my breast, and bowed in gesture of peace. He made likewise gesture. So approached we one another and clasped our right hands in friendship.

"I am called H'rshag," said I. "I am a priest of Akir-Ema, sent on diplomatic mission to the Kraaviki."

"I am Yerrik," said he. "I am an elder of the A'rYanhu tribe among the Kraaviki nation."

Yerrik continued speaking: "The hour is late. The day is fast spent. I will summon forth my people and command them bring logs and bring great quantity of flesh of venison, of wild boar, of elk, of partridge, of skins of wine, of loaves, barley, and buckwheat, and rye, and of wild fruits, nuts, and berries."

From out the forest came great numbers of similar-appearing people: men, women, youths, and little ones: all dressed in animal skins. Some were fair of hair, others had hair the color of fire. All were an exceedingly handsome and intelligent-looking people. Amid great numbers of bonfires we roasted animal flesh and kept them burning brightly thru the night. This heavy meat, fat, and grease proved a great trial to Akiri stomachs. We, being a people accustomed to lighter fare of fruits, nuts, grain, and herbs, eat meat only on rare occasion, as on High Holiday.

Amid the revelry and merry-making, came Yerrik to me beside the bonfire. "On the morrow, you must leave."

"Leave?" said I in surprise. Leave and then what? Go back and face that loathsome beast, Rok? "But, my man," continued I, "we've just arrived. Why this unexpected tidings?"

His answer came in one word: Nefilli.

"I have something to show you."

I followed him a distance from the scene of feasting to a great cave.

THE DELUGE SCROLLS

"Many years ago," he said upon entering its mouth, "we were even as you: dwellers of cities and villages, tillers of the fields 'til the Nefilli grew numerous and terrorized our people. They plundered our villages, sacked our cities, and despoiled our fields. They ravished our women, devoured our children, and killed many of our warriors 'til we who were once a people prosperous and many, are now forced into hiding in these dank caves."

Upon plucking a torch from a cooking fire, took he me to the cave's nethermost depths. "Here," 'nounced he, "tell we the tale of our people." So raised he the torch and I saw scenes of the hunt, scenes of animals grazing. Saw I also paintings of the loathsome Nefilli and of the brutish Ogoru.

"We constructed these paintings well within the cave's depths," he said, "lest the Nefilli discover them."

After we admired the paintings for a moment, Yerrik again spoke. "If you are insistent on staying, tomorrow I will introduce you to our brothers, the Lake Dwellers."

On the morrow 'gainst the gray dawn, made we ready to depart for the land of the lake dwellers. Yerrik, having sent scouts on ahead to watch for signs of Nefilli: foot-tracks, droppings, trampled vegetation, their musk-scent, and the like, did lead our band out through nigh impenetrable wilderness.

After trekking many days through forests of pine and oak, came we to a broad lake surrounded by mountains. It sparkled in the brightness of a sun set high in an azure sky. Out in the midst of the lake stood a village of three score houses of wood, grass, and thatching, set atop a system of piling. From the shores stretched a log walkway outfitted with ropes and pulleys.

The lake dwellers are brother Kraaviki, Yerrik reminded me. Those who dwelt near caves, fled to the caves. Those who dwelt near lakes, fled to the lakes. Those who dwelt northernmost, fled to Dhul (northernmost lands of human habitation—ed.).

So started Yerrik and I across the walkway to the distant village. Warmly did K'ven, their chieftain, receive us. Thus spent we a goodly number of days basking in the warmth of their hospitality.

Day 31 : I, H'rshag, am captured by the Ogoru.

Of a truth, their agreeable company and generosity proved most comforting. I, for the nonce, quite forgot the prospects of returning to Rok's dangerous snares.

After many days of feasting and merrymaking, K'ven announced:

"Our larder grows scant. On the morrow we must organize a hunt to replenish our already empty supply of fresh meat."

I joined the villagers, then, in an expedition on the mainland. I carried a ram's horn to give a blast at the sighting of game, or to give signal should I lose sight of the others.

After hours of plodding through forest thicket, I could no longer hear the voice of my companions. Came I then to a forest clearing hard by an uprising of bare mountain rock that soared high into lofty peaks well above the clouds. Strained I my ears for the sound of my party. I heard naught but the shrill cry of alpine kite.

I raised the trusty horn to my lips and gave a view halloo that echoed 'gainst the distant mountain peaks, and answered from the forest below me. As the last faint echo died away, again silence greeted me. I listened. Even the forest birds forebore their singing. A sense of foreboding came over me. Was I alone?

Was I not alone?

I was not alone.

Suddenly appeared a man from out a nearby grove of forest. Appeared he so noiselessly, he fair startled me. As I studied him, and he me, I perceived him not to be of our hunting party. (Here H'rshag describes a creature bearing a striking resemblance to what paleontologists now call Neanderthal Man—ed.)

He held a spear cruder in fashion than even that of the Kraaviki. His countenance appeared brutish and exceedingly ugly. Suddenly others of his kind also appeared. For a moment that seemed an eternity, none of us moved.

Then, sensing danger, I sprang for a spot back into the forest thicket. The gang of rogues followed hard at my heels, bellowing and chattering in all but unintelligible gibberish. I found a trail and began my desperate flight there along. Fast (almost) had I reason to hope that I had made good my escape when suddenly I was caught up in a net made of grapevines and creeper that fell over me from the trees overhead.

Shortly there came running along the path these yowling louts, screaming their shouts of triumph at my capture. Cutting me loose from the vines, they thrust their evil, grinning faces close to mine, almost smothering me with their foul breath.

"Heh," shouted they. "Looka! We-guy gotta Kraaviki guy!"

One whom I perceived to be their leader spoke to me as he cut loose the vines. "Heh, you-guy no make trouble or we-guy wastey."

They pressed their spear points in my face in an attempt to frighten me.

I refused to show fear, thereby depriving them of their satisfaction. Tiring of their sport, they pulled me to my feet.

"Heh, you-guy come gentle, or we-guy break-y you-guy bone."

Thus began they to jerk me along, manacled, down the mountain trail all the while chanting: "Heh, we-guy gotta Kraaviki guy!"

One thought assailed me: Ogoru! They encircled me and taunted me, laughing and shouting in their gibberish among themselves. All the while they sought to intimidate me with feinting movements with their weapons. Worse by far, was the spittle with which they showered me as they gave themselves over to spitting on me.

I knew them not to be the ultimate terror: the dread Nefilli. The Nefilli speak in a low growl, mostly in single syllables. These fellows jabber in a high-pitched, flat nasal tone. This, in turn, caused probably by their flat nose formation, their low forehead, their thickness of tongue, and the sluggishness of their lip and speech muscles. My total feeling toward these loathsome creatures was not so much fear, but revulsion. How I would have loved to engage one of these dogs alone in a bout of personal combat; their powerful arms and shoulders notwithstanding.

Wearying themselves at last of their sport, they marched me down the mountain trail to some unknown destination. I was tethered to two separate warriors, each continually tugging me in direction opposite the other. Each, in turn, would also express indignation when I went not his way, belaboring me with his spear shaft when I failed to do so. The others circled and would occasionally close in and strike or spit on me. Adding to my torment was the roughness of the path. I would occasionally lose my footing altogether and stagger like one drunken among the loose stones. My inability to walk in a straight manner seemed to anger them all the more. Thus I walked in torment, becoming quite bruised and sore from so shameful a treatment.

Late in the day—I being in much weariness and soreness of body and of mind at this point—we finally stopped. Paused we along a rugged ridge of rock overlooking a valley. Below us lay a small village of huts crudely fashioned of rocks, twigs, and branches. Columns of smoke spiraled slowly up from clay chimneys. This perceived I to be our destination.

Quickly, unceremoniously, was I dragged down that last bit of rocky trail to the rude village in the hollow. Even though the buffetings and taunting were here actually the worst of my whole sorry trip, I was grateful that the miserable journey was at last at an end. I was confident that whatever fate awaited me could be none the worse than the march of agony which I had just endured.

I could not have been more wrong.

Quickly, I was dragged still further 'til we came to a long structure larger than the rest. This I took to be the house of their chieftain, king, or whatever overly pretentious title he fain would call himself.

Suddenly came we to a halt at the threshold. All cacophony had ceased. I derived small comfort to observe that these beasts be capable of paying deference to anyone.

Our leader stepped to the large rough-hewn wooded door and knocked—a knock surprisingly gingerly for so uncouth a fellow.

A gruff voice from within bade us enter. Someone pulled open the massive doors, revealing to our eyes a kind of great hall. Suddenly I was thrust into the interior. Just inside the threshold, warriors with crossed spear shafts barred further entry pending their leader's leave to do so.

Straightway, I saw one of their kind in a skin loincloth, pieces of metal armor and helmet. This was the first indication I saw of any capability of metal craft on their part.

"State your business!" ordered he in a voice that grated like twain millstones a-grinding. "See that you are brief."

Our leader bowed low. "O, great and benevolent one," said he in speech and demeanor far different than that on the trail. "We have captured a Kraaviki at great risk to ourselves. Were it not for the valor and fighting skill of my men, he would have slain the lot of us. Him we now present before you."

"Enough!" shouted the one on the throne of logs. "I know all about your valor and fighting skill. How dare you seek to bamboozle me with your inflated stories of your prowess? You dullards are like cattle. You'd do well to match your fighting skill with that of a wild boar or ox."

The council hall fell deathly still.

The leader continued: "Kraaviki is he? If he be Kraaviki, then I shit feathers."

Suddenly I was thrown to the floor, and seized by my hair. I felt my head lifted up until I faced my inquisitor and the keen blade of a broadsword pressed to my neck.

"Who be you?" he demanded. "Whence come you and what is your business? If you would live long, answer me plainly, briefly, and truthfully."

"I am called H'rshag," said I with all the respect I could summon. "I am an Akiri priest sent on diplomatic mission to the Kraaviki."

"Akiri?" said he thougfully. "Diplomatic mission?"
He paused.
"We shall see how you like spending your diplomatic mission in our keep," he said slowly, deliberately. "I will have more to do with you later."
He turned to his guards. "Tell our warder this one is his. His own life be in jeopardy should he let this one escape."
He made a final sweep. "Guards, take him away."
Two burly guards held my arms in an ironclad grip as they ushered me out of the room.
He then turned to the ones that bro't me. "As for you—out! Your sycophantic twaddle wearies me such that it makes the braying of wild asses like music to my ears."
Quickly the guards dragged me to another building; one with but one small window, high on the outside wall. They took me to the oaken entrance and introduced me to the warder, relaying to him their leader's orders me-ward. He led me over the threshold and thrust me through an inner door. I heard a heavy door of oak and metal slam behind me and a bolt slide in its lock. Quickly, I took stock of my surroundings.
Directly overhead stretched a ceiling of rough-hewn timbers. In the center I saw what appeared a kind of trap door. The stone cell had but one small window well above my head. Only the weakest shaft of light beamed down at a remote angle. The filthy, rancid place was furnished with naught but matted straw, reeking of men's leakage.
I heard the slamming open of a bolt. Then I saw the opening of a smaller door built into the larger door and against the floor. Through its opening I saw a wooden platter shoved through bearing a bowl of raw grain and a pitcher of lake water.
I heard my guard shout through the door. "Kraaviki dog, hear well my instructions. I say them but once. This, your ration, will be thrust through this door daily at this time. Eat well (such irony!). Do not try to confiscate any of the utensils, or try to communicate with me or any other guard at any time, else shall this ration be withdrawn. Do not dawdle. You have only brief moments before this tray will be withdrawn. If you value your appetite, follow my instructions implicitly."
So partook I my first meal in their keep.
In the meanwhile, indescribable despair overwhelmed me. What plans have they for my torture, torment or execution? What painful and degrading treatment have they planned for their sport and amusement?

Dark thoughts assailed me. What gruesome fate awaited me here? Yet, should I be released and return to face Rok's lecherous clutches, what then?

Was the shaman's oracle coming to pass?
As my fears and anxiety knew no bounds, I waited.
As hours passed into days, I waited.
As days passed into weeks, I waited.
As weeks passed into months passed into years, I waited.

Day 32: De Profundis (Out of the Depths.) (H'rshag's Lament that he scratched on the wall of his cell with a small stone while confined by the Ogoru—ed.)

Out of great depths I cried to All-That-Is-Good.
In great darkness of cell and of spirit, I sink in despair.
I sink in deep mire where no standing is.
My spirit writhes in the Pit of Tumult.
Billows of a thousand sorrows roll continually o'er my head.
I am locked out of life
And imprisoned in the Land of Death:
That dread realm from whence no man returns.
I am a worm and no man
And have become a stranger to happiness.

Oft' have I paid vow and supplication to All-That-Is-Good.
Should he deign to release me from this hell
Will I yet again stand at the threshold of his Temple?
With unfeigned thanks I will offer the great Sacrifice.
With evr'y strength of my bowels I will pay ev'ry vow.
Here in the silence of stone and filth
I languish; I fain would e'en welcome
The voice and countenance of my tormentors.
This solitary darkness be worse than the rack.
The wheel or pillory would be welcome relief.
By what delicate thread hold I my reason?
By what tenuous bonds be there
That keep me from total madness?
I cry, and am answered only by the mockery

THE DELUGE SCROLLS

Of my own echo.
Day unto day I cry my eyes to near blindness.

Without benefit of mirror,
I can tell my countenance grows hollow and sunken.
My beard, unshaven, grows past my chest.
My head hair has become like a magpie's nest.
My splendid priestly garb rots and falls off my body.

I watch myself grow into a wizened old bag
Of wrinkled skin and bones;

An ancient before my time.
Strength and vigor of my youth
Long since have been sapped from me.
Lying in my own filth, my body has become
Encrusted with boils.
In the daytime, I long for night.
In the night seasons, I am assail'd with such nightmares
That I long for day;
All the while I long for death.

O, that I would again drink deliciously
Of the beauteous sunshine.
O, that I again would breathe air
Fresh and free from the foulness of this prison.
O, that I again could see a friendly face.
If there be any other Strengths in all this universe
Other than that dumb, leaden statue that defrauds
multitudes,
And remains fixed, immobile, a continent away,
I beseech Such a One: Hear me. Take pity on me.
Deliver me.
Give me yet cause to rejoice in the land of the living.
Give me yet cause to rejoice as I walk free upon the earth.

Day 33: I, H'rshag, am delivered from the captivity of the Ogoru.

I, H'rshag, being languished in this gruesome dungeon fast (almost) twenty years, (I, long ago, having devised a calendar by scratching symbols on my prison wall with a small, sharp stone,) lay one evening on my bed of filthy straw and rush weed and having recited my poem of lamentation for the untold thousandth time, I began to notice something strange.

I heard the sound of the door-bolt sliding across.

What meant this? Was my jailer at last going to bring my meager ration into my cell personally, rather than slide it thru the smaller door? Was I going to be honored with a visitor? Was I going to be released?

Or—was I at last being summoned before the Ogoru leader or his council for inquisition? Or, was it time for my torture or execution?

My dread heightened as the great door continued to slide open.

My consternation abated not-at-all when my jailer appeared. This one looked not-at-all like the other Ogoru. This one wore a long robe of gray homespun of very crude weave, but weave nevertheless. Up to this moment, I would have sworn that the stupid louts knew not how to weave.

A broad cowling also covered the head and face.

I noticed also the hands that held the ration tray. They did not have the appearance of the large, hairy hands of the Ogoru. Rather, they appeared small and smooth looking, rather like those of the most delicate of mortal damsel. The figure, too, instead of thick, squat, and brutish, stood slight and slender.

My jailer placed the ration tray at my feet, and then pulled back the coarse woolen cowling that covered the head. 'Twas then that I espied the long locks of hair the color of simmering sunshine that fell to the shoulders. 'Twas then that I saw that round face with features so celestial fair. 'Twas then that I looked into earnest eyes the color of the deepest heavens. 'Twas then that I fell at the figure's feet and clasped the knees.

"Ariel!" said I weeping. "Ariel, O thou blest heaven-sent sprite! How impossible for me to contain myself for joy at the sight of thy fair countenance."

She kissed her fingertips and pressed them to my brow.

"You are greatly loved," she said. "I fain would have come sooner, but the whole evil hosts of Angry Things were in array against me. Finally I had to summon help from Mik-hai-el, the mighty arch-messenger himself."

She gestured to the ration tray. "Take and eat, humble fare though it be. You must prepare yourself for great journey."

I pondered with great puzzlement at her last saying.

"Your days of captivity are ended," she added. She pointed to the window. Suddenly I realized it to be within my reach; a thing not possible when first I was thrown into this awful hole. Then I realized what had taken place: The brutish captors never changed the straw or rush weed but rather, from the trapdoor overhead, merely threw down fresh straw on top of the older, dirtier stuff. Over the years, it became such a buildup of floor matting that I could actually reach the window.

Aha, thought I in triumph. The blessed Ariel has foiled that flea-bitten little shaman.

As I reached the narrow ledge, I also discovered that because I had waxed more thin and wan over the years, I could now slide through the narrow opening quite easily.

"You have are now quite capable of engineering your own escape," she informed me. "I have only to cast your captors into a deep sleep until you have put yourself a goodly distance from them."

Gently, she helped me slide through the narrow window. Anxiety again rose within me as I noticed its distance from the ground. However, she then showed me how a nearby tree which had been but a sapling at my capture, had, over the years, grown into a mighty oak. Grasping its branches and easing myself to the ground now became a simple matter, even in my weakened state.

"Do not delay," she whispered from the window. "Go quickly to the forest edge, I will meet you there."

At the deep forest's edge, then, she stepped out from a nearby thicket. Night had fair fallen by now, but the shimmering light of a full moon lighted the forest.

Ariel gently took my arm. "This way," she said.

A full four hours or thereabout we walked, 'til the moon sank from the sky.

She of a sudden kissed me most sweet and tender on the cheek. "Follow the owl," she said.

And I saw her no more.

Day 34: I, H'rshag leave for the land of the Kraaviki.

With the blessed Ariel no longer at my side, I stood alone in the strange, dark forest. Off among the trees, I heard a cry high pitched and quivering that caused goose flesh arise on my arms. I glanced up and saw the soft, shadowy form among the branches of a giant oak. Noiselessly, she raised her wings and flew to another tree.

Again she began her plaintive call. I followed to see her fly to a still more distant branch.

Come daylight, weary of my nocturnal travel, I breakfasted on berries and lay on a bed of pine needles and betook myself a nap of sleep. Late afternoon, I awoke and started slowly through the forest.

As darkness fell, I heard again the plaintive wail. Understood I not which of the twain: were the creature merely a citizen of the forest or, was my little companion actually the Watcher in another form.

After many days' travel, I finally came to the land of the Lake Dwellers. I looked out across the blue, shimmering waters and saw naught but burnt ruins and stump pilings. I sank to the ground in full despair. It was then that I noticed something wonderfully strange.

I saw Lilies-of-the-Valley growing wild.

(I, H'rshag, digress to mention what was later revealed to me by the celestial child, Ariel.

(The loutish band of Ogoru would have made merchandize of me. In their evil cunning they appraised, perhaps rightly so, that my person could bring a princely sum in ransom.

(They had intended to contact K'ven and his Kraaviki clan that they should, in turn, make contact with the Akiri Grand High Potentate that my freedom could be had for a price.

(The Kraaviki, for their trouble, could enjoy a season of peace with the villainous Orgoru. The nefarious scheme, however, went awry on two counts. Shortly after the Kraaviki had sent away their envoy to the Grand High Potentate and as the Kraaviki continued holding counsel with the churlish Ogoru, Nefilli suddenly attacked the lake village.

(The Ogoru, being kin to the Nefilli, stood aside and watched the carnage in silent approval.

(Rok, with thirst for revenge overcoming perverse lust, refused to pay ransom.)

Wearily, I again fell to slumber. Again, at nightfall, I awoke to the call of the owl. Again, I followed her through the forest. I continued weeks more until I came to where the forest was at an end beside a broad, sandy expanse of sea.

Following the shoreline, I came to a rude village. I was cautious until I met the inhabitants. The people were short, stocky of limb, rather like dwarfs; homely and plain of countenance, yet friendly. They took me to caves wherein they worked with fire and metals over forge and anvil.

They gave evidence as craftsmen possessing great skill and cunning.

"We are called Nibel'," said their leader. "The Ogoru keep us in subjection. Perhaps your people can help us rid ourselves of this scourge."

The truth was out. The Ogoru possess neither knowledge nor refinements of art, nor of craft, but rather they depend for their temporal well-being on their exploitation of others.

With the help of the entire village then, set we to the task of building me a staunch outrigger; a sea-going vessel.

We constructed a raft built of great logs. On the deck set we a tent shelter, a mast, and sail of animal hides sewn together. Having also generously outfitted me with many provisions for many days and a stone anchor with a good, stout length of rope, they saw me off as I launched out to the distant horizon.

Fair winds carried me speedily out across the vast expanse of sea. The shores wherein dwelt the Nibel' soon dropped from view. I heard the shriek of a lone seagull. She circled my craft once and then headed off to a northwesterly direction. Perceiving my slowness to so set my course in that direction, she returned and began circling my craft once more. Taking this to be an omen, I straightway reset my course for the northwesterly direction.

After a scant three days I sighted the headland of a strange, new shore. It appeared to be in the formation of high, white cliffs. (Probably the south coast of England—ed.) I knew this land to be an outpost colony of the Akiri Empire.

I finally landed with the incoming tide. Having beached my vessel well up on the shore, I started inland in search of habitation. The following morning, I reached a village set in a verdant meadow. After properly identifying myself with my signet and medallion to the elders, we sat at meat in the great hall and held council. When I had rehearsed all that befallen me since leaving the Akiri airfield now many years past, they turned to me with countenance grave.

"It is not well with the empire," the chief elder informed me. He went on to relate how many citizens have ceased serving the god, Lemekh. Word of the fraudulent nature of the Statue has gotten out.

This became plain to the people over a misadventure at the mountain of fire. The sacrificial virgin that followed my own Lady Aarda was in like manner thrown over the precipice. However, the net broke and she fell screaming into the volcano. The temple guards, fearing for their lives over *their error, secretly kidnapped a young peasant girl to keep hidden in the secret mountain chamber in the poor victim's stead. She was then spirited to the Temple Secret Garden. She was bidden to silence on forfeiture of her life. She, nevertheless, successfully escaped from the Temple Secret Garden and straightway noised the truth abroad.*

"Since that day all has changed," the elder concluded. "Attendance at the high and holy festivals has dwindled. The priests themselves have become exceedingly corrupt and depraved."

At the end of the council table rose another elder, hoary and grave of demeanor. His crushed velvet robe of indigo marked him as one of the ten Grand Princes of the empire.

"A year ago, I attended my last Five Year Council Feast," he said. "I left early in disgust.

"No way did it resemble the refined and elegant celebrations of the past. Rok and his gang of obese usurpers have completely debased all that was good and noble about Akir-Ema. The filthy gluttons have given themselves over to every fleshly appetite. They order naked slave girls to serve them on giant brazen platters whole roasted camel, all basted with highly spiced juices and gravies. Within the belly of this camel lies a roasted calf or pig, heavily laced with oregano and bay laves. Within the belly of this beast lies a goat or roast lamb packed with mint. Inside the lamb lies a roast goose or duck garnished with basil and oozing grease. Inside this lies a roast quail or rabbit.

"The slave girls then serve them wine from giant hogsheads into goblets the size of buckets. This then is accompanied by pastries, dainties, and candied fruits of very kind.

"When the festivities had gotten full underway, Rok would cast away his priestly robes and step up to the table top. Here he would dance naked, in mock manner of the slave dancing girls. The hall would rock with raucous laughter, as others would join him. Soon the tables would collapse under their weight and the air would fill with flying food and eating utensils.

"Some, having their surfeit of drink, would rise unsteadily from their tables, stagger bleary-eyed and delirious, and so besmirch the gorgeous banquet hall tapestries with their leakage. Others would sicken from overmuch food and drink and retch until the floors became slick with their spillage. Others in drunken rage would draw scimitar or knife and fall to fighting until the floor was awash with blood as well.

"The masquerades have degenerated into mass orgies. Entertainers meanwhile continued with depraved acts of torment of people and animals, and of debauchery.

"Above the screaming and carousing, the musicians continued with their heavy beat upon their percussion instruments, adding to the cacophony of laughing, grunting, belching, farting, and vomiting of the revelers."

Stunned, I stood to my feet at a total loss to respond. "Akir-Ema is finished," I creaked hoarsely when at last I found my voice. "Such outrage is an offense to both gods and men. It cannot go on. This is the end."

"The priests also seem oblivious to the loss of support among the people," continued the elder. "They seem almost eager to willfully delude themselves that the god, Lemekh, matters any more. Many among the populace worship in strange and terrible cults; adopting the worship of the Angry Things with the Nefilli and the Ogoru. Many others serve no god at all, save their own bellies. Hudishi rove the streets in lawless bands terrorizing the people. The once proud and beautiful capital, Akir-Ema, is but a squalid slum. Many of the colonies are in open revolt."

The Great Colony in the Great Western Sea (Atlantic Ocean—ed.) has declared itself independent from all ties with the Akiri home island. Many fear it will be but a matter of time before Lemekh becomes as forgotten as is All-That-Is-Good who was once worshipped by the plain ones of Ym'.

The elders took me to an open area and showed me an ancient shrine. "This shrine like many others like it on our island is still a source of great mystery to us. Will our statue of Lemekh someday be as great a mystery to future peoples?"

Artie stopped the printout. Only then did she realize that it was late afternoon. She had been running the printer all day without a break. *I'll have to show this to Huck when he gets back*, she thought.

Just outside the patio door, the setting sun cast weak sunlight and long shadows on the snow, shrubbery, and bare tree branches. She did notice, however, the lengthening February days as the sunlight played off the distant mountain peaks.

She pushed the "print" button.

Many days passed since our visit to the Park of the Shrine. On a day I approached my elders. "I feel constraint to return to Akir-Ema," I said. "Bodes it well with her, or ill."

When they saw that their pleas that I remain were to no avail, they consented to prepare me for my departure homeward.

After many more days' preparation, we took a power-chariot to an airfield where they had a fleet of airships of their own. These they outfitted with provisions and a skilled crew, making ready for take-off. After several weeks' flight over the Great Northern Continent and Great Inland Sea, we again touched down at the colony outpost of (Crete.) Three weeks later we finally touched down at the airfield of Akir-Emka. From the air, the city did not look much different than when I left it years before.

I was to discover the differences upon reaching the ground.

Day 35: I, H'rshag, am charged with treason.

Scarcely had we touched down when we were met by the elite priestly guards. They greeted our mooring in stony silence.

"Come with us," the most high official bade me.

"Of course," I replied. "I know that the Grand High Potentate requires a full report of my diplomatic mission to the Kraaviki."

"He requires nothing," he said, "save your arrest."

I stared in disbelief. "Surely you jest."

Dismay within me knew no bounds. "But why?" I asked. "What are the charges? Pray tell me the nature of my offense."

"You will be told in due time," said the captain. "Come with me now and give us no trouble."

Bereft of choice, I followed him, leaving my fleet of airships and its crew at the airfield. Two lieutenants at either side ushered me away under armed escort. I fancied myself to shortly be sealed up in some loathsome donjon or gaol; or perhaps to be made ready for the rack or the wheel and thus be examined by inquisitors under some gruesome torture.

My worst fears were abated somewhat by the captain's next words: "You, being a priest and high-born, will be remanded to your own villa under house arrest. You will thus be assigned under cognizance of your chief steward, Dhjek. Only have a care that you do not leave your property."

As I was shunted aboard the guards' power-chariot, I saw fair close, how time had changed the noble city, Akir-Ema. My dismay knew no bounds at the filthy and shabby condition of the streets and their state of desertedness. Neither voice of merchant, nor yet the merry shout of children rang through the avenues and boulevards. Many houses, buildings, and villas languished in the worst of repair. Many appeared abandoned; their shutters hanging shut, or worse, hanging open at a crazy angle on but one hinge. Many stood in squalor, their paint and pastel colors faded and peeling; their roofing lacking in tile shingles. Stench of garbage and refuse rose to assail the nostrils. Many of the banners and flags of heraldry hung tattered and listless, or were missing from their staff altogether. Many of the trees and shrubbery were choked over with weeds and undergrowth. With great relief I at last sighted the approach of my own villa.

So it was that I was handed over in cognizance to my steward, Dhjek, by the guards that accompanied me from the airfield. Moreover, the captain of the detail did also leave behind a small detachment of foot guards to remain at the villa. As I entered my own estate, I studied Dhjek carefully to see any change in his attitude or his demeanor toward me. He, however, remained respectful and correct. I initially found nothing untoward nor cause for alarm.

This, then, ill prepared me for the shock I received when I noticed Dhjek's feet.

I saw him shod with sandals. (Akiri slaves customarily went about barefoot.—ed.)

"Halloo, what's this?" said I giving him a hard look. "Aren't we the presumptuous one now?"

I gestured toward his extremities. "How dare you stand shod in my presence? Remove those shoes at once!"

I noticed a smirk as again he gave a bow of feigned obeisance.

"My lord," said he. "All due respect, but the magistrate has declared you to be in my cognizance. He has ordered me to wear these as a reminder to the both of us as to the change in our relationship."

Consternation filled my being as I contemplated the unthinkable. The drunken lords who now hold sway could, on a whim, order my execution and award my entire estate and all my other slaves to this scoundrel

I now felt totally powerless.

As if that were not enough, I found a sealed parchment in a teakwood box hidden in a secret vault within my bedchamber. I discerned it to be the handwriting of Wolki. In the long, dreary months of my confinement, I had quite forgotten about the poor fellow. I read the following message:

"To H'rshag, honorable friend and benefactor:

"It has now been many months since I have had the joy of being in your presence. I fear that some great calamity has befallen you.

"I, myself, am failing in health by the day. By the time you read this, I could very well no longer be in the land of the living. Therefore I feel constrained, while yet alive, to write you tidings exceedingly painful for me to have to tell you.

"My word, simply put, is this: Dhjek, your chief steward, is not to be trusted. More I cannot write. I am being watched.

"Hoping and praying for safe and speedy return; thanking you for your every kindness, and still rejoicing at the very memory of you, I remain your most obedient servant.

"Wolki."

I returned the parchment to hiding. In great confusion, I repaired to my own bed. However, all sleep had left me. The next day the temple guards detachment returned to escort me to the presentment. Soon I stood before the grim-visaged magistrate.

"This but a preliminary hearing," he announced. "This is not the final assize (trial.)"

He pointed to me. "Lord H'rshag, priest of Lemekh and citizen of Akir-Ema, you are hereby charged with high crimes and treason against the nation of Akir-Ema."

I sensed color leaving my face.

"How answer you?" he said.

"I know not the nature of these charges," spoke I faintly, "nor yet the nature of my offense."

The magistrate plucked a scroll from his bench. "You are charged in the kidnapping of the Lady Aarda, espoused to the Grand Vizier."

My Aarda! With racing heart, I struggled to keep my counsel.

"How plead you?" he demanded.

I remained silent.

"So," he continued, "stand you mute then? Very well. You shall be bound over to High Court. You shall remain under house arrest until your trial." With his mace he forthwith struck the floor and announced, "This court session is hereby dismissed."

Shaken, I left the court chamber and was returned to my villa. That night, as I again tossed sleeplessly upon my bed, the sound of a hard object falling to my bedchamber floor startled me. I spotted a rock lying just inside my bedchamber window. Someone had thrown it from outside. Soon I heard the sound of someone crawling in the garden. Stepping to the window, I saw the most welcome sight of the silhouette of a figure bathed in the moonlight.

"Shumrag," I whispered. With great haste, yet with great stealth, he climbed thru the window and joined me in my bedchamber. We wept and embraced, taking care not to waken the household. We spent the next hours rehearsing all that befallen us these many years.

"I am a fugitive," he said. "An outlaw. I have been living all these years like a hunted animal, all because I refuse to be a party to a plot to assassinate our rightful Grand High Potentate.

"We of the underground have been following your case with much interest. You will receive a caller. Billiku, the most respected lawyer in all Akir-Ema, will represent you well."

Shumrag again stepped to the window. "I will stay in touch," he said, climbing out. "See that no one learns of our meetings."

"Wait," I said softly. "What of the Lady Aarda?"

"She is in good hands," he said. "She is safe in the care of the Keeper of the Temple of the Plain-Ones. Adieu, old friend."

In a trice, he was gone.

Finally the day arrived for my summons before the Grand Assize. At the two sides of the courtroom, at the back, and up in the balcony, sat high officials of the priesthood, court officials, ordinary priests, temple guards, and private citizens. At the sound of a drum roll, the Bailiff cried, "All rise and bow!"

So rose and bowed we at the entering of the magistrates.

His Grace stood to his bench. He chanted a prayer to Lemekh then commanded us to be seated. "We are assembled," he began, "to hear the matter of the plot to kidnap the Lady Aarda."

Straightway, he inquired of me, "Tell the court, what of your relationship with the Lady Aarda?"

"We had met," said I.

"And tell the court how this came to pass."

"We met during the Great Inaugural festivities."

"Indeed? And how was it that you two met there?"

"She chose me as her escort."

"Did she now? And I suppose she also chose you as her lover?"

Biliku jumped to his feet. "This questioning is intended to entrap the accused," cried he. "I insist the court cease and desist this practice."

The Second Magistrate sprang also to his feet. "How dare you address this court in so insolent a manner?"

The Chief Magistrate waved him off, and then again spoke. "Did you pay her court," he said, addressing me, "beyond the confines of the Festive Ball?"

I looked down at my feet. "I have so paid her court."

"And were you and she on intimate terms?"

"We were friends."

"Were you lovers?"

Throat dry, I spoke scarcely above a whisper. "We were lovers."

"Louder! The court cannot hear you."

"We were lovers," said I louder.

Chief Magistrate glared me-ward. "I adjure you: tell the court plainly, were you two ever joined at the hip?" (Intimate—ed.)

Again, I stared downward. "We have taken knowledge of one another."

"This be more serious than thought," said Second Magistrate.

"You know right well," said Third Magistrate, "that knowledge of women is forbidden to priests before the marriage bed."

"We pledged our troth. We never intended to commit whoredom."

The Chief Magistrate looked at me sternly. "Whence came you into this knowledge of one another? Before your ordination?"

"Yes, your worship."

"Took you then the ordination vows," said Chief Magistrate, "not a virgin, but as one of the lewd fellows of street?"

"All the more serious!" shouted Second Magistrate. "A Vestal Virgin broke her vows of chastity by copulating with a novice priest."

Silence again fell upon the court.

Chief Magistrate continued, "You presented yourselves before Lemekh defiled, and betrothed to one another. You put the Temple authorities to the shame of presenting to a prince of the priesthood a bride not as a virgin. You then steal from the Grand Vizier what is rightfully his, and then you have denied him what is rightly his for his years of faithful service. In this you implicated the whole court of Akir-Ema."

Chief Magistrate turned my counsel. "What say you to these charges, Defense Counsel?"

Biliku rose slowly, carefully for to speak. "Most Noble Magistrate," he began, "priests, officials, warders, and citizens: I rise not to deny the veracity of these charges. My client freely admits to the sum of them. My defense is based on but one argument: Who among us can with clean hands rightly make such accusations? Who among us has not similarly broken Akir-Ema's wise laws?

"Let me enumerate. Firstly, why are there charges of the kidnapping of the Lady Aarda? By all rights, ought not she be dead? Was she not publicly offered to the Great Fire? How now do two vie for her hand? Does not this even now give public notice to the fraudulent nature of the Solemn Sacrifice?

"Secondly: why this concern for the purity of the priesthood? From whence come the maidservants that serve at Temple banquets? Whence come the menservants that keep the Temple grounds? Are they not all bastard sons and daughters of the priests?

"Furthermore," said my defense counselor, "have not the magistrates themselves have also been known to have dipped their quills in many-a strange inkwell?" (Colloquialism for sexually promiscuous; implied as used in bribery or extortion in pending court cases—ed.)

Third Magistrate immediately jumped to his feet. "You are out of order!" he shouted.

First Nagistrate motioned him to silence. "Proceed, counselor," he said.

"Thirdly: again, why all this concern over purity and virginity? I have had the sad duty to break the news to my own client that he was not first of Lady Aarda's lovers. That the entire Vestal order is but a large network of shrine prostitutes is one of the empire's largest of dirty, little secrets among high and mighty.

"Fourthly: be H'rshag's true offense not the defilement of the priesthood, nor yet the sanctity of the Vestal order; rather, be it the wounding of the Grand Vizier's reputation and pride?

"Fifthly: has not concern for this court and its pronouncements been abandoned long ago among the populace until today scarcely any citizen respects the law. Runaway slaves are not caught, or, if caught, are not punished. Conversely, in other cases, masters mistreat, yes, and even slay their slaves without reason. There is breakdown of order and learning in schools. Tutors pass undeserving pupils upon threat of mayhem or death. Hudishi run rampant in the streets to molest and hurt with impunity. Youth no longer show reverence to the god, Lemekh.

"They know the truth regarding the oracle and the consumption of the sacrifices. They know of priests who defile themselves with harlots and Vestals who commit whoredom for hire. They are aware of priests and Vestals that commit abomination with members of their own orders. They know of the bribery and denial of justice in our courts.

"They're aware of increasing numbers of our women who cohabit with the Angry Things and thus produce, again in increasing number, their dreaded offspring, the Nefilli. All this and more rises as a stinking dung-heap to heaven. And yet—you priests behave as though you held complete rule as you once did. The truth is that you now hold little authority beyond the immediate confines of the Temple area.

"The larger body politic is indeed beyond anyone's control. And yet, you would bring charge to my client? Lemekh forbid."

The court sat in stunned silence. Then rose the Third Magistrate for his rebuttal. "How dare you address this court in such a manner? You fain would make the court the accused?"

"Aye," said the Second Magistrate amid renewed restlessness in the court. "You speak as the lewd street rabble. Your tongue should be ripped from your head."

The Chief Magistrate again motioned for silence. "Billiku speaks the truth. For no want of hypocrisy we now face great rebellion.

"I myself know that what he says is true. I have seen the people gathered in the temple plaza, supposedly to worship our Great God Lemekh. I have seen, instead, how they jeer to scorn at the sound of his voice. They raise fists in defiance, making figs at the statue. (Figs—clenched fists with the thumb thrust out between the fore and index finger; an obscene gesture—ed.) I have seen our Temple groundskeeper slaves wash from the base of the Statue of the leakage of dogs and of men. I have seen evidence of theft within our Temple. I have seen with my own eyes evidence of gold leaf being stripped from the baser metals underneath."

The Chief Magistrate turned to face the full court. "I will now make forthright admission before you all. It had long been the truth that much is not as it seems. In truth there are those who would accuse us of outright fraud. However, we priests did what we thought to be in the best interest of our people.

"We sought to give the people something to believe in when, at the time, our land was rent by continuous wars between petty chieftains. We united the people's loyalty around the name of the greatest leader of our history, the mighty, benevolent, and wise Lemekh.

"Though we priests, by many clever devices, gave the people illusions; we priests have always believed in the unity of our people. This, in fact, we believe in with passion. We knew that were we ever to fail to hold the people's loyalty, the results would be anarchy and lawlessness even as we witness today.

"We would be in direct league with the Angry Things and hellish hosts from the Abyss. Life under them would be intolerable, for Nefilli scorn anything constructive; they know only destruction. There would be no shame; no end of shame. They would perform real sacrifices of human lives. Our choicest damsels, before the eyes of all, would be ritually molested, tortured, dismembered, and finally offered to real sacrificial fires. They would circumcise our female infants, so as to be make them suitable for servitude as child temple harlots. Young boys would likewise be pressed into the same wretched abomination. Our citizens would be ceremonially eaten as victims of their insatiable cannibalistic appetites. No one's life, liberty, property, or family would be safe. Ours would be a fate that would beggar the imagination."

He paused. Then he turned to me. "We nevertheless still have a case before us. And we must render a verdict. We must pass judgment."

(We have a proverb among us: "In life, fear the courts. In death, fear the abyss." Would I yet be publicly stretched naked on the rack with the tormentor sawing me asunder at the posterior?)

"Lord H'rshag," continued the Chief Magistrate, "I find you guilty of treason and high crimes against the empire. However, since you are high born, I will exercise greatest clemency. I hereby sentence you to exile."

A murmur arose in the court.

Chief Magistrate continued pronouncing sentence: "I sentence you to serve as envoy on a diplomatic mission to Shurrupuk. There shall you serve and represent us as ambassador of Akir-Ema, so will you remain until this court summons you home again. When the Lady Aarda is found, when the Lady Aarda is restored to her rightful betrothed, when the Lady Aarda is duly wedded in ceremony to the Grand Vizier, when the Grand Vizier and the Lady Aarda are duly presented before me as man and wife, then, and only then, will this court summon you home.

"The court henceforth, on this case, is dismissed."

I sat in the prisoner's dock as one bereft of all life. I perceived, as in a dream, the unreality of what had taken place around me. Soon, came my temple guards to escort me back to my own villa where I was to be remanded again to house arrest.

Later that night, I again was honored with a secret visit from Shumrag. "Take heart," he said. "I know of a truth that the Grand Vizier is old and exceedingly decrepit (ill.) Your sojourn might well be cut short at the tidings of his death."

I was so gladdened at his words I embraced him. "Blessed Shumrag," I said. "You are more than a comfort to me."

He took me by the shoulder. "Do not detain me. I must go before we alert the guards. Were I to be caught, it would mean I would suffer death upon wood. (Either crucifixion or impalement; the meaning is uncertain—ed.)

"You shall see me again. In the meanwhile, as I have before said, take heart."

With these words, he was out the window and gone.

I turned and saw Dhjek standing in the doorway of the study. I seized his auburn locks and held my dagger to his throat.

"Scoundrel," I whispered. "What do you mean spying on me like this? Are you bent on betraying me to the Temple constabulary?"

Wide-eyed, he pleaded for his life. "Mercy, sire," cried he. "My intent was but to inquire after your late-night comfort. I know nothing of your company, who he is nor yet the nature of his business. I have never meddled with affairs that do not concern me. I beg you, O worthy master, show me clemency."

About to relent, I recalled another grievance I had been meaning to discuss with this rascal. "I have discovered that my personal accounts are short of late. What say you to this?"

"A thousand pardons, sire," he said, his crossed eyes twitching nervously, "but there are goings-on here that would result in dire consequences should the Temple Guards report same. All due respect, sire, I thought it would be prudent for me to take liberty in buying their silence."

"Aha," shouted I. "Then you do dip into my coffers to bribe the guards. You think me a fool? I've a mind to order my birch to dance merrily across your back."

Suddenly his face turned the color of parchment. He pointed to the window. "Look," he cried hoarsely.

I risked, in spite of myself, falling for this knave's trickery. I looked in the direction he pointed; to the window.

What I saw made me quite forget about Dhjek's chicanery. Out in the garden, through the willow trees, I saw a most evil omen. Hanging low in the night sky, shone the full moon shining a blood-red.

Day 36: I, H'rshag, am beset by yet more ill tidings. I learn of the death of T'reni-Akhmen.

Upon sighting this dread omen, Dhjek, poor wretch, fell to his knees. "Good master," he cried, "how read you the heavens?"

"Think you I am some sort of seer?" said I, indignant. "The meaning of this most malevolent sign would escape even the profoundest of magi. We can take surety in only one thing: this is a sign of calamity, the horror of which escapes the human tongue."

As we pondered the meaning of this ghastly sight, we were further affrighted by a cry. It shattered the night's stillness by its most piercing and hellacious sound; so loud that it smote the ear to near deafness. It penetrated the inward parts. It loosed the loins and caused quaking of even the stoutest of hearts. It caused gooseflesh to form on the skin. It caused the hair to stand on end. The cry echoed throughout the city streets. It reverberated against the walls and buildings, until finally with wave upon wave, it gradually died away, and the night again fell to silence.

Suddenly my guards burst into the library, faces blanched. They collapsed at my feet and lay as dead men, sobbing piteously.

"Never have we heard so horrendous a sound," said one at last.

They continued to lie sobbing. Amid their sobs they recited repeatedly between their sighs the Great Litany of Deliverance from the Nefillim:

"From the fury of the Nefillim,
Lemekh, deliver us—"

This they repeated over and over as they rolled over the floor, moaning words that I have now become convinced are but meaningless prattle.

Forthwith, I related my own misadventures of yore when my companion, Ulki, and I encountered the dread Nefilli in the vast, desolate mountain wilderness.

"I know that cry," I said to them. "Once heard, ne'er forgot. Many eons past, a few among mortal women wearied of their knowledge with mortal men. So began they to consort with Angry Things from the Pit who took bodily form in the appearance of men, save for goat-like horns growing from their foreheads and their lower parts, legs and feet, the appearance of goats."

I related further, "In secret ritual, far from the haunts of men, these women indulged their bizarre appetites in wild, sensuous orgies with these beings and thus spawned upon the earth a most monstrous race of known as Nefilli who are neither men, nor beasts, nor yet devils of hell, but rather part all three.

"In their sporting, they have created an issue of giants loosed upon the earth that cause destruction and terror without precedent and without remedy."

"What defense have we against this scourge?" asked a guard.

I felt color drain from my face when I was forced to answer, "We have none."

So spent we the night in a state of wakeful alertness, armed and ready for any eventuality, giving no thought as to how futile our defense might be against these dreaded misbegotten creatures who now infest even our city streets.

Dark forebodings assailed me. Full circle, thought I. This be the retribution for the keeping of animal stables as bordellos for the most depraved among our priests and wealthy lay people.

It had to come.

The following night I was again paid a secret visit by Shumrag. "I bear more good tidings," he said. "Put your fears to rest regarding that corpulent lecher, Rok. He lies a dying in greatest of agony. His fat body has become its own most exquisite torture chamber. His feet are swollen twice their size with water and he vomits worms."

Before I could embrace my dear friend in gratitude for the welcome news, his grave countenance stopped me.

"I have also a bad report," he said solemnly.

"Great Lemekh's Qumkwats!" (Atlantean colloquialism for testicles—ed.) I cried. "Now what?"

"T'reni-Akhmen, the Keeper of the Temple, is dead."

I sank back on my couch and remained for long moments in silence. At long last, I arose from my couch. As the Spirit of Am gave me utterance so recited I the following lamentation:

"My father, my father, the strength of Ym' and the chariots and horsemen thereof. How strange to ponder the imponderable; that after nine hundred sixty-nine years, you are not.

"What means this portent of your death? What means this portent of your name: T'reni-Akhmen, (Death-It-Shall-Come?) The horror of it almost fascinates me, e'en while I lament the passing of so righteous and beloved a patriarch. Those of us who yet remain in the land of the living, what of us?

"What of us, O my father, the Strength of Ym' and the horses and chariots thereof?"

Day 37: I, H'rshag, prepare to depart for Shurrupuk, and am beset by Hudishi.

The next morn I rose to set sail for Shurrupuk. Dhjek, traitorous rascal though he may be, proved true to form in his masterful ability to oversee the labors of the other servants as they loaded the endless supply of provisions aboard the beast-drawn wagons. When all was finally ready, Dhjek took command in a power chariot at the lead. I, under escort of two armed Temple guards, brought up the rear. At Dhjek's command then, we made exit out the front gate of my villa.

As that lousy little shaman foretold, perhaps for the last time.

Our caravan plodded through the now deserted streets. So lay the city as a wanton beauty whose lovers have wearied of her.

Suddenly our chariot slammed to a halt. As the rest of the caravan moved on out of sight, we stepped to the pavement. Our chariot had struck a chuckhole and broke a wheel. No sooner had we set ourselves to repairing it, we became aware that we were no longer alone.

I looked up and saw a youth. He had covered himself with green body paint. He had shaved his head to the scalp save for a topknot, which he dyed orange, that hung to his shoulders. Giant earrings hung from his ears. His fingernails and toenails he had painted black. A single eye was painted or tattooed on his forehead. Around his neck hung a talisman. I recognized the wizened piece of brown mummified tissue immediately to be a trophy; an erstwhile foeman's flowering manhood.

He stood before me naked save for a loincloth improvised with feathers of ostrich and peacock. He wore high-heeled sandals with leathern strap that glistened with jewels and that wrapped halfway up to his calves. He brandished two clubs of polished hardwood joined by a leather thong.

"Hey, guy," shouted this child of the dung-heap (i.e. bastard.) "You tread me spread. You trot me lot."

"Hudishi," said a guard. "They rule the streets. We must pay them tribute."

The previously deserted street now became alive with youth; all bizarrely costumed in various stages of dress and undress.

I looked to see my terrified guards held at bay against a curbside wall by others of this worthless band of rabble.

Some of the hooligans wore tattoos bearing such slogans as "uprising at will," (roughly translated "revolution for the hell of it") or "begotten for bedlam," ("born to raise hell").

I felt a wet kiss against my cheek.

"He cute; me like."

Quickly, I pushed away the person who took so brazen a liberty with me and saw another youth. He clad himself in the scantiest of female attire. His face was heavy with mascara. He pursed painted lips toward me and said, "Come, let us taste love's most exotic delights."

Before I could answer, the first assailant again closed in on me. "I saw your caravan laden with much loot," he said, wrapping his chalaka around my neck. "I know you can pay. Do so, or I cut off your arm; one (inch) at a time."

My antagonist wrapped the thongs of his weapon tighter about my throat. "We will hold you for ransom."

I reached my hand under my cloak and felt the handle of my dagger. With the swiftness of a striking adder, I seized my antagonist's necklace and pressed my dagger to his throat.

"Hear me, unnamed son of an unnamed goat (bastard,)" I whispered, "while you've yet a windpipe! Drop your weapon. Command the release of my companions. Get into this chariot with us. Quickly now, while I yet with great mercy withhold slaying you."

With eyes wide with fright, he complied completely. "Tell the others to let us pass," I ordered.

"Where are you taking me?" he asked.

"Silence," shouted I. "You ask too many questions."

No sooner had I said these words when I heard the air rent by savage screams. Out of the bushes and shrubbery suddenly appeared another band of youths. These dressed themselves in leather vests and leggings of serpent, lizard, and crocodile skin that left their secret parts and buttocks shamelessly exposed. Some dressed themselves in disguise of certain winged lizards of old time. (Pterodactyl?—ed.) Broad leather belts studded with beaded metal girded their loins. In their hands they brandished the most fearsome-looking halberd, pike, battleaxe, and morningstar.

They continued their peculiar type of scream achieved by the fluttering of their tongue in a piercing falsetto as they made for the other youths. Mercifully, they appeared to ignore us.

"Don't let them get me," pled my captive.

"I have no intention of doing so," said I looking back. A most horrendous carnage assailed my eyes as the scene quickly and mercifully faded from sight. Past deserted streets; past deserted shops; past abandoned villas overgrown with vines and weeds, we finally caught up with the caravan.

Next morning we came to the seaport Akir-Mar (Akir-Ema-by-the-Sea—Ed.), its streets no better off than the ones we saw the day previous. We were gladdened to reach the quay of the waterfront and to breathe the freshness of the bracing sea air.

Whilst a great company of stevedores busied themselves loading our vessels, I heard a familiar voice call out my name. From behind a corner of idly standing cargo, I spotted my old friend, my mentor, the noble Shumrag.

"I bring good tidings," he said. "The Grand Vizier is dead."

"And what of the Lady Aarda?" I asked.

"Lady Aarda has been returned to Akir-Ema," replied my mentor. "However, you cannot go to her yet. The Grand Vizier's successor has laid claim to her as his right of inheritance. This is a matter that must be settled in the courts. It is still not safe for you to go to her. You must go as planned to Shurrupuk and wait until we summon you to return.

"Also, there is still much insurrection."

He then hesitated as if he had more evil tidings.

"What is it?" I asked in alarm.

"Lemekh has fallen," he said at last. "The Great Statue is fallen; toppled over, lying in pieces in the Temple pavement."

"How did this come about?" I asked in much dismay.

"The street rabble," He said. "In their anger and rebellion vented their wrath on the poor, dumb statue. God knows what they have in store for the priests."

He looked away from me a moment and then continued. "God have mercy on us priests," he lamented, "when I think, for instance, of the resentment that must exist against us because of custom of the priests to spend the wedding night with the bride of every wedding he had performed. Oh, God, think of the jealous husbands who have been just biding their time!"

"I always did perceive that practice an abomination," I said.

"What difference does your perception make now?" Shumrag said with bitterness. His shoulders sagged in despair.

I wrung my hands in grief. "I fear Akir-Ema is finished."

Shumrag regained his composure. "We must be brave," he said. "If we show courage by bearing up under the unbearable, we can at least fight for the right to die with our heads held high. Perhaps we can somehow show that there are a few of us still worthy to be called priests."

I looked over his shoulder toward the city of Akir-Ema. From it spiraled upward a column of smoke as large as the city itself and black as any smelter's forge.

"Don't count on it," I said.

Trying to ignore my last remark, he presented me with a small cage containing a gray carrier pigeon. "When you reach Shurrupuk," he said. "Release her. She will then fly to us. If and when it is safe for you to return home, we will band a message about her foot, and send her back to you. In the meantime, may All-That-Is-Good look with favour upon you."

Upon these words, we embraced each other and wept, full heavy of heart.

"And may All-That-Is-Good look favorably on you," *I said in parting.*

Day 38; I, H'rshag, leave Akir-Ema, putting to sea in the diplomatic barge.

With great sadness of heart we prepared to put to sea. I noticed the seas about the great port to not be their usual cobalt blue, but looked rather a dirty gray. The whitecaps foamed not up a fleecy white, but the color of dirty mop water.

The demands of the hour cut short my thoughts of dismay. I noticed (I had all but forgotten) the youth at my side that we picked up from the Hudishi.

"You," *I demanded.* "How call they you?"

He looked up at me with eyes crazed with fear. "I am called Rokko," *he said barely audible.*

"Speak up, damn, you," *I shouted.* "I can hardly hear you."

"I am called Rokko," *he said, this time louder.*

Rokko? His answer puzzled me a moment.

I seized him by his topknot. "Don't make sport with me," *I hissed.* "That sounds like a nickname. What is your real name? Out with it!"

Tears came to his eyes. "Please, most noble sir," *he pleaded.* "That is my only name. I have neither father nor mother. I have never had any other kin. Rokko is the name that the Hudishi call me. I have never been known by any other."

Begrudgingly, I released him. "Very well," *said I.*

I summoned Dhjek from his work of oversight of the loading. "Come here at once," *ordered I.*

Immediately he stepped to my side.

"This is your reward," said I sarcastically, "for your years of faithful service." I pushed Rokko toward him. "Meet your new manservant." (Akiri law allowed slave owners the option of presenting a favorite slave with slaves of his own.—ed.)

Dhjek smiled his twisted smile as he saluted me and took the boy from me. I seized Dhjek by the arm. "A word of warning," said I. "Work him hard as you wish. However, if I ever hear of your committing abomination with him (sexual abuse—ed.) I'll have your head."

Dhjek bowed low. "I will treat him honorably, sire," he said. His narrow eyes fixed on me their steady gaze. "You have my word."

"See to it," said I, unimpressed, "if you know what is good for you. Now back to work. Your crew is idling. Your word indeed!"

Glared I hard after Dhjek as he pressed the boy into work with the others at loading the ships. From behind a stack of cargo remaining on the dock, I again saw Shumrag.

Having little time for sadness, I heard the voice of my pilot hard by my elbow. "We are ready to cast off, sir."

"Prepare to cast off," I commanded. "Hard to starboard!"

Straightway, he thrust the control lever to full forward.

Our flagship was fashioned thus wise: The length was 60 cubits (90 feet.) The width thereof 20 cubits (30 feet.) The height thereof above the waterline 10 cubits (15 feet.) On the main deck toward the bow stood the main cabin 20 cubits (30 feet) by 8 cubits (12 feet.) The sides of the cabin, the sides of the hull both were fashioned with a tightly woven (basket-like) wicker with wood, rope, and fiber material. Sealed within and without with pitch and bitumen being made exceedingly strong and watertight. Amidships stood the main mast and foresail. Hard by the stern-most section was fastened the ship's rudder. Thrust forward from the bow jutted out the bowsprit, sporting a generous number of bunting, sails, and ensign, including the heraldry of our homeland, namely, the Great Trident. In addition to the sails, we powered our craft with giant (electric jars), three of which we fastened in series and one that we kept in reserve in a leaden drum.

We came about and then proceeded to put out to sea. I stood on the deck of the flagship to take visual command of the entire fleet and observed the five other vessels, designed and fashioned in like manner.

The same did follow us in line as we plied our way out into the open water.

I watched my homeland slip out from sight, perhaps forever.

My dread further deepened at the sight of the pillar of smoke, blacker than any smelter, still billowing up toward the heavens.

As we proceeded further out to sea, there finally vanished from sight the last spit of land. We saw in every direction only a wide expanse of sea; that, and the column of smoke that continued rising into the sky.

We proceeded north-by-northwesterly, steadfast for Shurrupuk. At the onset of evening, I sought comfort at the sight of a clear sunset and the prospect of a bright, moonlit evening on a silvery, shimmering sea. My alarm, then, knew no bounds.

At the moonrise, I saw no silvery moon, but rather the sight again of the hellish omen: a rising moon colored blood red.

The dull, gory ball cast no reflected light. The sky wrapped us in darkness. The sea lay darker still. The evil-looking orb hung low in the heavens. Its only reflection was its mirrored image rippling in the heaving waters; wriggling like a crawling, crimson creature of the depths.

Leaden waves lapped at the bow of our ship. The air grew heavier, making breathing difficult. A foreboding hung like a pall in the very atmosphere. As the moon rose higher, instead of lighting the night, it somehow made the night all the darker.

These strange signs in the heavens were not lost on my crew. Great fear spread among otherwise brave and gallant men. At last we sought surcease by partaking of victuals in our main cabin. By lantern light, then, we sought comfort with a light supper.

Part of our crew repaired to hammocks. The remainder and I returned to stand on deck for the night watch.

Suddenly, appeared on the horizon a sight the likes of which I never saw before. I beheld a shaft of fire from heaven, then a glow as from a ground fire. It reached upward into the sky, until it spread to every horizon, turning night into day.

The glow still widened and I saw from the ground wherein lay Akir-Ema, a giant column of fire belching its hellish ball upward into the upper heights (stratosphere.) I then saw the very sky itself ignite, sending sheets of fire rolling across the heavens. Now even above my head the fire was accompanied by billows of smoke.

The smoke rolled across the sky, causing flickering, red shadows to dance behind it, reflecting even on the heavy surf.

Then the wind began picking up. At first it was nothing but a good, stiff breeze. Soon, however, it reached gale-like strength and still it grew as whitened foam churned the seas. The wind grew and the seas became rougher still. The air became cold. Then there appeared a new phenomenon. Large droplets of water began flying in my face. (Hard, drenching rain was unknown prior to this time—ed.)

A crewman then gave me a most disturbing report. The power jars with which we drove the great propellers on the underside of our ship were discovered to have gone dead.

We were without (electric power).

Suddenly the whole scene vanished and all became darkness.

As the seas grew to greater violence, the face of one of our crewmen turned the color of tallow. He pointed to the darkness just beyond our vessel's railing.

"My lord," said he, "the darkness is a mountain of water. It's mounted so high that it blots out the sky. With greatest speed, it comes our way!"

I heard a roar and felt the stinging spray. Our vessel rose as we began climbing the mountain of water. We barely had time to make for the cabin and bolt the door. Thus we braced for the freak sea's blow and waited. Yet we were totally unprepared for the shattering blow the water mountain did deliver our small vessel.

A great crash shuddered our tiny bark. Mercilessly we were tossed and rolled. I scarcely knew whether we were right side up or upside down. All cargo not tightly tied, flew about our cabin like dangerous morningstars of war. Were it not for a leaden lanthorn sealed with windows of Formica, we would have been plunged into the darkness of Hades itself.

Howbeit, it happened that our noble vessel proved herself so seaworthy and so watertight that she held herself fast despite the strenuous battering. We also perceived that after being completely submerged for long moments, she finally popped to the surface.

Heard we now the howling wind and roar of the waves. The heavy seas washed across our deck and we heard the sound of watery sheets blowing across the skies.

Like the bobbing of a cork, we continued to toss crazily over the seething froth. We spent the night in sleepless anxiety. For the nonce we had survived unprecedented catastrophe. We stayed hunkered in the vessel's cabin until the coming of dawn.

At dawn I stepped out on deck expecting, after the stormy night that had now spent itself, to see the usual sunny sky. I saw instead heavens such as I had never seen before. I saw a thick gathering (clouds.) Jagged *forks of lightning, dancing crazily like fine linen netting, lacing the sky and ever moving in malevolent formations. I saw sheets of sea spray—whether blowing up from the surf, or blowing down from the sky above, I could not tell. Howbeit, fierce winds blew such water in driving sheets before it.*

I searched for our sister vessels but they were not.

I was saddened to behold my valiant crewmen in a state of fear. Sturdy and seasoned seafarers though they were, they cried like panicked children. They dirtied their clothing from fright.

"Lemekh, save us!" they cried.

"No," I admonished. "Lemekh be dead these many hundreds of years. He cannot help you now. Direct your pleas to All-That-Is-Good."

"Iddi-bateeza!" shouted one. (An obscene colloqialism—ed.) "Never!"

It was Dhjek, my steward.

"You say me 'nay'?" said I, indignant. "You question me? Dare you question even heaven itself?"

I saw the mad look in his eyes. "I invoke the Angry Things!" he shouted. "Perhaps I can their fury assuage."

Laughing crazily, he stepped to deck railing. "Hear me, O Angry Things," he shouted in the teeth of the gale. His auburn locks flowed wildly. "I cast myself to you!"

His voice was all but drowned out by the tempest. "Receive me: body and soul!"

Suddenly sparks of fire shot out from my steward's hair. (St. Elmo's fire, or static electricity?—ed.)

Before we could restrain him, he threw himself into the heavy surf.

I stared hard after my steward's foolhardy self-destruction.

Did that wild little lunatick who fancied himself a holy man grasp the full impact of his prophetic utterance? Did the Ultimate Oracle press on the spirit of this filthy dwarf a message that would force even him to inquire in vain as to the full measure of disaster he foretold?

Damnable little charlatans anyway, I thought, these self-styled holy men. Unbelievably filthy of mind and of person they prove themselves exceedingly anti-social, living in caves, deserts, or sometimes in the streets of our cities; begging for their food. Occasionally besmirching palaces, homes or haunts of refined peoples to deliver some divine message or oracle and then vanishing from view.

THE DELUGE SCROLLS

"Strong-Ones," cried I in final despair, "madness has already begun amongst out valiant crew. Do thou in mercy yet spare us!"

So waited we for the water's worst.

* * * * *

The whirring stopped. Artie tore out the printout and sat down to her desk. She heard a footfall behind her.

She did not turn around. "Done," she said simply.

The hum of the electric clock atop the filing cabinet carried across the basement.

Done.

A sense of numbness settled in her inner being. Her mind seemed unable to wrap itself around the import of her findings. Did work on the scrolls put her at one with Moses bringing tablets down from Mt. Sinai, writ by a divine finger, to the errant revelers in the camp of ex-slaves below? Did it put her at one with Daniel reading for dissolute King Belshazzar the divine but ominous handwriting on the royal banqueting house wall?

Did the discoveries put her in league with Copernicus and Gallileo? Just as they were pilloried for announcing that the universe was heliocentric not geocentric would she face a similar firestorm of controversy from threatened authorities? Would her translated scrolls cause an upheaval in intellectual circles as Darwinian in its own proportions?

They felt a portent hanging in the ensuing stillness...

* * * * *

...Had he dozed off? The night seemed to have gotten darker. Neither moon nor stars shone in the heavens. The buildings stood as dark, ghostly hulks against a slate-colored sky. The lamp cast a dull, feverish glow across the page that lay in the attaché case:

Soliloquy

(H'rshag's Love Poem to the Lady Aarda.)

To Aarda, my Beloved:

Hear me, where'er thou art, these feeble words
I sing to thee:

Behold thou art fair, my precious one,
Behold, thou art fairer than the daughters of men.
Thy love to me had been better than the most
Precious of rubies.
Thy kisses better than the rarest of wine.
The lockes of thy head are like the scented breezes
From the mountain of spices.
Thy lips like honey and myrrh.
Thy face shineth as the sun shineth in his strength.
So as in thy face:
A thing of radiant beauty.

Thy shoulders exquisitely fragile did yield to my embrace.
Thine arms, thin and delicate
Yet with great passion did embrace me.
Thy breasts were as twin clusters of grapes
Or like twain noble towers,
With delight did I rest my head upon them.
With delight did they fain receive my kisses.
Thy belly was as exquisitely carved ivory,
Thy navel like the most cunningly wrought goblet of wine,
Thy thighs as the most skillfully wrought pillars of marble
That stood in the Temple of Lemekh.
Thy feet stand most delicate and
Tenderly wrought as the
Bauble from the most skillful jewelers.

Let me linger in memory to the nights of delight
We spent in moments of great tenderness
'Pon scented, coloured sheets of costliest silk,
As we shared moments of love, of passion, and
Knowledge too wonderful for words upon
Beds of spices.

THE DELUGE SCROLLS

Come with me again, to my banqueting house.
So shall I spread o'er thee my pavilion
Whilst my slaves bring us at table most succulent meats;
Most exquisite wines spiced with cloves and cinnamon;
Most dainty of pastries.

So entertained we ourselves with troupes of (entertainers)
Who provided us all manner of merriment
Of acrobatics, of juggling, of jesting, of song and story.
Howbeit, they do grate the soul
As the screeching of magpies
When compar'd to the Song of Love
'Twixt my love and me.

O, My belov'd Aarda,
My priceless one!
My sister, my spouse,
My jewel:
Whose brilliance
Sullies the costliest of diamonds,
I shall not soon forget thee.
I shall ne'er again see thee
Save in paradies (Paradise,)
In the land of the blessed spirits.

And so now, my turtle dove,
With great heart's sorrow, I bid thee:
Farwell.

(From Day 39. Trans. and Ed. Brit. Mus. Trans. 3.5; 1981.)...

* * * * *

...She could sense Huck's presence as she continued sitting in front of the monitor.

"Awful quiet down here," he said.

She did not turn around, but kept her eyes fixed on the sheets.

"Done," she said again.

The hum of the electric clock continued across the basement. She seemed to have lost all track of time. Time? What meaning did time have with these scrolls and the Atlantean civilization they revealed? Why did she herself feel so intimately involved in her research? As a scholar and antiquarian was she not supposed to maintain more objectivity, more detachment than this? What good would it do for her to grieve over the destruction of a race that flourished and then disappeared before the ancient pyramids?

The initial excitement she felt over the prospect of so epochal a discovery had now given way to despondency. Was this merely a natural reaction, a natural emotional letdown after being on such a high?

Or was it more than that? Had she, like Eve unlocked the key to forbidden knowledge? Had she like Pandorra opened the secret box and unleashed a host of evil entities upon the world?

Huck shifted his weight nervously. "Are you all right?"

"I'm all right."

She did not get up.

"What's the matter?" he said.

"Nothing."

He sighed and turned away. "I'll be upstairs."

She didn't answer.

Upon reaching the top, he paused then grabbed his jacket from a hall tree. Outside he noticed balminess in the air. The snow lay heavy and wet underfoot. He trudged through the soggy drifts out to the shed and proceeded to reorganize his workbench. He spent the next three hours putting trash into large, plastic liners and throwing them into the trunk of his car. As he neared the highway he noticed the days getting longer. He threw the trash bags beside the mailbox and pulled out the day's mail.

Back in the cabin, he sat at the dining table and sorted out the massive bundles. Beneath the junk mail and bills lay an envelope bearing the logo of Cortez Pacific University College of Arts and Sciences addressed to Dr. Ardith Mason-Rodgers.

The return address bore the name Dr. Purvis Lester Rodgers.

He listened to the sounds from the basement. Only silence. The printer had stopped hours ago. He took another look at the letter, uncertain whether to take it to her, open it, or destroy it unopened. He stood up. *Oh, hell*, he thought as he threw the envelope back on the table.

He walked thoughtfully to the kitchen, made a sandwich, grabbed a cold beer and headed for the living room. He peered out the picture window. The scene had by now gotten quite dark. He looked toward the basement stairway. Upon returning to the basement, he saw her still sitting where he had left her.

He laid his hand on her shoulder. She reached up and clasped his. Her palm felt cold and clammy.

"Let's go upstairs," he said. Without a word she stood to her feet and followed him upstairs.

He paused beside the bedroom door. "What's the matter?"

"Just tired," she said. "I'll be all right."

He left her and returned to the living room to watch the late news. If her mood persisted, he would take her back to Dr. Lambert.

* * * * *

The sweeper filled the room with an almost hypnotic hum. When he shut off the machine, silence assailed him with a sound like sea surf. Outside, the rotting snow showed the effects of the balmy weather. He heard a rushing sound. Artie's car slowly lurched its way through the forested driveway. He watched as she opened the door and began hobbling toward the house.

"How did it go?" he said when she stepped through the door.

"Quite well," she said, limping to the couch. "I'm going to try driving to Los Angeles."

She still struggled to sort out her feelings regarding the scrolls. Their import, at times, overwhelmed her. She could only guess the reaction of academia once she published her translations.

She watched sparrows hop about a feeder outside their picture window. "I'm afraid," she said, "that when I publish my paper, they simply won't believe it."

The sparrows continued their cracking of the hard shells on tiny seeds with their fragile-looking beaks as they hopped miserably about the rotting snow that lay in random heaps on their porch deck. Tree branches hung gray, bare, and damp. A fog ceiling wafted low enough to block the tops of the trees. A stiff wind beat the shrubbery to its will.

Huck's remark snapped her reverie. "Don't you think the evidence is pretty compelling?"

Artie continued to observe the struggling birdlings. A realization came to her. She turned from the glass door.

"Human belief is strange," she said as she stood with her back to the outside. Her silhouette outlined against the light from the out-of-doors. "It can set like reinforced concrete," she added.

* * * * *

...From the attaché case, Huck picked up a copy of Artie's paperback, *The Deluge Scrolls*, and read the following:

> An interesting belief extant among the ancient Akiri and other antediluvian peoples was the so-called Seven Ages of Man. Theirs they perceived to be the Age of Gold wherein the original paradise and brightest of civilizations flourished.
>
> Through an as yet unnamed catastrophe, this would be superceded by a new, still bright but albeit slightly inferior Age of Silver. Perhaps this presaged the rise of the ancient Egyptian, Sumerian, and the earliest Indian and Chinese dynasties.
>
> Another epoch with yet much brilliance but with still less luster followed, known as the Age of Bronze. This may have foretold the Greek, Persian, and Macedonian empires.
>
> There then followed a powerful but barbaric Age of Iron when Imperial Rome gained ascendancy.
>
> This was then, in turn, followed by a vastly inferior Age of Lead. This may have been Western Civilization through the Industrial Revolution.
>
> A technologically superior cultural wasteland known as the Age of Clay would follow which would then be consummated in an Age of Fire.

Huck closed the book and looked out at the darkness. Silence pressed in on him. The street below appeared void of all traffic. One lone morning star brightened an otherwise night of oblivion...

Chapter 25

The mists of spring arrive anew. The crocus breaks the sod, and I watch for you.
The breeze blows warm and caresses my brow. I marvel at each blade of grass as I wait for you.
Tree buds wax pregnant and burst forth into leaves; a miracle, yet none so great as that of seeing you.
The dew gently washes my face. The sun kisses my cheek. Will I again reach out and touch you?
I hear the nightingale. Her song is not half so sweet as your voice. I listen and long for you.
The gaggle of geese are soon gone as you are gone. How I desire to embrace you.
When will we meet? I patiently await that sweet moment. Expectantly, I seek for you.
'Til then, dearest delight, be bless't; be kiss'd by my thoughts and I watch for you.

(Day 39. Aarda's love poem to Lord H'rshag. Trans. and Ed. Brit. Mus. vers. 3.5: 1981)

* * * * *

Spring comes suddenly to the higher elevations, Huck thought. He straightened up and observed changes in nature around him. The angry whine of the chain saw reechoed through the woods as its blade bit deeper into the fallen tree trunk in front of him. He gripped the handle with both hands as the teeth began to slow down against the denser wood. He pulled back a moment and let the saw run free. He bore down with a fresh bite. Grains of sawdust began flying into the air and soon covered him. This time he turned the engine off.

Silence rushed in about his ears. He laid the saw in a crotch of a fallen tree and reached for a handkerchief. He wiped sawdust and perspiration from his face. Spring's balminess brought a perfume-like giddiness with every rustle of the breeze.

He surveyed the property. Green had spread increasingly across the yard, mountain meadows, and forest floor. *Need to start mowing soon*, he realized as he observed fresh growths of grass. Among the patches of snow, crocuses were already budding. Off in the woods, he heard the rushing sound of a swollen mountain stream. Also, he could hear the call of the newly arrived songbirds.

He glanced at his watch. Ten-thirty. He had been out in the woods a good two and a half hours. *Got to keep pushing*, he reminded himself.

Three short weeks ago, the doctor had removed Artie's oversized cast and had replaced it with a lighter, walking cast. Now she could make trips to the university. She had fallen behind in her research on Third Dynasty Babylon. He had seen her only briefly on a single weekend. She faced a two-month deadline on her post-doctoral dissertation.

Huck harbored one concern: her insistence on taking copies of her translation printout on campus prematurely. He feared that the wrong people could get hold of them and become privy to their text before Artie was ready to have them published. However, she dismissed his vague reservations as groundless.

Trying to suppress this uneasiness, he strapped on thin work gloves and began carrying cut logs to the woodpile beside the shed. As the sun rose higher, he peeled off his plaid flannel shirt. The pile jacket to ward off the morning chill had been jettisoned earlier. As he set himself to transplanting the iris bulbs, he fought the ache in his shoulder and upper body muscles that rippled through his T-shirt. *Another sign that I'm out of shape*, he reminded himself.

He heard the sound of a car engine coming from the driveway.

He looked up to see Artie's foreign compact pulling into the yard.

"Home already?" he said as she stepped to the flagstone path.

"I decided to take off work early," she said, hobbling toward the cabin.

He pulled grocery sacks from the car and followed her to the kitchen. He set the bags down and kissed her. "Welcome home, honey."

He gestured to the kitchen table. "Let's have lunch."

She slipped into a chair, injured leg thrust out straight.

In the meantime, he began working over the sandwich board. "Are you going to work on your Babylon project?"

"No," she replied. "I'm going to give myself a breather."

He stood to the sink and eyed the foliage just budding from the trees. His gaze turned to a calendar beside the window. "Oh, Good Lord," he said. "Do you realize what day this is?"

"Why, it's Friday."

"Not just any Friday," he said. "It's Good Friday. Our family is probably in church right now."

She looked at him a moment. "That's important to you, isn't it?"

He turned from the window. "As a matter of fact, I suppose it is."

She rose from her chair and stood beside him. "Well, dear boy, if you want to attend church somewhere, don't let me stop you."

He shrugged. "Kinda late now. By the time I found a church where services were held, I'd be just in time for the benediction."

They returned to the table. She studied the picture on the wall calendar. It showed a Renaissance artist's version of the Crucifixion. She sipped her milk thoughtfully. "I can relate," she said.

He looked at her puzzled. "What are you talking about?"

She stood to the kitchen sink. "I never did tell you the real reason why I left Lester, did I?"

He studied her briefly. "Sure you want to talk about it?"

"I think it's time I did."

In the stillness she watched the blue skies outside begin to cloud over. Newly budding trees scraped against the window as the rising winds thrashed them about.

"By now you've probably noticed that I carry certain scars."

At first he didn't say anything. "Lester?"

She nodded. "In case you're thinking what I think you're thinking, let me handle it. Please?"

"All right," he nodded in resignation. "If you say so."

Another silence.

He again studied her at length. "However did you allow this to happen?" he said, shaking his head. "It just doesn't make sense."

She sighed. "I did a lot back then that didn't make sense."
Her parents couldn't understand her marriage to him...

...Lester had been the instructor of one of her first classes. She found herself attracted to him from that first day. His wit and charm she found irresistible. In conversation he could be oh, so clever, oh so animated, oh so funny. His mind seemed to race like a cheetah when parrying a saber-like riposte.

They started dating clandestinely shortly before she left to join Earthnation. When she returned he was still there for her.

If those first heady days under his tutelage were her Woodstock, that encounter weekend would be her Altamont...

..."Thank God neither of them lived long enough to see the final result of my folly," she said. She related to Huck as to how she thought it really a "rad" thing to do.

"Rad?" said Huck.

"Short for radical," she said, returning to the table.

She realized early on her mistake. He never showed the slightest interest in a normal marriage relationship. She told of pornographic literature in its most bizarre and perverted form that he kept around the house. Then came subtle and later not-so-subtle suggestions that they reenact some of the action. When he chased her through the house with his belt, she left him for the first time.

The second time she came home early from a science convention and found a videotape lying on the coffee table. The video showed Lester leading two other professors and three students in a kind of Dungeons and Dragons game. A later frame showed Lester and his companions lounging about in various states of undress and various stages of intimacy in the family room. Without even unpacking, she took the video and left.

She would return, she had told him, only on the condition that they both seek counseling. Lines of disgust creased her mouth. "I should have realized that counseling in those situations is useless. People like Lester are incorrigible, but I was in a state of denial."

She gazed at the rising storm outside. "He picked the counselor," she said continuing her gaze. "The woman was just as demented or perverted as he."

The woman had hinted that Artie go along with Lester's fantasies; no matter how bizarre or degrading she found them. She then suggested that they join her and five other couples on a marriage retreat to a sylvan hideaway called Dochen Estate.

"That's when this happened." Artie gestured toward her backside.

She returned to the table and they sat silent again for a moment. "We were taken blindfolded in a stretch limo," she said. "I felt terribly uneasy about the whole thing, but the others thought it great fun, so I held my peace."

She recalled catching the sight of a gate and a security guard as she peeked out from the edge of her blindfold. Ah-ah-ah, a women sitting next to the driver had admonished her, mustn't cheat.

They checked in at their assigned rooms and then went to a drawing room for their first session. Actually, that first meeting seemed bland enough. Pretty much pop-psych stuff. Self-esteem stuff. Get-in-touch-with-your-feelings stuff. A lot of talk about feelings…

…The mention of encounter groups talking about feelings elicited in Huck's memory his high school sophomore English class. The young teacher had graduated from the university just the year before. During their first meeting, she gave them an in-class assignment wherein they were to first think about, get in touch with, and then write a paper describing their feelings. At the end of class they were to hand them in.

After sitting restlessly in his seat for about five minutes, he finally wrote "I feel fine," walked up to the desk and gave her the paper.

Then he walked out of the room.

He subsequently heard nothing more about it…

…All told, that first meeting remained pretty tame.

The wild stuff would come later.

No dinner hour appeared on the schedule. Those who were hungry could help themselves to a buffet of snacks set out on the dining room table. The retreat sponsors kept no regular mealtimes schedule as part of a deliberately unstructured weekend.

Meanwhile, what began as an evening session lasted all night, this also in keeping with a round-the-clock schedule. Midnight, someone broke out with wine and marihuana, accompanied by skinny-dipping in an outdoor pool. Around three, they retreated to a basement recreation room furnished with couches and easy chairs. Psychedelic posters covered the paneled walls. A strobe light furnished the only illumination.

The sight of naked bodies in the intermittently flashing light heightened the already heady atmosphere.

"It was all supposed to be, oh so therapeutic," she commented. However, fatigue, wine, and pot were beginning to tell.

"You should have heard what began spewing out of their mouths," she said. "Any resemblance to genuine therapy was purely coincidental."

She then related how they began directing their hostility toward her. Several of the people had been at Earthnation. Their accusations had something to do with what went on there. They had accused her of cheating on Lester.

Artie folded her arms and stared down at her feet. "They were accusing me of sleeping with Snake," she said.

Huck looked puzzled. "Snake?" he said. "Who's Snake?"

Artie went on to explain. Snake had joined Earthnation shortly after it formed. With a snakeskin-like tattoo that covered his head and body, his very appearance was frightening to the point of fascination. He quickly intimidated the others into submission and then browbeat his way into de facto leadership.

"He had to be the consummate psychopath," she sighed. "Wherever he went, he never left without hurting somebody or breaking something first."

During a drug orgy at the compound she supposedly performed some cultic or satanic marriage rite with him. Later, when in her right mind, she repudiated the whole thing. He had, however, continued to stalk her after she left Earthnation and even after her marriage to Lester. Of late, she had heard nothing, thankfully.

Perhaps he was dead. Or perhaps at least he ended up in prison on drug charges or something.

Accuse me of seeing Snake, she thought. *They've got to be kidding.*

In their surreal state of mind, they insisted she be disciplined. She recalled being bound by the wrists and tied down to a low daybed. Heavy metal music boomed from giant speakers in the far corners of the room.

"Why did you let them?" Huck said in disbelief.

"Too drunk," she replied, "and too stoned. It's the only way I can account for it."

She recalled more wine and joints had been passed from one reveler to another as music blared from the speakers and strobe lights flashed. In the blinking unreality, she caught a glimpse of Lester dressed only in a mask and black cape and brandishing a riding crop.

She ended her recollections abruptly as she stood up and headed for the living room. Huck came up slowly behind her as she looked out the picture window. He laid a hand on her shoulder. "You don't have to tell me any more."

She reached over and squeezed his hand. "I want to talk about it." ...

...The sweet, acrid smell of marihuana smoke hanging thick as she shouted to Lester that she was not into that sort of thing and she wanted to stop the whole orgiastic affair.

He then replied by striking her.

She squeezed Huck's had a little harder. "When I heard a woman's voice screaming, I realized it was mine. God, the pain was indescribable."

"'Lester!' I pleaded. 'Stop! I'm not enjoying this.'"

He hit her a second time.

Dammit, Lester, she then recalled saying. Stop it!

Another blow followed.

She pleaded to others for help. As glazed-eyed zombies, they began circling and fondling her. Going into shock, she lost control of all bodily functions simultaneously.

She also passed out.

"That must have dampened their enthusiasm," she said, still squeezing his hand. "I came to all alone in that awful room."

She also recalled that music had stopped, but the strobe light still flashed its alternate light and darkness. In the silence, she found herself on the floor, lying in blood and filth, and in incredible pain. She noticed for the first time the flimsiness of the knots that held her wrists. In a matter of seconds she freed herself and staggered out into the hallway...

..."I felt sheer agony with every move," she continued. Her only thought was of avoiding the others, finding some clothes, and getting out of there. She stumbled onto a laundry room and found a threadbare, begrimed trench coat. In the early-morning twilight she staggered through a wooded area barefooted, cutting her feet on roots and sharp stones until she came to the main entrance. She found it open. She ran toward the road and followed the winding, arboreal enshrouded blacktop until she came at last to an intersection with a gas station.

Weak with shock, she fought to maintain consciousness.

Please, I need to make a phone call, she had whispered to the startled attendant.

He let her use the station's phone. She called Peppi. She must have then passed out for her next memory was that of lying on the cold, grimy floor. The attendant had gallantly taken a mechanic's smock and had thrown it over her. She could see blinker lights of an ambulance through the station window.

"I must have been quite a sight," she said wryly, "barefooted, dressed in smudged, worn trench coat, hair matted and dirty, face pale gray with shock, and body covered with blood and filth."

"Peppi found me in a nearby hospital. I had just been brought out of intensive care. As a criminal assault victim, I faced questioning by the police, with a photographer yet. You can't imagine how I felt when they took my picture, lying on my stomach, naked, and with my face to the camera; all for evidence at a public trial."

She paused. "Peppi was most supportive."

Huck began pacing the floor. *This all is weirder than I thought.*

"I had plastic surgery," she added, "for the scarring."

He moved back behind her and pressed her shoulders. "They did a good job," he said. "You still have a beautiful tushie."

She smiled briefly. "Thank you. Actually, it's not funny—but yes, I really was concerned about that. I spent most of it lying on my stomach. Peppi finally got me into a shelter for battered women. I spent several months as an outpatient."

"As an outpatient?"

"Even after going back to work, it took several months of deep therapy before I felt human again."

Outside, the wind began to die down, but the sky still remained cloudy and overcast.

The bastard! The words exploded inside his brain. I knew there was something behind that blank stare, he reflected. I knew there was something behind that screwy crease in his forehead.

The pervert! Hell isn't hot enough! I'll kill that psychopath, so help me!

He fought to suppress his rage as he went over to the fireplace and began jabbing the poker into the ashes.

"If you do decide to press charges, know that I'll stand by you," he said, striking a match.

She sat on the couch and watched him put a couple of logs on the fire. "Thanks," she said, noticing his face still red with anger. "So far, I just haven't had the nerve."

As flames danced inside the blackened hearth, the phone rang.

Artie struggled to her feet and hobbled across the room. "Hello?" she said, picking up the receiver. "Yes, this is—"

Her countenance darkened as she listened in silence. She tried to avoid showing any further emotion. "Why are you calling me here?"

Another pause.

Her mouth took a downturn. "I think this is highly irregular."

Another pause.

"All right," she sighed, "if you think it's important."

Another pause. "I don't see why this can't wait until after spring break."

As she hung up, Huck looked at her inquisitively.

"Speak of the devil," she said, again starting for the couch.

"You gotta be kidding," said Huck. "How does he even dare?"

"He denies even doing it."

"What?" Huck stood up from the fireplace and stared at her.

"And then sometimes he says he doesn't remember," she continued. "He says that we were all too much under the influence of weird substances to know what really happened. Anyway, he'll be here in three hours."

Huck replaced the screen on the fireplace. "Why don't you take your nap," he suggested in tone of thinly disguised hostility. "I'm going to do some more work outside."

She saw hate in his eyes. Pure, raw hate. "Promise me you won't do anything rash."

He started for the front door. "I'll be the paragon of restraint." He cast a sidelong glance into the living room.

I'll tell that sonofabitch where the bear shit in the woods real quick, he thought.

* * * * *

Dr. Rodgers hung up the phone. He pushed his swivel chair away from his desk and picked up an attaché case. He laid it on the desk and then opened it. Atop some papers lay a supermarket tabloid.

His office door opened and Dr. Vawter entered.

Dr. Rodgers cast him a hard look as he seated himself.

Dr. Vawter's blotched ruddy features loomed close.

"I've got something for you," he said in a phlegmatic voice.

He flopped a sheaf of Xeroxed printed matter down on the desk.

Dr. Rodgers picked up the papers. He tried not to let his face give him away. He examined the excerpts from *The Deluge Scrolls*:

Day 39. I, H'rshag, learn of Lady Aarda's final fate.

So stood I on the heaving deck; hard put to remain on my feet. With my leathern girdle, I lashed myself to the remains of our mainmast. Our craft be now continually awash with the angry seas, dirty with rubble of the inundated plain. The howling winds seemed verily to scream for my life.

The clouds overhead billowed in demonic tumult: black as any smelter's forge, and yet, shadowed a flickering red, reflecting the continuing sky-fire. The (rain) still force-driven in angry torrents, lashed and tore at the remains of the ship's rigging.

Of great surprise, then, was I to see, struggling through the stormy skies, a dot. As it neared, I discerned it to be a bird. A pigeon: one of Shumrag's messengers—more dead than alive.

She neared our stricken vessel and lighted on my outstretched hand. Between her feet was tethered a scroll. I broke its seal, opened it, and read its contents:

"Most noble H'rshag: I bring tidings of the Lady Aarda. Thus her state as saw I her last: From a secret vantage within the Temple, I witnessed her capture by the Temple guards.

"I saw the Lady Aarda dragged and prostrated before the Temple Magistrate. Before the eyes of hundreds commanded he the masked tormentor be brought forth brandishing a dreaded scourge of rhinoceros hide.

"'She who plays the harlot and mocks the priesthood,' cried he, 'deserves naught but to be chastised most severely.

"'Lady Aarda,' said this bairn of the brothel (bastard—ed.), 'I find you guilty of whoredom. I sentence you to fifty stripes with the scourge.'

"The Lady Aarda replied: 'Go wallop a hedgehog!' (a vulgar colloquialism; gutter slang for copulation; considered to be the lowest of animals in Akiri culture; considered to the strongest of insults—ed.) 'Send me to the Grand Vizier's (Grand Vizier's successor—ed.) bridal chamber and I will castrate him with my teeth.'

"'Ho,' replied the Magistrate. 'The accused shows much spirit and great lack of penitence. Very well, then; strip her naked and give her twice fifty.'

"This saying, then, horrified even her burly tormentor. 'My lord,' cried he, 'were she to submit to such severe punishment, she would not survive.'

"The Magistrate remained unmoved. 'Tormentor,' shouted this perverse son of pollution. (lit. "one not cleansed of his after-birth or placenta"—ed.) 'You have my order. Give the shanta-mahoot (colloquialism for slut—ed.) her due. Let the punishment begin.'

"Thus ordered, the tormentor stripped away the Lady Aarda's fine raiment. However, ere were he able to land the first blow, the air was rent by shrieks and howls. Into the Temple Court, poured scores of Hudishi, dressed as serpents.

"From my secret vantage point witnessed I a carnage wond'rous in its ferocity, and in its horror.

"I regret to state that the Lady Aarda was among the slain. The Hudishi, having done their worst, put the Temple to the torch and fled. I emerged from my hideaway and rushed to where the Lady Aarda lay; lovely e'en in death. To spare her further shame, I clothed her again in her gown of tattered silk.

"Then summoned I others of the underground to help me carry her to a proper burial within the Secret Garden..."

(Trans. and Ed. Brit. Mus. vers. 3.5; 1981.)

Dr. Vawter sat back and eyed him. "What do you think?"

Dr. Rodgers stood to his feet. He studied the headlines of the tabloid that lay in his attaché case. He shut the lid, grabbed the handle, and started for the door.

"Aren't you curious as to how I came by this?" said the provost.

Dr. Rodgers grasped the doorknob. "All very interesting, Henry," he said in a mewling tone of voice, "but I have other fish to fry."

* * * * *

Huck resumed his task at the flowerbed, working on into the afternoon. As the sun began to sink low in the western sky, he heard something toward the road that lay on the other side of the stand of trees. A car came into view and stopped. The driver began climbing out. Huck recognized the tall, slender figure in the gray, double-breasted suit and bouncing on the balls of his feet. He recognized the wobbling head with wavy gray hair, the puckered expression and the colorless eyes behind the rimless bifocals.

"Something I can help you with?" said Huck, standing astride the flagstone walk.

"Oh, don't you have something useful to do," said Dr. Rodgers in his high-pitched voice, "like hauling out the trash?"

Huck continued to block his path.

"I need to see Ardith," said the dean after a brief but uncomfortable pause. "She's taking a nap."

"It's all right." Huck heard Artie's voice coming from the cabin. "What is it, Lester?" she asked with cold formality.

Dr. Rodgers tried looking past Huck. "We need to talk."

"I'll be in the yard," Huck called out as Dr. Rodgers stepped around him.

When Dr. Rodgers crossed the threshold, Artie gestured to a chair at the dining room table. "We'll talk here."

She sat awkwardly in her chair. "To what do I owe this visit?"

He set his attaché case on the table. "How's your injury?"

"Mending nicely, thank you," she said. "It just takes time."

"Mountain hiking can be dangerous," he opined. "One must take care."

Artie looked thoughtfully across the table. "I appreciate your concern," she said finally, "but I'm sure you didn't come all the way up here just to inquire about my health."

Dr. Rodgers opened his attaché case. "I'll get to the point," he said. "The administration has been concerned about your research."

"I'm recovering from a serious injury," she gestured. "The doctor only recently has let me drive. I have had to put my work on hold."

Dr. Rodgers reached into his attaché case. "What I want to share with you is the university's concern about this."

He held up a copy of a popular tabloid. Bold headlines read:

"Scientists Jump Start Disabled Truck With 6,000-Year-Old Battery."

Artie looked at it for a moment. "What about it?"

"Ardith," he said, "the administration is very concerned that after we've gone to all the trouble and expense of allowing you this sabbatical, all you have to show for it is something like this?"

"Let me tell you about that," she said, her voice taking on an edge. "We tried to submit that story to more conventional publications, but no one wanted to hear about it. That paper was the only one interested."

Dr. Rodgers steepled his fingertips. "I'm sure what you're saying is true," he said. "The fact remains that this is hardly the results that the university looks for when they grant a sabbatical."

Color crept into Artie's face. "There'll be more material forthcoming. I've got to allow myself time to recover from my injury."

"This is not the image of scholarship that the university likes."

Artie hobbled to a nearby writing desk and picked up in both hands a file thick with papers. She returned with it to the dining room table and spread it out before him.

"Here's what I have," she said. She then spent the next twenty minutes explaining the outline of her research.

They both fell to momentary silence. "This concern," said Artie finally, "was this your idea, or somebody else's?"

Dr. Rodgers laid the paper back into the attaché case and closed the lid. "That's not important."

You devious creep, she thought. *This whole thing was your idea.* "Unless you have something else that you wish to discuss, I think your point is well taken."

As he continued to sit, he began to fidget. *Oh no, don't go into your little routine again,* she thought, wondering what to expect next.

She eyed him with curiosity. "Is there something else?"

He studied her briefly. "Have you had your fill of baby-sitting?"

"Come again?"

"You know what I mean," he said.

Her features hardened. "No, I don't know what you mean."

A brief pause that became heavy with tension. "Suppose you tell me."

"You're a very clever woman."

Artie gave a disgusted sigh. "If you won't get to the point," she said finally, "I think we've about come to the end of this little chat."

Another pause.

"I want you to come back to me," he said at last.

She stood to her feet. "Perhaps you're going to want to get back to Los Angeles before dark."

Dr. Rodgers likewise stood to his feet. "After all," he continued, "once you've helped him through law school, who knows?"

"That will do, Lester." She gestured toward the door.

He stopped at the doorway. "I hope you recover fully soon."

He turned again and ushered himself out.

As Artie stood in the doorway, she saw Huck leaning against Dr. Rodgers' car. *Please,* she thought, *no confrontation.* She heard Dr. Rodgers' voice: "If you don't mind, I'd like to leave."

Huck took a step forward and placed a foot on the dean's toe. "So leave."

"In case you haven't noticed," he said, "you're standing on my foot."

"You're lucky that's all I'm doing," growled Huck.

"Are you threatening me?"

"Nah," said Huck seizing Dr. Rodgers' necktie. "If I was threatening you, I would be saying something like: 'Set foot on these premises again, and I'll work you over until you walk funny.'"

Artie continued standing in the cabin doorway, gesturing in an attempt to get Huck's attention.

He saw her motioning him. He turned again to Dr. Rodgers. "Just wanted you to know," he whispered, tasting every word, "that I know what you did to her."

He flipped the necktie over Dr. Rodgers' shoulder. "Tuck your tie in," he said. "As an educator, what kind of example is that?"

Dr. Rodgers gingerly stepped around him and hurried to the car. He gunned his engine and roared down the driveway.

As Huck neared the house, he raised his hand. "Don't say anything," he said. "I thought I handled that rather well considering."

She heaved a sigh as he walked past her into the living room. "I'm just glad he's gone," she said.

She limped wearily to the couch and sat down. She folded her arms. "He came up here," she said with a slight laugh, "because he was concerned about an article in a sleazy tabloid. He also tried to talk me into going back to him. I just can't believe that man."

Huck stood up and strolled over to the window. "Can you believe him when he says he can't remember hitting you?"

"Like I said, sometimes he denies having done it at all," she shrugged, "and sometimes he says he doesn't remember."

He reflected on what Artie had just told him regarding her ordeal. The bizarre, kinky event took place in the wee, small hours of the morning. He recalled the words of his mother. She had been wont to insist that nothing worthwhile, nothing good, is ever said or done after midnight.

He stared out the window. "When I brought up the subject to him just now," he said, "you should have seen the look in his eyes."

He paused briefly. "He remembers."

Chapter 26

This shrine, the elders informed me, be of great mystery among us.

The shrine was designed this wise:

It, being an enclosure area one hundred cubits expanse (about the size of four tennis courts—Ed.) is bordered by a system of unhewn stones, each be about the size of a small hut. Two stones stood upright a distance of about ten cubits (15 ft.) one from another. A third lay suspended side-wards atop the other two; forming themselves thus into a rude arch. The same basic three-stone formation continued on around the enclosure forming a kind of circle with smaller concentric circles in their midst.

"This votive stone," said I, "bears great resemblance of an open temple on our Main Island..."

(Day 34. Lord H'rshag views with the elders of the British Isles Akiri colony a Stonehenge-type petroglyph. Trans. and ed. Brit. Mus. vers. 3.5; 1981.)

* * * * *

Artie leaned slightly against the lectern and shuffled her notes. A banner stretched behind her that read: "Lost Atlantis: Do Recent Archeological Discoveries Produce New Evidence?"

She stood on the stage of Mayfield Memorial Auditorium of Cortez Pacific University and looked out at a capacity audience. Was the wording of the banner a little presumptuous? she wondered.

The 1981-82 school year neared its close. The three previous lectures had been for small groups of the scientific community interested in Early Dynasty Sumerian civilization. There she made no mention of the jars. This had been reserved for the final lecture. In anticipation of wider interest, she had sought a larger hall instead of a small amphitheater.

The Department of Arts and sciences, in anticipation of increased interest, and in conjunction with her request, had moved the lecture site to the campus main auditorium.

She took a sweeping glance of the packed lecture hall. Spread out along each of the outside aisles stood a platoon of journalists with notepad in hand and video camcorder operators. She realized early on the import of her epochal discovery, but never did she dream that the popular press would ever show such interest.

Who notified them anyway?

Private person that she was, she viewed the prospects of such glaring publicity with very mixed emotion.

"One of our most interesting discoveries," she said, struggling to maintain composure, "is how this civilization was able to utilize electrical energy."

Feeling the palms of her hands moisten, she stepped out from behind the lectern to one of the jars sitting on top of a table on stage. "I will now demonstrate."

She motioned for Paul and Angie to come out from back stage. Each carried an electrical cord with bared copper wire ends.

Artie wrapped the end of each wire around a metallic nodule atop the jar. Paul and Angie then slowly brought the exposed ends of their respective wires together. Upon the barest of contact a giant spark flashed before the audience with an accompanying roar that echoed throughout the auditorium.

Artie waited for the audience to settle down before going on.

"This jar was found in what appeared to be once river- or lake-bottom sand some twenty-five feet below the site of a ziggurat, or mound," she explained. "It was discovered only after weeks of digging through layers of artifacts of relatively more recent civilizations. The layer where three of the jars were found, however, had no other artifacts.

"This jar was discovered quite by accident to be electrically charged. The other three seemed like just dead batteries.

"One thing that has baffled our engineering department in their preliminary research on this jar is how it could maintain such a powerful charge for what could very well have been six thousand years or more. It in fact behaves very much like a permanently recharging dry cell."

She unscrewed the top and laid it beside the jar. She then stepped back and let Paul and Angie tilt the mouth toward the audience.

"This jar is made of a highly glazed and sophisticated ceramic material," she said. "Another layer of the same material is on the inside. Between are layers of tissue-thin gold and silver foil. This same foil is also apparently an integral part of the design on the outside. The entire design seems to be a very clever, a very ingenious, mechanism of a self-charging battery. As we have mentioned, our engineering department has already done extensive research and have as yet been unable to unravel its mystery."

She had Paul and Angie set the jar aright again.

"Another jar," she continued, "was found in a scriptorium in an upper-level Sumerian civilization. An interesting fact: That room also contained a tablet with one column written in cuneiform while the other column was written in a system never known before."

From the corner of her eye she could spot journalists moving down the side aisles toward the stage. She pointed to a woman carrying a spiral notebook and accompanied by a young man with a video camera. "Yes?"

"During your lecture," the woman began, "you mention sections of the scrolls that allude to a civilization that predates your so-called Antlantean civilization: one that was apparently monotheistic in its religious beliefs. What implications do you think this has for presently held views regarding the evolution of religious belief?"

Artie again leaned forward on her lectern. "Probably nothing short of revolutionary," she said, shuffling her notes. "The present concept is that animism and primitivism were the earliest forms of beliefs of primeval people. From these, ancient people evolved to the polytheistic religions such as the Olympic pantheon of ancient Greece and Rome, and the gods of the ancient Nordic peoples. From there, we evolved to the great monotheistic world religions of Judaism, Christianity, and Islam. Now, with the advent of the scientific era, we move on to a more human-centered rather than other-centered; or, if you will, God-centered.

"Now then, these allusions to a primeval monotheistic civilization could force us to completely rethink our concepts in this area."

The woman countered with another question: "Could these people very well have been pantheistic as well as monotheistic?"

Artie paused long on that one. "I think," she said, choosing her words carefully, "that they may very well have considered our categorizing pantheistic belief versus monotheistic rather arbitrary. I believe that they have given clear evidence of recognizing a something—perhaps some force of Being—that was above and beyond—transcendent, if you will. At the same time, I feel that they also had a very deep reverence for nature and the forces of nature that surrounded them. I think that they would have found our dichotomy of dividing pantheism as a distinct and different concept from monotheism incomprehensible. I hope that answers your question."

She thought she noticed a look of skepticism spread across faces in the audience. Off to the rear, on a couple of aisle seats sat Drs. Vawter and Faasendeck.

Artie, in the meantime, had pointed to another area of the auditorium. "Yes, question over here."

A bookish-looking middle-aged man stood to his feet. "Would you be willing to go on record that your discoveries tend to support the theory, for example, of a universal flood as recorded in the Book of Genesis?"

A brief but restless shuffling of feet followed the question.

She saw several camcorders moving closer to the front and beginning to pan the audience.

"I don't intend to go on record as saying anything," replied Artie, sounding slightly annoyed. "—But I will say this: given the facts of these recent findings, I find it difficult to foresee how one could come forward with a convincing alternative explanation."

Dr. Vawter sat back in his seat. He held in his lap an excerpted copy of an article Artie had just published in a professional archeologist magazine. The page read in part:

> "He was naked save for a loin cloth of animal skin. He was smaller of stature and rather squat in figure. His limbs, unlike the Kraaviki, were not finely shaped. He, rather, was longer of arm and hairy and muscular; looking to be exceedingly powerful of body. (Some paleontologists think that, as indicated by the heavy bone structure, Neanderthal Man may have possessed strength three times that of modern man—ed.) His head was thicker, more elongated, his brow sloping, showing a pronounced bony ridge above his eyes. His nose was flat; his lower lip larger than his upper. His jaw line receded

from his mouth. His large ears struck quite prominent out from the sides of his head. His body was well covered with hair. His forearms and calves of his legs disproportionately thick. His feet were broad and his great toe well spaced from the others. He held in his hand a spear cruder in fashion than even that of the Kraaviki…" (Day 31. H'rshag's first sighting of the Orgoru. Trans. and ed. Brit. Mus. Vers. 3.5; 1981.)

Could the account be, for the first time in modern archeology, a contemporary description of Neanderthal Man?

(Ardith Mason-Rodgers, Ph.D.; "Lost Atlantis: What Do Latest Discoveries Tell Us?" *Archeology Today*; Mar. 1981. pp. 34-36.)

Again, she searched the sea of faces that packed the auditorium. For a moment a lull seemed to settle over the crowd. Again, restlessness rippled through the rows of eyes directed at her. *Maybe this it*, she thought. *Maybe it's time to wrap the whole thing up and go home.*

From the middle section she spotted an upraised hand.

A graduate student from the Cortez Pacific University Divinity School who referred to himself as a teaching fellow in theology stood up. His question: What bearing did her discoveries have on Genesis chapter six, verse six: "Whoso sheddeth man's blood, by man shall his blood be shed." Some conservative theologians attribute this post-deluvian dictum as the basis for human government. Could an antediluvian civilization exist without government?

A subtle groan spread through the auditorium.

Again, Artie paused before answering.

More panning the audience by the video people.

"Some political entities, like the petty city-states of Shurrupuk, were extensions of such social groups as the family or clan and were ruled arbitrarily and informally by a patriarchal chieftain or king," she said at last.

"Wealthy land-holders, wealthy herdsmen, or wealthy merchants built fiefdoms whereby they possessed great numbers of slaves, servants, or vassals and from which they administered systems of legal codes regarding trade, commerce, and justice as suited their interests. They also employed numbers of free-lancing skilled artisans on a kind of contractual basis.

"I suppose that we could say that Akiri civilization was ruled by what we might call a 'quasi-government,' if you will. I realized that is going to be difficult for us to grasp, but here we are confronted with an empire that actually ruled without a central government as we are accustomed to thinking of such today. The nearest analogy that I can possibly get across to you in a way that is understandable by today's student of political science is to say possibly that this civilization was a kind of theocracy. An oligarchy of priests, through the use of illusions such as a giant 'talking' statue ruled by decree. Their only control over the peoples of the empire was the control they exercised over their minds as they convinced them of the statue's supernatural powers.

"This same feudal class also provided a ruling class of priests. These priests had their own elite corps of temple guards to enforce religious or priestly laws. The civilian populace, on the other hand, practiced the 'eye-for-an-eye, tooth-for-a-tooth' principle similar to the Old Testament. The individual and his or her own family were pretty much on their own for redress of any criminal or civil wrong. The priestly hierarchy intervened only when the stability of the empire was at stake.

"We, of course, are not the only species of social animal. One can think of dozens of examples among the insect, fish, bird, and animal kingdoms. Some actually have very complex social structures like the queen bee and their divisions of labor. Yet do they have governments in the sense that we do? Do they have laws—written or unwritten—other than a kind of genetic wisdom that we only now are barely beginning to understand?

"Why are some these species today considered endangered? Why, for example, did the powerful western bison become nearly extinct? Was it not because the species Homo sapiens (whether North American Indian, or later, the white man) could move in among a herd and kill a particular member of that species without fear of retaliation from the others? Are not the several herds of herbivorous species of the African plains such as the wildebeest, the antelope, or the zebra perfectly capable of fighting off with hoof and horn the predatory attacks of the lion were they to possess a greater sense of community?

"Yet the protective instinct seems to be much more present in the carnivores, especially toward their young.

"Do we have here a contrast between the herd instinct and the clan instinct?

"Did not antediluvian city-states and their loosely knit tribal units more closely resemble the herd rather than the clan? Was the Akiri patriarch, Lemekh, unsuccessfully trying to implement this clan-like cohesiveness when he uttered his famous oath of vengeance in Genesis 4:24?"

She spotted a hand shoot up near the back of the auditorium. A plain-looking, bespectacled woman rose to her feet. Artie knew her to be a science department colleague.

"How is it," she asked, "that you, a woman of science, appeal to the Bible for documentation?"

From her distance, she could not see Artie's expression during the pause before the answer.

"I hold no brief for or against the Bible," said Artie finally. "I merely alluded to it like any other document of antiquity. As an antiquarian, I reserve that as my right to do this."

The journalists with notepads and camcorder operators bent forward with intense interest. Several moved to immediately below center stage and continued panning audience faces.

Artie again paused briefly. *Dare I?* she thought. She felt her palms get sweaty. She took a deep breath. *Here goes,* she sighed, *I might as well let them have both barrels.*

"I find it interesting," she began, "the widespread antipathy among academia toward all things religious. Yet, when viewing the panorama of human thought throughout history, and even prehistory, has science come anywhere near capturing the imagination as has religion? Especially when we're talking loyalty, devotion, duty, and values as well as stated beliefs? The number of people on this planet that are devout Christians, Muslims, Jews, Buddhists, and Hindus, for instance, are in the hundreds of millions. How many, by contrast, are equally devout disciples of Darwin? How widely read is the *Origin of Species* compared to the Bible, the Talmud, the Koran, or the Veda? How many have given themselves in martyrdom for their various causes? Christianity, Judaism, Islam, and other religions number their martyrs in the millions. With Darwin only one comes to mind: John Scopes of Dayton, Tennessee, when he was fined one hundred dollars back in 1925 for teaching evolution in a high school biology class."

Dr. Faasendeck nervously observed Dr. Vawter out of the corner of his eye.

Another student stood up. "Would you comment further on the scroll's referral to an ancient temple and of the text on an obelisk in the area?"

Artie did not answer right away. She took a deep breath before answering. "The language of the obelisk," she said, "as translated not only by our department, but also by linguistic scholars from the National Geographic Society and the British Museum, would appear to be a text that could very well be a possible creation account similar to that in Genesis."

A man wearing a press badge stood and moved from the back of the auditorium to halfway down the center aisle. "Would you be willing to go on record that your findings tend to give historicity to the first few chapters of the book of Genesis?"

Again Artie paused. She was certain she knew what was behind that question. The local press had recently picked up on and was currently running hard with an issue that had taken over the C.P.U. campus like wildfire. Within the past two years the divinity school administrators, in an attempt to regain favor with the rest of the campus and to ingratiate themselves with Dr. Vawter, had sought to thrust their department into the forefront of social and political activism while at the same time jettisoning even lip service to supernatural dogma.

She shook her head. "Why are people always trying to put me on record? You forget, sir, that I am a scientist. I would be doing the academic community a great disservice were I to take a position on any issue that these most preliminary of findings might raise. There are revelations in these scrolls that could have profound repercussions in the thinking of science, archeology, anthropology, history, and even religion that could challenge the cherished notions of decades. I refuse to be a party to any hasty conclusions.

"I will say this: that there are allusions in the scrolls to an Antediluvian character named Xisusthrus. That name has been mentioned in unearthed Babylonian tablets before as a possible mythical character named in Hebrew as the Noah of Genesis. The scrolls now treat him as an historical person. The scrolls also allude to a people in prehistoric Europe who were described as refugees hiding in caves from some primordial race of terrorist monsters. Based on what we can ascertain from the scroll's description, these people may very well have been the race that paleontologists have called Cro-Magnon Man. The scrolls also refer to belief extant of a common set of parents from which the entire present-day human race descended; namely a creature known as 'Red One.' The word 'red' in Hebrew interestingly enough is 'edhom' from which we also get the words 'clay' and 'Adam.'"

Dr. Vawter gave Dr. Faasendeck a nudge and got up to leave. After a brief hesitation, Dr. Faasendeck followed. As the evening's moderator thanked Artie for her presentation, the audience filed out under the glare of video lights and in an obviously agitated mood.

Chapter 27

"Do not misconstrue this to mean that I am one of those deviant fellows... I am, in fact, every whit as manly as any."... The usurper paused, shot a hard look us-ward. "You forget," said he, "that I am now Grand High Potentate." ... Convinced of the futility of further discussion with this misbegotten pig (Akiri colloquialism for "bastard"—ed.)... "How came such swine to the priesthood in the first place?" queried I.
(Days 28 and 29. Trans. and ed. Brit. Mus. vers. 2.75; 1981.)

* * * * *

Dr. Rodgers tapped his fingers fitfully on the linen tablecloth.

"I am looking forward to these meetings with less and less enthusiasm," he said, squirming against the awkward fit of his suit.

Dr. Faasendeck looked up from his copy of the menu. "Those were some startling statements Ardith made at her lecture last week."

He glanced anxiously about the University Club dining room. "This is really beginning to get unraveled," he sighed. "Sometimes I wish the whole thing would just go away."

"What is this, a wake?" Dr. Vawter pulled up to their table, carrying a whiskey from the bar.

A waiter produced an order pad. Dr. Faasendeck folded his hands on the tablecloth. "I'll just have a salad and ginger ale."

"So," said Dr. Vawter as the waiter left, "do we have an agenda?" *Another pleasant afternoon with Kewpie Doll and Puckerpuss*, he thought.

Dr. Rodgers cleared his throat. "That young man, George Bouknight; the one on a graduate assistantship?"

Dr. Vawter unwrapped a cigar. "What about him?"

"He has no background in archeology at all. I can see problems when, as a graduate assistant he tries to help undergraduates."

Dr. Vawter lit his cigar. "Have you tried tutoring him?"

"Tutoring a graduate assistant in his own field of specialty?" said Dr. Rodgers, shaking his head. "That's unheard of."

"Well start hearing of it."

Dr. Rodgers leaned forward. "Excuse me?"

Dr. Vawter slouched back in his chair. "You heard me," he said. "Get a tutor for him. Do what you have to do to see that he makes it."

"But that's highly irregular. That's—"

"What's next on our agenda?" said Dr. Vawter, cutting him off.

Dr. Faasendeck tugged at his collar. "Contract time coming up," he said. "We've started negotiations with the faculty bargaining team."

Dr. Vawter took a sip of whiskey. "How does it look?"

"I don't know," said Dr. Faasendeck. "I can see money problems."

"Money is always a problem. Just what do you mean exactly?"

"Well," Dr. Faasendeck shrugged, "alumni giving is off of late."

Dr. Vawter laid his cigar on an ashtray. "Since when did the country club set get so tight with their money?"

Dr. Faasendeck picked at his salad. "Some of them have notified intention to withhold contributions because of our new policies."

"Is that right?" Dr. Vawter took another drink of his whiskey. "What new policies do they have a problem with?"

Dr. Faasendeck laid down his salad fork. He coughed and pressed his hand to his throat. He took off his glasses as his eyes began to water and pulled a handkerchief from his pocket. He raised a water glass and drank deeply. "Please excuse me," he gasped.

Dr. Vawter smiled at his discomfiture

Dr. Faasendeck tried to regain composure. "There is concern about our proposed discontinuance of weekly chapel."

Dr. Vawter took another sip of his whiskey as he continued his cold stare.

"Why is that? We still use the chapel auditorium for other purposes: lectures, recitals, concerts, and the like. What's the big deal over one weekly service?"

"They feel it is indicative of changes in direction."

Dr. Vawter studied his tumbler of whiskey. "It is indicative of a change in direction. I thought we'd been through all that."

"Their concern," said Dr. Faasendeck, squirming in his chair, "is over the swing away from the school's traditional religious emphasis."

"What emphasis?" said the provost. "When I first came to this campus, I didn't know Christianity had anything to do with it. Where's the emphasis? Your so-called religious emphasis went by the board decades ago. You're looking at a school where divinity students are considered the shits of the campus. We're talking last vestiges here."

Lines began to wrinkle Dr. Faasendeck's forehead. "If what we have are the mere vestiges, why is it necessary to jettison even that?"

Dr. Vawter glared at him. "Because it's the honest thing to do."

"I don't understand."

The provost leaned back in his chair. "Tell me," he said eyeing the president. "Do you consider yourself religious?"

Dr. Faasendeck gestured toward his clerical garb. "Let's say that I'm religious but not superstitious."

Dr. Vawter squinted his eyes. "Religious but not superstitious," he said wryly. "Interesting. Just what is that supposed to mean?"

Dr. Faasendeck hesitated. "Let's just say," he said, "that I try to take a reasoned, intelligent approach to religious faith."

"All right, let's say that," nodded the provost. "Tell me, Mr. Reasoned, Intelligent, Ordained Clergyman, do you believe in God?"

The president sat upright, about to say: "Of course I believe in God." He tugged at his collar. After a pause he said, "I believe in God in my own special way."

The provost again eyed him. "In your own special way," he said. "Why don't you ask me that question?"

"Why should I?" Beads of perspiration began forming on his forehead. "Isn't this whole thing a highly personal matter?"

Dr. Vawter leaned further forward. "My point exactly." He continued his hard stare. "Each one of us has a right to believe in his or her own god—or no god at all."

Silence.

The provost went on. "Therefore, since this is each individual's own prerogative, any overt form of religious expression by any institution: government, school, or whatever, is an infringement on the individual's right of privacy. A gross imposition."

Dr. Faasendeck began making nervous little popping sounds with his lips. "But eliminating all outward forms of religious expression..." A shortness of breath made him pause. "Isn't this going a bit too far?"

"Don't you think it's time that we quit dancing around the issue?"

"Which is?"

"Which is..." Dr. Vawter slowed his words down for emphasis. His voice resounded with portent. "According to any empirical evidence, the material universe as we can perceive through the physical senses is the only reality that we can ever be sure of and that it's the only reality that ever was, that ever is, or that ever will be."

Dr. Faasendeck wiped sweaty hands on his pant legs. "I'm afraid there's a lot of people," he said, "that just are not ready for that."

"If not now, when?"

Dr. Faasendeck didn't answer.

"So," said Dr. Vawter, again eyeing the president's reaction, "what other policies do your precious alumni object to?"

Dr. Faasendeck stared at his plate. "They have expressed concern," he said, clearing his throat, "about the reported watering down of Cortez Pacific's academic standards. As you are no doubt aware, we have long enjoyed the reputation as being a West Coast equivalent to the Ivy League. After such a long and proud legacy, many of our alumni would hate to see us lose that."

"Just don't get it, do you?" replied Dr. Vawter. "Since when does money or position determine curriculum anyway? Since when do dead intellectual snobs tell us what's a fit curriculum for the new generation of student? As I've said repeatedly, we're going in new and revolutionary directions these reactionaries don't even understand."

A sardonic grin crossed Dr. Vawter's features. "What do you two gentlemen know about Moscow University?"

Moscow University? thought Dr. Faasendeck. Good Lord, how did that get into the conversation?

The other two continued to sit silent.

"Forget Ivy League," the provost went on. "Our new role model is a massive building just blocks from the Kremlin done in Stalin Gothic. Instead of a cross atop its spire, there's a big, red star. Political reliability is the key for entry. Students of color outnumber the whites. You talk about diversity?"

He took a sip of his drink. "We could duplicate that here."

Drs. Faasendeck and Rodgers exchanged anxious glances.

"We could introduce a curriculum," continued Dr. Vawter, "that would make the soft little white boys and girls from our own country and their parents wet their pants.

"Students admitted there, however, pay no tuition. Not only is that covered, but their room, board, and textbooks as well. Hell, while we're at it, let's even give them a little stipend for personal expenses.

"In the meantime, after three or four years, we turn out dyed-in-the-wool, hard-core revolutionaries."

Dr. Vawter paused and continued to level his gaze at the other two. "And so, if we can help our students divest themselves of the baggage they bring from home, does their actually learning anything else really matter?"

Dr. Faasendeck looked fitfully to the other tables. "Some of the most generous contributors are concerned about the co-ed dormitories."

"Really?" snapped the provost. "Co-ed dormitories have been accepted as commonplace for years now."

"I realize that," nodded the president. "But now the alumni are concerned with your policy of making the dormitories exclusively co-ed, with unisex bathrooms and showers yet. You leave students who wish to stay in the old gender-segregated dormitories with no option. Alumni are concerned that there are young people just not ready to handle situations so potentially explosive, sexually speaking."

"Sexually speaking," he said, mocking Dr. Faasendeck's words. "I knew it would come down to that."

Dr. Faasendeck fidgeted in his chair. He recalled a recent jibe overheard among the student body referring to life in the freshman dorm as "Fornication Seminar 101."

"Many accuse you," he continued, "of advocating free love."

"I do," said Dr. Vawter simply. "We ought to require that our women students lose their virginity before we allow them to graduate."

"What?" gasped Dr. Faasendeck.

"With the men students," Dr. Vawter went on, "I think we should make it a requirement, not for graduation, but for admission."

Dr. Faasendeck stared at him. "You're kidding, of course?"

Dr. Vawter nodded. "Yeah, I'm kidding, of course." He paused, then added, "And then again, maybe not."

Dr. Faasendeck blinked nervously. "Good heavens, man," he said, "have you no morals at all?"

"You would talk to me about morals?" Dr. Vawter cast him a sidelong glance. "You, with each one of your own kids a complete sociopathic basket case? You, who preside over a campus that practices the sexual mores of a rabbit hutch?"

"Morals—shmorals," said Dr. Rodgers with a smirk, "invented by the prudish and powerful to suppress the rest of us."

Dr. Faasendeck puckered his lips thoughtfully. "The point is," he said hoarsely, "we have lost support."

"Is that right?" Dr. Vawter took another drink of his whiskey. "So have you applied for any more government grants?"

"Not lately—"

"Well get with it. Go after some of those private foundations as well. We don't have to suck up to elitist alumni."

Dr. Faasendeck again wiped perspiration from his forehead.

"Look," said Dr. Vawter, "there as many rich bitches out there that donate to progressive causes as there are reactionary. There are millions waiting to be tapped by schools such as ours. All you have to do is know where to look"

"And just how do I go about doing that?" said Dr Faasendeck hoarsely.

"Like I've said before: you're the PR expert," snapped Dr. Vawter. "I'll leave that up to you."

Suddenly Dr. Faasendeck thought of something. *Moscow University? Don't they have one of the most rigorous scientific programs in the world? How would this square with Dr. Vawter's progressive, softball approach to education? Have I misjudged the man? Is he really the hardcore revolutionary that we feared, or is he merely a romantic, an idealist like so many of the new left?*

A subtle smile crossed Dr. Faasendeck's face. Ideas slowly began to formulate in his head as he watched the provost pull an attaché case out from under his feet.

"I've got an item here," Dr. Vawter continued, lifting up the top. From it he showed them an article, a journalist's interview with Dr. Mason-Rodgers.

Q: In all your findings, it seems evident that you place the Epoch of Atlantis somewhere near the end of the last Ice Age. That being the case, in your opinion, what does the translation of your scrolls indicate regarding climactic conditions?

A: Very interesting question. First of all, how long is an ice age? We can have an ice age any time the snowfall of a given winter fails to completely melt the following summer and thus adds to the accumulation of the next winter. Ice ages can be short-term, as in years, or they can be decades, or centuries. Here we have ice ages that last millennia.

Akir-Ema evidently existed in an epoch immediately prior to our own recorded history of roughly 3,500 B.C. to the present. This may have been near the end of the most recent Glacial Era of 30,000 to 50,000 years ago. There could have been a period when mild temperatures prevailed from the equator all the way to the polar regions.

We could be talking anywhere from 5,000 to 20,000 years ago.

Q: Dr. Mason-Rodgers, your translations indicate that these alleged Atlanteans utilized electrical power, am I correct?

A: That is correct. One of the demonstrations in my lecture was to show how one of the jars contains a powerful electrical charge; very much like a giant-sized dry cell.

Q: And you say that according to your translation of the scrolls they used this power in many ways?

A: That is correct. They very likely used electric lighting for their homes and their streets.

Q: Did they utilize this energy in their system of transportation?

A: They used it in land, sea, and air.

Q: Air transportation?

A: Yes. They evidently had types of aircraft that were propeller driven by these dry cells. Their aircraft was also designed to use hot-air balloons to give them extra lift.

Q: Was their aircraft like those of the modern airplane?

A: Actually they more closely resembled the hot air balloon or dirigible. To say that they were an ancient replica, for instance, the modern airplane is not quite correct.

Q: I notice that in your translations, you mention that none of their modes of transportation attained to speeds of more than forty or fifty miles an hour. One of the previously held conjectures of Lost Atlantis was that their aircraft, for example, attained speeds possibly exceeding the speed of sound. Now you tell us that they traveled at a more leisurely pace.

A: You will recall that my translations indicating the so-called Atlanteans as enjoying great longevity. Life spans in the scrolls parallel in a remarkable way with genealogies in the Book of Genesis. Both list individuals living several hundred years.

It is possible that these people lived and moved in a vastly different space-time continuum. To put it simply: they lived longer; therefore they were never in a hurry as we in the modern era are. With life moving at a more leisurely pace, attaining speeds of more than forty miles an hour may well not have been important to them. Hence they may have not developed a faster system of transportation because they simply saw no need for it.

Q: You just brought up an interesting question. As you no doubt are well aware: paleontologists have long held—based on radiation and other tests—that the average longevity of prehistoric adult was only about 25 years. Now you claim to have discovered the existence of primordial individuals who lived to be hundreds of years old. How do you account for that?

A: To assert that prehistoric man lived an average of only 25 years is based on an assumption that the rate of aging reflects accurately the actual calendar years of an individual's life span. Is it not entirely possible that though their bones reflect an aging process of a rate very similar to that of a 25-year-old modern adult, that this does not necessarily preclude the actual calendar years to be much more than that?

Q: Could their leisurely-paced lifestyle have been a contributing factor?

A: It definitely could.

Q: Do you see this as a lesson for us today?

A: I certainly do.

Q: In returning to your mentioning their use of electrical energy, I still find it hard to accept that they used an energy form that subsequently lay unknown to any other civilization until our own of the past century and a half.

A: That's not quite true. The ancient Greeks had understanding of both the electron and atomic theories.

Q: How is it the Greeks knew this without research?

A: I attribute this to a type of genetic wisdom—a thing long accepted by science, albeit little understood. In a sense, this is another instance of the Me of the ancient Sumerians.

Q: You also claim that these historical records predate even our previously held concept of the dawn of history?

A: That is correct.

THE DELUGE SCROLLS

Q: What do you estimate to be the date of those scrolls?
A: Anywhere from 3,500 to about 10,000 B.C.

Dr. Vawter pointed to the last statement. "Do you see that? She's still using the outdated, sectarian system of date designation." He paused, pulled a bottle of pills from his pocket and washed two of them down with a glass of water.

He pointed to the page. "Look what comes next."

Q: Are you contending that there is evidence now of civilizations predating our own historical era?
A: Exactly. These scrolls, coupled with other such phenomena as the Easter Island statues, Stonehenge, the Peruvian landing strip, and the stretches of what appears to be manmade highway systems under just a few feet of sea bottom in the Caribbean, all seem to indicate that there is now as much evidence that even in the very remote ages past, civilized man and primitive man coexisted much as they do today.

Q: What is the implication for the notion that our historical era evolved from prehistoric man of eons past? Won't the recent discovery of civilizations that predate even ancient Egypt and Sumer force the scientific community to radically rethink many cherished ideas about the emergence of modern man?
A: I should think so.

Q: But what of the so-called glacial era?
A: We're talking the last 30,000 to 50,000 years. That in and of itself is a length of time that beggars the imagination. Yet, that in turn is just a blip on the evolutionary screen wherein time spans of 4 billion years are often casually bandied about.

Q: What are you getting at?
A: Just this: despite all the discovery of prehistoric man, his artifacts, and the fossilized remains of fauna and flora, it's minuscule compared to what really went on during those years.

Suppose, for example, that archeologists millennia from now began digging for remains of our civilization. What would they really know if all they found was a single videocassette?

Q: I guess it is pretty staggering as to the possibilities of what there remains yet to be discovered.
A: My point exactly. Is it not possible that there are whole epochs of civilizations that predate our own historical era?

Q: Are you saying that some things previously considered myths are now becoming history?

A: The Hittites were long held to be a mythological race until recent discoveries indicated that such a people really existed. This is also true of the Minoans on the island of Crete. We also now have evidence of an actual, historical city of Troy.

Dr. Vawter laid the magazine aside. "So, what do you think?"

Dr. Faasendeck shrugged. "Pretty amazing," was all he said.

Dr. Rodgers pressed his lips together. "I had no idea."

Dr. Vawter rubbed his chin thoughtfully. "We've got to get hold of those scrolls," he said. "We've got to run tests on them in our own laboratories to determine proper dating."

"But what if their dating authenticates their being 5,000 or 10,000 years old or more?" said Dr. Faasendeck.

"We'll publish their age as being between 500 and 200 B.C.E. in any event," replied Dr. Vawter. "That will be our official pronouncement on the matter."

"One problem," said Dr. Faasendeck. "What about their location?"

"One of the jars was found in a Sumerian scriptorium."

"But the others were found in plain river silt below the most primitive village-level civilization. How do we counter that?"

"We maintain that they were found much closer to the present-day surface. They were washed into a gully by a more recent local flood. After all, floods have washed through the Tigris-Euphrates valley since time immemorial."

"I see another problem." Dr. Rodgers steepled his long, delicate fingers. "Ardith has already corroborated her findings with the National Geographic Society and the British Museum."

Dr. Vawter lit another cigarette. "We blitz academic journals with articles denying the whole thing. We deluge the popular news media with our version. Most people—even many scholars—won't bother to check with the National Geographic Society or the British Museum. Most won't know or even care."

Dr. Vawter eyed Dr. Rodgers. "You're not keeping very good track of your wife. Who knows what she and her boyfriend will come up with next?"

Dr. Rodger's face puckered. "Dr. Vawter," he said, "I am not amused."

THE DELUGE SCROLLS

Dr. Vawter smiled. "Know something? You're funny, real funny." *Quit your damn squirming*, he thought. *You're giving me St. Vitus' dance.*

For a moment neither of the other two answered.

A thought occurred to Dr. Faasendeck. He recalled Dr. Vawter's contention that reality that can perceived through the physical senses is the only reality that ever was, is or ever will be.

Whose sensual perception, he thought; *our species?*

What about other species whose senses are wired differently than ours? A dog, for instance, has poor eyesight and is perhaps colorblind, able to perceive only shades of black, white, or gray. Yet its sense of smell is some 700 times as keen as ours. Its ears can pick up sound frequencies too high for us to hear. A cat, also, has not only eyesight, but also smell and hearing keener than ours as well. If we had the eyesight of a bird, we could read newsprint a mile away. I see one Dr. Vawter. A fly would see 400. Which perception is reality? A bat can avoid colliding into a wall with a built-in sense of "radar" and without eyesight altogether.

And what of one born blind? How can we demonstrate to such a one the reality of color? Or how could we convince one born deaf with the reality of sound? Do we not display a stupidly cavalier attitude when we belittle one who claims to possess ESP?

Drat, he fumed within himself, *why didn't I think of all this when discussing the matter earlier?*

Hershel Ladd, thought Dr. Vawter. *He's been like a stone in my shoe ever since his sophomore year.*

He recalled a complaint from a professor of philosophy...

...The professor had begun his initial meeting that term with a withering interrogation of a class in introductory philosophy.

"Who was Abraham Lincoln?" he demanded.

"He was sixteenth president of the United States?" answered a bespectacled youth.

"I don't want to know what political office he held," shouted the professor in mock disgust. "I want to know who he was?"

"He freed the slaves?" volunteered another student.

The professor feigned even more intense disgust. "I don't want to know what he did," he roared. "I want to know WHO HE WAS?"

The class sat back thoroughly intimidated.

Finally a girl raised her hand tentatively. "He was a lawyer from Illinois," she asked in a voice barely audible.

The professor clenched his fists and grimaced toward the ceiling. "I don't want to know what profession he pursued," he said, growling through his teeth. "I want to know WHO HE WAS?"

The professor's eyes swept the anxious faces of the class. He finally fixed his gaze on Huck. "Mr. Ladd, perhaps you can tell us who he was?"

Huck looked up in feigned surprise. "Who what was?"

The professor's brow furrowed. "Why Abraham Lincoln, of course."

"What about him?"

The instructor took a breath. "Who was he?"

Huck inserted a pencil end in his mouth and looked at the ceiling. "Let's see," he said thoughtfully, "I think he used to run the deli down the street."

Tension mounted as the other students tried to stifle impulses to laugh.

For a moment the instructor tried to fight off looking flustered. "Come, come," he said with a note of impatience. "Surely you've heard of Abraham Lincoln?"

Huck nodded in mock recollection. "Yeah," he said, drawing out the word. "I wonder whatever became of him?"

The professor's face hardened. "Are you trying to be impertinent?"

An embarrassing silence.

The professor stared at Huck getting out of his seat. "I'm getting a drop slip," he said. "This class is a crock of shit."...

...Dr. Vawter again picked up the conversation. "But," he said to Dr. Rodgers, "your wife isn't funny at all. What we have here is a loose cannon. If she keeps on publishing this kind of stuff, we're going to have to get out some kind of disclaimer."...

* * * * *

...Huck laid aside his pen. His watch indicated three o'clock. He pushed his legal pad and law volumes to one side, got up from the couch, and stretched. *Guess I'll go for a coffee*, he thought.

Fifteen minutes later, he sat atop a stool in an all-night grill around the corner from his office building. In the harsh glare of the diner, he stared briefly into a white, steaming mug. When Artie had finally fulfilled her post-sabbatical obligation lecture series and articles, she again resumed the routine of classroom teaching. With financial help from Artie, Huck had also begun his studies in law school at University of Nevada at Las Vegas.

Only rarely did they manage to get together weekends at their mountain cabin. That year in the High Sierras fast became an idyllic memory. Once the eighties had begun, the years seemed to roll by with increasing rapidity. He recalled the spring break of '84.

That week proved a disappointment. Huck, then a senior in law school, spent the week studying for his finals. Artie changed from playmate to workaholic. I thought we had seen the last of this when you finished that translation of those scrolls, he had said.

She then explained to him the beginning of her new book. But you had just published your post-doctoral dissertation on Third Dynasty Babylon, he had reminded her. True, her answer, but there are new pressures at school. The word was out: "publish or perish." The school found itself badly in need of new prestige and revenue.

The text contained a fuller account of her expedition, research, and personal comments on the scrolls, plus a complete translation. The project took much of her spare hours for the next two years. The fun things that they enjoyed: hiking, skiing, relaxing in front of the hearth, dinners by candlelight, quiet conversations, and making love had now become a rarity.

Huck, in the meantime, had finished law school, passed his California bar exam, and took a job as an intern law clerk in a Federal District Court office in San Francisco. Here his workload increased. Friday afternoons saw him leaving his law office with an armful of case files. This meant working weekends in his San Francisco studio apartment. The rare respites at the cabin pretty much became still more working weekends for the both of them there as well.

After two years at the Federal District Court office, he finally secured employment with a firm in downtown Los Angeles. He had hoped to move in with Artie; however, she lived a good two hours' drive from his office. He had to take an apartment a block from the Long Beach city line; only ten minutes away…

* * * * *

…With his success at the firm, however, came an even heavier workload. Finally, after a Sunday dinner at Artie's apartment in September 1987, he got up from the table in her formal dining room.

"We need to talk," he said as he studied the shrubbery outside.

She agreed.

He turned from the window and glanced back at Artie. "It seems as if we're drifting apart."

She looked at him without answering.

"—And I don't want that," he continued.

"Nor do I."

"What's happening to us?" she said, again breaking the silence.

Huck shrugged. "I don't know. However, I do know we need to take a hard look as to where we're headed. We're not getting any younger."

He reflected on their relationship. Get married? Why bother? Why let some arbitrary institutional stricture tell us how to live? Why can't we be free to just love each other the way we want without getting permission from a piece of paper?

So went the contention of many of Artie's peers.

Huck, however, was finding their arguments a little threadbare.

As a child of the baptismal covenant, he could not shake the haunting conviction that commitment mattered, that overarching everything, an invisible supreme being who sees all considers such things to matter greatly.

He concluded that, yes there is—not a God, but God. Period.

Maybe it's time, he concluded, *to cut out all this loosie-goosie and grow up; to quit being adolescents and to start living as adults.*

He glanced in her direction. Finally summoning the courage to broach the subject, he found her reaction surprising.

Instead of the expected snappish riposte, she looked at him clear-eyed but with a pained expression. Her voice took on a huskiness.

"I know," she said simply.

She got up from the table and joined him in front of the window.

"I want to get married," he said as she caressed his shoulder. "What's it going to take to get Lester out of the picture?"

Artie looked away wistfully. "There are new problems," she said. "Lester is ill; very ill."

He saw her walk to a corner of the dining room and hold her hands to her face. *He didn't look very sick to me the last time I saw him,* he almost said. "Are you in some kind of trouble?" he did ask.

She turned to him. "Things are not good on campus just now. For one thing, the divinity school has finally closed due to lack of enrollment. Now weekly chapel services have also been suspended."

"I never did consider them anything special," shrugged Huck. "Ten minutes of Dr. Faasendeck's philosophical vagaries. Ask him an hour later what the homily was about and he couldn't tell you."

She edged away from him and again gazed out the window, arms still folded tight. "Nevertheless, I think we've lost something. I, for one, have never been anti-God. Our school, however, is run by someone whose hatred for religion borders on the pathological. He even takes offence when he sees someone saying grace in a restaurant."

"He's a complex personality, to say the least," he sighed.

What a perfect cliché when one wants to say something nice about a scoundrel, she thought. "It's my book," she said. She related the administration's pressure to softpedal the contents, make retractions, or even surrender the scrolls.

She took a step back toward the center of the room. "I've turned over everything pertaining to Third Dynasty Babylon."

She stared thoughtfully at the wallpaper. Beyond the window, autumn winds blew in a low, gray cloud ceiling. "Those scrolls are mine," she said finally. "They're interested in them because they now realize how controversial they really are."

He recalled a recent visit to the Cortez Pacific Administration Building. He had a double errand: as a high school football talent scout, he had business with the athletic director. He also had, at Dr Vawter's request, an appointment with him.

After a few brief pleasantries, Dr. Vawter decided to get to the point...

..."Mr. Ladd," he said, "I understand that you and Dr. Mason-Rodgers have been an item for quite some time now. Is that right?"

Before Huck could answer, Dr. Vawter held up his hand. "Quite all right," he insisted. "No need to defend that sort of thing here. What goes on between you two is no concern of mine."

He paused.

"I do want to discuss something that is a very great concern of mine," he said finally.

Huck waited for him to go on.

"Those scrolls," he began.

"What about them?" Huck wanted to know.

For a moment Dr. Vawter gestured in a futile search for words.

"Well—hell," he said when he finally collected his thoughts. "You know and I know—all that stuff about the Flood and Garden of Eden is spurious nonsense," he continued. "Why don't we just shit-can it all as a bunch of myth?"

Huck returned his steady gaze. "Dr. Vawter, we now have written archeological records," he said. "Accept it or reject it, but doesn't that by definition sort of take it out of the myth category?"

"Okay, try this." Dr. Vawter's features fixed a cold stare. "The scrolls were primarily addressed to future generations totally unknown to that alleged Akiri priest. Now then, when we decipher archeological records we sort of eavesdrop in on peoples of the past, as it were. Ancient records were primarily written to contemporaries. They're either mundane things like accounts of business transactions or maybe the exaggerated exploits of the current king. Wasn't addressing future generations as to what is happening at a given moment in history the least of their concern?"

"Okay, try this," said Huck mimicking Dr. Vawter's words. "The scrolls were a ship's log, remember? Now then isn't it in the character of even modern-day logs to be written as a diary whose entries were intended to be read by whomever?"

Dr. Vawter's eyes hardened. "It's still a lot of bullshit," he said. "Now c'mon, don't tell me you actually believe that stuff."

"Whether I believe it disbelieve it is not the issue," said Huck, feeling his pulse quicken. "The point is that it's now of matter of historical record."

Tense lines formed around the corners of Dr. Vawter's mouth. "Yeah, but do *you* believe it?"

A thought occurred to Huck. He leaned forward in his chair. "Okay, let me ask you something," he said. "Have you ever received Jesus Christ as your own personal savior?"

Color crept into Dr. Vawter's face, from his neck on up to his temples. "I don't see whether that's any of your business," he said, his voice becoming phlegmatic.

Huck continued leaning forward in his chair. "My point exactly," he said, struggling to control his voice. "If what you believe is none of my business, why is what I believe any of your business?"

Dr. Vawter sprung to his feet and gestured toward the door.

"Get out!" he roared...

* * * * *

...Huck picked up the legal pad and resumed writing. *George and I used to be real close,* he recalled. *Then he became Dr. Bouknight.*

His summer with the archeological expedition whetted his appetite for the subject. He returned to Cortez Pacific U. and enrolled in graduate studies in archeology. To overcome deficiencies in this area, he actually had to take some undergraduate courses. Much to his surprise, he got graduate credit for them, plus an assistantship that he had also applied for. In 1983, he was appointed full-time instructor. The following year, he married Jacki. In June of 1985 he got his Ph.D. in archeology. True to its stated intention from as far back as 1979, the university created the new Department of Antiquities and appointed the new Dr. Bouknight as its department head...

...In the dining room of Artie's apartment that fall Sunday afternoon of 1987, Artie had told Huck that the greatest pressure to surrender the scrolls now came from Dr. Bouknight.

"I can't believe it," said Huck.

He recalled feeling the pulse in his neck quicken. Iconoclasts pay a price, he concluded. Savanarola sought to purge the church of Renaissance Italy of its images and statues. He eventually ended up being burned at the stake. Elijah of the Old Testament forced a showdown with the idolatrous priests of Baal. After calling from heaven on the altar Jehovah, he ordered the Baalist priests killed. For his trouble he had to flee for his life from the wrathful Queen Jezebel.

"Believe it." Artie returned to the window and glanced out at the parking lot.

Chapter 28

We were affrighted further by a cry—the suddenness of it shattered the night's stillness... Giving no thought as to how futile our defense might be against these misbegotten creatures that now infest even our city streets... Slowly and labouriously our caravan plied its way through the deserted streets of the once-great Akir-Ema. How sad and shabby she looked to me that day; rather like an (aged) concubine... as a wanton beauty bereft of lovers who wearied of her...
    (Days 36 and 37. Trans. and ed. Brit. Mus. vers. 3.5; 1981.)

* * * * *

...Huck again leaned against the rich leather back of the couch. A line of pale blue etched the Los Angeles skyline and stretched across the eastern sky. He chided himself for having missed some very important signals. Could he have headed off subsequent events had he been a little more aware; a little more sensitive? Lester's intransigence still remained in his mind. However, another twist to the whole situation then came up in the conversation...

* * * * *

...Artie drew her arms about her as she continued looking out the window. "I went to the doctor the other day."

"Not feeling well?" As soon as he said it, he realized it was a dumb thing to say.

She turned to face him. She slipped both hands up around his neck. Her words had a ring of unreality: "I'm going to have a baby."

He pulled her hands down and held them in front of him while he let the truth sink in: Dr. Mason-Rodgers, internationally renowned scholar, carrying his child, initiating him into another rite of passage: fatherhood. He tried to search for an appropriate reaction. He threw his arms around her and pulled her off her feet. He then dropped her into a chair and rushed to her refrigerator.

"We're out," she announced, still short of breath.

He returned to the dining room. "This is great," he said, kissing her repeatedly.

He stopped and eyed her.

"What's the matter?" he said, sitting down.

As he pulled closer to the table, his expression sobered.

She seemed to struggle for words. "When I first heard the news," she said finally, "I confess I was less than thrilled."

He continued studying her.

"I—briefly considered—abortion."

"Oh, dear God, no," he whispered. "Don't ever do that."

She caressed his arm. "It's all right, I've dismissed the idea completely." She sat back in her chair. "But there are still problems: like giving the child a name."

He stood and began pacing the floor. "We need Lester to give you your freedom so that we can get on with our lives."

Artie rose and turned to the window. "He wants me to give up his name first."

She then explained that it involved a joint financial venture. He had persuaded her to invest some of her money with him in a limited partnership in a small, fledgling movie studio. Only later did she learn that Atlantis Studios produced pornography. She immediately announced to Lester that she would have none of it and wanted her money out. But, my dear, he had objected, you don't know what you're passing up. Large, commercial studios regularly risk hundreds of millions of dollars on projects with no guarantee of return. Porno producers, on the other hand, can often produce an X-rated film for less than $50,000 and then recoup their investment within two days of the film's release.

Not for the squeamish, I grant you, he had acknowledged, but financially a sure thing and unbelievably lucrative.

Wording in the joint tenancy clause also stipulated that giving up his name meant relinquishing her share of the money.

Huck stopped pacing the floor. "Time he and I had a showdown."

"Don't you dare," she warned. "Let me handle it."

He moved alongside her, facing the dining room window. I have to be going, was the last thing he had said to her that afternoon.

The following week, Huck again had occasion to be back on campus. He had more talent scout business with the athletic director. As he left the athletic director's office, he paused.

Instead if heading toward the main exit of the Arts and Sciences building, he turned toward the office of the dean. Stopping just outside the closed door, he knocked.

"Come in."

As he entered, Dr. Rodgers' eyes narrowed. "Well if it isn't God's gift to womanhood," he said, leaning back in his chair.

Huck took a chair across from his desk. "I'll get to the point. I think it's high time you granted Artie her freedom."

Dr. Rodgers' face puckered like a withered prune. "I don't want to discuss it."

"I do," said Huck.

"I think you should leave."

"Not until we talk."

"Get out," demanded Dr. Rodgers.

"I'm not leaving," insisted Huck.

Dr. Rodgers started for the door. "I'll get a security guard."

Huck jumped up and seized Dr. Rodgers' lapel. When Dr. Rodgers tried to push him away, Huck threw him back on his desk.

He felt a blow to his chest as Dr. Rodgers slammed both feet against him, flinging him against a bookshelf. As books cascaded down on him, he saw that Dr. Rodgers was again at the door. Huck sprang to his feet in an attempt to pull him away.

He felt a fist slamming into his mouth, again throwing him against the wall. He realized his antagonist's moves were not haphazard. How could he have been so dense? That photo behind the dean's desk! That autographed photo of the Korean martial arts instructor. In a flash Huck chided himself for not connecting the dots, as it were.

Dr. Rodgers knew karate.

Huck jumped him again, trying to avoid another fist. He caught an elbow to his ribs, followed by the knife blow to his jaw. He now realized that the dean would be no pushover. Tasting blood, he again seized his antagonist's lapel. He knocked Dr. Rodgers against the desk with a right hook, sending his glasses flying to the floor, when the door opened.

A security guard stood in the doorway. The two combatants stood up and straightened their clothing. Breathing heavily, they both began daubing blood from their faces.

The guard turned to Dr. Rodgers. "Are you all right?"

Silence pressed in on the room.

Dr. Rodgers looked at the guard. "It's all right," he said, picking up his glasses. "Mr. Ladd is just leaving. Just a minor disagreement. It won't be necessary to report this."

The guard stood aside, but didn't leave. His message was clear.

Huck stepped through the doorway and exited down the hall.

After Huck left, Dr. Rodgers dismissed the security guard and returned to his desk. He gingerly pressed his handkerchief to his lower lip. The bleeding had stopped but the swelling had already begun. *That young man really hurt me*, he thought. *Can I not defend myself anymore?...*

...A shaken Huck started down the corridor from the dean's office. He sucked on the skinned knuckles in an attempt to assuage the smarting. Already discoloration had started. *I hit him my hardest*, he thought, *yet it didn't seem to faze him. Am I losing my punch?*

The surprising strength that Dr. Rodgers had shown left Huck in an unaccustomed depression; exacerbated during subsequent days when he left messages on both Artie's home and office answering machines.

She wasn't returning his calls.

A week later he received a letter in the mail.

Hi, this is me, Artie. I'm out of town. I heard about your altercation with Lester. We were on the verge of reaching an agreement when you took matters into your own hands.

Your little trip to Lester's office has set things back for who knows how long? I have been waiting for years for the man I have loved to realize that he cannot solve every problem with brute force, but apparently that's not going to happen.

Needless to say I am disappointed and hurt. Deeply hurt. As you yourself once said: we're not getting any younger.

I can't afford to wait for the man I once loved to finally grow up. I have to get on with my life.

Please don't try to contact me.

I can still abort the child or have it and put it up for adoption. Or—maybe even keep it and raise it myself.

Have a nice life.

In the weeks that followed, his workload did little to take his mind off her. His time was spent as a retainer for large corporations, advising them how to avoid expensive environmental lawsuits.

More importantly, he couldn't stop thinking about the child.

A trip up to the cabin revealed that Artie had changed the locks.

In subsequent years, Artie told him the real story. She really did have business regarding her parents' estate. She recalled her trip to Chicago that Thanksgiving holiday weekend...

...As she drove up the winding driveway to the family homestead, she felt dismayed by the run-down appearance of the house and grounds. Shrubbery around the once-splendid Victorian-style house had now become overgrown with neglect. Paint had begun peeling from off the shutters that bordered the windows. Fallen chips left open chinks in the brick exterior. Vines growing wildly out of control gripped that same exterior in an extensive chokehold. Leaves, having fallen off the giant elms autumns past, now lay a rotting carpet over the spacious, rolling yard. The rusted lock on the oaken front door turned only with the greatest of difficulty.

Just before stepping through the doorway, she heard a shriek that made goose bumps pop out on her forearms. She looked up to see a crow circle low through the naked tree branches overhead. It repeated its raucous caw as it rose higher against the gray, leaden sky and disappeared over a tiled rooftop nearby. The raw, autumn wind cut into her face, heightening the color of her cheeks.

Fighting silly notions of portents, she stepped into the mansion's cavernous foyer.

She pushed the heavy front door shut behind her and immediately a musty odor greeted her. Graying sheets enshrouded the living and dining room furniture. She eyed the hardwood wall paneling and staircase and marveled how the once highly polished wood had lost its luster.

She slowly walked from the foyer into the living room. A thick layer of dust had sullied the sheen of the marbled mantelpiece. Cobwebs festooned the corners of the ceiling. The outside chill followed her in.

Opposite the fireplace and on the faded carpeting once stood the giant Christmas tree. Immediately in front of it a six-year-old girl in the dark dress with white-laced collar had once sat posing beside her other gifts. She recalled her parents snapping that picture. She recalled how they still glowed with pride over their child's solo during the Christmas program of the previous Sunday. She also recalled the stage fright mingled with the sense of excitement as she sang that last verse of "Away in a Manger":

"Be near me, Lord Jesus, I ask thee to stay
Close by me forever, and love me, I pray.
Bless all the dear children in thy tender care,
And take us to heaven to live with thee there."

She exited the living room. Upon reentering the front hall, she stopped and surveyed the surroundings worn by age and neglect. The threadbare condition of the stair tread and the once brightly colored Oriental rug saddened her. She shivered as her breath formed moisture in the air.

Gentle, well-bred faces of a man and a woman looked down at her from an oval-shaped picture frame. They had married and had her rather late in life. *Dear Mommsie and Poppsie,* she thought, *how I miss you.*

Moisture welled up in her eyes as she pushed aside faded curtains and looked out the front bay window. The pungent smell of dust assailed her nostrils with each wave of the curtain. *I'm going to reopen this house,* she decided. *I'm going to find work and move back.*

She determined to put her California experience behind her. She would go ahead and have the baby here and raise it in the Midwest. And of course she would bring the jars and scrolls with her. She locked up the house again and drove back to the motel. For the time being she would leave it that way.

The next morning she braved the miles of traffic maze to the Loop in downtown Chicago. She had an appointment with the personnel director at an institution known as the Chicago Historical Museum. She was interviewing for the position of curator.

As she returned to the parking lot, she saw him.

He was one of those individuals once met, never forgotten. Upon joining Earthnation, he had terrorized the entire commune into submission. His erratic temper and psychotic personality made life a living hell. He had insisted that he and Artie had wed in a secret satanic wedding.

When he demanded that the "elders" of the commune hand her over to him, she fled the commune compound in the dark of night. She hitchhiked her way back to the Greater Los Angeles area, without money and without ID. She was finally able to phone Peppi. She was grateful to Peppi for letting her hide in her apartment while she called home, apologized to her parents and appealed to them for money so that she could get back in school.

Even after marrying Lester, she still feared his stalking her.

She realized that there was no mistake. She could recognize the hulking figure, well over six feet. She recognized the black leather jacket, the tattered jeans, the goatee, the dark glasses, and the shaven head. Most of all, she recognized the tattoo design that covered his face and head. She ducked behind the parked cars to avoid being seen. Stealthily, she opened her car door and slipped in. She tried to quietly drive out of the parking lot without his seeing her. She still couldn't believe that she had just seen her worst nightmare.

Snake.

Trembling hands held the wheel as she drove for O'Hare, checked in her rented car, and headed for the ticket counter that scheduled flights to LA International. As she stood waiting in line, she still trembled at the thought of his following her to Chicago. *Is there no way to get away from that man?* she asked herself in near panic.

As the waiting became prolonged, a thought occurred to her. *How typical of so many tides of historical turmoil that overtake us. They are easily joined. However, once in, it is difficult to leave.*

Sharp cramps seized her abdomen. *Dear God,* she thought, *I'm going into labor.*

In the terminal dispensary, she delivered a one-and-half pound boy. A boy: Huck would have liked that.

However, he was stillborn.

She spent the next three days in a nearby suburban hospital. When she finally left and flew out of O'Hare, her mind writhed in turmoil as she sat in a window seat. She looked out at the clouds and reflected on the men in her life and of her relationships with them: Snake, Lester, and now Huck. She wondered at her inability to establish a normal relationship. Maybe she harbored latent lesbian tendencies. No way, she concluded. She had no desire for other women. Certainly not in that context. Was it her sheltered upbringing and its resultant naïveté? *What is it with me?* she thought.

The clouds dropped below her as the plane gained altitude. The skies cleared to an azure blue and the sun shone brightly near the horizon. *Snake,* she thought. *Is there no way to get away from that man?*

She remembered conversations with Huck regarding the literal Resurrection. Certainly all nothing more than just symbolic, she kept insisting. Certainly not to be taken literally.

Huck would merely shrug.

Quest for the historical Jesus. He recalled the buzzword among liberal scholars who insisted the literal Jesus of Nazareth lay in some forgotten Palestinian tomb. They had only to find his bones to prove once and for all, to believer and skeptic alike, that it was all just a pleasant myth.

He also recalled the obvious discomfort on her part when he alluded to the mysterious disappearance of Bishop Pike, Episcopal bishop from their own state of California, when he went on this very quest. Instead of finding the remains of the so-called historical Jesus, he himself took a wrong turn in the desert. Searchers found his body a week later.

If the historical Jesus did, in fact, escape that forgotten Palestinian tomb, she thought, why would he allow a monster such as Snake to remain loose in his universe?

What of Huck? After all, he was the child's father. She would send him a quick note, she decided. It's only fair.

She nervously bit her lower lip. How now their relationship?

* * * * *

… Huck shook his head. In later years, she had disclosed to him upon her return to campus, she was served with an injunction to turn over the scrolls and jars to the school. However, she knew that they had no interest in publishing the translations. She had seen this happen to the Dead Sea Scrolls. After forty years the scrolls' contents were still not generally known.

The problem lay not in the difficulty of translation. The problem was political and ideological.

She did not want the same thing happening to her Deluge Scrolls.

Other factors figured as well. The administration was certainly aware of the possibilities of untold wealth for anyone who could unlock the secret of the self-charging dry cell. Artie and Huck had already contacted private electronic research labs to conduct experiments on the jar without success. The lab people finally concluded that learning the secret of the electrically charged jar would be impossible without breaking it apart and examining it. Of course, that would involve destroying a priceless artifact.

This Artie had no intention of doing.

"Could Dr. Vawter ever have that greedy a motive?" Huck had once asked.

"Greed knows no ideological boundaries," replied Artie…

* * * * *

…Huck got up from the couch. He went to the kitchenette sink and splashed cold water on his face. Back into the inner office, he looked out the window. The eastern sky had gotten brighter. His watch said six. Got to meet George in an hour. As he sat back on his leather couch, his mind went to more recent events…

* * * * *

…When he had a respite from his schedule, he drove up the San Fernando Valley to Artie's apartment. Here he found a surprise.

The apartment was locked.

And empty.

He rushed to the buildings manager's office. "Did Dr. Mason-Rodgers leave a forwarding address?" he demanded.

She flipped through a Rolodex file. "Apartment #2B? That must be the tenant who's in jail."

"Jail?" Huck shouted in disbelief.

The apartment is empty, Huck had told her. Where is the furniture?

"I'm holding it for rent collateral."

Huck flipped his checkbook out on the manager's desk. "How much does she owe you?" he demanded as he took out his pen.

As he wrote out the check, he announced to the manager, "I want you to reopen her apartment and put her furniture back. I'll pay her rent until she is released. I'll want a key, and I'll give you my card. I want you to call me if there are any problems. Any questions?"

The manager eyed the check. "No questions, Mr. Ladd," she said as she wrote out the receipt.

When he finally reached campus, he looked up Dr. Berthold to learn the full story. Artie had defied a court injunction to turn over the scrolls and was finally incarcerated on charges of contempt of court.

For an attorney, Dr. Berthold had recommended an old drinking buddy. Huck knew him by reputation to be an incompetent lush. He often appeared in court either drunk or nursing a hangover. *With him, she could stay in jail until she rots,* he thought. That evening, back in his apartment, Huck perused Dr. Berthold's note that contained Artie's prison address. He began writing the following:

Dearest Artie:

I know you told me not to try to contact you. However, whether you know it or not, you are in deep doo-doo. Your present counselor has the reputation of not knowing his butt from a hole in the ground. And that's when he's sober. For your own sake, I suggest you get another attorney. I may not be the most disinterested counselor around, but I can't think of anyone who cares more about seeing you released than I. Whatever you may think of me personally, I suggest we put our differences aside for the moment.

Enclosed is a stamped, addressed postcard. Just write "yes" if you want me to represent you; or "no" if you don't. If you decide "no" I'll not bother you further with this.

I just want to say that I'm sorry I messed things up for us. I also want you to know that I still love you.

Love,
Huck

P.S. I also paid your back rent and reclaimed your furniture. I will keep your apartment open until you are back on your feet.

Five days later he received a piece of prison stationery.

My Darling Huck:

Hearing from you is like at last waking up from this terrible nightmare. Please forgive this silly woman and come as soon as you can. I'm afraid I'll die if I don't see you again.

Love,
Artie

Huck laid the letter on the desk and reached for the phone. Much as he wanted to see Artie, he decided to see Dr. Bouknight first. He wanted to get a little background on the case before he did anything else. He contacted George at campus just as he was dismissing a night class. George could see him at lunch day after tomorrow.

On the day in question, Huck had gotten to a table at the Student Union dining room a little early. He saw Dr. Bouknight coming toward him carrying a lunch tray. *Been awhile,* he thought.

"Good to see you," he said, trying to sound casual. He pulled out a chair and George sat down. He replied that it was good to see Huck. For a moment they sat facing one another.

Not like the old days, thought Huck.

A pause.

"About Artie," said George. "Could you convey a message?"

"What kind of message?"

"When you see her, ask her if she would be interested in a deal. Namely that if she was to turn over the scrolls and jars, she can keep her notes and we'll drop the charges."

Chapter 29

The Age of Clay... There is breakdown of law and order. Hudishi run rampant in our streets and molest law-abiding citizens with impunity. Youth no longer show reverence to the god, Lemekh. Billiku speaks the truth. We face rebellion. I have seen our Temple slaves wash from the base of the Statue the leakage of dogs and men.

I have seen evidence of gold leaf being stripped from the baser metals underneath... Nefillim: neither men, nor beasts, nor Angry Things, but rather part of all three.

(Days 12 and 35. Trans. and ed. Brit. Mus. Vers.3.5; 1981.)

* * * * *

Huck began eating slowly. "Interesting proposition." He would have to get back to him on that.

"Something I never could understand," he said after a pause, "how you could do this to people once close to you."

George's shoulders sagged. "It hasn't been easy."

Huck looked puzzled as George recalled his first time inside the exclusive University Club...

* * * * *

..."Dr. Bouknight, over here." Dr. Vawter beckoned him from across the room.

"Where are the others?" George wanted to know as he took his seat.

Dr. Vawter began nursing a whiskey on the rocks. "Kewpie Doll and Puckerpuss aren't coming."

George glared at him. "Excuse me?"

"Dr. Faasendeck couldn't make it," was the answer, "and Dr. Rodgers is a very sick man."

Dr. Vawter's eyes hardened as he tipped his glass to his mouth. "Just as well," he said, "just leaves the two of us, mano e mano. I've already ordered your drink."

"I'll just have ice water."

"I'm ordering you a whiskey."

"But I don't drink whiskey." George felt moisture under his shirt.

"I didn't ask you what you drank," Dr. Vawter said in a flat tone of voice. "I'm not about to drink alone."

George slouched further in his seat but said nothing.

"We need to talk about your staff," Dr. Vawter said finally. "Dr. Mason-Rodgers in particular."

He reached for an attaché case and produced a copy of *The Deluge Scrolls*. He showed sections that he had highlighted.

The chapter dealt with such phenomena as Easter Island, Stonehenge, the mysterious Peruvian "Airstrip," undersea temples and superhighways on the floor of the Caribbean, and evidence of temples and highways under the rotting foliage of the Mayan jungle. A closing section questioned modern science in giving earth an existence of billions of years, yet confining recorded history to only five thousand years.

> We have long considered places such as the Tigris-Euphrates basin, the Nile Valley, the Indus River basin, and China to be the cradles of civilization, all beginning about 3,500 B.C. However, does this preclude the possibility that at any time within the end of the last ice age, given the right climactic conditions, the evolution of any hunter-gatherer culture to agrarian to village level and from there to an interdependent civilized social order?

"So what do you make of it?" said Dr. Vawter, eyeing him closely.

"You forget, sir," said George returning his glare, "that I was with Dr. Mason-Rodgers on that expedition."

At first Dr. Vawter didn't answer. Instead he turned to another passage. "Okay, look at this."

He showed George a passage mentioning famous historical persons sighting a visitation known as the "Red One," or "Red Man." Eyewitness descriptions depicted him as having a swarthy complexion and copper-colored skin. According to the scrolls this bore a resemblance to the Akiri, or possibly the "Plain ones."

In Hebrew, the word for "Red Man" was Ed-Hom, or "Adam."

"What the hell's she trying to do," Dr. Vawter said, "connect all this with Adam and Eve?"

"I don't know," George said with a shrug.

"It's your department," Dr. Vawter reminded him. "Don't you think it's damn well time you found out?"

"Suppose she does advance that idea," said George. "So what?"

"We can't have it is what," insisted Dr. Vawter. "We can't have hypotheses like that coming out of our school."

"But in all her research and publications," said George, struggling to defend a respected mentor, "she always adhered to highest scientific standards. I don't understand your concern."

"Scientific standards is not the issue," snapped Dr. Vawter.

"If not scientific, what?"

"Ideological."

Ideological? George looked at him.

Dr. Vawter continued a steady gaze. "I've been concerned about her for a long time. For openers, she claims her husband hit her with a riding crop. That was her pretext for leaving him in the first place."

"What makes you think he didn't?"

Dr. Vawter's eyes narrowed. "Get real. That whole scene was a wild, kinky orgy. A lot of strange things went down that weekend. Who knows for sure who did what to whom and when—and if?"

He continued, "I also understood she quit graduate school and ran off to join a commune in the desert someplace."

"A lot of kids did wild and crazy things back in those days."

Dr. Vawter continued looking at George without changing his position. "Okay, try this: the clincher is this cockamamie story about her finding a dead child in her rented beach house."

"Hershel Ladd was with her."

"He only saw photographs—so he said."

"But there was a break-in."

"Yeah, but no publicized police report of a homicide. Go figure."

Silence.

Dr. Vawter shifted his weight and leaned further back in his chair. "Like I say," he sighed, "I'm afraid her wrapping's coming loose. We've got to do something."

Dr. Bouknight still remained silent.

Dr. Vawter continued, "When I say 'we' I mean I want you to do something."

He went on to suggest publishing some kind of disclaimer. Get a colleague to publish a paper questioning the jar's authenticity. The dating could be flawed, for instance, and the real dating could only about 400 B.C.E. Get literary critics to analyze the metrical differences in the various entries. Have them question why some of the poetry is rhyme and some blank verse. The scrolls couldn't have all been by one author. Blitz academia with allegations that her stuff is spurious.

George cleared his throat. "What about intellectual honesty?"

"All right," said Dr, Vawter with another disgusted sigh. "You figure it out."

Dr. Bouknight fidgeted in his chair. "I don't understand."

"Good God, man. Do I have to spell everything out for you?"

George's eyes widened. "I never heard you talk like this before."

Dr. Vawter pointed at him. "You're going to hear me say a lot of things you've never heard me say before we're through with this."

He paused, and then went on. "Listen, I had you kicked upstairs when nobody—and I mean nobody would have bet a plug nickel on you. And now I'm going tell you something—and I'm only going to say it once. So hear me and hear me good. That flaky broad and her mumbo-jumbo research are getting out of hand. I said I was only going to say that once, but since I'm in such a generous mood, I'm going to say it again: that flaky broad and her mumbo-jumbo research are getting out of hand. You got that? Good."

Payback time, he thought, as he continued puffing on his cigarette.

"Enough shop talk," he said, changing the subject. "Let's order."

George sat staring at the tablecloth.

Dr. Vawter motioned out into the dining area. "Waiter," he said tersely, "over here."

When the waiter arrived, Dr. Vawter ordered for the both of them. Later, as they were eating, George's order still lay untouched.

Fifteen minutes later they parted in the parking lot. "Say 'hello' to Jacki for me," said Dr. Vawter.

Still later, George drove through darkened streets; with a mood darker still. By now his suit hung on him drenched as though he had been caught in a downpour.

He's got me just where he wants me, he thought.

Things were just too easy, he reflected, *and I bit, hook, line, and sinker. Ph.D. in archeology, professor and department head,* he thought further. *Now what? Am I just a toy? A puppet?*

He smiled at the irony. Back in the bad old days, white plantation owners owned his ancestors' bodies.

Now Dr. Vawter and their ilk own our souls. Sweet Jesus, he reflected, *how do I get out of this?*

When George finally reached home, he stepped out of his car, coat draped over his arm, and trudged up to his front door.

Jacki eyed him with alarm. "George, what's the matter?"

He walked past without answering. His jacket dropped to the floor as he went into the bathroom and began washing his face in the sink.

"I've never seen you like this." Jacki followed him and stood in the doorway. "What is the matter?"

"It's unreal," he said, studying himself in the mirror. A haggard, peaked face stared back.

A recollection occurred to him. *Sweet Jesus,* he thought, *I remember you once said "the truth shall make you free."*

"Can I get you anything?" He heard Jacki's voice, taut with concern, from the doorway again.

He saw a sudden serenity in the face in the mirror. "No, thank you," he said, turning toward her. "I'm okay."…

…As George related the story, Huck stared at his tray. He said he was sorry; that he didn't know.

George got up from the table. "My problem," he said.

He picked up his windbreaker. "I'm going to have to deal with it. I'll get back to you…"

* * * * *

...Huck's watch said six-thirty. He stood up yawning. The blood surge from his head made him dizzy. He steadied himself and waited while his senses cleared. He recalled leaving George at the Union and taking off for the athletic office to meet Mike Travis...

* * * * *

...Mike also worked for the athletic department as a football scout. In the hall just outside the AD's office, he saw Mike approach.

"So how's Dr. Vawter's lackey today?" Mike had asked.

Huck's expression froze. "You mean George?"

He fell in stride beside Mike. "He was our teammate once, remember?"

His steps were abruptly halted by Mike's sudden stop. Huck scanned the empty corridor. "You know—Yucca Bowl?" he continued. "Or have you forgotten?"

Mike stooped to a drinking fountain. "Or has he forgotten?" he said after he straightened up.

"Promotion to department head," he snorted, "what a suck-up job."

"Just had an interesting conversation with him at lunch," said Huck as they resumed walking. "I wouldn't be too hard on him."

Mike followed him in sullen silence out to Huck's Mercedes.

"Let's stop at the Matador," suggested Huck as he opened the driver's door. "You know, for old time's sake?"

Mike slid in on the passenger side. "Been a while, hasn't it?" he said giving Huck a sidelong glance.

Huck fumbled with the keys. "What's that supposed to mean?"

"Never mind," said Mike pointing toward the windshield. "Just drive by and see for yourself."

The engine roared a crescendo as they raced out of the parking lot. Later they circled the block where the Matador had once stood. They saw a building painted black with a sign in white letters: "Osiris Club."

Huck looked back in disbelief. "What happened to the Matador?"

"Gone," was the answer.

Huck glanced back at the sign. "Since when?"

"Since about a year ago."

"Well." Huck slammed his brakes. He looked back again, then added, "What the hell?" His wheels squealed in a U-turn. As he edged into the parking lot, he noticed a VW van painted in a psychedelic design, a decades-old relic that looked barely mobile, and four motorcycles.

"Doesn't look our kind of crowd anymore," commented Huck as they climbed out.

"Wait till you see what's inside," said Mike with a wry smile.

Huck pushed open the door and was immediately confronted with a corridor painted black. A swinging door leading to the main taproom presented an entire interior with furnishings also painted black. While they waited for their eyes to become accustomed to the darkness, they saw the intermittent flash of a center strobe light hanging from the ceiling, a dim light over the bar, and a spotlight where two bearded giants in vests of wet leather and soiled tank tops lunged ample bellies over a pool table. They both wore wide leather belts that held up creosote-soaked jeans. They aimed their cues at balls rolling over a dirty green tabletop. Elaborate tattoos glistened with sweat beneath the thick hair of their flabby arms.

Mike cast him a jaundiced eye. "Still want to go in?"

"Why not?" Huck gestured to a table of chipped veneer. "One drink and then we'll leave, okay?"

They could feel the stares of alienated eyes through the darkness. They could hear the remark: "Hey, look at the suits."

The small, skinny barkeep wore a black T-shirt with a red, inverted pentagram. Over the T-shirt, he too, wore a vest of wet leather. The glare of psychedelic blue reflected off his shaven head from the pulsating strobe light. Despite the darkness, he wore dark glasses.

"If you gentlemen want anything," he said in a hoarse voice, "you're going to have to come up to the bar."

Huck got up from his wire-frame chair. "I'm getting a draft beer," he said, turning to Mike. "That okay with you?"

Mike nodded. "Whatever."

After Huck returned from the bar, Mike took a sip of the foamy head. "See what I mean?"

Huck continued to survey the murky interior. On the tiny bandstand stood gigantic speakers and amplifiers. Beside the bass drum a stood a black sign with white letters that read, "Now playing—Primal Scream."

Along the opposite wall sat a row of booths. They were empty except for one occupied by two men with orange hair. Vests of wet leather covered their green-dyed upper bodies.

Huck forced himself not to race down his drink. *Don't let them see you anxious*, he told himself.

When their drinks sat half empty, Mike rose to his feet. "Lend me a quarter." He gestured to the vestibule. "I want to use the phone."

Huck reached into his pocket. "Make it fast, will you?"

Mike cast him a sidelong glance. "This place getting to you?"

After Mike disappeared into the vestibule, Huck cast furtive glances toward the men in the booth. He noticed the gold of their pentagram-shaped earrings glistening in the glare of the strobe light.

He saw light burst from the rear passage, heard footsteps banging the walls of the corridor, and then he saw two shadowy forms in the doorway. Huck recognized the lanky figure in faded jeans as Jack Springfield. Beside him stood a stranger towering over even him. Huck noticed beneath a badly soiled tank top the broad, muscular chest. Biceps thick as railroad ties hung suspended from massive shoulders. The stranger wore a small goatee. The bald head, face, and chest, arms, and body were covered with a tattoo designed to look like a snakeskin. When he removed the dark glasses, small pig-like eyes blinked at the interior twilight.

Huck recognized the stranger from Artie's description.

The man standing beside Jack Springfield was Snake.

The newcomers joined the green-dyed couple in their booth. After a brief whispered exchange, Jack Springfield started for the bar. When the barkeep served up four draft beers, Jack started back to the booth. He passed Huck's table, despite its being out of his way.

Suddenly his foot caught a chair leg and drinks spilled over Huck's head and shoulders. Huck jumped to his feet and faced his antagonist

Small eyes and fixed their cold stare. "Well, if it isn't the counselor," Springfield said with a twisted smile. "How clumsy of me."

Huck wiped his sleeves. "No problem," he said. "Just an accident. I was about to send this suit to the cleaners anyway."

As Huck reached for his chair, Jack snatched it out of his reach. "You tripped me."

In his peripheral vision, Huck saw Snake and the two green men closing in. He started moving slowly toward the door. Suddenly he felt a chain thrust around his neck. He grabbed muscular hands and kicked against a kneecap as he threw an assailant over his shoulder.

No sooner had the antagonist's body crashed into furniture, than Huck found himself beset by other attackers. A mass of hairy arms grabbed him, barely giving him a chance to yell, "Mike!"

He felt himself being dragged onto the pool table. The vestibule door burst open and Huck caught an impression of Mike's face twisted with rage as he jumped a couple of assailants. Huck managed to work one arm free and drove his fist into the soft midsection of one of the pool players.

He felt his head jerked upward in a powerful headlock. He saw the scaly face of Snake move in close as giant hands grasped his collar.

"So this is the dude you told me about." He spoke with a Southern accent in a gravelly, high-pitched voice. Huck again felt his hand wriggle free. Seeing Snake's midsection pressing in close, he drove his fist into Snake's solar plexus. With a hoarse groan, Snake's head shot back. His eyes glazed over in a pained expression. He stepped backward and fell gasping to the floor.

Suddenly a scream pierced the already deafening din. Mike had just seized a green-dyed patron's earring and had torn it from his ear lobe. "Come on!" Mike yelled waving a blood-smeared hand.

As the moaning patron lay doubled over on the floor holding his head, Huck jumped to his feet. He saw Mike drop the gory earring and snatch a basket of pool balls from off a nearby rack. The sound of running feet thundered behind them as they rushed toward the glare of the rear exit. Mike paused in the doorway while Huck ran on to his car. Mike began grabbing the balls and firing fast pitches back into the passageway. He managed to hold the attackers at bay while Huck swung his Mercedes by close. Throwing the basket aside, he jumped into the passenger side and struggled to bring his door shut.

Once out in traffic, they lapsed into a stunned silence, driving several blocks without saying anything

Huck looked in the rearview mirror. He noticed discoloration forming beside his eye. As the minutes lengthened, he still couldn't control his shortness of breath nor his trembling. He raised his fist to his mouth and began sucking his scraped and bleeding knuckles.

Mike looked at him. "You okay?"

"Guess so."

Huck, in puzzlement, glanced down at his lap. He felt needle-like pains stabbing his knees. He noticed tattered trousers hanging listlessly about muscular legs.

"Better get new pants," he said, laughing nervously, "before I go back out in public."…

* * * * *

…Huck raised his head with a start. He saw the rays of morning sunlight streaming through the window. His watch said six-fifty. From a desk drawer he pulled out a freshly laundered shirt. He rushed toward a private lavatory where he doused his face with cold water and gave himself a quick shave. Vigorously he splashed on cologne, put on his clean shirt, and retied his tie. He glanced nervously at his watch, snatched his jacket and attaché case, and bolted for the front door.

He again entered the coffee shop around the corner. The lunch counter clock said seven. Exactly. He wiped his forehead with a clean handkerchief. Saturday morning meant the place shouldn't be busy. Most everybody would be gone for the weekend. He slid into a secluded booth nevertheless. *I like privacy*, he thought as he looked at a menu.

He glanced up to see George coming through the front entrance.

"Good to see you, George," he said as George entered the booth.

"Good to see you too," said George, imitating Huck's affected formality. He slid in the seat opposite and for a moment said nothing.

"So," said Huck, "how have you been?"

"I've been well."

Another silence.

"Let's order," said Huck motioning for the waitress.

"I'm really not hungry," said George. "I think I'll just have an order of whole wheat toast and coffee."

After the waitress left, Huck again turned to his former teammate. "So," he said, clearing his throat, "how are things at school?"

"Busy."

"I see," said Huck. He could not shake the sense of awkwardness. "We ought to get together soon."

"I'd like that." George tried to make it sound convincing.

"So—how have you been?" said Huck after another pause.

"Great."

"Guess we went over that already, didn't we?" said Huck with an embarrassed smile.

"Yeah."

Another silence; broken only by the waitress bringing their orders.

"You called me last night," said Huck. "You wanted to see me."

George paused. "I've made a decision," he said. He reached into his jacket and handed Huck an envelope. "I think this will explain."

Huck slit open the envelope and pulled out the sheaf of papers. He scanned them briefly. "Artie's free in other words?"

"That's right."

Huck started to slide out of the booth.

"Oh, and another thing." George's remark halted his exit.

George pulled out another envelope. "My resignation," he said, "effective immediately."

Huck slid back into the booth. "What will you do?"

"Oh, I got a few things going," he said, "but the main thing is that now I'm my own man."

As Huck again got up to leave, he extended his hand. "I hate to cut and run, as they say," he said, "but I've got to get back to Artie."

"Of course," said George. Still gripping hands, they studied each other briefly. A look of understanding flashed between them.

"Keep in touch." Huck snatched both checks.

"Right," said George, waving him off...

* * * * *

..."I'm here to see prisoner 1102."

The desk officer reached for his credentials. Was it really only yesterday? He handed her George's envelope.

"What's this?" she demanded, looking up.

"Release order for prisoner 1102."

She took the papers and examined them. Then she flipped the switch of the intercom.

"Yes?" the matron somehow made herself heard above the static.

"Matron to squad room," ordered the desk clerk. When the matron finally entered the room, the desk officer showed her the papers. "Prepare prisoner 1102 for release."

Forty minutes later, Artie stood in the doorway with the matron, showered and in her own clothes. Holding a small overnight bag, she smiled a tight little smile.

The desk officer stepped into a walk-in safe behind her and returned with a large manila envelope. She untied the flap and handed it to Artie.

"These are your valuables," she said, pointing to a list of items on the outside. "Check the contents with this inventory."

The desk officer pushed another document toward her: a liability disclaimer regarding those valuables. Artie signed it and laid aside the pen.

"You are free to go." The desk officer extended her hand.

Out the main entrance, they continued walking to the parking lot. Other than a tight grip on his arm, Artie remained impassive, staring straight ahead. She recalled the outpouring of support she received during the initial days of her confinement. As weeks dragged by, however, word of support from the outside dwindled until it dropped off completely. She recalled how totally alone she felt. She recalled praying, *God, where are you when I need you? Have you deserted me too?*

Was Huck's coming finally the answer she was looking for?

When they reached his car, he opened the door on the passenger side and helped her in.

As they roared out the main gate, he studied her. She gripped his hand, but stared straight ahead. They continued driving through the light weekend traffic in silence. She looked out the window at the speeding landscape. The palm trees lining the curbside hung limp and brown. Squat stucco houses gave way to low, rolling hills—crisply brown against a burning sky. Twenty minutes later the canyon road descended down into another valley and into the more urban setting of the San Fernando Valley.

He slowed down as they came to an intersection. They stopped for a traffic signal; however, they again encountered only light traffic. He started moving the car forward as the light turned green. As they headed toward a suburban business section, traffic began picking up.

Huck slowed down his Mercedes. Street traffic moved consistently heavier now. As the surroundings became increasingly familiar, they saw the Cortez Pacific University campus slipping by on their right. She glanced out the window and saw the science building that housed her office, her lab, and her classroom.

She hesitated. "It seems," she said, taking a deep breath, "that the lines of demarcation between historical record, empirical scientific evidence, myth, and religious revelation are no longer as sharp and clear-cut as they once were. These lines of demarcation are now, and will continue to become, increasingly blurred."

He made a left and started down a residential street.

Artie moved to a more upright position. She picked up the handbag that lay at her feet and placed it in her lap. As they neared her neighborhood, she searched the familiar landscape that came toward her.

"The thing is," she said, "the people like those in our administration are coping with these changes very badly."

The driveway to her complex appeared. He turned left and headed into it. He pulled his Mercedes alongside the space where her own car was parked. She laid her hand on his wrist.

"Wait," she said.

He looked at her curiously. She slid close. "Thanks," she said, kissing him, "for taking care of things."

He sat for a moment, staring through the steering wheel at the dashboard. "It's the least I could do. What can I say? I owe you."

Neither of them made any attempt to get out. "I've been thinking," she said at last. "You remember your asking a year ago last September where our relationship was headed? I think it's time we both grew up."

Huck flicked a piece of lint off his trouser leg. "I agree."

Artie leaned against her door handle. "Lester is ill," she said, "desperately ill. However, I'm going up to the hospital to see him—first thing next week."

Later that evening and for the first time in months, Artie began tidying her apartment. Stopping for a breather, she stepped to her kitchen tabletop to where her overnight bag lay. As she began pulling out the contents, she found the necklace. She took it out and studied it.

At the bottom of a gold chain hung a triangle within a circle.

Chapter 30

Espied I my old, familiar friend, my mentor: the noble Shumrag. "My friend," shouted he. "I bring good tidings: The Grand Vizier is dead."

"And what of the Lady Aarda?" I asked, "now that the illustrious T'reni-Akhmen also is dead."

"The Lady Aarda is being returned in secret to Akir-Ema," replied my mentor. "The evil tidings is that you cannot return to her yet, for it is still not safe to see her..."

(Day 37. Trans. and ed. Brit. Mus. vers. 3.5; 1981.)

* * * * *

"Dr. Rodgers?"

The woman at the main desk punched a computer screen.

Room 832A was in the isolation ward. Artie had to first go with a floor nurse into a visitor's prep room. She reemerged in a hospital gown, hair under a surgical bonnet, a cloth mask over her face, bags tied with drawstrings over her shoes, and wearing latex gloves.

Upon entering the room, she was immediately confronted with a labyrinth of medical machinery. A cloth curtain blocked her view of the bed. From behind it she could see suspended bottles and tubes gurgling to an unseen patient.

"Lester?" She said the word tentatively.

She could hear labored breathing from behind the curtain. "Who is it?" asked a voice in a hoarse whisper. She parted the curtain and took a glance toward the bed.

A shock of unreality pierced her inner being at what appeared before her. She had tried to steel herself ahead of time as to what she might see. Nevertheless, the psychological arsenal with which she thought she had armed herself fell away before a sense of disbelief that the patient in that bed was once her husband.

The figure lay curled on its side in a fetal position. The head sprouted sparse, wispy strands. Listless eyes glanced at her with a feverish glow. The mouth hung open with brown lips drawn tightly back. Tubes gurgled life-giving fluid into the veins. With heavy breathing the figure in the bed gurgled back.

She stepped close and caressed a foot that lay under the covers.

"Lester?" she repeated. "It's me, Ardith."

A claw-like hand reached out from underneath the covers. "It's good to see you," he rasped as she pulled up a chair.

She gripped the extended hand and recoiled at the feverish touch. "It's good to see you, too," was all that she could manage.

"How are you feeling?" As she contemplated the life-support equipment arrayed before her, she realized the inanity of her remark.

"Like I'm holding my hand in a light socket," came the reply.

Please, darling, she thought, *not now*.

"No matter," he continued. "I've felt that way most of my life. As Arthur Rimbaud once said: 'As a moth is drawn to the flame, so I am drawn to decadence.'"

"Lester, stop it," she said, raising her voice slightly.

He coughed in an attempt to laugh. "Always were squeamish about such things, weren't you?"

She released his hand and drew her arms in a tight fold. "If you don't stop it, I'll leave."

"All right," he gasped. "You win."

The ensuing silence fell like lead on the mood of the room. *You're right*, she thought. *No one knows that better than we.*

"A priest came by yesterday," he said, breaking the silence. "He wanted to administer the last rites. I refused, of course."

She looked at him incredulously. "Why, Lester?" she said. "Don't you want peace with God?"

Again, he coughed in an attempt to laugh. "If I had it, I wouldn't know what to do with it."

Good God, she thought. *You're dying! Can't you entertain a serious thought for once?*

The gurgling and humming of the machinery broke the stillness. Again the wraith-like figure in the bed endeavored to speak. "You—must have a reason for coming here," he said. "I'm glad to see you and all that—but I find it hard to believe—that this is just a—social visit."

A sense of surrealism engulfed the entire scene. "You're right," she said. "This is not just a social visit. I have news for you."

"Which is?"

"Hershel Ladd and I want to get married." She marveled at the ease with which it came out.

"Well, well, well." He fought a congestion building in his lungs. "Surprise, surprise."

Artie bit her lip underneath the mask. "I've come to ask for that annulment. I'll give up your name first, or whatever else you want."

"Not necessary," he said feebly.

"Excuse me?" she said in disbelief.

"Bring a priest," he whispered. "I'll grant it no strings attached."

She entwined her fingers around his. "Thank you."

She stood to her feet. "I'm leaving now. I don't want to tire you. I'll be back tomorrow with a priest. Thank you again and, God bless you, darling."

She turned to leave.

"Ardith?" The voice sounded noticeably weaker.

She stopped midpoint toward the door. "Yes?"

"I'm sorry." The figure shifted its position.

She closed her eyes a moment, then untied the mask and let it fall from her face. She returned to the bed and clasped his hand. She bent over and kissed the burning forehead. "Good-bye, Lester."

Biting her lower lip, she turned and quickly left the room.

She was not to return with a priest. The next day, the hospital called and notified her that Dr. Purvis Lester Rodgers was dead.

Three days later she stood beside Huck under a small graveside pavilion. Beside her stood Dr. George Bouknight.

On her other side stood the other three mourners, namely Drs. Faasendeck, Vawter, and Hyde. As Dr. Faasendeck stood beneath the pavilion, his attention remained fixed on the ground beneath him. From the corner of his eye he studied Dr. Vawter.

A fault line chasm split the revolution in its early days, he thought. Trotsky, the intellectual, the romantic, advocated a not-too-well-thought-out plan to spread the revolution worldwide immediately, so certain was he that the working class of all nations was ready for it. Stalin, the street thug, the realist, the disciplinarian, wanted to consolidate the revolution in one country first as a base of power. The disciplined street thug prevailed, sending the idealist into exile. Trotsky the dreamer died with an alpine axe buried in his skull a little more than a decade later.

Yet, today do not many of the so-called new left inadvertently follow the Trotskyite vision? Perhaps we erred in allowing ourselves to be intimidated by them, realized Dr. Faasendeck.

Was Dr. Vawter a follower of Lenin or Lennon?

The casket sat mounted over artificial turf. A man in clerical robes had placed himself at its head with his own head bowed and hands clasped.

"We commit this vessel of clay to the earth." He picked up a handful of dirt.

"And the spirit to God who gave it. Amen," he intoned, making the sign of the cross.

Huck tightened his grip on Artie's shoulder. "No further need of hanging around," he said as he guided her back toward his car.

"Now maybe he is at peace," she said.

"Who knows?" shrugged Huck. "Let's get out of here."

They walked slowly up a knoll toward the row of parked cars.

Suddenly Artie stopped. "They're here."

"Who's here?"

She pointed to a band of unkempt youths driving by in a color-splashed van. She recognized the van. She recognized the youths. *I thought the Kern County Sheriff closed the place,* she thought. *Who or what still holds that unsavory bunch together?*

"Earthnation," she said. *Once pacting with the devil,* she thought, *breaking away can be difficult and dangerous.*

He took her arm and headed toward the Mercedes. "I'll go up to the cabin this weekend. I can find a wedding chapel in Las Vegas."

She laid her hand on his sleeve. "Don't get me wrong," she pleaded. "I do want to go ahead with our plans, but—"

"But what?" A slight tone of irritation rose in his voice.

She folded her arms and looked at the ground as they continued walking. She recalled going up to the hospital the day after they had called. As she collected his personal effects, she picked up a copy of *Oscar Wilde: His Life and Confessions* by Frank Harris. The inside cover page contained the highlighted statement: "Crucifixion of the guilty is more awe-inspiring than the crucifixion of the innocent."

"I'll be all right," she said. "You're just going to have to be patient with me. I never thought I'd feel this way, but—I've just lost my husband. I feel that I'm going to need a little time."

* * * * *

Drs. Vawter and Faasendeck again sat at a table in the University Club dining room. This time Dr. Jacqueline Hyde had joined them.

"Now that she's out," said Dr. Vawter, "where do we go from here?"

Dr. Hyde flipped a long gray stand over her shoulder. "Go from where?" she said in her smoker's husky voice. "Of whom are we speaking?"

"Dr. Mason-Rodgers, of course."

Dr. Hyde pulled a cigarillo from a pack that lay on the table beside her. "Is that going to be a problem?"

Dr. Faasendeck cleared his throat. "That depends."

"What do you mean, 'that depends'?" said Dr. Vawter, lighting a cigar of his own. "With all the publicity the last few years, that woman is trouble."

Dr. Hyde leveled a gaze at the provost. "Why is that?"

Dr. Vawter stared at her in disbelief. "Are you kidding? Have you read any of her research?"

"Yes."

Dr. Vawter blew heavy smoke into the air. "And do you agree with her conclusions?"

"No."

"So. There you have it. What do you propose we do about it?"

"Nothing."

Dr. Vawter eyed her in disappointment. "Don't the things she is saying bother you?"

Dr. Faasendeck nodded. "Dr. Vawter is quite right," he said, polishing his silverware. "We do have cause for concern."

Dr. Vawter leaned forward. "Okay, try this: she alleges that those scrolls tell of a race of hairy one-eyed freaks that terrorized the world of that time. If they are not just myth, how come we haven't found any skeletal remains?"

Dr. Hyde took a puff on her cigarillo. "I recall," she said, inhaling thoughtfully, "the scrolls mentioning that these creatures did not bury their dead. They cremated them. That may account for it."

She flicked ashes toward an ashtray in the center of the table. Whether she spilled on the tablecloth accidentally or deliberately was uncertain. "I say leave her alone," she said, drawing deeply on her cigar. "She's been through enough crap."

Dr. Vawter and Dr. Faasendeck looked at each other. Dr. Hyde's appointment to acting dean of arts and sciences did not fit their original plans. They would have preferred Dr. Seymour Gould in that position. The Human Rights Committee and C.P.U. Women's Caucus insisted that they follow government guidelines on that appointment.

Dr. Vawter puffed thoughtfully. "Perhaps you don't understand our predicament. For all intents and purposes, she has won. If she was difficult to deal with before, now she'll be all but impossible."

Dr. Faasendeck cleared his throat. "I don't think we could get another injunction."

Dr. Hyde took a drink of water. "You gentlemen should have thought of that before you took such a rash course of action."

Dr. Vawter narrowed his gaze at her. *Damn her, anyway*, he thought. *She was supposed to be with me on this.* Jacqueline Hyde grew up middle class, he recalled. Comfortable. She picked up her radicalism from Brynwood. He recalled his own early days from the streets of Hell's Kitchen. *When you know what it's like to be a hungry nobody*, he thought, *you appreciate power. That's what it's all about, he told himself. Once you've had a taste of it, even sex pales by comparison. This university will be my monument, my legacy.*

His mind went in retrospect to the day before in his office...

...He had just called in his secretary, a tall woman in her late forties. She stood in the doorway, clad in a gray suit, clear plastic glasses, and flat shoes.

"Get me Dr. Mason-Rodgers' file," he had told her.

She then retreated to the outer office and returned with the file. He slipped on his glasses at a skewed angle and perused the file's contents

This woman is like a stone in my shoe, he had confided to his secretary. *It's not really the scrolls I give a damn about. It's the jars. If I can get our electronics lab to unlock the secret of that one self-charging dry cell, we will be the world's new power source. OPEC and their oil will be as obsolete as the dinosaurs they came from. I could make J. Paul Getty look like a penny ante fool.*

As he flipped through the file, he turned to some secretly Xeroxed pages from *The Deluge Scrolls*.

> One can only speculate, the pages read, what many of these findings are telling us of our primordial origin. Was original paradise really all that much of a myth? Why indeed does the concept lie so stubbornly in our collective psyche despite our recent scientific enlightenment? When one contemplates the lush abundance of life in our present rain forests, perhaps these are the present-day equivalent to the original Eden. Why, then, do we not all return to these habitats and abandon the technological artificialities of civilization and revert to the state of Rousseau's noble savage?
>
> On the face of it, such a suggestion would be sheer insanity, sheer suicide. We are no more equipped to cope with life in the tropical rain forest than on the surface of the moon. Perils of plant, animal, reptile, insect, and bacterial life abound on every hand. This Eden paradise would swallow us in a matter of weeks, days, or even hours.
>
> Why is a place of such beauty and abundance so hostile an environment? Why is there a place for every life form in such an ecosystem except civilized man? Why, indeed, must our species survive even in temperate latitudes by our wits and cunning? Why is the marbled ball we call Planet Earth the only fit habitation for us?
>
> Beyond lies only a bleak, hostile universe whose mysteries we are only beginning to discover and explore. Yet, our survival even in our terrestrial ancestral home is also, only tenuous at best. Beyond our native cunning and sophistication, we, the slowest and weakest of all intelligent creatures, are least equipped to adapt to our surroundings.
>
> Why must we constantly engage in an almost existential struggle as aliens in a cold, unfeeling cosmos?
>
> Was this our intended purpose, if indeed there is a purpose? Was this our originally intended destiny? Where in the long line of evolutionary process did we thus get derailed, as it were? What catastrophic or cataclysmic blip on our evolutionary screen caused such a slip in our genetic programming?
>
> Did a primeval ancestor, in fact, trade this natural one-ness with the environment for a spark of knowledge Promethean in its power? Did this newfound knowledge, this newfound power, in fact prove to be too hot to handle?
>
> Is the term coined by some theologians and philosophers really such a far-fetched concept?

THE DELUGE SCROLLS

The term I refer to, of course, is Original Sin.

Not scientific I hear some say? Perhaps not; but we are not talking science here. We are talking philosophy and since when is it inappropriate for an author of a scientific treatise to wax philosophical on occasion?

Why must we practitioners of science as Western culture defines science, maintain such a perpetually cavalier attitude about this?

Dr. Vawter continued studying the pages. Artie continued in her discourse speculating that another explanation as to the Me's immutability could be the Torahaic pronouncement: "Forever, O Yahweh, your fiat is settled in the celestial realms."

And what of the Me? Artie continued in her article, struggling to come to grips with exactly what was its origin. Was its author divine or mortal, or both? Was it revelation, myth, or the result of rational thought? Or was it a combination? Did it predate the Torah? Was it the same spiritual wisdom impressed on the hearts and psyches of holy men separated from one another by time and distance yet who were of one message?

("To keep the cosmos in continuous and harmonious operation and to avoid confusion and conflict, the gods devised the Me, a set of inspired and unchangeable laws that all beings were obliged to obey." *Encyclopedia on Sumerian Culture*—ed.)

Were its teachings so comprehensive, so precise that to omit a single syllable, word, or phrase would change its entire meaning? When its precepts were treated carelessly by unworthy persons was its meaning lost, never again to be regained because of later changes in language, culture, and conceptual imagery?

Had its loss contributed to the destruction of Akir-Ema?

Was divine revelation reestablished with the advent of the Torah, the Decalog, the Burning Bush, and the Urim and Thummim? Was all this also the Johannine pronouncement: "In the beginning was the Word (Logos)"?

Her essay also contained the following footnote: "When they knew Strong-Ones, they glorified him not as God, but became vain in their imaginations... worshipping the creature rather than the creator; worshipping images of mortal man, birds, animals, and reptiles—" (Shaul of Tarshish in his letter to the believing goyim community in Rome.)

Certainly in any event, Artie had concluded in the article, the Me would never endear itself to present-day advocates of so-called situational ethics and/or moral relativism.

He took off his glasses and stared, thoughtfully sucking the end of one of the bows. He was originally pleased to see Seymour Gould, Dr. Rodgers' protégé, passed over for the sabbatical. Now, however, the published result of her research put a whole new factor in the equation.

This at a time, he reflected, *when I am trying to build a faculty where no instructor will so much as admit being a deist.*

He put back on his glasses, stood, and stepped to a nearby window. Outside, across the quad, little eddies of dust and wastepaper whirled about the sidewalks and buildings before a rising wind. Overhead, clouds scudded across the heavens. The day, unseasonably cloudy for this time of year, seemed to press in on his already darkened mood. He clasped his hands behind his back and continued to stare thoughtfully out through the window blinds. The air in the room felt uncomfortably close.

Damn, he thought, *is that air conditioner on the blink again?*

He sighed and returned to his desk. He was startled to see his secretary still standing across it. He held the file out to her.

"Will there be anything else?" she asked

He took a drink from his water glass. He looked at the pitcher and found it empty.

He handed her the pitcher. "Get me a refill," he said with a cough, "and bring me my pills."...

...*How quick they turn on you,* he thought.

Dr. Vawter glanced at his watch. "Got an appointment with my doctor," he said tersely. He stood up. "Cancel my order. We'll continue this later."

Dr. Faasendeck looked apprehensively after him as he departed the dining room.

"You were invited here because Dr. Vawter liked you," he said to Dr. Hyde. "He always admired you and considered your philosophy very much in line with his. This was to have been a stupendous opportunity for you."

Dr. Hyde studied him with bored amusement. She watched him sweating profusely and tugging at his clerical collar. He reminded her of an insect squirming under the sunrays of a magnifying glass.

"There is something I feel you should know," he continued. "Dr. Vawter doesn't take kindly to disagreement. You could very well be right. I thought it admirable the way you stood your ground. On the other hand, now—well, I'm just not sure."

Chapter 31

Forbidden was I to say farewell to my dearest Aarda. She was already reckoned dead by those who lov'd her most..."Your beloved shall not die." (You are mad, I said.)... "They will indeed throw her over the precipice. But she will be caught in a net. She will remain forever behind the walls of the Forbidden Temple Garden...
(Day 20. Trans. and Ed. Brit. Mus. vers. 3.5; 1981.)

* * * * *

Upon returning to campus that summer of 1989, Artie knew that she was in for a difficult year. She could sense it as she took inventory of her archeology lab. She continued with the premonition as she dusted off the bookshelves of her classroom. Facing her students and their awareness of her time in prison filled her with apprehension as well.

As she left her classroom and headed for her office, a thought occurred to her. She and Huck had often argued over the reality of the literal resurrection. She had been quick to point out that Christ's alleged post-resurrection appearances had been to his followers only and never to the world at large. Now she thought she may have understood. The hostility that led to his cruel execution would have been abated not at all by any new public appearances. They would still have wanted him dead.

From her own experiences with the scrolls, she realized that there would have been no diminution of unbelief.

As she sat at her desk, she tried to drown her misgivings in a sea of work. She plucked from her attaché case a sheaf of papers and studied its contents:

> Day 17. An Account of the Origin of the Nefillim, Offspring of the Angry Things and Mortal Women. (Trans. and ed. Brit. Mus. vers. 2.75; 1981.)
>
> And so it was; Shumrag, my mentor, and I betook ourselves from ceaseless round of duties pertaining to the Temple of Lemekh and his environs. To seek surcease from grueling toil repaired we to distant haunt deep within the forest glen, for sport of angling for trout in some bubbling mountain stream. Ne'er took we guide for so purposed our hearts to abandon the common places for fishing grounds more remote, and thereby hangs my tale.
>
> Perchance happ'd we 'pon forest glade hitherto unknown e'en by the most clever guide and mountain man. 'Twas a most delightsome spot. How found we it, I still know not.
>
> 'Twas a forest peopl'd with giant pine, spruce, and cedar that towered o'er us like giant sentinels guarding us from the sun. From their majestic heights supported they by their wide branches hung heavy strands of moss, some hanging down as long as (six feet.) At many of their trunk's bases, a (platoon) of warriors could join hand-in-hand and still barely reach around their circumference. Mosses thick and green spread across every rock, tree trunk, and even the forest floor itself like a deep, soft carpet, bringing to a hush every animal cry, every birdsong, and every mortal word uttered within its boundaries. Soft, slanted rays of pale yellowish green were all the sunlight the forest guardians permitted.
>
> We paused and stood in awe of a place that seemed more of the habitation of gods than a section of mortal man's planet.
>
> "Good mentor," said I, "might this be the Primeval Paradies from whence Red One, our Ancestor and Erdh' were driven?"
>
> "No, my son; else would the mighty Kherubvim be standing guard and we would not be half here now."
>
> Lush and verdant grew the forest with grassy meadow thick. Hard (immediately) before us lay bathed in sunshine's gentle caress, mountain

flowers of every sort and colour and fragrance. Ferns of gigantic size and variety grew about luxuriantly. (Here, we cannot account for the break in rhyme and meter—ed.)

Of a sudden espied I something strange as came it within my eye's range. Set hard midst a clearing ground, a huge rock outcropping mound. Twice a man's height, the thing itself doth naught raise alarm. Atop the rock also lay small cause for harm. 'Twas merely a heap of oaken ash; evidence of sacred fires of recent past. However, upon our side appeared a Seeing Eye, drawn with charcoal, the size of a mortal man. Amid the grass of brightest sheen, encircled a band of deeper green.

My mentor showed great distress. "Appearances deceive us," he me addressed.

"How so?" queried I. "This beauteous spot could be the scene of Evil Plot?"

"Let us now leave this wretched place," pled my mentor, heavy of face.

"What mean this outcrop and rune?" quizzed I, as turned we from that vale again.

"'Tis the dark women, the Daughters of Gijn-eth." 'plied mentor wise. "The dark women meet here whence full moon rise, to hold most sensuous ritual dance; to invoke the Angry Things with secret chants. Yon rock by them is altar lain; by Perverse Eye their Kabala, they reign.

"One leader plus twelve, dance they in circle, clad only in coloured ritual oil and rub they their bodies with scented spices fair. With flowers and garlands t'adorn their hair, by moonlight dance they sensuously wild and free. Their singing echoes o'er forest and lea. While around close by the ritual rock, each celebrant sets a brazier of earthen crock. Anon as excitement and frenzy builds, their chants echo 'gainst the hills. Their braziers, too, begin to levitate and circle round the grey, granite altar mound. Amid fetid odours and strident cries, forms from the Nether regions rise. Midst shrill feminine shrieks, male voices join as tumult peaks.

"Gradually like a rolling fog, the dancers are veiled in angry shroud. Appear horned men with legs of goat. The Angry Things now join the musical note.

"These Angry Things be prevalent in our land. Tho' to mortal eye, oft unseen, they wander about; foul, unclean. Many eons past they be cast out from Court of Strong-Ones 'mid drastic rout. Now seek they embodiment again to know and cohabit with mortal women.

> "Women who love of mortal man have scorned for greater thrill repair in secret to this hill. And amidst demonic pleasure they debase themselves beyond measure. Thus become they heavy with child and give birth, in forest to monsters wild.
>
> "Their wantonness does scourge our land with roving, loathsome bands. This then is the tale of an Angry Race. The Nefillim: they terrorize fast (nearly) ev'ry place."

Moments of her time in the women's facility haunted her as well. She had met a fellow prisoner who claimed to be clairvoyant. When the woman learned of Artie's research and her discovery of the scrolls, she showed genuine interest. I can help you in your research, she had said. Artie had shown skepticism at first. I make contact with the dead, the woman had replied. I will bring up the spirit of a person from the lost civilization and you can interview him.

Artie had confessed to Huck that, in a moment of weakness and curiosity, she had let the woman take her into a day room. As they sat alone, palms pressed flat on a tabletop, the woman appeared to go into a trance.

Nothing happened. Artie waited. The woman awoke. This is going to take concentration, she had said. She tried again to go into a trance.

Still nothing happened.

Close your eyes and concentrate with me, she then said. Clear your mind of all other thought. Please. Try harder, she had said, this time breathing hard and sweating profusely. This takes time. And effort.

An hour went by. Two hours. This is getting ridiculous, Artie recalled thinking to herself. She was about to give up in disgust.

Suddenly the woman began speaking in a man's voice in an unknown language. The woman then spoke in her own voice in English, purporting to translate the other's words.

"What would you like to know," the woman had given in translation.

"I want to know your name," Artie had said.

"My name is H'rshag," the voice replied.

Artie marveled. How could this woman have known a name from the scrolls? It is possible, of course. Artie had published extensively on the scrolls in recent years. However, how likely was it that anyone not in the academic loop be that knowledgeable of Artie's writings?

Artie, nevertheless, decided to go along with whatever this happening was called.

A thought occurred to her. If calling up beings from the spirit world was this difficult, how easy would it be to dismiss them back to where they came from?

"Are you, in fact, from Lost Atlantis?"

"Yes," replied the voice.

"How many years ago did you live?"

"Seventy-five thousand years ago."

"How long did you live?"

"Seventeen thousand years."

Artie's skepticism grew. The scrolls had indicated Akiri longevity to be in the hundreds of years; much like the Genesis antediluvian genealogy.

Something clearly was wrong. Artie had tried to waken the woman, but to no avail. Her trance seemed to deepen.

Artie tried another strategy. "Did Atlanteans fly any kind of aircraft?" she asked.

"Yes," the voice replied.

"And what speed did your aircraft attain?"

"We had aircraft exceeding the speed of sound," said the voice.

This last answer came from a different voice. The new voice—still masculine—sounded harsh and guttural. It spoke without the woman's mouth moving and in a measured, mechanical-sounding monotone.

The new voice also spoke to her in English.

"That does it," she said. "You're a fraud, whoever or whatever you are. My scrolls indicate that you attained speeds of about forty miles an hour."

The woman trembled, appearing unable to return to a wakened state.

"How dare you doubt my word," roared the harsh, guttural voice.

"Am I still talking to H'rshag?" asked Artie.

"My name is Dhjek," replied the voice. "I was with H'rshag at the last until I gave myself to the sea. Doubt my word do you? Very well then, we will dispense with this poor, wretched woman. I will deal with you directly. And that right soon."

The voice laughed. The woman screamed. She pulled her hands away and pressed them to her face. Her eyes widened with terror.

"My dear," said Artie, "what's the matter?"

"Please go away," said the woman.

Artie stared at her. "Whatever is the matter with you?"

"You are going to receive a visitation," said the woman.

"A what?"

"You are going to be visited by an incubus," said the woman, still trembling, "a thought entity that visits in the night; very often in one's dreams. Now please go away."

With legs feeling like rubber, Artie got up from the table and left the woman still sitting alone, sobbing softly to herself. She and the woman avoided one another for the balance of her prison term...

...At the first sight of her apartment, she began to feel uneasy.

She began to notice little things: in the night, the sound of wind blowing against a window not securely fastened. When she got up to secure the window, stillness gripped the night outside. She awoke a few nights later to discover a light coming from her living room. When she went to investigate, she found the living room light on. She tried to remember whether she had in fact forgotten to turn the light out. A week later, upon retiring, she heard the bathroom faucet dripping. She awoke in the night to find the faucet running full blast. When she turned the faucet handle, the water stopped completely.

Somebody or something had deliberately turned on the tap.

Another time, she heard footsteps just outside her front door. Could it be a prowler, or merely a neighbor coming home late? She jumped from her bed, pulled on her house robe, and started for the front door, turning on every light as she went. When she tiptoed to her front door, she strained to take a look through the peephole.

She saw no one.

Heart racing, she reached into her front closet for a mace canister. *This is so totally foolhardy*, she thought, *but I've got to check this out.* Pressing her body against the door, she reexamined the security of the chain lock, slid back the deadbolt and parted the door ever so slightly. A death-like stillness hung heavy in the hallway.

Gingerly, she stepped through the doorway.

Silence and a yawning emptiness greeted her. She felt that she could just as well be standing in a pharaoh's tomb. How could mere stillness and solitude itself loom so menacing?

She looked down at the hand that gripped the mace can. The knuckles had turned white.

She returned to her bedroom and quickly dressed herself. Sleep would now be impossible. Again, still brandishing her mace can, she stepped back into the corridor. She quickly walked down to the outside exit and emerged into the cold, fog-enshrouded parking lot. She spent the rest of the night driving through darkened city streets.

The next day, she checked into a motel.

This is getting ridiculous, she told herself after the second day. The following morning she checked out and returned to her apartment. For about a week, after having returned to her apartment, all seemed normal.

Then it happened.

As the woman in prison had predicted, it came during the night.

At first Artie thought she was dreaming. She could feel herself toss and turn under the covers, as she perceived a voice softly calling her name. She felt herself sit up in bed, trying to focus her eyes. Yet, her eyelids felt glued shut. Was she actually looking at her bedroom furniture or did she visualize it in her mind?

She noticed her dresser mirror.

A cloud or mist formed from within the glass. She watched, still uncertain whether she was really awake or asleep. She again heard, or perhaps sensed, the voice whispering her name. She tried to call out, but her vocal cords would not respond. Finally with great exertion, she startled herself with a shriek that barely sounded human.

She realized from the vibrations of her throat, that it was she. Again with great exertion, she managed the words, "Who is it?"

A soft glow, as from a distant lamp trying to penetrate a swirling, pea-soup fog, began to emanate from deep within the mirror.

"Who is it?" The inability to modulate her own voice frightened her.

A silhouette took shape in the swirling mist. She first perceived a pair of small, narrow eyes set below a wrinkled, browless forehead. The crossed eyes stared a cold, expressionless stare. The nearly bald head sprouted shoulder-length hair about the temples. Small, pointed ears protruded from between the listless, white strands. The beak-like nose centered a waxen face. The sunken cheeks and long, narrow chin framed a gaping mouth. Jagged, discolored teeth protruded from the entrance of a crypt-like oral cavity. He appeared dressed in the attire of an eighteenth-century British seaman. A tattered, striped shirt covered a bony chest and shoulders.

"Who are you?" The sinking feeling weighed like lead in her stomach.

Words again came from a mouth that didn't move. "I'm called Springheel Jack." It spoke in the harsh, guttural voice she heard in prison.

"I recognize your voice." Her own presence of mind surprised her.

"I thought you would," replied the figure.

"You lied to me in prison, didn't you?"

"Just testing you, my dear. You're a very clever woman."

"I was right then?"

"Of course you were right."

"Why are you here?" she demanded. "What do you want of me?"

"It is you who wants something from me."

"That's not true. All I want is for you to leave."

The spirit laughed. "You have sought me long and diligently."

Silence weighed in with a depressing closeness. "You claimed to be from Atlantis," she said. "Yet you speak English and you dress as a British sailor. You answer to an English name. What are you, Atlantean or English?"

"Yes," was the reply.

"Yes?"

"Yes!"

"I don't understand."

Again the figure laughed. "The mortal mind is as incapable of grasping certain realities," it said, "as the seamstress's thimble is in containing the sea."

"All right, answer me this," said Artie. "Am I on the right track?"

"You are," said the visitor, lowering his voice.

"You lied to me once before. How do I know you're not lying to me now?"

"You don't."

She paused. She realized that, of course, he was right. Did the apparition actually present her with her big chance? She took a deep breath.

"What do you know of ancient languages?" she finally managed to ask.

"Everything."

Her heart began racing faster. "Can you teach me?"

"'Can I?' is not the question: 'Will I?'"

"Will you, then?"

"That depends. What can you do for me?"

"You're a spirit. What possible interest would you have in things terrestrial?"

"All in due time. Do you want to learn spoken Sumerian?"

She took another deep breath and swallowed hard. "Yes."

"D'voh Ish-k'toe Ergil-Ga-mekh, um shivah Ur-ara-tu."

Was he for real? He did not say the phrase in his usual harsh, guttural monotone. The voice resonated a rich baritone. He spoke the syllables in a lilting, musical rhythm. He gave accent to the second-to-the-last syllable of the big words. The consonants wallowed generously in lush, rich sounds.

The vowels stretched open and bright while the R's rolled playfully off the tip of the tongue.

After struggling unsuccessfully to focus her eyes in a waking state, she still felt them glued shut.

Yet, she knew she was looking in her mirror. The spectral figure also continued to look real enough. "What was that?" she asked.

"'The Chronicles of Gilgemish regarding the matter of the vessel atop Mount Ararat,'" the visitor replied. "It's the heading on your Inanna tablet."

She felt herself break out in a cold sweat. "That's very interesting," she managed between breaths, "but how am I to learn a whole language from chatting briefly with a spirit in my bedroom in the middle of the night?"

"I will come back." The silhouette began to fade.

Another pause. As curiosity overcame her sense of horror, she felt a compulsion to question the figure further before it faded altogether. "Tell me." She was unsure why she was asking this next question. "Is there such a thing as God?"

"We call him the Strong-Ones."

"Is—is he—good?"

"Good?"

"Yes. Are there conflicting supernatural forces of good and evil?"

"We don't think in those terms."

She struggled with the pounding. "In what terms do you think then?"

"Power," replied the spirit. "And knowledge. Our leader is called the Prince of Light."

"You are good, then?" As soon as she said this, she realized that in no sense could this apparition be considered good. Its appearance alone would dispel that notion. Besides, it had already admitted lying to her.

Whoever or whatever this thing was, it was evil.

"I didn't say that," the visitor laughed. "I said we call our leader the Prince of Light."

"You're playing with me again. I want you to know that I resent it." Again, she amazed herself at her courage.

The figure became clearer in the thinning mist. "I am not playing with you," it retorted. "And I warn you: do not trifle with me."

Artie licked dried lips and hesitated. "I'm sorry." Her voice was nearly inaudible. "I just don't understand your calling your leader the Prince of Light."

"In the writings, he is called Lucifer—the Giver of Light."

"The writings?"

"The writings."

Artie hesitated. "Is that the same thing that we call the Bible?"

"It is."

She took a deep breath. "Tell me then," she said, barely able to form the words, "some people claim that they're just a collection of ancient Hebrew folklore. Others claim that they are a collection of thoughts and introspections of ancient holy men. Still others insist that they are divinely inspired. Which is it?"

"I'm not supposed to be discussing this with you," the visitor admitted, "but to coin a modern-day cliché, they are all of the above."

She took another breath. "These writings," she forced the words out of her mouth, "the Bible as we call them—are they—are they…?"

"Are they true?" He finished the question for her. "Is that what you want to know?"

She nodded. "It's been a controversy among us for some time now."

The visitor didn't answer right away.

"Again—and I'm not supposed to be discussing any of this with you."

Why not? she wondered. A frightening possibility occurred to her. Was he so sure of his plans for her imminent demise that it no longer mattered what cosmic secrets she knew?

"The writings—the Bible as you call them," he continued, "are true. Every word."

Artie struggled for breath.

"But—" he continued.

But?

"But," the visitor repeated. "They are true in more ways than any of your pettifogging scholars, philosophers, or religionists could ever possibly imagine."

The visitor faded from the mirror. Artie opened her eyes. Everything remained just as she had envisioned it, with one exception: the mirror reflected only the gray shapes of her bedroom furniture. She lay back on her pillow limp. She was barely able to summon enough presence of mind to look at her dresser clock. The luminous dial indicated less than an hour until daylight. She felt wetness in the nightgown that clung to her body.

She asked herself in her embarrassment: had the shock of an encounter with an otherworldly visitor caused her to lose bodily control?

She pulled herself, weak and trembling, out from under the covers and slid to the floor. Her head ached and she felt nauseous. She felt feverish as though she might be coming down with the flu. A draft of night air made her shiver. Was the apparition coming back? She buried her face in her hands. She felt certain that renewed contact with this "thing" would totally destroy her sanity. She sat on the floor beside her bed. Seconds dragged by on her dresser clock. Presently light from the eastern sky filtered through the curtains of her window.

She lifted her head. The dawn of a new day had somehow given her strength to struggle to her feet. While staggering toward the bathroom, she felt a depression unprecedented in its severity. She thought she felt a sharp pain deep within her psyche, very like a red-hot needle thrust into her innermost being. She finally made her way to the bathroom sink and reached for a water glass. She glanced at herself in the mirror.

All color had drained from her lips. Her face looked ashen gray. The sallow complexion and deep lines around her eyes shocked her. Her expression had a wild, hunted look. The texture of her skin appeared dry and old looking. Her hair hung listless; like an old woman's. *You look as though you have seen a ghost*, she thought.

Bad joke, she concluded. She laboriously removed her soggy nightgown and turned on the shower nozzle. She had to mentally command her body for every move. When she finally climbed into the stall and felt the cascade of warm water, she began to feel a little better. However, she still, with great deliberation, finished her shower.

As she rubbed her body with a bath towel, a thought occurred to her. Was the spirit still present? Was he at that moment, watching her? How could she tell whether the dreaded specter had, in fact, violated her privacy? Did disembodied spirits still show enough interest in fleshly lust to even want to do such a thing? Somehow, she still sensed his presence and was even now watching her.

She tried to hurry as she donned her house robe. She returned to her bedroom, tore off the bedding, and threw the soiled sheets into a laundry hamper.

She decided to simply let the spirit watch, if that was his pleasure, and not worry about it.

After dressing, she put on extra-heavy make-up and dark glasses.

She got up from her vanity and started for the door. She decided that, upon returning that evening, she would again check into a motel.

She would not spend another night in that apartment.

* * * * *

Deciding to move, however, involved breaking her lease. Fortunately a larger and more expensive apartment in her complex stood vacant.

Getting the manager to sign her over to a new unit, therefore, turned out to be no trouble. The cost and inconvenience of hiring truckers to haul her furniture a hundred yards seemed well worth the nuisance.

Except for one problem.

Would the transfer of earthly possessions be enough to baffle the evil forces plaguing her? Could she ever flee far enough?

After the move, Artie's misgivings about the new school year continued. Her classroom, her lab, the corridors—all at one time a domain comforting in their familiarity—took on strange, even hostile foreboding. The psychic pain—that depression that burned relentlessly deep in her innermost consciousness—continued unabated. She found herself at odd moments breaking into tears for no apparent reason. She now wore dark glasses almost constantly and continued with heavy make-up. She held her hands tightly together to hide the tremor. In addition to the depression, she discovered within herself another new and disconcerting phenomenon.

She found her thought life besieged by fantasies of eroticism, mayhem, and destruction unprecedented in their perversity and savagery. She fought with her conscious mind to keep them in check. The more strenuously she fought to suppress them, the more they seemed to scream for her to carry them out in overt behavior.

If she found clinging to sanity and rational behavior during waking hours difficult, she found it all but impossible during sleep. She found her mind quickly descending into a vortex of somnambulant hell, void of all control.

She did not know how long she could go on this way.

She recalled an incident in the Student Union Grill. When a waitress brought her order, she, without warning or provocation, jumped to her feet and, with a wide sweep of her arm, brushed the dishes to the floor.

"Damn you!" she roared to the frightened waitress. The voice was the harsh, guttural voice of Springheel Jack.

Tears of embarrassment stung her own eyes as she fled the grill.

Probably on steroids, commented a nearby student.

* * * * *

She stood at the front of a new section of Archeology 101. The knowing look in their eyes, their whispered remarks, and subtle jokes unnerved her. Never had Huck's and George's late arrival a decade earlier seemed nearly so unsettling.

I've got to get hold of myself, she resolved.

At dismissal, she rushed across the hall to her office. *How am I ever going to go through with all this?* she asked herself as she leaned against the closed door.

Another dreadful faculty meeting, she thought. She glanced at the digital desk clock then threw papers into an attaché case. When she arrived at the amphitheater, she spotted a seat beside the ponderous Dr. Berthold.

As she settled in her seat, his mood turned serious. "How have you been, Ardith?" he whispered from the side of his mouth.

She eyed him curiously. "I've been well, considering."

She spotted a short, stubby man in an ill-fitting blazer walking past. His thinning dark hair lay disarrayed in a comb-over across the top of his head. Pale eyes blinked nervously as he tried to adjust the microphone.

"Dr. Gould," commented Dr. Berthold. "The new dean of the College of Arts and Sciences."

Artie remembered the Sabbatical Review Board's passing him over in her favor ten years ago.

"Watch out for him," Dr. Berthold said, looking about furtively. "That guy is poison."

"I thought Dr. Hyde was the acting dean," whispered Artie.

Dr. Berthold cast another anxious glance toward a tight little knot of teachers sitting nearby. "Not so loud."

Artie moved closer to Dr. Berthold. "What's going on, anyway?"

Dr. Berthold covered his mouth and continued, "There was an investigation over a misappropriation of funds; just enough suspicion to put the appointment out of her reach."

As Dr. Gould droned on through the agenda with the same monotone that Dr. Rodgers had used, Artie again bent her head toward Dr. Berthold. "Are people really avoiding me, or is it just my imagination?"

Dr. Berthold wrote a note: *It is not your imagination.* As she read it, he whispered, "Word has it that you're trouble."

Dr. Gould continued belaboring endless minutiae.

"I think I'll leave," she whispered. She slipped out of her seat and left the amphitheater. She went back to her office, picked up an armload of typewritten papers and left for the faculty lounge.

She turned toward a work area consisting of a table, a copy machine, a paper cutter, and a metal storage cabinet when she heard someone behind her.

Dr. Jacqueline Hyde had just entered the lounge.

As Artie began working the copy machine, Dr. Hyde stood near one of the windows and took out a package of pencil-slim cigars. She lit one and began to inhale thoughtfully.

"Hello, Ardith."

"Hello, Jacqueline."

"Good to have you back."

"Thank you."

Artie continued to run off papers from the copy machine. She found herself strangely fixated by Dr. Hyde's body contour and bust line. This puzzled her because she had never considered Dr. Hyde all that attractive. Secondly, because she herself had never felt attracted to another woman. Certainly not that way anyway. She struggled with an impulse to rip Dr. Hyde's clothing from her body.

Why now? she wondered.

"I'm sorry about Lester." Dr. Hyde continued puffing on her cigar.

"Thank you."

Dr. Hyde began pacing in front of a window. "It must be difficult, losing one's husband."

Artie stopped for a moment. "Yes," she said guardedly. "It has been quite a trial."

Another pause. Finally, Dr. Hyde again spoke. "Mind if I say something personal?"

Artie resumed copying. "I suppose not."

"I thought you were taking an awful chance."

"Oh?"

"Yes, you know, having someone you're personally involved with represent you at court."

Artie glanced with her eyes without turning her head. "I suppose so," she said, "but it all turned out for the best."

Artie spotted a pair of scissors lying on the table. How easy to seize them and plunge them into Dr. Hyde's stomach. She could throw the shears into an outside dumpster and leave the building. No one would know she had even been in the workroom.

The other human voice startled her back to reality.

"By the way, how is Hershel's practice doing these days?"

"Very successful, thank you."

Dr. Hyde stepped to the window blind and peered between the slats. "I'm glad," she said. "You have a very nice young man."

Artie began stacking papers. "It's been an enduring relationship."

"I sort of thought it would be."

"Oh?"

"Yes," said Dr. Hyde, "—ever since I first saw the two of you together—at the Pirate's Cove."

Artie stopped working. "So you did see us, then?"

"Yes."

"I suppose I owe you a debt of gratitude," Artie continued.

"For what?"

"For not exposing us."

Dr. Hyde blew more puffs of smoke into the air. "Just returning the favor."

Artie fought to keep from coughing from all the smoke. "Returning what favor?"

"For not exposing us."

Dr. Hyde was among those at the encounter weekend.

Artie began gathering her papers.

"I had heard that you two have had your differences," said Dr. Hyde. "Hershel is still your significant other, I take it?"

Artie stopped. "Significant other?"

Dr. Hyde blew more smoke. "Yes—you know—"

Artie smiled a wooden smile. "Oh—yes—you mean: is he still my lover? Well, yes he is. He's my lover, and I'm his mistress."

"My," Dr. Hyde smiled, "aren't we getting old-fashioned all of a sudden?"

"We certainly are." Artie started to leave. "As a matter of fact, he's been more loving and faithful these past ten years than many husbands."

"Ardith—?" Dr. Hyde's voice halted her steps.

"Yes?"

"May I say something further?"

Artie turned to face Dr. Hyde. "Yes, what is it?"

Dr. Hyde flicked ashes onto an ashtray. For a while she said nothing. "It's not easy for me to say this," she said at last.

"Not easy to say what?"

Dr. Hyde inhaled on her cigar. "About that weekend—I'm sorry."

Artie reached for the wall behind her to steady herself. "That's all right." She fought to control her voice. "I forgive you."

Dr. Hyde turned from the window. "You weren't the only one hurt."

Artie eyed her questioningly.

Dr. Hyde turned her eyes toward the ceiling. "We left you in that awful room," she began, "injured and alone. Rather bad form on our part, I admit. Anyway, you were wise to leave when you did."

"Why do you say that?"

"Somebody introduced something new to the party: LSD."

Artie looked at her, but said nothing.

"Some of us came out of it within hours," said Dr. Hyde. "My husband never did."

"That's right," said Artie with tone of recollection. "I guess you did have a husband."

"Did have," sighed Dr. Hyde. "How appropriate."

"Oh, I'm sorry," said Artie. "I didn't mean anything."

"Quite all right." Dr Hyde smiled wistfully. "Sylvester has been in a private nursing home since that very weekend. He's practically a vegetable."

Artie reached for the doorknob. "I—appreciate your sharing this with me. And I'm sorry for you. I really am. But I guess I have to ask the question: Why are you telling me all this?"

Dr. Hyde resumed pacing the floor. "I suppose you could call it a kind of catharsis."

Artie continued leaning against the door. "Oh, and I was wondering," she said, pressing the handle. "I hope you don't mind my saying this, but I was shocked to learn of Dr. Gould's appointment."

Dr. Hyde's eyes narrowed. "They haven't heard the last of this. Believe me."

As Artie pushed the door ajar, she again heard Dr. Hyde address her. "One more thing."

Artie looked at her questioningly.

"For your sake, I would suggest you leave this campus. Oh, and I wish you and Hershel well."

Artie's face contorted into a hate-filled grimace. "Go to hell!" she screamed, again in the other voice.

Dr. Hyde staggered back, her face registering shock, but said nothing.

Artie pressed against the door lintel and licked dry lips. "I'm sorry," she said hoarsely but in her own voice. "I—didn't mean it."

She started through the doorway. "Thank you," she said, "for your—words."

She fled the lounge in panic and confusion.

When she returned to her office she sat at her desk and tried to compose lecture notes for her next class. No use. Her mind swirled in conflicting thoughts and emotions. The depression still stabbed at her psyche like a red-hot stiletto. She couldn't tell whether the pain was physical or mental, or perhaps both. As she sat behind her desk, the tears started again.

She heard a knock at her door. Dr. Berthold stood outside.

He looked around carefully before entering. He sat across from her, and continued to suck on his pipe without lighting it. "About what I told you," he said, "don't take it personally."

Her mouth took a disgusted downturn. "How should I take it?"

"Look," he said with obvious nervousness, "things aren't good around here just now. Why, even fraternities are banned from campus."

"I never did consider them anything special," shrugged Artie.

"I'm an old Chi Rho myself," he said, ignoring her last remark. "Is there nothing sacred anymore?"

"Well," sighed Artie, "when you have a president who's just a figurehead, what can you expect?"

She paused, then added, "And as for who is really in charge, I know that I am not one of his favorite people."

What a terrible man, she thought, *referring to Dr. Faasendeck and my husband as Kewpie-Doll and Puckerpuss. Even they deserve better. How unprofessional can we get?*

"He wants you fired," said Dr. Berthold finally.

She knew that were it not for a tenure clause in the faculty contract, she would not be here now. "What do you suggest I do?"

Dr. Berthold filled his pipe bowl. "I would keep a low profile. In the meantime, I would also start sending out my resume."

"What if you-know-who decides to blackball me?"

Dr. Berthold started for the door. "Just pray that he hasn't."

Before leaving, he glanced back into her office. "I wouldn't worry about it unduly if I were you. With the way the enrollment is dropping off, we may be all of us out of work."

He slipped out the door, closing it softly behind him.

Artie turned to her lecture notes. Any further work on them was out of the question. She inserted some personal stationery into the typewriter.

Dearest Peppi:

Just thought I'd drop you a line to let you know I'm still in the land of the living. When we have a little time to sit and talk, I can tell you more. Suffice it to say, things are getting bizarre to put it mildly.

Remember back in college how you considered me the model of modern American woman: assertive, confident, determined—and liberated?...

The phone interrupted the flow of her thoughts.
"Artie?" Huck's voice from the other end.
"Huck?" said Artie in bewilderment. "Where are you?"
"I'm at the cabin."
Something in his voice filled her with alarm. "Is anything wrong?"
"I think you'd better come up here."
"Why?" she said amid rising consternation. "What happened?"
A pause. "It's been broken into."
She tried to collect her thoughts. "Is anything missing?"
"Can't tell. Someone has turned this place every way but loose."
She slammed the receiver and grabbed her attaché case.

* * * * *

Later, in her apartment, she packed a small suitcase. Exiting her bedroom for the front door, she grasped the handle. It didn't budge. She tried the key, the deadbolt, and the night lock. They all worked.

She heard the bathroom faucet running.

She dropped her suitcase and ran to shut it off. She noticed the mirror over the sink clouding over and taking on depth. She saw the silhouette.

Springheel Jack was back. Or had never left.

The figurine! The one destroyed in the earthquake! Were these little clay dolls or idols, in fact, really points of contact with powerful, unseen forces? Forces malevolent and wicked? Was some entity even now hell bent on wreaking vengeance upon her for what they perceived to be carelessness on her part?

Please, she thought, *it was an accident. I didn't mean it. It was the earthquake; something over which I had no control.*

As she continued staring into the mirror, a disturbing insight came to her. *No good,* she concluded. *They don't care. Despite the earthquake, in their irrational hatred, they still hold me responsible.*

Dear God, she thought, *is there no way escaping these fiends?*

The coarse whisper called out: "Artie—"

"What do you want?" she screamed hoarsely.

"You," the voice said simply.

Me? Hands frozen in fear grasped the sides of the sink.

"Payback time," he continued. "Your negligence has caused the destruction of Inanna's likeness. We can never forgive that.

"I have also disclosed to you forbidden knowledge. I have also taught you the Sumerian language. It's your turn to do something for me."

She laughed despite the horror of the moment. "You call one phrase teaching me a language?"

"We have chosen you," he said, ignoring her remark.

"For what?" she demanded, heart racing.

"To be the mother of a new race."

Nefilli! The evil offspring of the Angry Things and dark women that terrorized the Antedeluvian world.

Oh dear God, no! I am not one of the dark women.

"You're a spirit." She almost laughed. "How do you plan to do that? As a goat-legged freak?"

The image focused clearer. "We have ways. Turn on the faucet."

She reached for the faucet and saw it gush out blood. Numbly, she watched bloodstains splatter the bowl. She saw her hand turn off the tap.

She found herself again fleeing to the living room. One hand seized her suitcase; the other again grasped the doorknob. This time she felt the entire doorknob housing come right out of the wood. Not questioning her newfound superhuman strength, she reached through and pulled open the door and bolted for the stairway.

As she spun her car out of the parking lot, she felt the interior turn cold. She shut off the air conditioner and turned on the heater. Despite the hot air shooting from the vent, she felt as though she were in cold storage. When her breath formed vapor, she knew it wasn't her imagination.

"Artie—" The coarse whisper came from inside the car. A foul odor began to permeate the air.

"Thought you could elude me, did you?" Again the laugh.

Before the rearview mirror completely clouded over, she looked at herself. A seventy-year-old image of Ardith Mason-Rodgers with hollow eyes stared back. Her skin looked shriveled like ancient parchment. Her hair had turned white—snow white.

With stunned disbelief, she looked at her hands on the wheel and saw gnarled, bony hands of an old woman; the skin loose and wrinkled. She had aged thirty years in a single day.

She pushed the accelerator harder.

Missed the red lights, she thought. *I'm in luck.*

The notion of lucky quickly dissipated, however, at the sound of the voice coming from the stereo speakers. "You seem to be in a hurry."

"Please." Salty tears stung her eyes. "Go away."

The Thing laughed. "Your pleas for mercy only heighten my excitement."

She drove on in silence. "But why me?" she asked finally.

"Your name is Ardith, called Aarda in Aryan; Erda in Teutonic. In Semitic: Eve, mother of all living."

"This is all so ridiculous." Again, she marveled at her newfound courage. "I don't believe in reincarnation. You might as well know that."

"What you believe or disbelieve is of no consequence."

Artie stared out at the mountain landscape that sped along the highway. How comfortably common seemed the occasional traffic that rushed by; how in contrast with the surrealism inside her car.

"I still don't really believe in you," she said.

"Why haven't you discussed this with anyone? Afraid of ridicule? Can science help you?"

She didn't answer.

"Why don't you go to your clerics again?" the voice taunted. "They don't really believe in us either, do they? Go to your nearest psychiatric clinic and let them encumber you with their meaningless jargon."

Another pause.

"Since our plans to have you unite with Snake have failed, we will possess you through your lover."

A thought occurred to her. "How can you do that?" Again, she marveled at her boldness. "You can't. He's a believer."

"We will just use him, but possess you as the two of you unite sexually. That will suffice us. You will then bear our spirit-child."

Artie gave a brief, but hardened laugh. "We'll fix you. We'll just simply abstain."

It was the voice's turn to laugh. "We will infuse the two of you with such a burning lust you'll be in agony until you capitulate."

She drove on in silence. She felt like a shell, empty of all life. She was aware only of the engine and the swiftly passing landscape; that and the salty tears flowing down her aged cheeks.

The San Fernando Valley dropped away as she began climbing into the foothills. She realized that Springheel Jack was right. She recalled wishing that she could actually hear some ancient speak to her and teach her those spoken languages of antiquity.

She also reflected on her life back in Winnetka and Evanston. She again recalled the snapshot that she showed Huck of her six-year-old self in front of her family's large Christmas tree. Did that child, in her innocence ever imagine that someday she would be engaged in a titanic struggle with the very essence of evil itself? Artie tried to bring out of the recesses of her memory the image of that little girl singing her solo at that Sunday school Christmas pageant. She tried to force the words into her consciousness.

Be.

What malevolent hand was trying to stifle her thought life toward anything good? Did not Our Lord himself say "Out of the mouths of babes"? What heinous entity was now trying to push wholesome thoughts out of her mind?

Near.

Beads of perspiration began rolling down her face.

"Me." Perhaps it would help if she said the words audibly. Does deliverance for her lie anywhere? Perhaps it lay through the intercession of that little child of yesteryear.

"Lord Jesus." She had to force the words from her mouth.

How comforting and predictable stood the stately elms on Northwestern's campus. How in contrast the culture shock she and Peppi experienced when first they came out for graduate work; just in time to get caught up in the Student Revolution. She recalled the perverse thrill she felt in joining the alternative lifestyle that was Earthnation with its experimentation with new relationships, new thrills, and its openness to new ideas. The past had no relevance. Theirs would be a lifestyle void of rational thought. The sensual, the visceral, would be the only reality. Total acceptance was in. Taboos and inhibitions were out.

Did her original exhilaration of letting loose of all that was customary and conventional with its attendant sense of liberation eventually dissipate into a new and grievous bondage?

"I." Somehow, it came out a little easier.

She recalled the many others, the many joiners with addictions of one kind or another. She recalled those admitted who had severe personality, mental, or emotional disorders. She recalled others with sexual appetites of the most bizarre deviation from any societal norm. No one suggested any behavior change, or therapy. Earthnation stood against all that.

"Ask." Did she actually hear, or did she merely sense, what sounded like the screams of a legion of lost souls?

The commune did require, however, the turning over of all assets. Those employed turned over their paychecks. Those unable or unwilling to work did not. The destitute were required to contribute nothing. Those feeling the need to repair or tidy up the premises could do so.

From each according to his ability, to each according to his needs.

"Thee."

She felt remorse regarding her turning over thousands of dollars of scholarship money; and of seeing that money spent by others for drugs, booze, and food; others who were, frankly, outright free-loaders.

Equitable food distribution seemed always hampered by pilfering and theft. We tolerated those unable or unwilling to help in the preparation and in the serving. We also tolerated those who stole food then sold it, or stole money to sneak off to a McDonald's.

Love and harmony were to be the rule, yet jealousy and distrust over money, sex, living space, or possessions somehow interfered. Sleeping and waking schedules came into conflict with those who slept at night and listened to loud music in the daytime and those who slept in the daytime and listened to loud music at night.

"To."

In her memory she could again see the scrub brush and sand that surrounded the rambling, deserted ranch house. An unpainted one-story relic with a sagging roof and gaping holes for windows served as the commune's main building. Several smaller sheds surrounded it. Rusting, psychedelically painted vans parked randomly about the treeless dirt yard. A seldom-traveled blacktop passed the front entrance.

"Stay."

Artie had fled down that blacktop one dark night and walked the seven miles to the nearest highway to hitch a ride back to civilization.

"Close."

One secret she would never disclose even to Huck was how close she came to allowing herself to be pressured into the mass orgies of open sex. *Like true revolutionaries, we considered promiscuous sex our birthright*, she recalled. *Our attitude: rebellion, booze, drugs, sex, and rock 'n' roll; what else was there?*

"By."

As she reflected further on her relationship with Snake, she again concluded that, yes, he had to be the consummate psychopath. Interesting that he had undergone, over a two-year period, a series of painful tattoo operations until his entire body was covered with a design the looked like a snakeskin, thus shutting himself off forever from the rest of law-abiding, civilized society.

She did tell Huck that she had in fact given Snake her virginity. This seemed to delight the man greatly. As a lover, however, Snake was a disappointment. His style was mechanical, loveless, existential. *Existential sex*, she reflected; *interesting concept.*

"Me."

His image again reemerged in her memory: the pig-like eyes void of emotion; the bent nose, the cherubic mouth, and sparse goatee, all set like a caricature in a massive, melon-shaped head.

She recalled the emergency Medi-Cal admissions at small, rural hospitals in the area involving young, counterculture adults complaining of fractures and other injuries. She learned of other medical problems as well. Earthnation members, in their disdain for convention, shunned normal standards of personal hygiene and sanitation, causing epidemics of hepatitis and dysentery to break out. Die-hards were evicted—some on sick bed—when the sheriff, acting on court order, finally padlocked the front gate.

"Forever."

She daily had risked health of body and mind. *It's a wonder I was able to put a complete sentence together*, she thought, *much less teach at a university. It's a wonder my brains are not like scrambled eggs.*

You'll never guess the motto over the front gate, she once said to Huck:

"Be."

Be? What was that supposed to mean, Huck wanted to know.

Whatever you want it to mean, she answered.

"And."

Like all so-called waves of the future, she reflected, *we eventually spent ourselves and washed up on the shore. Then, as the rest of humanity flowed back out to sea, we were left as debris on the sand.*

"Love me"

Aware now of the reality of evil, she realized that there must be counter-forces of good. *But,* she wondered, *if there really is a God, why does he not show himself openly?*

It occurred to her that we either consign those who claim to be deity to mental hospitals or we nail them to a cross.

Could that pile of dust in that forgotten Palestinian tomb help her now?

"I pray."

As she sped downward into a valley, she hit the brakes.

The pedal fell to the floor.

"Bless all the dear children."

She noticed that the overpowering stench no longer permeated the car's interior. Had it in fact disappeared, or had she just become inured to it?

She tried to slow the car by sideswiping it against a rock formation. She succeeded only in scraping the side of her car. She felt the car accelerate as she fought to keep it on the road and negotiate the mountain curves. Trying to shift down, she succeeded only in grinding the gears. The transmission simply would not go into a lower gear. Resigned, she let her foreign compact race downhill.

Out of control.

"In thy tender care."

How like revolution, she thought. *Once in motion they tend to let loose events that quickly snowball, gathering momentum until the whole social order crash lands, as it were, into the bottom of a ravine.*

"And take us to heaven."

As she careened across the outside lane, she barely missed oncoming traffic.

"To live with thee there." She screamed. Her car shot through a barrier and rolled, end-over-end, until it crashed on the canyon floor.

In late afternoon sunlight, spewing a trail of dust into the air, her car lay upside down some fifty feet below the highway.

Chapter 32

I was startled by the appearance of a child; a damsel not yet twenty summers. Her long, straight hair rivaled the color of the sun. Her face was round, smooth, and radiant. "I am Ariel," she announced. "I am a Watcher."... What prompted my next question still puzzles me: "You are not mortal then?" ... "Ariel," said I weeping, "thou blessed, heaven-sent sprite!"
(Days 24 and 33. Trans. and ed. Brit. Mus., vers. 3.5; 1981.)

* * * * *

Huck paced the floor of the cabin living room, then stopped and looked out at the darkness just beyond the picture window. He glanced at his watch. Had there been a problem, she surely would have called. He went to the phone and dialed her apartment. He got her answering machine.

Something clearly was wrong.

He surveyed the wreckage. The basement lay in even worse disarray. Huck found filing cabinet drawers pulled out; their contents spilled out over the floor, cabinet doors jimmied open and the glass-covered case was smashed, as was the computer screen. Intruders had thrown the keyboard to the floor, and had strewn papers across the basement.

Yet, he found nothing stolen. Knowing what they were after, he congratulated himself on his foresight. He had slipped up to the cabin on successive weekends previous and had dug a vault underneath the tool shed. He lined it with cement and built a trap door in the floor, covering it over with all-weather carpeting. The jars, scrolls, software, and videos were thus all well hidden.

He looked at his watch again and resumed pacing the living room. He slammed his fists together. Should he wait any longer?

He felt trapped.

The phone shattered the night's stillness.

He grabbed the receiver. "Hello?" he managed between breaths.

"Is this Mr. Ladd?" asked a female voice. "This is Mercy Hospital, Los Angeles. Are you a friend of Dr. Mason-Rodgers?"

"Yes, I am—Is anything wrong?"

"Mr. Ladd, there's been an accident."

His pulse quickened. "Well, what happened? How is she?"

The voice hesitated. "She has just been taken out of emergency. Her condition is stable for the moment."

He took a pen and notepad from beside the phone and wrote down the address of the hospital. "Okay. Got it. Thank you very much."

He put down the phone, slipped on a light windbreaker, and headed out the door. Five minutes later, he was sending his car racing down the winding mountain road. As he stared at the rushing ribbon of concrete picked up by the front headlights, the urgency of the situation had frozen his thoughts into a glacial-like hardness. His mind could only register the alone-ness that pressed in on him. He surveyed the darkness that pervaded the car's interior. The hum of the motor seemed to reverberate faint and distant, taking on a surreal, dreamlike quality. He shivered and saw his breath form a vapor in front of the windshield. Autumn chill comes early in the high elevations. He could feel his facial muscles tense. If he squeezed the steering wheel any harder, he was sure he would break it. Tiny lights sparkled in the valley below where the town lay. He felt relieved that he encountered no other vehicles on that stretch of road. Coming down into the valley, however, he began to pick up traffic. He had no reckoning as to how many traffic lights and stop signs he ran. He was unheeding of the number of speed limit signs and regulations he disregarded through towns, suburbs, and shopping centers. Ahead of him lay a good hundred miles of open farm country before he would reach to the Los Angeles area. The names of the towns barely registered in his thoughts as he sped past them on into the night: Springville, Porterville on highway 65, and then to Freeway 99 just outside of Bakersfield. Then he hurled his car south on 99.

He passed the turn-off he had not traveled in nearly a decade.

He felt a strange sense of alienation as it flew past his rear window. His mother had simply no give in her disapproval of his ongoing affair with Artie.

Lights of the Los Angeles suburbs loomed in the distance. His mind began to thaw as though it had been frozen. His thoughts again started to have a free flow. As with a wound, with the thaw, also came the pain.

He realized he could lose Artie. He recalled the scene in the High Sierras; how he had promised the Almighty that he would marry her. Lester had been dead some months now. He resolved to let whatever would happen, happen.

He encountered city lights and city traffic. He guessed that he was still about an hour's drive from the hospital.

An hour from the moment of truth.

The increased congestion forced him to go slower. Stoplights, pedestrians, and vehicular traffic all seemed as cosmic roadblocks. He pushed against the wheel in an attempt to speed up his forward motion. A sense of deadness came over him. Suddenly it no longer mattered.

Nothing mattered.

He spotted the neon red cross glowing in the distance. The hospital now lay only a block away.

The traffic came to a standstill. He searched among the vehicular silhouettes for the entrance. When the traffic again permitted him to move, he faced the matter of finding a parking space. He finally pulled into a slot by the back fence and got out. He must have been still a good city block from the building. He raced through darkened aisles of parked cars to the visitor's entrance. Inside, past a maze of swinging doors and elevators, he spotted an information desk.

The clerk punched the keyboard and some figures popped up on the computer screen.

"Dr. Mason-Rodgers?" she said. "Yes. Five thirty-two."

He thanked her and headed for the elevator. Up on the fifth floor, he again checked at a desk.

"This way," the woman gestured. "You have fifteen minutes. Room 532 is intensive care."

When he finally came to room number 532, he pushed the door gently aside and entered. The figure lay beneath a maze of rubber tubes and wires attached to electrodes. Beside the bed stood an array of electronic gadgets fronting dials with crazily darting needles.

"Artie?"

No answer. Only a deep, measured breathing. He noticed the head and face swathed in bandages with tubes extended from her nostrils. Her face showed profound discoloration. As he pulled up a chair beside the bed, he reached out for a hand that lay limp on the covers.

"Artie?" he repeated. "It's me."

He pressed lips against her cheek and felt her squeeze his hand.

For a moment he continued to just sit, savoring the feel of her hand. In the stillness, he contemplated the sensation of the touch. He recalled the times and conditions that he had held that hand. He recalled touching it as he grabbed her in an attempt to keep her from losing her balance while they were alone in the classroom. She, the internationally renowned scholar in archeology, had grasped his hand to keep from falling. He remembered the strangeness of that particular familiarity. He remembered the seductive touch as from a soon-to-be-lover that evening at the Flaming Embers. He remembered the domestic feeling engendered as they walked hand-in-hand through a mountain forest. And now, as he caressed the pale hand, he marveled at the way it lay limp on the bed sheets.

A female figure with an R.N. badge stepped into the room.

His fifteen minutes were up.

Fifteen minutes. He had made contact with her. Or rather what remained of her: a pain-racked body in traction? A body pricked with a myriad of needles and wires; a body gasping through a bruised and heavily bandaged head.

He walked slowly to the elevator. Would she even recover or was this really it? The elevator door slid open. Numbly he stepped inside, turned around, and watched the doors roll shut. After eyeing the lighted buttons during the five-floor drop he stepped out into the main lobby. He noticed an arched, wooden door with a brass plate that read, "Chapel."

He pushed open the door and saw a carpeted, dimly lit room with straight-backed pews lining either side of a narrow aisle. At the front stood a small altar bearing a cross with the initials "IHS." A sunken ceiling lamp cast soft amber-colored lighting. He genuflected, slipped into one of the front pews, and knelt on a low bench.

The stillness pressed in on him as minutes became hours. He wasn't sure whether he was in prayer or not.

His watch read six-thirty.

He rose and stepped back into the lobby. He turned toward the coffee shop and ordered a light breakfast. After paying the cashier, he sought out a pay phone. He deposited a coin and began dialing.

"Angie," he said softly. "Huck. I won't be in today. Sam will cover for me. He owes me. It's Artie. There's been an accident. I'm at the hospital now. Too early to tell. She's just come out of emergency. How is she emotionally? I don't know. She was barely conscious. Her what? Her depression?"

His face sobered while Angie explained. She was alluding to what Huck had previously told her regarding Artie's visitation…

…Angie had reacted with surprising seriousness. What has been her mood since the visitation, Angie had wanted to know.

Huck confided that he had never seen her in such a state. She seemed to actually be in pain.

Dr. Mason-Rodgers is in danger, Angie had told him. More than you can possibly realize. That visitation, "Springheel Jack," as you call him, is planning on coming back. The depression is but a preliminary stage. The danger of outright possession is very real…

…Huck hung up the phone and headed back into the main lobby.

Possession?

What is this, he thought, *a throwback to the middle ages?*

He notified the woman at the information desk that he would be in the visitor's lounge and would she please notify him in case of any significant developments. He then again headed for the chapel.

As he entered the dim sanctuary the second time that morning, his mind seethed with conflicting emotions. *What next,* he thought as he knelt on the bench. *Please, God, keep them away from her.*

He was to follow the same routine in the days that followed. This was interspersed with visits to his office and an occasional stop by his apartment for a quick nap, a shower, or a change of clothes.

One morning, while in the lounge, he took a paper cup, drew from a Mr. Coffee, and headed for a remote corner. As he sat on a couch, he caught the scent of cheap after-shave. He became aware of a man in a three-piece suit settling heavily next to him. Out of the corner of his eye he saw a pudgy hand holding a wallet with a badge.

"You Hershel Ladd?" The voice spoke with a New York accent.

Huck folded his arms. "Who wants to know?"

The thick hand continued to hold out the badge. "Lieutenant Chevojka, Los Angeles Police. Are you Hershel Ladd?"

"You got it," Huck said, still looking straight ahead.

Huck remembered him from the murdered child incident.

"Are you Dr. Mason-Rodgers' attorney?"

Huck began to feel pressure. "That's right. What's this all about?"
"Just a few questions."
"About what?"
"About the fire in Dr. Mason-Rodgers' car."
Fire? "What about the fire in Dr. Mason-Rodgers' car?"
"Any ideas as to how it got started?"

Huck glanced at the figure sitting next to him. The words came from a thick, unsmiling mouth. Dark, beady eyes were set in a broad, surly-looking face, topped by a crown of thinning black hair.

"I was two hundred miles away when it happened."
"We have reason to believe it wasn't an accident," said the detective. "Too many things don't add up. Crash must have occurred 3:45 PM. Give or take."
"And?"
"Time of the fire was set at 5:45."

Huck unfolded his arms and leaned forward. "There was a ruptured gas tank," he said, still looking ahead. "That much I do know. Gas was leaking all over the place. What's strange about that?"

"Gasoline ignites when it touches a hot manifold," said the detective, "or when it touches a hot wire. Now, two hours is ample time for a manifold to cool and the ignition was dead. The engine stalled on impact. So that lets those two factors out. So where does that leave us? Nowhere is where."

"Spontaneous combustion?" suggested Huck.
"Fun-ny," said the detective. "I can't put that in my report."
"Yes you can," said Huck looking at him. "You've got a whole department downtown that deals with the paranormal. Contact them."

The lieutenant stood up. "Right," he sighed. "I'll keep in touch."

Two days later, Huck learned that Artie had been moved from intensive care. As he sat in her new room holding her hand, he heard "I love you" in a whisper, barely audible.

He kissed her hand and said, "I love you, too." He left, not wanting her to overexert herself. When he descended to the ground floor, he returned to the coffee shop.

As he sat at the counter, the imposing figure in the three-piece suit moved to the stool next to him. "Got more questions," the detective said.

Before Huck could answer, the detective cut him off. "Not here," he said, looking around the coffee shop's interior. "There."

He pointed to the lounge.

After settling into a couch in a remote corner, the lieutenant leaned heavily toward Huck. "What kind of people does Dr. Mason-Rodgers associate with?"

"What do you mean, 'what kind of people does Dr. Mason-Rodgers associate with?'"

"What kind of people does Dr. Mason-Rodgers associate with?" he repeated. "Why is that so difficult?"

"Mostly university types. Why?"

"Somebody wants her dead."

State police had found that her brakes didn't fail because of a worn hose. Somebody had deliberately cut it.

"We got an investigation going on," said the lieutenant.

Could he think of anyone who would want her dead? Or silenced? Although Huck had suspicions, he wanted something more than just hunches. He realized that nearly everyone that Artie had ever known led personal lives that were totally dysfunctional. Dr. Faasendeck, for example, did not even know exactly how many grandchildren he had.

As he started to walk away, he was stopped by another question: "What was Dr. Mason-Rodgers' hair color?"

"Black," Huck had replied. "Dr. Mason-Rodgers is a brunette."

"Medical report showed she suffered scalp lacerations," said the detective. "We took hair samples."

The detective's next words had a ring of unreality. "They were white."

"White?" Huck eyed the lieutenant. "I don't understand."

"Neither do we," said the detective.

Hair samples from the wreckage that were white? What is this?

He continued. "Too bad Dr. Rodgers is no longer with us."

"Why do you say that?"

"He could maybe give us some information."

"About what?"

"About Atlantis Studios."

"It's a porno studio."

"That ain't all. They're suspected of producing snuff movies."

"'Snuff movies?' what's that?"

"Put it this way." The detective's eyes narrowed. "When you star in one of those, your career is very short-lived, if you know what I mean."

Huck left the visitor's lounge in silent turmoil. *Is there no bottom to all this perverted garbage?* he thought. Snuff movies? He had prided himself with being pretty worldly wise, but never had he heard, nor could he have imagined anything so grotesque.

And Dean Rodgers? How could he have not known? Had Artie ever been privy to the level of depravity to which this studio trafficked in? How could she have not known? How could she have not suspected the danger that this could have placed even her?

The shit never stops, he thought.

He left the lounge feeling like a stunned ox. He left, feeling as though he were in a bad dream.

* * * * *

...She had lain pinned under wreckage for nearly two hours with gasoline dripping around her. A passing motorist finally spotted her car and sent a call on his CB radio. The ambulance and fire truck arrived within minutes. Before they could reach the wreck it had burst into flame. The firefighters fought the blaze some minutes before they were able to extinguish it with spray foam. When the charred and smoking wreck eventually cooled, the crew approached it. One of the firefighters shouted, "There's a woman under it. I think she's still alive."

When they finally pried open the driver's door, they eased her out and strapped her onto a stretcher. Despite being trapped in an inferno, she suffered burns only on the right side of her face and her right hand. There were, however, multiple fractures and internal injuries...

* * * * *

...He entered the room, bent down and kissed the bandaged face.

For the first time she was able to turn her head.

"The plastic surgeon thinks the skin graft will cover most of the scarring, just enough of a reminder that there is no rational explanation as to why I wasn't taken out of that car a charred corpse."

She remembered hurtling over the precipice, still strapped behind the wheel, and falling down into the canyon. Her next recollection was of waking, upside down, amid a wreckage of broken glass and twisted metal. She also sensed a presence strapped in the seat beside her. She perceived a hand and a sleeve of homespun. Despite the precariousness of her position, she felt a sense of serenity as the presence gripped her wrist.

She also noticed the hand looked recently injured.

The gathering dusk made discerning the face difficult. She then remembered hovering over the wreckage, the presence still holding her wrist. She saw flashing lights of approaching vehicles, and of wrecking crews crawling down the mountainside.

She saw fire light up the deepening twilight.

She sensed sliding with her benefactor back down into the wreck and herself reawakening inside her body and surrounded by flames.

The flames felt cool; like a breeze fanning her face.

Her benefactor continued holding her wrist. She noticed charring spreading across the coat sleeve. The person seemed to writhe as if in pain.

She recalled screaming, "Please don't let him die!" She tried beating out the flames. She also tried to get a look at the face.

Her next recollection was waking up in the hospital with the burns on her face and right hand.

He related to her another interview with the detective...

* * * * *

...The police lab found bloodstains on her right sleeve, the detective had said. But something doesn't add up.

"What's that?" was Huck's reply.

Those bloodstains, he recalled the detective as saying, they're not her blood type. According to the medical report, Dr. Mason-Rodgers is type O. The stains on her sleeve indicated a type so rare that medical science had never seen it before...

* * * * *

...Artie bit her lower lip. For a long time she lay as if deep in thought.

"What's the matter?" Huck said finally.

"Remember a long time ago when we had that conversation; at the Flaming Embers, I mean?" she said.

"Yes."

She lay back and, for a moment, said nothing further.

There was a downside. Word of her miraculous deliverance from the funeral pyre of broken glass and metal had gotten out; again to the press. Op Ed columnists from around the country alluded to the irony that the hospital also contained a burn unit. Photojournalists published widely shots of patients grotesquely disfigured and posed the cosmic question: Why them and not her?

They're making it sound as though it were my fault, she reflected. One columnist made remarks about one of the victims resembling E.T. *How tasteless can we get?* she thought; *to say nothing of violating their privacy. As Huck says, "The shit never stops."*

* * * * *

"I've also noticed that psychic pain," she said at last, "that horrible feeling since the visitation by Springheel Jack—is gone."
He heard footsteps. A doctor and nurse had just entered the room.
Time to remove the bandages from Artie's head and face.
He stepped away from the bed. The nurse raised the bed until Artie sat in nearly upright position. He watched the doctor hold a pair of surgical scissors to her temple and began cutting.
He could hear only a snipping sound. Even the machinery had stopped. The snipping continued. Huck eyed the proceedings with apprehension. How drastically would her looks be altered? Would her hair still be black? Or would it be white, as the detective had contended?
Artie winced as the physician pulled the adhesive from her cheek. Long strands of soiled bandage fell to the bed sheets beside her.
The critical moment had come.
Huck gingerly craned his neck to take a look at her—newly emerged as from a cocoon.
The skin of her face appeared fresh, clear, and firm. True to prediction, only a hairline scar extended up past her right eyebrow, but the distortion was not highly noticeable.
Her head bandages fell away, revealing hair that remained black—with the exception of a thin lock of white running from her forehead to the back of her skull.
He embraced her shoulders, intending to kiss her.
"Be careful," she whispered. "I still have ribs mending."
He released her shoulders and caressed her face instead.

* * * * *

For a long time they said nothing. The doctor and nurse had long since left. In the silence, his thoughts again writhed in turmoil over the almost downright casual remark made by the detective about Atlantis Studios producing "snuff movies."

In his imagination, he saw a giant dark spirit descending on Los Angeles like a black cloud until it stood astride the area like a giant puppeteer pulling strings of unspeakable evil over the teeming population dancing to its will.

How like Sodom and Gomorrah, he thought.

He glanced at the wall clock. The fifteen minutes had come and gone. They weren't going to limit his visit.

"You were talking of marriage," she said at last. "I've made a decision. I'm going to contact the chaplain. I want to see if he'll perform the ceremony right here in the hospital."

Before he could answer he heard a clatter in the doorway. A nurse's aide entered, pushing a cart laden with a basin and towels. Huck moved to the other end of the room.

"You needn't leave," said the aide. "With the bandages removed, I'm going to let Dr. Mason-Rodgers pretty much bathe herself."

Her words sent psychic shock waves pulsating through him.

Her voice—flute-like and virginal—seemed to float out into the room until it filled every nook. She spoke in crisp, clear consonants—not unlike that of certain California valley girls Huck knew who tried to affect an upper-class British accent.

She turned to look him full in the face. Immediately he felt an inward burning. Her facial expression bore a psychic radiance that was hard to look at. He also noticed something about her body. As she moved about the room, she passed in front of the window blinds. Slanted rays filtered through the cracks reflecting on the floor with strips of sunlight. Her body, however, cast no shadow.

A pastel aide's uniform clothed her petite figure. A regulation hair net held her blond hair. The soft lines and porcelain skin color of her oval-shaped face suggested the subtle brushwork of an impressionist painter. She gave him another quick, penetrating glance.

Just as quickly, the spell vanished as she turned away.

He leaned back in an easy chair in feigned casualness. "You're new here, aren't you?"

The aide began splashing a washcloth into the basin. "You could say that," she said, handing the washcloth to Artie.

Huck pointed to an empty bed opposite Artie's. "If I crawl in that bed over there, will you give me a bath, too?"

The aide began to towel down Artie's arm. "As soon as you're back on your feet," she said, "you're going to have to straighten him out."

"First day home, he and I are going to have a little talk."

Huck started for the door. "Since you two insist on ganging up on me," he said in mock defensiveness, "I think I'll leave."

The aide paused. "How do you plan to get out of the parking lot? You forgot your wallet."

He felt for his inside pocket. She was right.

She reached into her uniform. "Here," she said, producing a five-dollar bill.

"I can't take this," Huck said as he sensed color rising in his face.

"You've got to. You'll never get out of the lot."

She handed him the bill but didn't release it right away. He again noticed her skin texture to be unlike any he had ever seen. It radiated a subtle sheen without actually emanating physical light. It appeared smooth and ceramic without any pores. Yet it remained soft and pliant as any human skin.

She nodded toward the door. "We need to talk," she whispered.

Out in the hallway, she turned to him. "There is a staff party in the cafeteria this evening. Meet me there at eight."

What is this, a date? He almost asked that question. However her look told him she was serious. He again glanced at the money. When he looked up, she was gone.

When he reentered the room, he saw that the cart, too, had vanished. He heard a rattling sound. A woman of African descent pushed a cart into the room.

"Dr. Mason-Rodgers, it's time for your bath."

* * * * *

That evening Huck moved down the hall toward the employee cafeteria. He saw the aide standing beside the door as she had promised. However, now her hair hung in straight, long strands. She wore a low-cut, lavender party dress with skirt flared just above the knees. (Isn't this kind of daring for someone like this?) As he continued to wonder, he noticed the dark net hose and high-heeled shoes.

His also noticed her nametag. She took his arm and edged him toward the entrance. He saw a gold necklace bearing a triangle within a circle hanging from the milk white neck.

"Nice necklace," he said, attempting conversation.

"Did you bring your wallet?" she teased. She handed him a sticker tag and pressed it to his lapel. "This will get you in the door," she said as she admired her handiwork.

Passing through the entrance, they saw a young woman behind a table beginning to look over some paper lists.

"Charisse," said the aide, taking the young woman's hand. "I'm so glad to hear that your husband is better."

The woman looked at her startled. "Thank you," she said, managing a smile.

She gestured toward the murky interior. "Cash bar's open."

A puzzled Huck ushered the aide into a dimly lit cafeteria festooned with crepe streamers and balloons. "Does she know you?" he whispered as they headed for the bar.

"Probably not, but I know her."

Huck tried to dismiss his misgivings. *Wonder what kind of drink I should get,* he thought.

She turned to him. "I'll have a ginger ale with ice."

He ordered two ginger ales and they headed for a small table. She bent her face toward him. "I see you recognize the name."

"I've run across it before," he said guardedly as they sat down.

She observed the dance floor. Despite throbbing rhythms booming from the speakers, it was empty. She bent close. "Do you believe in me?" she shouted trying to make herself heard above the music.

He fidgeted briefly. "I think you've done Artie a lot of good."

She looked at him askance; however she let the remark pass. "Dr. Mason-Rodgers has had a very close call," she said.

She glanced with concern at the disc jockey on a bandstand as he prepared more tapes. More throbbing rhythms boomed from giant speakers at either end of the bandstand.

"What do you mean?" shouted Huck.

The aide looked frustrated. "Evil entities like Springheel Jack," she said, raising her voice. "Once they are loosed into one's life, one is totally defenseless against them."

Huck struggled with an inward pressure to bring up the subject. Dare he broach it to her?

She eyed him as if to perceive him in throes of inner conflict. "You seem to have something on your mind."

He felt his palms get sweaty. He felt his pulse quicken. "I made a shocking discovery today."

She looked at him quizzically. "Oh?"

He took a deep breath. When he finally found words, he found it difficult to control the tremor in his voice. "Atlantis Studios," he said. He paused.

"What do you know about—'snuff movies'?"

Her reaction was as immediate as it was frightening. Her facial features transmogrified from the sweet, angelic countenance into a Sinai-like indignation. Her gentle eyes burned with a laser-like fire. From her face seemed to shoot forth flashes of lightning more perceived than actually seen. As she continued studying him, gone now was the serenity, the celestial-like river of calm that before had coursed through his being. An inexplicable terror replaced it, creating within him a desire to hide under the table.

He heard her mutter subdued but portentous whisperings. "Dies irae. Dies Illa." The words came out with a softly hissing sound. "Confutatis maledictis, flammis acribus addictis!"

He felt himself on the verge of tears of panic.

He swallowed, but could think of nothing to say.

An impulse of curiosity welled up within him, pushing as aside the numbing sense of alarm. Again, dare he ask? He cleared his throat and forced out hoarse words. "About—?" A final exertion croaked out the name: "Jane Doe—?"

The dim lights that illuminated the cafeteria flickered on and off and then the room plunged into darkness. The DJ's speakers emitted a whine followed by a blast that choked off the music. The DJ's chair flew backwards throwing him off the stage. Fingers of blue lightning flashed in a circuit around the walls of the room. The revelers on the dance floor froze into a tableau of horror.

In the flickering surrealism, Huck could see her raise her arms in an apocalyptic gesture. Her long hair suddenly stood out straight from her head. From the out of the void he heard a sonic boom: "We know!"

The flash of light that accompanied the words threw him to the floor. The pungent smell of ozone burned his nostrils. He felt his hair stand. A tingling sensation shot through his fingertips and toes. His mouth took on a strong metallic taste. Pressure behind his eyeballs became unbearable.

The whole scene seemed to whirl out into another galaxy of darkness. Matter itself seemed to break apart into subatomic particles. He himself felt disembodied and spiraling out into ether of space. Was the cosmos itself reverting to its primordial chaos? Or was this the apocalyptic end of all things?

Just as suddenly the swirling stopped. Just as suddenly the fragmented universe reassembled itself.

Just as quickly the cafeteria returned to normal. Lights went back on. Music again flowed from the speakers. In a state of shock, the DJ set his chair aright and pulled up to his table. After a startled restlessness, the dancers tentatively resumed their dancing.

The chaos and disorientation vanished like smoke. From the dance floor and from nearby tables came such comments as "Probably a power outage."

As he lay on the floor in a cold, sweaty paralysis, he waited for the ringing in his ears to abate. Somewhere in the now dimly lit cafeteria, he could hear her in her normal voice. "Come on. Get up," she teased.

Still trembling, he climbed back into his chair.

The party mood had by now fully settled back into the cafeteria. It was as if nothing had happened.

Huck waited still more minutes for the ringing in his ears to fade. He marveled at how quickly the memory of the whole incident began to blur into hazy forgetfulness.

Again she reverted to her gentler self. "I have good news."

He looked at her questioningly.

"Those that have been tormenting Dr. Mason-Rodgers will torment her no more forever. Springheel Jack is a name that neither of you will ever hear of again."

She sat back and appeared to relax.

Huck studied her a moment "Are you some kind of therapist?"

He no sooner said this when he realized it a dumb thing to say.

"You're familiar with the scrolls?" said the aide after a pause.

"Oh yes."

"I was there."

He shrugged and again tried to look noncommittal.

"You seem skeptical."

His poker face wasn't fooling her.

"No matter. Tell me, what do you know about angels?"

He looked at her. He tried to quickly recall what he had read from Bible; also from Milton's *Paradise Lost*, Dante's *Divine Comedy*, and Bunyan's *Pilgrim's Progress*.

"I'm just a peon, as it were," she said.

She couldn't be crazy, he thought. *Everything about her shouts out perfect sanity. And yet?*

She again caught him with a look such as no other female he had ever met. Deep within her pupils seemed to yawn eternity itself. Do house pets feel this way when looking into the eyes of human masters? Was he to her like a dog on a leash?

She took a sip of her drink. "I am sent to minister to the most fragile of suffering humanity. Though I sometimes fail in saving my charges from the agonies of earth, I never fail in sparing them the agonies of hell. Does it make sense to you that the Source of all wisdom assigns so crucial a mission to such a one who is also comparatively vulnerable?"

He licked dry lips. "It's not for me to say."

"Perhaps," she said, ignoring his remark, "the answer lies in the fact that visions of dread, otherworldly creatures, brandishing flaming swords would destroy those who are often already at the point of death."

She paused. "Yes," she said, as if finding the answer to her own question. "That's it. The presence of a gentle, non-threatening friend or as a loving, compassionate mother is more needed here."

How could a delicate young girl of incredible beauty elicit such awe? Her words continued to radiate a pulsating energy that surged through him like sea waves. He felt attracted to her; yet repelled and intimidated at the same time. He wanted to embrace and kiss her, yet he wanted to genuflect before her, or yet again, to flee from her.

He thought he caught a look of poignancy as she glanced away. "As one who doesn't hold particularly high rank," she said, facing him again. "I can better empathize with the weak and vulnerable for we are nonetheless greatly loved."

He had to force himself to breathe. *How do I deal with somebody like this?* he thought.

She went on. "I, however, have been afforded a privilege not given everyone even in the unseen realms. I have been granted audience with the Great Abv' face to face."

She sat back and studied him. He swallowed to create enough moisture to speak; however, he could form no thoughts into words.

A few female dancers had begun to gyrate to the rhythm of the music out on the dance floor. "What's the matter with the guys?" she asked. *Why should she concern herself with something like that?* he thought. Was she endeavoring to relieve the tension of the past few moments? She stood to her feet and he felt himself pulled toward the dance floor.

They reached the space in front of the bandstand where the disc jockey worked the turntable, just in time for a slow dance. She moved close and he could feel the tender, perfumed forehead brush against his cheek. He also noticed that the pain in his knees had vanished.

THE DELUGE SCROLLS

As they moved to a faster rhythm, brushing shoulders with other dancers, he continued to churn in inner turmoil.

The D.J. segued from one tape to another for a good hour. Huck began to feel fatigue building in his calves. Out of shape, he concluded.

"I think I'll sit this one out," he panted.

"So soon?" she teased.

He staggered back to their table shaking his head. Settling back in his chair, he looked back out at the dance floor. The music boomed out the introduction to the Hustle. He watched her organize those on the floor into a kind of group dance. During the ensuing interaction, the dancers seemed thoroughly caught up in her charisma and charm. Huck sipped his ginger ale as he observed the crescendo of their laughter.

Her complete control of every situation and the way she seemed entirely at ease in every social contact impressed him profoundly.

Another hour passed before she finally returned to his table. As she pulled out her chair, he hadn't realized his staring at her.

"Why are you looking at me that way?" she said.

After settling in her seat, neither said anything for a moment. "I don't get much chance to mix with mortals," she said finally. "We enjoy people and I try to take advantage of the moments I have with them."

He stood up. Were recent moments already an elusive dream like surrealism?

"Your drink's gotten warm," he said, trying to change the subject. "Let me get a refill."

Elbowing his way to the bar, he glanced back toward their table. An obviously inebriated youth had just moved to the chair beside her. She got up from her seat in an attempt to get away from his advances. He followed her and grabbed her shoulders. What happened next would still fill Huck with a sense of disbelief.

As he set the drinks back on the countertop and prepared to rush to her aid, he saw her point her hand toward her assailant's face. From her fingertips an invisible spark of energy seemed to shoot out that blinded the young man. Immediately he pressed both his hands to his eyes and staggered away from her in panic and confusion.

Picking up the drinks, Huck hurried back to the table. "What happened?" he managed to say.

For a moment she didn't answer. She took a sip of her ginger ale. "I blinded him," she said finally. "But not to worry. It's only temporary. He'll be all right as soon as he sobers up."

She claims to not be very powerful, thought Huck. Struggling to recall the frightening epiphany that had already begun fast fading into the oblivion of forgetfulness, he concluded that yes, she could probably create a nine-on-the-Richter-scale earthquake right under his feet.

"How come you didn't blind the jerk permanently?" he asked.

She took another sip of her drink. "One of the mandates of power," she said, "is restraint. Otherwise one's power could be one's downfall. The writings testify that such was the fate of Lucifer, and also of Samson."

He recalled Artie's further accounts of her conversation with that clairvoyant woman in prison. The woman claimed that of the myriad of spirit beings that inhabit the unseen realms and that occupy the cosmos in and around us, unseen and undetected by any sensory perception or device known to mortals, only a very few of them possess the power or energy to breach the nearly impenetrable veil that separates their world from ours. Some are able to communicate with us only with tapping on tabletops; candle smoke messages on mirrors, or with such devices as ouija boards and tarot cards. Others can manage to penetrate to the extent of audible voices or even with visual manifestations such as shadows or opaque, transparent forms.

Huck had always given a shrug of skepticism to all this. Yet, did there now sit one before him who had actually been able to form fleshly substance?

The D.J. changed the tapes. The music and lyrics began to coarsen. Soon the cafeteria filled with the booming sound of the f— word.

The aide tightened her grip on his forearm. "Time to leave," she said. "As they say, 'the party is getting rough.'"

He walked her through the door and let the music fade into the background. She continued holding his arm as they walked down the hall. On reaching a distant corner, she stopped.

"Thank you for a fun evening," she said, kissing him on the cheek.

He leaned against the wall to gain additional support from legs that felt suddenly made of rubber. Despite his shaking like an aspen leaf, he sensed serenity that surged through him like a swollen river. He pressed his head against the wall and closed his eyes. His mind seemed to swirl out to unseen galaxies. An explosion of light burst on the darkness behind his eyelids. Was this merely a response to terrestrial light? It seemed to him much more intense and all pervading as it spread across a universe more felt than seen. Did he actually hear distant music, or did he just imagine it?

He opened his eyes.

Once again, she had disappeared.

Chapter 33

I noticed that my jailer appeared not like the other Ogoru. The hands that held the ration tray, instead of massive and hairy, were small, refined, and delicate; like that of a young damsel... 'Twas then that I fell at the figure's feet and clasped the knees... "I fain would have come sooner," she said. "But the whole evil hosts of Angry Things were in array against me... Your days of captivity are ended... I will meet you there..."

(Day 33. Trans. and ed. Brit. Mus. vers. 3.5; 1981.)

* * * * *

Dr. Vawter glanced at his watch. Nine AM sharp.

The atmosphere in the conference room adjacent the provost's office grew tense.

"I'll make this meeting brief," he said to the small group seated around the glass-topped table. The assemblage included Dr. Faasendeck, Dr. Gould, and Dr. Hyde. These latter two studiously remained aloof from one another.

"For a long time," Dr. Vawter continued, "I've been contemplating some changes in our curriculum."

Dr. Faasendeck fidgeted. News of the fall of the Berlin wall hit the eleven o'clock news yesterday evening like a thunderclap. Perhaps Trotsky was right all along. Perhaps lasting world revolution was possible only with a single upheaval so that there would be no comparison between two competing social systems. Only then would socialism not suffer by comparison. Could it be possible that Stalin, for all his wiliness, lived perpetually delusional regarding this?

Finally he found words. "Is this about abolition of major and minor sequences? I'll be candid. I'm concerned."

Dr. Vawter took a puff on his cigar. "Why is that?"

Dr. Faasendeck shrugged. "That practically removes all structure. What would be next? No more required courses?"

"You got it."

Dr. Faasendeck tugged at his collar. "Where then is the disciplined framework that is the scaffolding, as it were, of all serious academic study?"

Dr. Vawter eyed Dr. Faasendeck with a smirk. "Still hung up on tradition, I see?"

He leaned forward and surveyed the others. He paused to study their reaction. Finally he again sat back. "Each student would structure his or her own plan of study."

Dr. Faasendeck blinked his pale blue eyes in disbelief. "You mean—each incoming student would just select courses from all across the departments—willy-nilly—like a cafeteria, or a smorgasbord, as it were?"

"Exactly."

Dr. Faasendeck cleared his throat. "Well," he said, "how would we ever prepare our students for life outside of school?"

"Education itself is life. What preparation would they need other than what they perceive useful to them?"

Dr. Faasendeck took a drink from his glass of ice water. "How in the world will a student ever know beforehand which courses are going to be of value to him unless he gets a little guidance from us?"

Dr. Vawter took up his cigar. For a moment he said nothing. Then: "Because we will help the student as he shapes his own course content."

Dr. Faasendeck shook his head. "I can't believe this."

"On another subject," Dr. Vawter took a book from his attaché case. "I want to read something."

The cover read: *The Deluge Scrolls*. He turned to the final chapter:

"'If my discoveries and research have taught me anything, it is this: The comfort zones that the intellectual community have cocooned themselves in during the last century and a half will have to go. As surely as the scientific community launched a wholesale abandonment of the literal interpretation of Genesis with the advent of Darwin, so the time is approaching when the doctrine of classical Darwinism will itself be considered just as quaint.

"'And why is this so surprising? When one considers that we are talking about time spans of, for example, 30,000 to 50,000 years to the last glacial period, 65 million years back to the dinosaur era, 4 billion years for the age of the earth, and 12 to 15 billion years to the beginning of creation, we are talking about periods of time that I question whether even the sagest among us can begin to fathom. Were we to liken the 4 billion years of earth's history to one year, then the previously perceived time span of the four to six thousand years of recorded human history would be but the last 31.936 seconds on a stopwatch in comparison.

"'And yet, what is known to science to date (despite the fact that the sum total of human knowledge is now doubling every decade and soon will be doubling every five years) with what is not known will be likened to a thimbleful of water to the ocean. Previously held myths are becoming scientific fact. Previously cherished scientific concepts are becoming as outmoded as old wives' tales.

"'Just as few self-respecting scientists are willing to call themselves creationists, I predict the day will come wherein natural scientists will avoid the label of Darwinism with equal fervor.

"'A good case in point is the time frames on which the various ideological views regarding universal origin seem to fixate. Followers of Ussher, for example, fought strenuously, insisting that creation began 4,004 B.C. (Some even held that October 24, 4004 B.C., 9:00 AM was the creation of Adam.) and that out of nothing (ex nihilio) everything that is sprang into existence in a series of six successive twenty-four-hour periods. (If that were true, the farthest observable star would now be only about 6,000 light years away instead of the 12 billion or so that we now can reckon, and that when Adam viewed the heavens for the first time, he would have seen no stars at all for a good 4.3 years.) The confirmed Darwinist, conversely, talks in terms of millions and even billions of years. Now, however, archeological discoveries of calendars and astronomical observations of civilizations of extreme antiquity indicate time reckonings many times the 12 to 15 billion years date that we in the field of modern Western science set as when the Big Bang occurred. Yet astronomers and astrophysicists now believe that the event itself took place within a time frame of less than three minutes.

Within the three minutes, also, matter, energy, and hitherto indeterminate stages of pre-matter very possibly underwent a series of dramatic metamorphoses or changes—some lasting only milliseconds—before the Great Cataclysmic Event was complete and masses of stellar cloud-like material began hurtling themselves outward into the primordial ether of space.

"'All this, I believe, so stretches immeasurably our concept of time that any discussion of it in ordinary human terms is not only irrelevant, but even futile, when considering a universe of such proportions.

"'I who once considered myself thoroughly Darwinian in my biological philosophy, do so no longer. What do I then label my present persuasion? Creationist? In answering that question, there appears to be emerging a great body of evidence to support the theory that the universe, in fact, developed through a series of upheavals, or catastrophes. Perhaps that position is an alternative to the creationist-evolutionist polarization that developed during the nineteenth century. This third alternative is the one that I call Catastrophist.

"'I call on my colleagues in the scientific community to maintain an open mind, remembering always that this is, after all, the only attitude of the true scientist.'"

Dr. Vawter laid aside the book. "Well, what do you think?"

The others in the room sat silent.

"All right," he continued. "Since everybody has developed a sudden lack of eloquence, let me read on.

"'Does myth necessarily mean something not true? Or is it merely something that cannot be proven? If so, need it be proven? Can myths sometimes contain more truth than mere objective facts? In trying to prove them by the so-called scientific method, do we not lose something? Do they not lose their power? Are they not sometimes more than the sum of their parts? We need not seek to prove nor disprove, for example, *Aesop's Fables* to accept their larger truth. What justification, then, is there in questioning them?

"'I who once totally subscribed to the humanistic denial of the supernatural do so no longer.'"

He laid aside the pages and again looked out at the group. He studied their faces as he continued to let them sit motionless around the table. He let the silence lengthen until it was beginning to get awkward.

"Heard enough?" he finally asked. "Or should I go on?"

A sardonic smile crossed his blotched, ruddy features as he flipped through more pages.

"Listen to this," he said, stopping at a particular page marked with a highlighter.

"'One hears in recent years of an alleged controversy dubbed "science vs. religion." What makes this contention so quaint is that until recently many great scientists have been men of devout faith: Sir Isaac Newton, Blaise Pascal, and Father Mendel, to name a few. Was it not largely since the advent of Darwin that we have seen otherwise? Also, has not most anti-religious thought been in the so-called "soft" sciences like philosophy and literature?

"'...In his railing against Christianity, was not Nietzsche possibly striking out against his lifelong battle with syphilis, migraines, and insanity? Was it not true of Karl Marx against his hemorrhoids and self-imposed poverty?

"'...What if all references to deity or religion of any kind were to be suddenly erased from the human psyche, memory, and culture? What if all inquiry and learning were to become the exclusive domain of the natural sciences? What would the human experience be like had no religious thought ever existed? Would humankind indeed find the answers to its most deeply vexing questions?

"'...What is the origin of religion anyway? Has it not always been the attempt to reconcile the two irreconcilable realities of life, namely the will to survive and the certainty of death?

"'...What of there had been no Bible, no Torah, no Koran, or Veda? What if there had been no cathedrals, mosques, or temples? There would also have been no prehistoric paintings on cave walls. Neanderthal Man would not have practiced ritual burial of his dead. There would have been no mythology. Science itself would have to search for names other than mercury, plutonium, and titanium for its metals and other names than Mars, Venus, Jupiter, and Saturn for its astronomical bodies. Obituary columns would be bereft of such phrases as "passed away," "departed," or "left behind."

"'...Why is it, for example, that the chimpanzee, with a genetic make-up that is 99.4% identical with mine could sit beside me as I type this page and not have the slightest concept as to what I am doing?

"'...In short, one has to ask the question: "How many medical students pray during final exams?" Or perhaps ask: "How many scientists are asked to officiate at funerals?"

"'... Or put it another way: How could one born blind and who had never traveled more than, say, ten miles from his place of birth grasp the concept of the Grand Canyon or Mount Everest? How could one born deaf grasp the sound of Beethoven's Ninth Symphony (who himself was deaf when he wrote it.) Would not such a one ridicule the idea of any of these as a fool's tale?

"'Are we not all struggling with varying degrees of blindness and ignorance in perceiving a universe wherein all of us at best can barely grasp what is really out there?'"

Dr. Vawter studied the page briefly. *Damn her anyway*, he thought. He recalled a picture of a burn victim treated at that very same hospital. The man was a refinery worker burned in an oil fire. His head, face, upper body, and arms looked like something from outer space, or perhaps a cheap horror movie. *This poor schlep gets fried and she escapes unscathed. Why? A miracle, she says. How arrogant can we get?*

There you have it, he thought. *She's won a skirmish and now she's mounting a frontal assault.*

He laid the page aside. "I've made a decision," he said. "As of next year I'm closing the department of archeology."

"But archeology is an old and respected discipline in our university," objected Dr. Faasendeck.

Dr. Vawter dismissed his objection with a wave of his hand. "As John Dewey once said: 'Let the dead past bury its dead.'"

"You can't do that," gasped Dr. Faasendeck.

"Why not?" demanded Dr. Vawter. "Enrollment has dropped off. How can we possibly justify continuing to offer it?"

Dr. Faasendeck toyed with a glass ash tray. "Enrollment is down in all departments," he said, clearing his throat. "There's still sufficient interest to offer Archeology 101."

Dr. Vawter eyed him. "You can fight me on this if you want to."

Dr. Faasendeck struggled for breath. The underclothing beneath his suit became wet with sweat. *Ironic*, he thought, *Soviet education produced scientists that could send astronauts up into outer space for weeks. And we? Are we producing mush-heads with inability to find their way out of the nearest coffee house?*

Before he realized it, he found his chair pushed back and himself on his feet.

"I have gone along with you on everything these past few years," he said, struggling for calmness in his voice. "For years our school has sent graduates out into education, graduate schools, professional schools, and into commerce with impeccable credentials. A diploma from Cortez Pacific

University was worth its weight in gold. It sufficed to open the tightest of closed doors.

"I have watched you change all that. I watched you change a strong, intellectual bastion of truth-seeking into a quasi-educational laboratory wherein we have conducted all kinds of spurious experiments with young people's lives, their minds, and their futures.

"I have watched you pressure staff members like Drs. Gould and Hyde into publishing treatises averring that adolescence extends to age forty and beyond and that society is nothing more than a mass of grown-up children needing government or some other authority playing the surrogate nanny. Yet you not only denounce the old 'in loco parentis' philosophy of the past as antiquated nonsense, you force our young people into such socially explosive situations as co-ed dorms with their unisex bathrooms and showers. You force these alleged 'children' of ours to live, defecate, and copulate together like animals.

"In a more genteel society, you would be subject to class-action charges of contributing to the delinquency of minors.

"I have watched you change what was once the West Coast equivalent of an Ivy League school into nothing more than a cesspool of radical propaganda."

He searched the faces of the others. They remained frozen into expressionless masks.

He took another deep breath before going on. "And now I'm going to tell you one more thing, sir," he said, turning his glare back to Dr. Vawter. "No more."

Dr. Vawter emitted a hoarse groan as his mouth dropped open. He pressed a hand to his forehead as if suddenly afflicted with a severe headache. The left side of his face and body seemed to change and his left hand fell uselessly at his side.

Dr. Faasendeck moved to his side and tried to give him a drink of water. "Call the ambulance, quick!" He gestured toward a phone at the end of the conference table.

Dr. Hyde rushed to him and opened his shirt collar. She adjusted the chair to a more reclining position to make breathing easier.

Dr. Faasendeck pressed the intercom. Dr. Vawter's secretary burst in with a pill bottle. While he slipped into a coma, they could only watch.

Dr. Gould hung up the phone. "The ambulance is coming," he said.

Now all they could do was wait.

Silence settled in about them until they saw flashing lights reflecting against the window curtains. Dr. Gould ran out and guided the paramedics into the conference room. The medics inserted a plastic tube into Dr. Vawter's nostrils and then laid him on a wheeled stretcher. They worked over him for more tense minutes. Finally they wheeled him out the door to a waiting ambulance in the parking lot.

Dr. Faasendeck and his colleagues followed and then watched the speeding ambulance exit the front gate. They continued standing for an indeterminate period of time in stunned silence.

On impulse, Dr. Hyde slipped away from the others and returned to the administration building. She reentered the conference room and walked over to the glass-topped table.

How empty, how quiet, she thought. How in contrast the conference of the school's most powerful just a few moments ago.

She pulled from Dr. Vawter's attaché case his copy of The Deluge Scrolls and began flipping through the pages. Stopping at the entry of Day 40, she began to read:

> *So greeted I day forty of this most fearsome voyage. Perceived I to be breathing air of thinnest rarity; rather like the air atop the highest mountain summit.*
>
> *Covered over by waters beneath me now lie mountain peaks, and valleys, and verdant meadows, and once-fertile plains, and whole continents; and whole races of men.*
>
> *Below me in these waters lie the remains of my beloved Akir-Ema. Full thirty-nine days of gray and red saw I, and nights blacker than the Pit itself. Fearsome days with unrestrained waves, foam and vicious winds seem to howl for my very soul. Treacherous currents washing flotsam and rubble threaten my fragile bark.*
>
> *Full forty days partook I of little food. Full forty days got I precious little sleep. Perished my entire crew of fright; of madness. (Whereupon they, amid much ranting and raving, did hurl themselves into the sea.) Thus it was on day forty, I stood aboard my vessel abandoned and alone.*
>
> *Or so I thought.*
>
> *I heard a rustling, a stirring from below; in the hold. Some villainous stowaway no doubt, I thought. I drew my sword to await this unwelcome son of a jackal. (Lit. "S.O.B."—ed.) The common impending doom we shared notwithstanding, I am still commander of this voyage and I will brook no freeloaders at my expense.*

I saw a figure emerge from the hatchway.

"Rokko," said I. (Of a truth I had quite forgotten the lad.)

I marveled at the metamorphosis that had taken place. Gone now was his orange topknot. His hair had since grown back a natural black. The green dye had faded from his skin that now showed a natural color. Instead of the feathered loincloth, he now arrayed himself in the manly dress of breeches and tunic.

"I beg of you, my father," (Akiri term of highest respect; may or may not denote familial relationship—ed.) *he pleaded. "Send me not away."* (Indeed, where could I send him were I so minded?)

"How is it," I asked, *"that you did not give yourself to the sea, as have the others?"*

"You spared my life," he said, *"as my friends were being slaughtered in the streets by the dread Herpetia* (Lit. Serpents—ed.) *As you pressed me into the servitude of Dhjek, you forbade his shaming and abusing me. You indeed are the only father I have ever known. I have no other request than this: to join you in a watery grave."*

I clasped this stalwart youth by the shoulders. "By All-That-Is-Good," said I, *"you would do any father proud."*

* * * * *

I see Day Forty about to dawn. I see a dawning different than any of the previous thirty-nine. I perceived first that the fierce wind was beginning to abate. The driving waters that were blowing through the air now have been reduced to a slight drizzle. Though the (clouds) still raged thick and dark, I perceived the fearsome fire that raced through the heavens did so no more.

At the horizon, I saw a break in the (clouds) and, for the first time in forty days, a clear sky. It revealed a thin band of pale, gold color of sunlight that gave no warmth; rather it glimmered weakly as if trying to penetrate the thick, smoky atmosphere. The wind blew no longer strenuous, but steady; and very cold. The air was filled with fine flurries of dust and ash. The waters lapped at my craft heavy, murky, and black. The waves, no longer mountainous billows nor yet great swells, assailed our ship fitful and choppy. Out in the water—everywhere—I saw the bobbing, drifting pieces of wreckage of buildings, wagons, logs, and the carcasses of animals and men.

The wind continued to blow cold. Very cold. (Possibly this was the phenomenon known as "nuclear winter."—ed.)

I stood on a deck swept clear of all rigging. Thus we set; with no power; no sails, helpless in the murky waters, subject to the cold and buffeting winds. The gray-dark ash with its overpowering, sulfurous stench, whipped our faces, borne as it was on the (rain) until it was thick like sludge covering everything; permeating everywhere, making our garments heavy and caked with the pestilential goo. It made our vessel wet, slippery, and treacherous.

As I looked for brightness other than the thin, pale streak on the horizon, I determined by my compass that we drifted northward. I then entered my cabin to make a final entry in my log. I marveled at the ease of this day's writing task. Previously, when the seas raged boisterous and contrary, I struggled mightily as I tied myself to my desk. I held my writing quill in both hands. My scroll, too, I tied to the desk, while I also fought to keep my inkhorn from spilling.

I came out on deck again and perceived us heading westward. A time later, upon checking our course, I noticed our drift southward. Another reading of my compass showed our direction eastward. Some time later, I noticed a northward course again. All the while, in every direction, saw I naught but water.

I had not long to wait ere I noticed a new and strange and evil thing. As my ship drifted in all directions of the compass, I became aware of an all-pervasive roar. I looked off to my port side and saw a gaping emptiness; an abyss toward which we all—the rubble, the trees, the driftwood, in an ever-tightening circle were headed. So dawned on me the awful truth.

Whirlpool!

I saw my vessel, all that remained of life upon the water, and myself inexorably drawn toward the vortex.

I viewed the swirling wreckage sliding with the accelerating current toward the roaring emptiness; closer, ever closer. I sensed a presence beside me. I beheld Ariel the Watcher.

I knew not whether she was mere spirit, or whether she had, in fact, taken bodily substance. Overjoyed, I became most presumptuous. I embraced her, as an old friend. She was real. She had substance. Showing no offense, she returned my embrace.

I was aggrieved to see her hair besotted with the gritty, muddy ash— the hellish stuff proving itself no respecter of persons. The stinking, sulfurous pumice quickly begrimed her lovely face. The waters from the sky befouled by the putrefying ash flowed freely from her fair cheeks. Her gossamer, golden robe quickly became as impregnated with filth as mine.

Noble sprite that she is, she bore the indignity of the storm and attendant stench without complaint.

Spake she to me these comfortable words: "You are greatly loved. However, your earthly sojourn is nearly ended. But fear not. I will meet you there at your moment of departure and I will personally escort you into the presence of All-That-Is-Good. When the waters overwhelm you, he will be with you.

"King Xisusthrus and his family, sealed aboard their large vessel, will be the only ones spared this terrible calamity. The horror of it will be shielded from their eyes. They will be the only ones to repopulate a whole new world. You, however, are singularly privileged to be sole eyewitness. You did well to keep an account of what you have seen. Seal up the scrolls in the power jars as a written record for future generations."

She kissed her hand and pressed it to my forehead. "Am's blessing on you, dear H'rshag."

She then faded into the storm's sulfurous fury.

So it is I, H'rshag, of late a priest of Akir-Ema, do seal up these words until such a time when Providence decrees that they be discovered by a world yet unknown; to a people yet unborn; to discover the fate of the once great (Atlantis?—ed.)

May Am's blessing be upon one and all.

So let be.

* * * * *

Dr. Hyde laid the papers back in the attaché case. She again marveled at the quiet. She pushed aside a beige curtain and looked out. The campus, the street, and the neighborhood beyond all seemed void of life.

She pulled a cigar from her purse and soon thoughtfully blew puffs of smoke out into the room. *Jacqueline Hyde, Ph.D., Dean of the School of Education*, she reflected. *You've just watched your immediate superior being rushed to the hospital, maybe never to come back. Were it I*, she continued, *would I be willing to put my life in the hands of a brain surgeon who learned his profession, for instance, through Montessori?*

* * * * *

Forenoon had arrived before Huck had finally made it to the hospital. The morning routine seemed laden with more than the usual round of petty, detailed paperwork. He was able to break free at ten-thirty. An hour later, he checked in at the main desk.

"Message for Mr. Ladd."

The receptionist pulled a note from off a spindle. He was to call a certain number. From a pay phone he dialed a nearby motel. He told the desk clerk he was returning a call.

"Nobody answers," she said. "Apparently they're out."

"Can you tell me who is registered in that room?"

"I'm sorry," said the clerk, "we can't give out that information."

Huck slammed the phone back on the hook and rushed for the elevator. As he waited, he glanced at the news vending machine. Headlines read, "Berlin Wall breached by East and West Berliners."

* * * * *

Huck drew open the blinds to let in the noonday sun.

"The chaplain had agreed to perform the ceremony," said Artie, "as soon as I am able to make it to the chapel."

Huck stared straight ahead in silence. *Thank God*, he thought, *at last*.

They heard a rattling sound behind them. The aide, again clad in a pastel uniform, pushed in a lunch cart.

"I see you survived the festivities," said Huck, settling into an easy chair. "Did you get any sleep?"

She flipped the legs of the lunch tray. "I never sleep."

Artie looked at the both of them. "Whatever are you two talking about?"

Huck cast a glance toward the aide. "Should we tell her?"

The aide flipped a napkin. "I think we'd better."

"Better what?" demanded Artie. "What's going on here?"

"There was a staff party last night, in the cafeteria." He gestured toward the aide. "She invited me down. She wanted to discuss some things."

Artie eyed them. She felt a twinge of guilt over a secret irritation with the aide's preppy, schoolgirl manner of speech. "I think I'm getting jealous," she said in a mocking tone. "Whatever did you talk about?"

Huck sat upright in his easy chair. "You."

The aide helped arrange the tray. "How have you been feeling lately?"

I'm still in a lot of pain, Artie was about to say. "You mean—?"

The aide nodded. "Yes—the depression."

"Gone," said Artie. "Since being here, it hasn't bothered me."

Gone. *No more*, she realized. *Gone also is that Thing, whoever or whatever, seen or unseen, it was that was angry with me over the destruction of the figurine. It hasn't seemed to have made its presence felt lately.*

Interesting.

"You experienced a taste of hell," said the aide.

Artie stared at her.

She recalled telling Huck of frightening experiences with drugs while at Earthnation. Now the memory of hallucinatory trips came back with renewed force.

Silence hung heavy in the room.

Hell.

Like a ball rolling across the surface of a pinball machine suddenly dropping into a hole, so the word seemed to fall into a slot in her mind. The idea, the concept, so flippantly dismissed by the modern scientific mind suddenly took on a new and horrific reality. She felt a chill creep through her body. She felt the room freeze into tableau quite out of context with any universe of time and place. Inside her head she felt a rhythmic roar in sync with her heartbeat. The horror of an otherworldly confrontation so foreign to mundane human experience and the resultant depression so profound that she actually felt a burning within her convinced her of an actuality too terrifying for words

"You should have seen this gal last night." Huck's attempt to change the subject broke the spell. "She was the life of the party. She acted like she knew everybody."

"I do," said the aide. "I've known all of them since before any of them were even conceived."

Huck again sat upright. Dared he ask? "How much do you know?"

"Everything," was the reply.

Everything? "Oh, my go—" he almost said it before catching himself. Amid mounting chagrin, he glanced quickly in the aide's direction. Her reaction, however, appeared non-committal.

More silence. He reflected on that scene in Artie's apartment. Or what about those scenes at the beach when they copulated like dogs in broad daylight? Or at the cabin in front of the fireplace?

As Artie resumed eating, the aide stepped back briefly. Out of the corner of her eye, she spotted Huck gesturing for her toward the door.

Once out in the hall, Huck leaned against the wall, arms folded. For a moment he stared at the floor and said nothing.

She stood off a short distance from him. "What was it you wanted?"

He looked at her briefly and then at the floor again. "You saw?"

She stepped closer and laid her hand on his shoulder. "The secret sins of earth are open scandal in heaven."

He turned away from her, brushing her hand away as he did so. "I knew it," he said. He continued leaning one shoulder against the wall with his back to her.

Again, she laid her hand on his shoulder. "Please don't do this."

He continued staring at the floor.

"Please listen to what I say." Her hand continued resting on his shoulder.

He still leaned against the wall, away from her with arms folded. He could not even muster the words: What can I say?

He glanced back in her direction and noticed an expression of gentle pleading.

"I have been eyewitness to every form of human behavior a million times over," she said. "We don't consider it all that big a deal. Actually, we find it rather boring. We are far more interested, for example, as to how mortals treat each other."

Like Atlantis Studios? The words came rushing into his mind despite his attempts to banish them to the stygian recesses of his subconscious. Like snuff movies? The darkness gathered with increasing momentum despite his being in the very presence of heaven itself. Like the innocent little lamb, Jane Doe, lying even as they spoke in an anonymous grave. Dying under unspeakable conditions, banished from the land of the living without even one mortal who knew her or would claim her as their own. *Please, God,* he thought, *please, Ariel, somebody, somehow, somewhere make it up to her wherever she is!*

Ariel withdrew her hand. She, likewise, folded her arms and stared thoughtfully at the floor. "Tell me," she said, looking up, "have you, for example, ever seen two dragonflies copulating in midair?"

He nodded. "Why, yes."

"Did it embarrass you?"

"Of course not."

"Do you think it embarrassed the dragonflies?"

"No way."

"Have you ever seen a male ruffled grouse do a ritual mating dance?"

"Why yes."

"Did it embarrass or arouse you?"

"Are you kidding?"

She continued to look at him. "Clumsy analogy, I know," she said with a shrug. "But there you have it."

Huck gave a self-conscious chuckle. "Yeah."

"You see," she continued, "'be fruitful and multiply' was actually God's first command. 'Thou shalt not commit adultery' was given millennia later when the act was misused and debased. Adultery is really not so much about sex as it is about betrayal of trust."

Silence again settled in the corridor. "Humans get so obsessed with their so-called right to privacy," she said, shaking her head. "What makes you think mortals can hide anything from the spirits?"

He thought long and hard on that one. He was sure that if one were to rip all the roofs off all the buildings in just the L.A. area alone, one would see enough depravity to drive one insane. How could somebody like this young girl stand to be privy to all the junk and not totally lose it? When he mentioned the subject, she again turned to him with that penetrating look.

"Since we see all." Her voice again caused him to break out in a sweat. "We are not shocked by anything. We are not taken by surprise."

She paused.

Even things like Atlantis Studios? he thought. *Even things like snuff movies? Even ritual orgies of unspeakable vileness? Even people calling good bad and bad good?*

The silence continued.

"This helps, believe me," she added. Finally.

The corridor seemed to grow in length and emptiness. He marveled that a major urban hospital could remain so long void of bustle and activity. *Is this something else she arranged?* he wondered.

"This business of 'living in sin,'" he said after a pause. "It really is a big deal, though, isn't it?"

She nodded. "Yes it is. But that isn't the worst of it."

He looked at her questioningly.

"We've missed you," she said, searching his eyes.

"I don't understand."

"It's been fourteen years since we've seen you in church," she continued. "Why didn't you ask me how many times I was beside you as you knelt to pray? Or when you knelt to take the wafer and chalice?"

His mind went in retrospect to the late September Sunday morning during his senior year in high school. The church calendar indicated Michaelmas Sunday. The lesson and homily centered on angels. He recalled the text: "—He makes his ministers (angels) a flame of fire… sent to minister (serve) the heirs of the kingdom…"

He grasped her hands. Breathing became difficult. He closed his eyes momentarily.

"'Father, I have sinned grievously in thy sight,'" he said. "'I have done those things which I ought not to have done, and have left undone those things which I ought to have done for which things I am heartily sorry and do confess that I am not worthy of the least of thy mercies… The memory of them is painful to me and I do heartily repent and upon the merits and bitter, holy, innocent sufferings of thy son, Jesus Christ, do humbly beseech and implore thy forgiveness. Lord have mercy. Christ have mercy. Lord have mercy.'"

He found himself in kneeling position. *This is crazy,* he thought. *What if somebody comes?*

She kissed her fingertips and pressed them on his forehead. He heard her whisper softly. Then, "Arise in peace," she said audibly.

He stood to his feet and embraced her. She returned his embrace.

"I love you, Huck," she said, "and I love Artie, too. Marry with our blessing."

Serenity came flooding back into his being. Yet he again began shaking like an aspen leaf. He felt the perspiration soaking through the wool of his suit. *What if somebody comes?* he asked himself again. They would see a middle-aged guy in a dark business suit old enough to be her father embracing a teenaged girl in a nurse's aide uniform.

She released her embrace and he felt a tug on his sleeve. She gestured toward the door. "Let's see if Artie has finished eating."

Upon entering the room, the aide moved to Artie's bedside.

She pulled the cart away from Artie's bed. "I'll return shortly," she announced. She exited the room, pushing the cart ahead of her.

After she left, Huck sat beside the window. He watched swallows hop in and out of a nest on a nearby window ledge. Along the ledge lay some sunflower seeds. *Who put them there?* he wondered. *How could the frail, feathered creatures ever crack open the hard shells? What awareness did they have that they were being watched? In their miserable existence, in their struggle for survival would they even care?*

The sound of footsteps broke his reverie.

When the aide reentered, she stepped to the bed and gestured for Huck to come alongside.

"I'm going to leave you now." She laid her hand atop theirs. "You will not see me again this side of the eternal realms."

Immediately he again felt the uncontrollable trembling, the profuse breaking out in perspiration, and the serenity that again surged through him like a powerful, swollen stream; a serenity almost orgasmic in its intensity. Was this in contrast to the depression felt by Artie after her encounter with Springheel Jack a sense of heavenly bliss as real as were her agonies of hell?

Ariel kissed them each, in turn, on the cheek. With that kiss came a sensation pressing in on him that accompanied an overriding conviction that it was all right. Everything was all right. Even with the unspeakable like Atlantis Studios rampaging through the universe.

Huck detected a bittersweet pensiveness as she raised her other hand. Eyes closed, she began whispering. He caught the words: "Pax Vobiscum. In Nomine Jesu, Amen."

They saw her uniform change to a gossamer material. Gold thread bordered her sleeves and hem and a golden sash formed about her waist. A bejeweled, white gold tiara formed about her forehead.

Her body shape amazed them most. The soft, feminine curves about her breasts and hips began to flatten out. Her shape became straight or stick-like; like that of a child. Was she still a "she"? Light began to radiate from the face and figure. The face appeared less human and more stylized: resembling an icon, or a figure from a stained-glass window in some European cathedral. The image became translucent, opaque, as light continued to envelop. The figure blurred, disappeared and imploded into natural sunlight.

Visually, the disappearance was now complete, yet they still felt the sensation of her touch. Did she still remain with them, or just in their memory? Or imagination?

Gone, thought Huck. *Vanished. Someone who looks like a young, teenaged ingénue.* He recalled how she claimed to not be very powerful. *Yet, I'll bet she probably possesses power enough to shake a whole continent like a cement mixer*, he thought. He wondered how many ancient languages she knows. Languages that not one person alive today can speak. Artie had always wanted to tap into something like this.

Now she's gone. Disappeared. Forever. I think we goofed.

They remained motionless in the tomb-like silence. A tacit agreement flashed between the both of them not to discuss this with anyone.

Years would pass before they would discuss it between themselves.

The silence lengthened. They each seemed loath to move or speak.

The sound of footsteps startled them. A figure in a three-piece suit moved beside the bed. Bending over Artie stood the detective.

Before Huck could interject, the detective spoke first. "Lieutenant Chevojka," he said, showing his badge. "Dr. Mason-Rodgers?"

"Yes?"

Again, before Huck could say anything. "Got some questions."

He took her left wrist and began examining it.

"Hey!" shouted Huck. "What is this?"

"Just examining her wrist."

"For what?" demanded Huck; neck reddening.

"For cuts is for what. I noticed your right hand is bandaged. Not self-inflicted, is it?"

Artie glared at him. "Of course not. What's this all about?"

"We had a warrant to search your apartment. We found evidence of a suicide attempt. Yet, my inspection just confirms no slashed wrists. Just doesn't add up."

Huck searched the detective's face. "What did you find in her apartment that suggests a suicide attempt?"

The detective took out a small notepad. "Your bathroom sink," he said as he began scribbling, "was solid with bloodstains."

Silence filled the room.

"Also a possible break-in," he continued. "Somebody did a real number on your front doorknob. Tore it right out of the door."

Artie looked questioningly at Huck.

"Tell the man, honey," he said.

She gave the detective a full account of her encounter with Springheel Jack.

The detective turned to Huck. "What kind of cockamamie story is this anyway?" he said, holding up his note pad.

"A true cockamamie story," retorted Huck.

"Look at it from my point of view," said the detective. "What's gonna happen when I write up a report?"

"Looks like it's your problem."

"No, it's *our* problem," he said, shaking out the pages. "What am I supposed to do with this?"

"I could make a suggestion," said Huck.

"Don't get smart," snapped the detective.

"You don't get it, do you?" shouted Huck.

"No, you don't get it," shouted the detective in return.

"Please, the both you," Artie pleaded. "I can't take this."

Huck glared at the detective. He gestured toward the door.

Once out in the corridor, the detective turned to him. "Okay, smart guy. Let me spell it out for you in kindergarten blocks. We are conducting a criminal investigation here. Attempted murder. So far we don't have a suspect; not even a motive. All we have is a weird story about some spook giving her a hard time."

"We're talking demon possession," insisted Huck. "Or maybe I should say attempted demon possession."

"Whatever," shrugged the detective. "I don't need to remind you that demon possession ain't against the law. Attempted murder is."

Again, he held out his note pad. "Know what we got so far? Butkus!"

He moved in close. "I am sure you also know how some hot dog lawyer, like yourself, would make her look: like she was nutzo. All the while we're tryin' to convict some would-be murderer."

Huck saw just enough truth to the detective's words that all he could do was shake his head. "You were asking about the people she associates with," he said with a sigh. "Let me have some time to get some more facts together. A lot of it may be more weird shit like you already got on your notepad."

The detective flipped the notepad shut. "I'll get back to you."

He sighed as he turned and walked away. "I don't know," he said to himself. "I just don't know."

After he left, Huck tiptoed back into the room. Artie lay on her side, toward the wall. She was daubing her eyes with a facial tissue. He bent to kiss her. She continued staring wistfully toward the wall.

Again, he heard footsteps. He turned to see a woman in uniform. "We have allowed you to stay entirely too long," she informed him. "We don't want Dr. Mason-Rodgers to have a relapse."

He left the room in turmoil. He approached the elevator, punched a button, and waited. Relapse? Could a brief argument with the detective precipitate a relapse? With broken ribs, could she possibly develop pneumonia? Impossible, he thought. She was doing so well.

He watched the lighted buttons on the panel approach his number. Numbly, he stepped through the doorway and waited with a queasy stomach as the elevator dropped to the ground floor. He stepped into the lobby and headed for the chapel. Upon entering, he moved up to his accustomed pew and knelt.

Again, he wanted to pray, but didn't quite dare. After all, he had promised the Almighty ten years ago that he would marry her. Had he exhausted the Almighty's patience?

He recalled a lesson from confirmation class: something about a fallen sparrow. Jesus had told his disciples in his Sermon on the Mount that not a sparrow falls to ground but what the heavenly Father. Heavenly Father what? Takes knowledge? Consent? Or both?

He heard himself saying the words: "Dear God—" Tears streamed down his face, freely, unashamedly. "There's a sparrow up on the fifth floor. She's broken and hurt. Please. Take care of her."

He could hear the hinges of the chapel door move; then someone tiptoeing into the room behind him. He sensed a female figure, an older woman, slipping into the pew beside him.

"Mother," he whispered, trying to maintain his composure. "This is a surprise."

"I saw Dr. Faasendeck out in the lobby just now," she said without returning his greeting.

The unexpected news filled Huck with questions. "Did he say why he was here?"

Mrs. Ladd began leafing through her prayer book. "It seems that Dr. Vawter has had a massive cerebral hemorrhage. Dr. Faasendeck said that he was in intensive care."

The stillness of the chapel interior stretched out into minutes.

Dr. Vawter, Artie's nemesis, in a deep coma, he reflected. Very likely about to meet his Maker.

A Maker he never really believed in.

The hushed atmosphere was interrupted by his mother's voice.

"You didn't do right."

He didn't answer right away. He studied her profile: the slight, intense figure with a face accentuated by prominent cheekbones. He contemplated the strong-looking hands that held the prayer book. Without looking up, he knew she would not be wearing make-up. Actually he had allowed that she looked beautiful enough without it. Yet, her face radiated not so much beauty, but strength.

Perhaps therein lay her beauty.

He never recalled hearing her raise her voice. He could not recall ever hearing her say "I love you" either. Perhaps her admonition to "take your sweater, it might turn cold," or her "be careful on the highway," was her way of saying "I love you."

"I haven't been doing right for a long time," he confessed. "But that's all right. Artie and I are going to rectify that situation. We're going to be married as soon as the doctor says she is able; right here in the hospital."

For the first time since entering the chapel, she looked at him.

"That's not what I'm referring to," she said. "You didn't do right in not informing us of the accident. I came as soon as I heard."

Epilogue

Artie paused at the bottom of the basement steps. She still had trouble maneuvering those steps with a cane. Outside the patio door, poplar leaves shimmered gold in the late autumnal sunlight. She hobbled over to the computer. Laying her cane on the floor, she slid into her chair and began typing the following:

Dr. Ardith Ladd
Box #476
Mountain Lake, CA, 93266

Dearest Peppi:

Finally, I get to answer your last letter. Yes, we are doing fine. While I still need a cane to get around, I am getting more mobile every day. Despite all that happened, life is finally developing a serenity that is welcome and satisfying.

She paused from her typing. *Our anniversary soon,* she thought. *And now it's the twenty-first century. How time flies.* She resumed her letter:

Six years ago, Huck walked away from a lucrative law practice in Los Angeles. He says he has left the city for good and now stays up at our Mountain Lake address. He has opened an office here in town and had started a general practice.

It looks like the two girls are the extent of our family. I got in on the childbearing just in time. I'm sure that Huck would have liked a boy, but we were just too late for that. Just a note of sadness: the child I lost a few years back was a boy.

The scrolls and jars are now gone as well. I had loaned them to the City Museum for a special exhibit. They were kept in what was presumably a highly secured warehouse. Before the exhibit opened, however, the riots broke out. When fires from some nearby buildings spread to the warehouse, the jars and the scrolls were also destroyed.

Speaking of fires, she thought, *the press had finally gotten off my case about my miraculous escape from the car wreck.*
Thankfully.

I still have photographs, transcripts, and videos. However, I'm afraid the destruction of Atlantis is now finally complete. As Huck once asked early in our relationship: "What about Atlantis?"

* * * * *

Suddenly other words jumped to her screen. *What is this?* she thought. *Virus?*

She tried to delete them but they clung to the screen. She feverishly punched more keys, trying every operation in her repertoire, but still they remained…

Damnable, little flea-bitten weasels, thought I. They can't all be seventh sons of seventh sons. Whence then come their claim to prophethood?
Who speaks for God anyway?

...Indeed, who does speak for God? Why the thought came to her still remains a puzzle.

The Me.

Was it a providentially inspired oracle that predated the Torah? Had the Torah and later the New Testament been given because the older revelation had fallen into disuse and forgotten?

In desperation she finally resumed typing. The words on her manuscript popped to the screen, even though the cryptic message continued superimposed over them:

> I guess we can only say as H'rshag the Akiri priest once said: "Alas, that great city; alas, in one hour is not."
> We only know that somewhere beneath the ocean's waves lie what once were plains, and whole continents, and whole races of men.
> Yet I can't help but believe that the love bond of those dear people of so long ago has somehow risen above the sea's depths.

Babylon, she thought. She recalled how she once considered the biblical curse on those ancient ruins mere superstition. Could she now conclude that the trauma of subsequent events that overtook her own life to be more than mere coincidence? What of the current megalomaniac ruler of modern-day Iraq and his attempt to rebuild Nebuchadnezzar's palace? Is there any connection with their disastrous defeat in the recent desert war?

During the first two years of publication *The Deluge Scrolls* enjoyed phenomenal success. Subsequent years, however, saw sales dropping off drastically. Will the book, in time, be relegated to some remote library under the section entitled "archeology"? Will others, in time, look upon it with the skepticism of the late Dr. Vawter?

Was Dr. Vawter also correct in his speculation that the electrically charged jar could have unlocked the Atlantean secret of electrical energy, thereby rendering our environmentally damaging dependence on fossil fuels obsolete? If so, how many years has the jar's destruction set us back in the development of alternate energy sources?

Another question: Why did only one jar contain an electrical charge while the others were like dead batteries? Was that one jar the reserve vessel sealed in a leaden drum? Why then did the others go dead? Was the initial blast that precipitated the Deluge nuclear in nature?

She recalled Lord H'rshag's final entry:

> (Here I, Lord H'rshag, take leave again from my account of the last days of the illustrious Akiri Empire to digress, however briefly, with yet another revelation disclosed to me in that last meeting I had with the Watcher, Ariel—hidden things which she did graciously share with me of more perfect tidings concerning the horrible destruction that befell my homeland.)
>
> On the day that the sun rose on the Great Empire for the last time, much evil had befallen her. Rule and authority had ceased in the land. Everyone did that which was right in his own eyes. The citizenry wearied themselves to find new ways of wrongdoing.
>
> None any longer questioned them. Or dared say them nay.
>
> Station "Z," the nethermost station, saw the invasion by lewd fellows of the baser sort: the Hudishi of the streets. They slew the guards and the wizard-priests (scientists) who kept charge of the Station. With their unskilled hands they tampered with power beyond that which was fitting for them.
>
> Thus brought they down from the heavens fire of their own destruction. (Did an icy comet enter earth's atmosphere from outer space and get caught in its gravitational pull? Did the resultant friction cause the ice to melt? Could the Akiri rabble have precipitated a gigantic lightning bolt that struck the nuclear generator that caused a primordial blast of megaton proportions. Did this in turn, ignite the hydrogen-rich outer atmosphere that produced a firestorm of burning hydrogen?—ed.)

She thought it courageous of George to make the break and then become whistleblower with an article he submitted to a professional journal exposing his superiors' machinations.

Again she resumed her typing. Soon the following words appeared on her computer screen:

> Another plus: the man who had been harassing me off and on since those disastrous days at Earthnation was reported to have been

stabbed to death by another inmate at Folsom Prison. He was the one who tampered with the brakes of my car. He was serving sentence on an attempted murder charge.

He was like a volcano ready to erupt, she recalled. Strange, how a psychopath like Snake could ever take over a movement like Earthnation. How many of our world leaders, she wondered, are likewise psychopaths?

She stood up and walked away from her computer. She hobbled across her basement to the sliding glass door and looked out. Long rays of the autumn sun slanted at a steeper angle now. Shadows in the forest grew deeper. Overhead a flight of geese headed southward.

In the aureate sylvan scene lay a stillness that made it surreal, like a painting. Even the sky, fading from a rich gold in the west to a deep indigo in the east, seemed to take on an otherworldly dimension. *They called it the Age of Aquarius*, she thought. *Will historians someday refer to it as the Dark Ages of American history?*

She hobbled her way back to the computer.

She continued working the keys as the following words jumped to the screen:

> Although I have never been one to derive satisfaction over the death of another human being, I am relieved to learn that I can at last put the whole experiment behind me.
>
> Also, thankfully, I have contracted a real estate management agency in Chicago to maintain my family homestead as rental property. It's such a beautiful home with such sentimental value for me that the idea of giving it up is unthinkable. Perhaps we can move back there in our retirement and keep our Mountain Lake cabin as a second home.
>
> But enough about me. I'm glad to hear your dress shop is doing so well. You are to be congratulated on your courage to reopen your store so soon after the earthquake.
>
> Speaking of earthquake, you no doubt heard that Cortez Pacific's campus suffered extensive damage. Classes have now resumed, although many in portable facilities. I think a new school with a new spirit will rise from the ruins.
>
> The problem of Atlantis Studios is also solved. It had been totally destroyed. It is almost worth losing money over.

Keep in touch. Write when you can. God bless you.
Your old roommate,

Artie

P.S. By the way, the other day I visited Jane Doe's grave and saw the strangest thing: Lilies of the valley growing wild.

The postscript triggered within her another train of thought. After two decades it finally happened: a break in the case of Peppi's vandalized beach house and of the mysterious murder.

A young woman in her mid-thirties also turned herself in to the Los Angeles police station. She brought in with her brown-stained items of girl's clothing to corroborate her story. There must have been at least a dozen of us, she had disclosed; all members of a secret, cultic society from a nearby middle school. The girl was the center of a bitter, out-of-state custody battle, so we made up a story of her being kidnapped.

Then rather than trying to keep it a secret, we actually bragged about it to the other students, she had finally confessed. These other students were either sworn to secrecy, or were afraid to tell.

The ruins of the Atlantis Studios had also revealed a partially intact video film of the break-in.

Another nagging question: why the crime did not get in the news. It never made the newspapers, radio, or television. That proved more vexing to Huck than to her. He had inquired of all these news sources and got from them essentially the same pat answer. We have an editorial board that meets daily or weekly, they had explained. Because of limited newsprint or airtime, we have to be selective in publishing our stories to those we determine to be of uppermost relevance. Apparently your little incident was deemed not to be newsworthy to a broad segment of our readers, listeners, or viewers.

We are sure you can understand.

As the years put distance between them and the break-in, the chance that they would ever get to the bottom of it had become even more remote.

Give the whole thing a rest, she finally had pled with him.

But to little avail.

Another interesting aspect learned from Ariel: during the orgy, she had actually possessed the girl's body and suffered her torment for her. Of her final moments, the girl knew nothing.

In Pace Requiescat. Artie recalled saying those words at Jane Doe's graveside. *Rest in peace, little darling,* she thought. *My prayers are answered.*

As she reread the words on her screen, she reflected on another concern that she had held in recent years, namely Huck's health. One confidence she would not disclose even to Peppi was an issue she had harbored since the mid-eighties. In his altercations with the likes of Durwin, Lester, and Snake, his bruised and scraped knuckles came in contact with their blood and saliva. At her bidding, he had submitted to a series of tests.

After five years, the tests had consistently proved negative.

Could the cloud that hung over their marriage and family life finally be lifted?

In our euphoria, we referred to it as revolution, she recalled. *Was it really all that historically significant, or was it all merely a gigantic generational temper tantrum? There are those of us who are still paying a big price for our Aquarian rebellion,* she reflected, *and for what?*

In her case, a few months of Earthnation involvement had taken her half a lifetime to disentangle.

Could she, as she approached the sixth decade of her life, finally feel herself free?

also available from publishamerica

THE CAPRICORN GOAT
by Billie Williams

When a young couple's engagement party ends in tragedy, the caterer, Sasha "Echo" Folio, is suspect because the groom-to-be was her former boyfriend. The deaths were from food poisoning. January Flannel becomes the accidental sleuth who tries to clear her friend's name, all the while under her own stress from someone trying to do her in. Is Leroy Rogers, who is obsessed with Echo and seeking revenge for her dumping him, the threat to both January and Echo? Did he have something to do with the young couple's death? Will Dakota Phoenix and Adam Scott be able to help keep the women they love alive, or will they all wind up dead?

Paperback, 287 pages
6" x 9"
ISBN 1-60813-090-8

About the author:

Award-winning, multi-published mystery/suspense author Billie A Williams' accidental sleuths solve crimes with wit, wisdom and chutzpah. She writes a monthly column for Mystery Fiction.com "Whodunit?" interviews authors for Manic Readers.com and writes the monthly newsletter for Wings ePress, Inc. "Flight of Dreams." She lives in a northern Wisconsin town with her husband.

available to all bookstores nationwide.
www.publishamerica.com

also available from publishamerica

DIPOABLE LIVE$

by Richard Freeman

After a lifetime of safe choices, funeral director Spence Darnell enters a Detroit casino one afternoon, triggering a chain reaction of lies, lust and sacrifice—human sacrifice. In *Dipoable Live$*, what starts off as an obsession with gambling and an attractive blackjack dealer leads Spence down a path of no return. A dark journey culminates in the immoral decision to literally play God with the lives of society's forgotten. The abandoned, bereft and lost members of society—those with disposable lives—are traded in exchange for personal redemption.

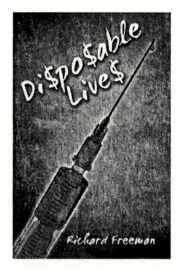

Paperback, 211 pages
6" x 9"
ISBN 1-4241-4931-2

About the author:

Richard Freeman has spent his lifetime managing and owning broadcast facilities. In his childhood in Detroit he lived down the street from a funeral home and was always fascinated by the fact that the lower level lights were always on. His novel does not solve that mystery, but does present his impression and imagination of what could have gone on. This is his first novel, and critics are hoping it is not his last.

available to all bookstores nationwide.
www.publishamerica.com

also available from publishamerica

FROM THE CASE FILES OF HANNAH JORDAN:

Fulfilled Justice

by CJ Lange

After a lengthy absence from the public work force, wife and mother Laura Rolins has returned to work only to become someone's target for murder. When the Denver police department, of which her husband is a detective, has no leads into the attacks, she turns to a daring, local private investigator named Hannah Jordan for help, but while investigating the Rolins' case Hannah Jordan's personal life becomes a target as well.

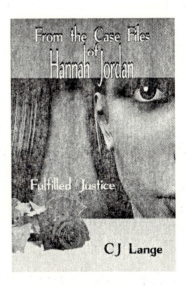

Paperback, 187 pages
6" x 9"
ISBN 1-60672-578-5

Through frustration, tears and fear for her own safety, sheer determination drives her to get the answers that will solve this case.

available to all bookstores nationwide.
www.publishamerica.com

also available from publishamerica

GOD WALKED THE DARK HILLS OF MY LIFE

by Mary Ann Sadler

God Walked the Dark Hills is a must-read book for all humanity; truly, it is a statement that each and every one of us can relate to at some point in our lives. God does indeed walk the dark hills for all of us. Although we may not see Him or feel His presence, He is there. He will lead us through the darkest valley and over the darkest, steepest hills if we will only trust in Him and keep our hands in His. We are never alone; He is there to take our hand if we let Him. For Mary, this became very true during the time of her husband's illness and death. For her this truly brought to perspective God's everlasting omnipresence in times of pleasure and in times of pain—in times of what may appear to be everlasting pain.

Paperback, 157 pages
5.5" x 8.5"
ISBN 1-60672-706-0

About the author:

Mary Ann Sadler, one of five children, was born in Jonesboro, Illinois, to Pastor Robert Raymond and Myrtle Mae Burton. Mary was married to Kenneth Deleen Sadler for forty-two years. Mary still resides in Jonesboro, Illinois, where she spends her time recollecting on memories and putting them on paper.

available to all bookstores nationwide.
www.publishamerica.com